THERE'S
SOMETHING
IN THE
BACK
YARD

THERE'S
SOMETHING
IN THE
BACK
YARD

RICHARD SNODGRASS

VIKING

VIKING
Published by the Penguin Group
Viking Penguin, a division of Penguin Books USA Inc.,
40 West 23rd Street, New York, New York 10010, U.S.A.
Penguin Books Ltd, 27 Wrights Lane, London W8 5TZ, England
Penguin Books Australia Ltd, Ringwood, Victoria, Australia
Penguin Books Canada Ltd, 2801 John Street, Markham, Ontario, Canada L3R 1B4
Penguin Books (N.Z.) Ltd, 182–190 Wairau Road, Auckland 10, New Zealand

Penguin Books Ltd, Registered Offices: Harmondsworth, Middlesex, England

First published in 1989 by Viking Penguin, a division of Penguin Books USA Inc.

1 3 5 7 9 10 8 6 4 2

LIBRARY OF CONGRESS CATALOGING IN PUBLICATION DATA
Snodgrass, Richard, 1940–
There's something in the back yard/Richard Snodgrass.
p. cm.
ISBN 0-670-82821-1
I. Title.
PS3569.N55T46 1989   88-40626
813'.54—dc19   CIP

Printed in the United States of America
Set in Garamond Number 3
Designed by Fritz Metsch

For Jane Welch

In vain do individuals hope for immortality, or any patent from oblivion, in preservations below the Moon.

Sir Thomas Browne

PRELUDE

According to some of the Hopi stories, when everyone lived in the First World, far under the surface of the earth, the first people didn't look like people at all; instead, they looked like insects, like ants. And when that world, the First World, was eventually destroyed by fire, the insects, the ants, crawled up into the Second World, which was still under the surface of the earth, where they became other creatures, like tadpoles, with gills and webbed fingers and bulging eyes. And when the Second World was eventually destroyed, this time by water, they crawled up into the Third World, still under the surface of the earth, where Hurúng Wuhti, the Woman of Hard Things—or maybe it was Spider Grandmother—decided to make creatures that looked a lot like people as we know them, except that they had tails. Now, the people, of course, were ashamed of themselves, because they knew (even if the gods didn't) that people weren't supposed to have tails. But as it turned out they were more like people than they could ever imagine: they didn't need fire or water or some natural catastrophe to destroy their world, they mucked it up so badly by themselves that it soon became unlivable. And that's when they entered the present world, that's when they climbed up onto the surface of the earth, this, the Fourth World, and people came to look just as they do today, like people. But as to how this world turns out, what people make of the Fourth World, the Hopi stories, at least the ones told outside the kivas, don't say, the outcome hasn't been determined yet, the stories are still going on. . . .

ONE

1

One morning, in a house a few miles north of Flagstaff, Arizona, a man by the name of George Binns was sitting in his study on the second floor, sitting at his desk staring at a blank sheet of paper, a sheet of paper on which he hoped to begin a poem, or maybe a short story, or maybe even a sketch for a novel—hoped to begin something, at least—as he thought about his lover's thighs (which, though he thought they were very lovely thighs, had nothing at all to do with the poem or short story or anything else he hoped to write; but that was only part of the problem), when he heard his wife call out:

"George, look out the window."

George, in response to her command, promptly looked down at his shoe—or, rather, down at the baseboard register beside his shoe, the place where his wife's voice usually came from when he was in his study, knowing, even as he looked there, that this time Mary Olive's voice came not from downstairs in the kitchen but from their bedroom, at the other end of the second floor. He looked at his watch: 8:42. What on earth was she doing up at this hour? She usually slept till noon, it was an unspoken agreement they had: she took over the house in the evenings (and, usually, late into the night) and he had the peace and quiet of the mornings to himself; or, as they used to joke about it at parties in New York, he worked daylight and she worked graveyard.

"George. Look out the window. There's something in the back yard."

There's something in the back yard. Twenty-five years of marriage had taught him that such a statement from Mary Olive could mean

7

anything from the presence of an unfamiliar butterfly to a crew of workmen ready to take off the rear of the house. (That had happened once, years before, when they lived in Pennsylvania, when he was teaching at Penn State: a crew of workmen arrived one day to start an addition on the back of the house. The problem was that they got the wrong house; George ran out to stop them just as the backhoe bit into the rear walk, the flagstones popping up like tiddlywinks. Mary Olive had seen the men and equipment arrive while she fixed lunch, and announced it with those same words: *There's something in the back yard.* Even then she did things like that, he thought to himself now; she played her little games even then.) The blinds in front of his desk were still closed against the morning sun. He listened; he didn't hear the sound of heavy equipment. Somewhere up in the trees, on the hill behind the house, the magpies were making a fuss about something—*rak rak rak rak rak rak rak rak rak rak*—but that wasn't unusual; in the distance he could hear the growl of a chain saw—Don, their nearest neighbor, half a mile down the road, probably working on his woodpile. Offhand, George couldn't imagine what she could be so upset about.

"George!"

George sighed. He leaned forward over his typewriter, took off his glasses, and lifted one of the slats of the blinds; then he stood up and opened the blinds. Mary Olive was right: there was indeed something in the back yard. Through the branches of the trees, the twin pines on the terrace in the back yard whose branches filled his study windows, he could see something standing in the dry wash at the far end of the yard. Something that, from this distance and from this elevation, partly blocked by the branches of the trees, appeared to be a brightly colored eight-foot-tall bird.

Calmly, keeping his dignity, his control of the situation, George left the study and went down the hall to the bedroom at the other end of the house. He was in his early fifties, a tall, heavyset man— you might want to say he was more than heavyset, you might say he was large, you might say he was fat, even, but that isn't quite it either—with a full head of wavy salt-and-pepper hair and a strong jaw. From the back he appeared to be of normal proportions, but head on (or as best seen in profile) his chest and stomach swelled out in front of him, not in a potbelly that drooped over the tops of his trousers, but in a graceful arc, a natural buffer, so that it was possible to imagine that, if he ever fell forward, he would rock back and forth on the ground. Mary Olive stood at the bedroom window, peeking through the curtains, through the crack between the closed blinds and the window frame, clutching her nightgown about herself as if afraid that what she peeked at might peek back. He joined her at the window, looking over her head.

"Didn't you hear me, George?"

"Yes, dear. That's why I'm here."

"There's something in the back yard."

"I know, dear. I can see it."

She turned and looked up at him. "You don't seem very worried about it."

"We don't know if it's something to be worried about, do we, dear?"

He smiled reassuringly, not really looking at her, and stretched his neck away from his collar. She was also in her early fifties, a slim, erect woman with high cheekbones, quick though cloudy blue eyes, and her tawny-gray hair pulled back into a straggly bun. She was a handsome woman—she looked nearly the same at fifty as she had at thirty; on the other hand, a thought that occurred to George at those moments when he wondered what he missed in life, at thirty she had already looked fifty—and could be striking if and when she wanted to be; the thing was, she no longer seemed to want to be, or at least that was the way it seemed to George. He particularly disliked seeing her in the mornings, before she washed and dressed and had her coffee—in the mornings her skin was oily, the circles under her eyes were as dark as bruises, and her features often appeared to have slipped down a notch during the night. As he stood close to her now, looking over her hair and out the window, she smelled of cigarettes, sweaty slept-in clothes, and last night's wine.

"Can't you see it from your study?"

"Not very well. The trees are in the way."

"What do you think it is?"

"I don't know, dear."

From this window, without the branches of the pine trees in the way, the something in the back yard no longer looked like a brightly colored eight-foot-tall bird. From this window, the something in the back yard looked like a man in a cape with a very tall, very blue, very pointed hat. George and Mary Olive stared for a moment in silence through the gauze curtains, through the crack between the blinds and the window frame, a totem pole of lookers. Then Mary Olive turned around quickly and stretched up and gave him a quick sloppy kiss on the cheek.

"Mary Olive! What was that for?"

"That's because you came when I called. That's because you're my big brave protector."

He looked at her to see if she was making fun of him, but from the smile on her face—a half-smile really; it was the other half, the unknown half, that bothered him—he couldn't tell. He wiped the slobber from his cheek and looked back out the window.

"So what are you going to do about it, George?" Mary Olive stared up at him, into the side of his face.

"About what, dear?" George said, afraid for a moment she meant the kiss on his cheek.

"About whatever it is that's down there in the back yard."

"I'm going right down and take care of it, of course." He bent over slightly and patted her on the shoulders, repeated the form of her shoulders, outlined her, patted her into place.

"My big brave George."

"Well, what did you think I was going to do about it?"

"You're absolutely right, George."

"We have to know what it is, don't we?"

"Of course, George."

"Harrumph," said George. And thought: *Is she laughing at me?*

Mary Olive advanced on him, lips puckered. "Give us another kiss, George. You always look so handsome when you're trying to act sure of yourself."

"What do you mean?" George said, drawing back. "I am sure of myself."

Mary Olive smiled at him, pulled up the corners of her mouth at him—a quick jab of a smile—but before she said anything else he turned around and left the room, clomping stately, determinedly, landing with his weight on his heels so the house reverberated with his progress, so she would be sure to hear him, down the stairs and through the first floor of the house to the back door.

The July morning was already hot, even though the sun had yet to clear the peaks of the mountains to the east; George stepped out the back door and into the hot air, into the smells of dust and pines and the dry grass. The upper yard extended some twenty feet or so from the rear of the house on a built-up terrace; beyond the terrace wall, a retaining wall of native volcanic stone, the lower yard—it was more of a field than a yard; he kept the grass on the terrace watered and trimmed but ignored the lower yard, the field, the sparse brown grass in the sandy soil—sloped gently for another hundred feet to a split-rail fence along the bank of a dry wash. The wash was five or six feet deep and twice as wide; George had called it a gully when they first moved here, a year earlier, but Don, their neighbor, who was also in the English Department, had insisted that, in this part of the country, such a thing was called a wash. On the other side of the wash, the forests of pine and aspen climbed the foothills of the San Francisco Mountains. George walked across the terrace, through the grouping of white wooden lawn furniture sitting under the twin pines, and stood on top of the retaining wall, looking down at the end of the field. Up on the hillside, a dozen or so magpies continued to clatter in the trees, talking to themselves about something, their black-and-white wings flashing as they flew from branch to branch, not alarmed really, just noisy, the same as they were most of the time, giving their repeated rasping call—*rak rak rak rak rak rak rak*—that George thought (he was proud of this simile and tried to use it in practically every poem and short story and letter he had written since they moved to the West) sounded like a car that wouldn't start. But from where he stood, on top of the terrace wall, he couldn't tell much more about the figure in the wash than he could from the second-floor window; in fact in some ways, without the extra elevation, he could tell even less, the figure half hidden from view now by the split-rail fence, except that from here it appeared the figure was wearing a tall blue dunce cap.

George turned around, back toward the house; Mary Olive stood in the upstairs window, shrouded in the gauze of the curtains, clutching her nightclothes about herself, watching him. He shrugged, held out his palms to show he still didn't know who or what it was. She said something to him behind the glass and shook her head and flicked her hand at him, motioning him to go on down and look at it. George clenched his teeth and growled in the back of his throat—how dare she flick her hand at him, as if he needed to be told what to do; he had half a mind to go back in the house and throttle her (*Throttle,* he thought: *now that's a curious word. Why would you say you wanted to throttle someone unless you wanted them to do something more or faster? I've got to remember to look up the meaning when I get back to the house*), but he turned and went down the terrace steps and marched out across the yard.

Halfway down the slope, however, he wondered if he wasn't being a bit hasty. He wondered if he shouldn't have a weapon of some kind, something to hold in his hand, at least—the figure in the wash was holding a long stick, a staff. But it was too late now; no matter what the guy was holding or how big he was—and as George got closer he could see the guy was very big indeed—he couldn't turn back now, not with Mary Olive watching from the window. When he got to the fence he was breathing heavily and sweating and he rested his weight, rested the bulk of his stomach, against the top rail. The figure in the cape and the blue pointed hat was poking the end of his staff among the rocks on the bank of the wash, his back turned toward George, and George was glad the guy hadn't noticed him yet, that he had a moment to get himself together. He had no doubt that he could handle this situation, that he could take care of this fellow, whoever this fellow was, find out what this fellow wanted and what this fellow thought he was doing here—find out if he was a fugitive from a service-station opening, or the entertainment for a kiddie party who got lost, or just a kook—George just needed a little time to figure out how.

2

The hat wasn't a hat at all: it was a mask, a blue, cone-shaped mask several feet tall, topped off with white feathers and strands of red yarn tied at the very point, and more tufts of feathers and more red yarn sprouting out from the sides, where the ears should be; a fox skin was wrapped around the neck as a ruff. The figure wore a white kilt with a thick red-black-and-green sash around the waist, the ends of which cascaded down at the side, and moccasins; tied around his shoulders was a long blanket or cape that draped down the back to his knees. The cape was spotted in tropical colors—red and yellow and green—and undoubtedly had been very beautiful at one time, though now the material was old and the colors faded. The figure's chest, arms, and legs were painted alternately blue and yellow. In his right hand he carried a long staff with small ears of corn tied around the top and tipped with feathers; in his left hand was a small sack and a bundle that included an earthen jug and a white arrow-shaped board with an ear of corn tied to it.

It was a kachina, or at least George thought it was a kachina. There were pictures of kachinas all over the Southwest, and especially around Flagstaff—there were kachina restaurants, kachina drive-ins, kachina motels; his checks from the bank had kachinas on them, his students at the university wore T-shirts with kachinas on them. They were one of those things he had always meant to learn more about since they moved here—he was going to learn more about the Grand Canyon and Southwestern wildflowers and take weekly hikes in the mountains too—but he never got around to doing it. Now he wished he had, oh, how he wished he had, because he realized, standing in front of this tall masked figure poking around his back yard, that, besides knowing that kachinas had something to do with the Indians, something to do with the nearby Indian reservations—Don and Sally talked about kachinas all the time, why hadn't he paid more attention; he thought they were dancers of some kind, gods maybe—he really had no idea what a kachina was.

George's bowels gave a watery *ker-chunk*.

The kachina, if that's what it was, appeared to be looking for something, using the butt end of his staff to prod among the rocks. As the kachina turned toward the fence, George could see that the face of the mask was smooth, with no protruding features; there were only two long black rectangles painted like slits for the eyes, and an inverted black triangle painted for the mouth—an expressionless face, neither friendly nor fierce; neutral. Finally the kachina stopped his poking around and sighed, then noticed George and looked up. They stared at each other for a long minute, and George thought: He's looking at me as if he's wondering what *I'm* doing here.

George's bowels gurgled profoundly; he was afraid he might have to run for the house.

"Hello," George said, clamping his buttocks hard.

The kachina cocked his head, hesitated, then nodded once.

"Ah . . . may I ask what you're doing?"

The kachina shifted his footing on the edge of the wash so that he could get a better look at George; as he moved, the rattles inside a turtle shell tied to his right leg just below the knee gave a dry whisper, like branches rubbing together. Otherwise the kachina was silent, the mask expressionless. George stretched his neck away from his collar, cleared his throat.

"Who are you? What are you doing down here?"

The kachina turned his head slightly, as if to ask George the same question.

George tried to think if it could be someone he knew, someone playing a joke on him. The only person he could think of was Don, but this fellow was at least a foot taller, even without the mask, and sixty pounds heavier than Don; besides, from what George could see, this guy's skin was reddish-brown—it was either an Indian or somebody using, in addition to everything else, body makeup. George had Indian students in his classes, but he didn't know any of them very well, they were generally withdrawn and kept pretty much to themselves—after a year he still couldn't tell the difference between the Hopis and the Navajos. He was almost sure it couldn't be anyone he knew. But who was it, then? George moved away from the fence so he wasn't leaning on it, so he could stand as tall as possible. His bowels seemed secure.

"This is my place. I—I mean we, my wife and I—we own this house."

The kachina looked past him as if he hadn't noticed the house before. Then he looked at George and nodded—was he approving? George, in a sudden flight of whimsy, almost said thank you; he blinked, a very slow, determined blink, trying to clear his mind, trying to start over. I've got to get hold of myself, he told himself, I own this property, this is my place, I'm in control here. The kachina seemed to look at George curiously, as if wondering what the problem was, then turned around so he faced the hillside, the turtle-shell rattle punctuating his movements. On the back of the cape, worked into the splashings of tropical colors, was a drawing, a vague image of a large bird with a man's head; a second fox skin, which hung from the kachina's waist, stuck out below the bottom edge of the cape, almost touching the ground, as if the kachina had a tail. Up in the trees, the magpies were still clattering. *Rak rak rak rak rak rak rak, rak rak rak.* The kachina raised his staff toward the peaks of the mountains, rising above the forests on the hillside. The magpies quieted down.

That was just a coincidence, George told himself.

The kachina turned around again and thumped the end of his staff in the dirt, apparently pleased with himself.

This is ridiculous, George thought, nobody's going to believe this. Here I am trying to talk to some guy wearing a cape and a blue cone on his head. He's probably some crazy and I'm going to get myself killed.

The kachina shook his head, looking at him intently, as if to say, You don't have to worry, I'm not going to hurt you.

George laughed to himself: I'm being silly, he doesn't look dangerous. I don't have to worry, he's not going to hurt me.

The mask was expressionless as before, there was nothing about the features that could change, that could give expression one way or another, but for a moment George had the idea that the kachina, with his small upside-down triangle for a mouth, was smiling at him.

I've been working too hard lately, George said to himself, there's too much pressure in the modern world.

The kachina nodded, and continued to smile.

George looked back at the house, but from this distance he couldn't tell whether Mary Olive was still watching him from the window or not. He thought about it for a moment—*This is insane. Do I dare? Yes, the question: do I dare?*—then grinned to himself and shrugged a little *What the hell* cleared his throat, hitched up his pants, and started to climb through the rails of the fence for a closer look.

The kachina stepped back a little, onto the floor of the wash, to give him more room. The turtle-shell rattle clacked.

George was halfway through the fence, one leg on one side, one leg on the other, when he got stuck, his stomach wedged between the rails, his belt hung up on a splinter. He flapped his arms, trying for leverage, then looked over sideways at the kachina.

"Tight squeeze, ha ha."

The kachina tilted his head sideways, bent over a little, to get a better view.

George sucked in his stomach and got a handhold on the rail above him and pushed his way through, tearing his belt free from the splinter and landing with an "Ooof!" on his hands and knees.

He stood up, brushed himself off. "I keep meaning to lose some weight but you know how it is."

The kachina, with rolls of fat layered on his waist above his kilt, just looked at him.

George harrumphed, straightened his shoulders, tried to regain some of his lost dignity; he moved a couple of steps closer to the kachina, down the edge of the wash.

"Well, now. Can't you tell me something about yourself and what you're doing here?"

The kachina thought for a moment, then raised his staff in front of him, a sudden motion. George thought the kachina was going to hit him and ducked, stumbled backward over a rock and sat down heavily on the edge of the bank, his eyes closed, ready for the blow, his arms thrown over his head. When nothing happened, he opened his eyes slowly and peeked between the cracks of his arms. The kachina stood where he was, his staff still raised in mid-gesture, looking at George. George laughed, embarrassed, trying to appear as if he'd meant to sit there all along. He shifted his weight to get a stone out from under him.

"Ha ha, yes, ahem. Well, can you tell me at least if you're supposed to be an Indian? I mean, are you an Indian? Or if you're not, is that what you're dressed up to look like? I mean, is that what this is all about?"

The kachina looked at him blankly.

George was getting disgusted with himself. *I'm not handling this at all well.* "What I mean is, we haven't lived here very long. We don't know anything about Indians or kachinas or things like that. I've never seen anything like you before."

The kachina looked down at himself, then cocked his head sympathetically at George: *Oh.*

The sun had cleared the mountains and the tops of the trees, backlighting the kachina against the shadows of the hillside, the dark green of the forests. George searched the features of the blue mask, the black slits painted for the eyes, the small black triangular mouth, the blank face that nonetheless seemed concerned and friendly, almost as if the kachina was searching

George's face in return (*He doesn't know what to make of me, any more than I know what to make of him*), though he still couldn't make out the eyeholes or the eyes, the breathing space for the mouth, some sign of the person inside. But in the strong, angled sunlight, the feathers and red yarn at the point and on either side of the mask glowed, as if illuminated from within, and the entire figure was ringed with light, dazzling. George laughed a little, shook his head slowly.

"This is all very peculiar."

The kachina shook his head slowly in return, mirrored him: *It certainly is.*

The two stared at each other for a moment; then George flinched as he heard a cry from the direction of the house and turned around. Mary Olive was shuffling across the yard and down the terrace steps toward them, still in her nightgown, George's black raincoat thrown around her shoulders, waving a broom over her head.

"Hold on, George! I'm coming! I'm coming!"

"Oh good heavens," George said and looked back at the kachina. *Now what?* the kachina looked at him.

"I'm afraid to think."

George stood up, brushing off the seat of his pants. The kachina stood behind him in the wash, peered around him, looking up through the rails of the fence, his head cocked, watching the woman with the broom charging toward them, amazed.

3
———

Mary Olive was trying to run but the long nightgown hobbled her, so halfway down the field she stopped and reached down and hiked the bottom of the gown up over her knees, and then kept on coming, holding up the edge of the gown with one hand and waving the broom in the other, the broom held in front of her as if it were dragging her down the hill, clipping along at a good pace until her slipper flew off and she stepped on something, a stone or maybe a clump of weeds, and she yelped and jumped up and down as if doing a war dance (George looked at the kachina to see if he was offended; the kachina looked at George to see if he knew what was going on) and limped the rest of the way, using the broom as a crutch. When she got to the fence she leaned against the top rail as she looked at the bottom of her foot, and George went over and took the broom away.

"I was coming to save you, George," she said absently, putting her foot back down and trying to walk on it.

"I don't need saving. I'm all right. Everything's all right."

"Did he hurt you?"

"Hurt me?"

"Poor George." She felt his upper arm as if she were kneading bread dough. "I saw him hit you. I saw him knock you down."

He pulled his arm away; she was beginning to pinch. "He didn't hit me. I tripped."

"Oh." She looked disappointed, then giggled.

George frowned. He looked at the kachina in the wash; the kachina was twisting his head back and forth, apparently trying to get a good view of the two of them through the eyeholes of the mask. Standing on the bank, George was just a little taller than the top of the feathers at the point of the mask. Then he realized he was holding the broom the same way the kachina was holding his staff, the upturned bristles like the feathers on top of the staff, as though he were mimicking the kachina. George handed the broom back to Mary Olive.

"Don't turn your back on him!" she yelled.

George ducked and stumbled and almost fell again, catching himself against the fence. Mary Olive waved the broom over the top rail, trying to keep the kachina at bay, yelling "Hyah! Hyah!" as if she were prodding cattle. The kachina hadn't moved; he stood there, his feathers stirring in the occasional warm breeze, tilting and shifting his head, looking from one to the other, twisting his head to look at them as a bird might. George felt like a fool.

"For heaven's sake, Mary Olive," he said. He grabbed the end of the broom so she'd stop waving it around. "He's not going to do anything."

"How do you know that?"

"I just know. Now take it easy. Everything's under control."

"Did he say who he is?"

"No, but I'm pretty sure he's one of those kachinas."

"Well, of course he's a kachina," Mary Olive said.

"Dear, we don't know enough about the subject to make that kind of judgment. Let's just say he appears to be a kachina."

"Dear, let's just say that until we find out what the big chief here is doing in our back yard we don't take any chances."

"Mary Olive," he said through clenched teeth, "I know what I'm doing."

"Of course you do, dear," she said, and looked down at her dusty toes.

"Oh for . . . ," he growled in the back of his throat. He looked at the kachina, then went over to the edge of the bank and turned his back to it.

"George!"

He held out his arms, a limp crucifixion: "Ta da!"

"Don't do that," she said. "You don't know what he's going to do."

"I'm just trying to show you that there's no reason for you to be so worried."

"You tell me what's reasonable about finding a thing like that in your back yard."

He looked over his shoulder to see what the kachina thought of the goings-on. But the kachina had evidently given up on them; he was back to poking around the rocks along the bank, ignoring them. George put down his arms and went back to the fence.

"What's he doing now?" she whispered, peering around George's stomach.

"He seems to be looking for something," George whispered back.

She looked at George sarcastically. "We can't have a drunk Indian digging up our back yard, George."

"Drunk Indian?"

"There's drunk Indians all over this town. We can't start letting them hang around here."

"Mary Olive, we don't even know if he's an Indian, much less if he's drunk."

"Why are you whispering," she whispered.

"Because you were whispering," he hissed.

"Well I'm not whispering now," she said loudly. "What are you going to do about him?"

"Keep your voice down!" He waved his hands. "I'm sure there's a perfectly understandable reason why he's here and why he's doing what he's doing—whatever it is he's doing."

"And you're just going to let him stay there?"

"I don't think we have much choice about it," George said, looking away.

"It's our property, isn't it?"

"Actually, no. Our property line ends with the fence. Technically, he's on government land."

He was glad he thought of it: it hadn't occurred to him that, if it was an Indian inside the mask, it might be a drunk Indian. Mary Olive was right about that, as much as he hated to admit it: Flagstaff was filled with Indians who came from the reservations to get drunk, the nearest town where they could get booze, sitting in clumps in the drainage ditches on the roads outside of town, filling up the street corners on the weekends—there were a few blocks of Santa Fe Avenue, a main street in town, where George was afraid to walk, even in the daytime. No, he didn't want any trouble with a drunk Indian.

Mary Olive had an unpleasant look on her face.

"Now, now, dear, there's nothing to worry about, I'm sure of that," he said, leaning across the fence to pat her shoulders, mold her, he hoped, into a reasonable and controllable shape. "Everything's going to be okay. We'll just leave him alone and he'll leave us alone and he'll do whatever it is he's doing and go away again. Everything's going to be fine."

Mary Olive looked at him as if to say *Oh yeh?* and started back up toward the house.

"Where are you going?" he said after her.

"I'm going to the house and call Don," she said, turning around to look at him and thumping the broom once for emphasis. Then she continued on up the slope.

George harrumphed; it was a good idea, he only wished he had thought of it first. Don had lived around here a long time, he would know whether kachinas showed up from time to time in your back yard, if it was just one of those quirks of living in the Southwest that you had to get used to. The day was getting hotter, his shirt stuck to his back, his collar pricked against his neck. A bluebottle fly wouldn't leave him alone. George watched his wife stop to slip her foot into her lost slipper; then she reached back with her free hand to adjust the raincoat around her shoulders, a slim, rigid figure, her shoulders set in the coat as if it were on a hanger, and continued up the hill, walking the broom like a bishop's crosier. He looked back at the kachina. The kachina was standing there, watching him watching her, his feathers glowing in the sunlight, a bright tropical figure against the backdrop of pine trees. And for a moment George could have sworn that the same blue, cone-shaped mask, the same painted, expressionless face that he earlier thought was smiling at him was now grinning at him, downright laughing: *Hello George.* George snapped his jaw and pushed his way back through the rails of the fence, headed back toward the house.

4
—

In the kitchen, Mary Olive dropped George's raincoat over the back of a straight chair at the table, snapped the broom into its holder behind the closet door, and—taking her by surprise—felt the air go out of her momentarily, not as if she'd been punched in the stomach but as if there were a small painless slit somewhere deep inside her that was slowly leaking. And thought: I married a lump.

She went over and leaned against the counter, lighting a cigarette as she looked out the window. The counter formed an L under the window, a corner where the long counter that ran under the cupboards and her shelves of cookbooks joined with the shorter counter that jutted out into the room to divide the work area from the table where they ate most of their meals. It was her favorite spot in the house, inside the corner, her only favorite spot besides her bed, the only place in the house—she would have said the only place in northern Arizona, the only place west of the Hudson River—where she felt comfortable; within reach were the few things she thought necessary to give her pleasure, the few things that gave her pleasure these days: the radio, cigarettes, ashtray, Bic lighter, telephone, window with something to look at, a stool to sit on, the register opening with which to talk to George when he was upstairs in his study, her jug of wine. For a moment she pressed her pelvis into the jointure of the two counters, into the corner, against the rolled edges of the wood, and for a moment she felt safe and held. For a moment she felt that, whatever it was in her that had been leaking, she had been able to seal it up again.

She took a long drag on the cigarette, letting the smoke curl out her open mouth and up across her face before she blew it away. Out the window, George stood among the white wooden lawn furniture on the terrace, under the pine trees, his back toward the house, looking down the yard and scratching his head as he tried to figure out what to do with the masked figure in the wash. A lump, if ever she saw one. The man would be the death of her. They had come here from New York City, where George had taught for a dozen years at Hunter College, and she, after a couple of dumb jobs, including staff writer for *The Plumber's Journal,* had been managing editor of *The Little Review,* had been responsible (everybody said, anybody who knew) for making it one of the most prestigious literary magazines in the country. In many ways their lives in New York, after she got the job at the *Review* (she was aware that she had gotten it through George, through contacts they had made after his first book was published, after he began to be invited to the best literary parties; she just didn't like to dwell on it), had been ideal, at least by her standards: a beautiful apartment, dozens of literate, interesting friends, the excitement of being, if not a driving force, at least included in the mechanisms of the publishing world. She had no idea that George was even thinking of leaving it, had no idea that he was even mildly unhappy beyond the complaints that everybody made about crime and violence and bad air, until one night at (appropriately enough) another party.

It was at Thom McCann's place—no relation to the shoes; he only began putting the "h" in "Tom" for a joke while he was at Yale and then got used to it; he was the publisher of, the money behind, *The Little Review,* Mary Olive's boss—one of his many parties crowded with writers and publishing people and his rich friends; Mary Olive had just speared the last piece of smoked salmon on the buffet table—she sighed now, sitting in her kitchen on the outskirts of Flagstaff, Arizona, thinking of smoked salmon on a buffet table; yes, Thom McCann certainly knew how to throw a party: lots of expensive munchies, lots of expensive or interesting people, and lots of black-haired, high-assed Puerto Rican boys (his stable of lovers, though the boys were known to swing both ways) to keep the liquor flowing—when McCann, halfway across the room, put his arm around George's shoulders and, loud enough for most of the room to hear, said, "What do you think about that, Mary Olive? George here says he's thinking of taking a job in Arizona."

She finished the salmon, licked her fingertips, and made her way over to the group, taking a fresh glass of white wine from a tray as it went floating, shoulder-height, by.

"Oh, really? This is the first time I've heard anything about it."

The group was smiling, including George, though George's smile was a little queasy, like that of a man who had just been pushed on a ride that he was afraid might go too fast.

"So what about you?" Thom McCann pressed, as only Thom McCann would, the point. "Would you give up your job with us to go with him?"

McCann—a short, tonsured man in his fifties, the only man Mary Olive ever knew who would invite people to come informal to a party and then himself wear a dinner jacket—reached up and patted George's hair, as one might pat a friendly but too large guard dog. The others laughed, but whatever other emotions were going through George's mind at that moment, his eyes asked the same question: Yes, would you go? In response, she gave him a sugary-sweet smile, batted her eyelashes half a dozen times at him, and looked him straight in the eye, affecting a Western drawl: "Well honey, he's my *hus*-band, isn't he?"

George blanched at that—the other listeners howled, of course, and Thom McCann clapped him on the back; they all assumed it was a good joke—but George read it not as a joke, or as a declaration of love and loyalty (which, at the time, she actually thought she meant), but as a threat. The more she thought about it later, however, she decided George's interpretation was probably right. Over the months, as it became apparent that George was seriously considering the move (they had still never talked about it directly, sat down together and discussed it; the plans just seemed to roll along by themselves, as if all the intermediate steps were foregone conclusions, and what she did learn about them usually came at

other parties, usually came from what she heard George tell someone else what he planned to do), she supposed she could have
stopped it, if she had put her foot down, if she had stopped to
think what she was getting herself into. But the truth was she was
curious just how far he'd take the idea, though she should have
known the answer to that from the beginning: he followed the
idea, as he did everything else, to its logical conclusion, and accepted the job in Flagstaff. By the time Mary Olive did realize
what she had gotten herself into, she found herself sitting in the
front seat of their car, the back seat filled with their house plants
and bonsai trees (no one thought they'd make it—the plants and
trees, that is—especially the bonsai, but they all seemed to thrive;
even her plants let her down), riding across the New Jersey Turn-
pike. It was a case, she told herself later, when she was in a lighter
mood, a much lighter or perhaps drunk mood, of having taken
the inductive method too far.

She survived the trip, and the growing realization of what she
had allowed to happen to her, by cataloguing, out loud of course,
and for George's benefit—when he was on the spot he stretched
his neck like a worried turtle; on this trip, however, in response
to her, he stretched it so often she told him he looked like one
of those toy dogs with its neck on a spring that they saw in the
rear windows of certain cars—the seemingly endless procession
of McDonald's and Burger Kings, Denny's and Pizza Huts, the
franchise restaurants and company-designed service stations and
motels that made the outskirts of any American city look the same
as the outskirts of any other American city, so that Pittsburgh was
indistinguishable from Oklahoma City—My God, she thought, it
really looks like this: it had been a favorite subject of hers at Thom
McCann's parties and other literary gatherings, she had made endless jokes and put-downs about the sterility of American culture
and the sameness of American life; and now, after she had been
sequestered for a dozen years in The Apple, it was a shock to see
that the country really looked the way she said it looked—so that
Columbus, from the freeway, looked the same as Albuquerque.

So that driving into the outskirts of Flagstaff at first seemed no different from driving into the outskirts of any other town or city they had passed along the way, but that impression changed, changed quickly and terribly, when they got into the town itself: driving down Santa Fe Avenue, through the very heart of the town, with the rows of two- and three-story stone buildings on one side of the street and the railroad tracks and lumber yards and oil depots on the other, a frontier town that had been dragged reluctantly into the modern world, a working town, a tough town; with a hodgepodge of signs for Trading Posts and Indian Crafts and Finest Turquoise (and kachinas: pictures of masked dancers on signs and store fronts and billboards, grisly, stamping, unhuman things), and the streets clogged with tourist cars heading for the Grand Canyon and pickups filled with brown- and red-skinned families, Indian children standing up in the truck beds, their faces to the wind, as she had seen dogs do, and the men and women with long black silky hair and broad pug-nosed faces, black eyes like evil buttons, jammed into the cabs and leaning out the windows; and with the drunks, at midday, on the main street of a supposedly civilized American city, Indians alone or in clusters, standing in doorways or along the curbs, their faces puffy and enflamed with booze—one man's face was bleeding, blood poured from his forehead where somebody had hit him or he had run into something and he was too drunk, too dumbfounded, to know what to do, another lying facedown in the gutter, actually lying in the gutter at noon, his clothes stiff and shiny from dried sweat or who knows what else, while his friends stood above him, grouped around a parking meter as if they were about to sing, taking turns drinking from a brown paper bag and ignoring the man at their feet—that was when she found something worse than the sameness of other American cities. She felt as if George were driving her into a world devoid of people and buildings and life altogether, a blanked-out place where nothing had survived and nothing would survive, as if she would never be around anything human or civilized or worthwhile (the way a Beethoven quartet was worthwhile, a good play, or a witty conversation carried on over smoked salmon and wine among clever people) again. She had cried, saying over and over the only words that came to her, "This is it, this is it," meaning it as a question, meaning that, after all she had lived for and struggled to make of herself, was she going to end up among drunk Indians and signs for turquoise?

And George, good old George, had reached over and patted her knee, squeezed it actually, the first time he had done that in years, driving down Santa Fe Avenue, rubber-necking to see the buildings and the mountains and the people, his voice filled with enthusiasm and wonderment: "I know what you mean, I feel the same thing. This is it. A new life. This is what we've been looking for."

The man was thick. The man was a lump.

The man would be the death of her. If she let him.

Well, she had sat by and watched George dig himself—no, dig them—into a hole for the last time. There was no telling what this kachina business might lead to—how could George know if it was dangerous or not; it was big enough to be dangerous, certainly—and she didn't want to find out. She had seen it happen, in too many other situations, too many other times: George, a friend, for a little while at least, interested until something else presented itself to distract him, to lost dogs and damaged birds and bewildered souls alike. She had seen him wander off with panhandlers, with some guy who just stopped him on the street asking for money, not only listening to his story, but going with him to buy the guy's dinner and maybe take a look at where he lived, to find out more about him. She had seen him befriend the young women in his classes, talk to them, bring them home for a drink or dinner, listen to their problems, become uncle and sometimes father and, yes, often lover, had watched their faces go from respect to admiration to love, then to bewilderment and hurt as he left them, as he wandered off to help the next one. Lump. She stubbed out her cigarette and dialed Don's number, but it was Sally who answered the phone.

"Oh, Mary Olive, dear, how good it is to hear your voice!"

Mary Olive could imagine the woman's plump and leathery face, her cocker-spaniel eyes brimming over with sincerity; in the background she could hear Indians singing and drums, one of the records Sally played at full volume for inspiration as she worked on her sculpture. (Help me, Lord, Mary Olive thought, I'm surrounded by fools and pygmies.)

"It's good to hear you, too," she cooed.

5

When George came in the back door, Mary Olive was standing at the counter in the kitchen, talking on the phone. From the expression on her face he guessed she was talking to Sally; Mary Olive looked at him, rolled her eyes, and smiled sweetly: "Is that so?"

She held the phone away from her ear and looked bored. George leaned against the doorway to the dining room, waiting to hear if Don would come over. The kitchen was the darkest room in the house; the pine trees on the terrace formed a canopy over the windows, blocking out most of the outside light, so that, except for a few moments in the early morning when the sun first cleared the mountains, there had to be a light on in the room. The floor was dark tile, a checkerboard of brown and black; the walls were lined with wood cabinets, pegboard to hold Mary Olive's Le Creuset pots and pans and her collection of antique eggbeaters, and her shelves of cookbooks. Cooking had always been one of the things she loved to do; in New York, even though she worked at the *Review,* she cooked gourmet meals in the evenings and won for herself a reputation as one of the finest cooks among their circle of friends and acquaintances, which meant among some of the most cultured and literate people in the city. It was one of the things she said, had told people, she was going to do when she got to Arizona, was one of the things she looked forward to: to spend more time cooking and baking. Since they got here, however, the only cooking she had done was to make endless varieties of hash: roast-beef hash, corned-beef hash, chicken hash, ham hash, beef-and-ham hash, browned hash, hash with vegetables—and, after they had lived here for a few months, hash with a definite Southwestern flair—mutton-and-squash hash, beef-and-*posole* hash, chicken-and-green-chili hash, chicken-and-red-chili hash, Pueblo pork-and-corn hash, Navajo hash. . . . True, she made a grand production out of it, treating hash as if it were some kind of delicacy, some kind of gourmet specialty—George doubted whether there was any other hash, by whatever name, in Flagstaff, Arizona, prepared in a Cuisinart and cooked in an imported copper-bottomed skillet—though George couldn't tell the difference between what she made most of the time and what they could buy in a can: as far as he was concerned, a hash was a hash was a hash. He waited for her to change the menu herself, to stop whatever little game she was playing, but she never did, and he learned to accept hash. He wondered whether doing something to brighten the room—maybe put in a new tile floor, paint the woodwork, add some more lights—would make a difference with her cooking, inspire her to return to her soufflés and chicken and broccoli in white sauce and linguini in clam sauce. . . . He knew he was kidding himself. As he watched, she wedged the phone between her chin and shoulder and lit a cigarette:

"And what did the doctor say?"

She exhaled the smoke in a thin blue line, aiming it at the ceiling—it reminded him of the thin blue flame you saw burning at night—a safety flame?—at refineries and pumping stations— then pointed the cigarette at his shoes: his shoes were powdered with light-brown dust from outside. Mary Olive frowned. George took a dust rag from the broom closet and wiped his shoes clean; she pointed to the trail of footprints leading from the back door to where he stood. He dusted off the soles of his shoes as well, then dropped the rag on the floor and moved it around with his foot, tried to make a little joke out of it, a dance, moving the cloth with his toe back and forth, to erase his tracks. She smiled, a thin slit of a smile. He put the dust rag back in the closet, dropped it on the floor of the closet, and went into the dining room.

It was a newish, nondescript two-story frame house, a house that would have seemed just as at home in a suburb of Cleveland or Newark as it did sitting on the edge of a pine forest in northern Arizona. Their furniture was a collection of things they had gathered moving from one job to another in his early years of teaching, the things they bought in New York during the dozen years they lived there, and the antiques, many of them Oriental, that Mary Olive inherited from her family. On the walls of the dining room were a small Byzantine icon of the Virgin and Child, a Japanese woodcut entitled *Samurai and Attendant Watching a Crane,* and a print by Paul Jenkins; as George wandered around the room, the long-stemmed crystal wineglasses inside the cherrywood cabinet tinkled softly among themselves. The surface of the Queen Anne dining-room table was covered with a layer of dust; he resisted the temptation to write "Dust Me" with his finger, a reply to her worrying about his dusty footprints in the kitchen.

Between the table and the large red Chinese vase sitting under the window, effectively blocking the passageway on that side of the table, was the Electrolux. Sometimes the vacuum cleaner turned up in their bedroom for a while, lurking in a corner; sometimes it curled on the landing on the stairs for a week or so, ready to attack unsuspecting ankles; but most of the time the low, squat tank could be found where it was now, sunning itself in the patch of sunlight from the window, its little wheels slightly pigeon-toed, its long snout curled peacefully in front of it on the rug, testament and proof that Mary Olive had every intention to vacuum—she was scrupulous to a fault about putting things away, picking things up, making sure that everything was in its place and that there was a place for everything, but she hated to vacuum and dust—even though they both knew she wouldn't turn the machine on for months at a time. (*I should be able to talk to her about that,* he told himself. *I should be able to say that it's her job to run the vacuum, like it's my job to earn the living. I should at least be able to tell her to get this damn thing out of the middle of the dining room if she's not going to use it.)* George had begun to feel the vacuum cleaner was almost another presence in the house, the way it turned up here and there, as if it were an old friend, or an infirm pet that didn't do anything except take up space. He touched it with the toe of his shoe—it was such a lowly, ugly thing; *Hello, old-timer, how are you today?*—and went back to the kitchen.

"You don't say?" Mary Olive said. She held the phone away from her ear and stuck her tongue out at the receiver. George pointed that he was going upstairs.

On the second floor, he stopped in the bathroom, then went on into his study and opened the rest of the window blinds. The room had been an enclosed sleeping porch, with a wall full of windows across this half of the back of the house; the trees screened his view of the wash from the window in front of his desk, with only glimpses of the kachina through the branches, but from the window at the far end of the room he could see it unobstructed. The brightly colored figure was still digging with his staff along the bank of the wash. George watched it for a moment, laughed a little to himself; there was something about the idea of such a thing poking around in his back yard (*What on earth is he doing down there? Who can that be?*) that tickled him. Then he went back to his desk. He listened at the register, but he didn't hear Mary Olive talking on the phone; he lifted the receiver of the extension on his desk, but there was only the dial tone. From the top drawer of his desk he took his monocular and went, quietly, back across the room to the side window, training the instrument on the house on the opposite hill, across the small valley filled with pines and aspens, half a mile away. It was a low, dark house, all wood, built close to the trees, the original lines of the architecture—it had started out as little more than a cabin— lost among the many added rooms. In the small circle of the lens he could see the back steps full of the Pikes' collection of dogs— a couple of Irish setters, a collie mix, several hounds, and Cable, their old Labrador; as he watched, the dogs scrambled to their feet, all except Cable, and stood looking up at the screen door expectantly. In a moment Sally appeared at the door, shooshing them out of the way so she could get out. She was a plumpish woman in her early forties, dressed in a peasant skirt and blouse, with her long black braid draped over her shoulder and down her breast. George watched her walk down the back path, watched the swing of her heavy-shouldered body, the setters prancing about her, toward Don's cabin.

"I talked to Sally and she said she'd go tell Don," Mary Olive's voice came from the register. "He's working out in the woods."

George watched Sally walk out of sight into the trees, then he went back to his desk and sat down, careful not to make any noise.

"Did you hear me?" said her voice from the register.

"Yes, dear. Did you tell her about the kachina?"

"Absolutely not. She'd be over here with her feathers and rattles wanting to dance with it. I just told her we needed Don to come over right away and look at something."

George put the monocular back in the center drawer of his desk, perched his reading glasses midway down his nose, and swiveled around to the stand behind him, to his twelve-pound library-sized *Webster's Third New International Dictionary*. He hunched over the stand, looking for the "K"s, while talking back over his shoulder.

"What was that about a doctor?"

"Don went to the doctor about his throat again."

"What'd the doctor say?"

"Don won't tell her."

There was a squeak from the register, then another: the sound of a cork being eased from a jug of wine. Already, he thought, she's starting already, at ten o'clock in the morning. He shook his head, then read.

> ka·chi·na *or* ka·tci·na *also* ka·tchi·na *or* ca·chi·na \kə-'chēnə\ *n* -s [Hopi *qačina* supernatural] 1 : one of the deified ancestral spirits believed among the Hopi and other Pueblo Indians to visit the pueblos at intervals (as to bring rain) 2 : one of the elaborately masked impersonators of the kachinas that dance at

agricultural ceremonies 3 *or* **kachina doll** : a doll representing
a kachina made from cottonwood root and given to Hopi children
by the kachina dancers

He read it over several times; they were calling both the spirit
and the masked dancer a kachina. Hmm. Then how could you tell
them apart? He thought about that for a moment, his finger poised
reflectively on the side of his nose, pleased in an academic sort of
way and interested all the more by finding a contradiction in the
terms, then swiveled back around to his desk, looking casually,
lost in thought, out the window, through the branches of the trees,
across the terrace, and down the field to the wash, where the
kachina, to his shock, was gone. George pulled off his glasses and
stood up abruptly, sending his office chair crashing back into the
dictionary stand. Then the kachina stood up again, having bent
over to look at something on the bank, the blue conical mask once
again moving around in and out of George's view through the rails
of the fence and the pine branches. George sighed, blinked a
couple times, ahemed, and sat back down again.

"What's the matter, George?" Mary Olive's voice said from the
register. "Do you see something?"

I can't make a sound, I can't make a move. It's like being bugged.
"No, everything's okay," he said, and swiveled around again, back
to the dictionary, looking for the "H"s.

"Is he still down there?"

"Yes, dear. He's still there."

"What's he doing?"

"Can't you see him from down there?"

"Yes, but I can't see what he's doing."

"I can't either. I think he's just poking around."

"Do you think I'm silly for worrying about him?"

Yes. "No, dear. I don't think you're silly for worrying."

She was quiet for a moment and he wondered what she was
doing; he listened, but he couldn't tell. She probably wasn't doing
anything. Her spot at the counter was almost directly below him;
he pictured her sitting on the kitchen stool, drinking her glass of

wine (*Already*), smoking, staring out the window. He felt sorry for her, in a way: for all her bluster, she was a very bothered, very insecure woman. He tried to help her, she needed him to take care of her; she depended on him to take care of things, to handle little emergencies like this—like clogged drains and broken toasters and finding a kachina in the back yard—to protect her, she was so afraid of everything. He smiled to himself, pleased with himself, content with his purpose, satisfied with his role—*My big brave protector,* she joked, but he knew she meant it—and scanned the column, resetting the glasses on his nose for the small print, for "Hopi."

"Do you see Don yet?" she said.

"No. Not yet."

"Sally said he'd be right over. But I wouldn't put it past her not to tell him."

"Now, now, dear. Be kind."

Sometimes it was like living with an invalid; sometimes it was like living with a child. Oh well, at least she didn't get in his way. *Sometimes it's like living with no one at all.* He waited but she didn't say anything more; he heard her moving around, muttering to herself. He shook his head and stretched his neck away from his collar and read.

> ho·pi \'hō(,)pē, -ַpi\ *n, pl* hopi *also* hopis *usu cap* [Hopi *Hópi,* lit., good, peaceful] 1 a : a Shoshonean people of Pueblo Indians in northeastern Arizona b : a member of such people 2 : the language of the Hopi people 3 : FRENCH BEIGE

That didn't tell him much. He was about to look up "Shoshonean" when he noticed, a few lines under the entry, after "hoping" and "hopingly":

> hopi way *n, usu cap H & W* : the ethical and behavioral code of the Hopi people depicted dramatically in the annual ceremonial cycle and including rules for each of the roles which a person of either sex and at the various age levels is expected to assume throughout life

Now, that was something: to have an entire moral code taken from your name. Of course there was the American Way, but that didn't have very good connotations: "Buy now, pay later, it's the American Way!" This sounded different, though the dictionary didn't give the specifics of the Hopi Way. But if the code was "dramatically depicted" during the ceremonies, the guy in their back yard might be one of the depictors. Interesting. George flipped on to the "S"s.

sho·sho·ne·an \shə'shōnēən, shō'-, ¦shōshə¦nēən\ *n, pl* **shoshonean** *or* **shoshoneans** *usu cap* [*Shoshone* + *-an*] 1 : a language family of the Uto-Aztecan phylum comprising the languages of most of the Uto-Aztecan peoples in the U.S. 2 a : any of the Indian peoples whose language is Shoshonean b : a member of any such peoples

Nothing there; on to the "U"s.

uto-aztecan \'yü(,)tō+\ *n, usu cap* U & A [*Ute* + *-o* + *Aztec* + *-an*] 1 : a language phylum comprising the Nahuatlan, Taracahitian, Piman, and Shoshonean families 2 a : a people speaking a Uto-Aztecan language b : a member of such people

Aztecs; the other names sounded ancient, and from Middle America, too. Interesting, and strange. George turned around in the swivel chair again, back to his desk, and after checking out the window again—yes, the kachina was still there; and for a few seconds, as he caught glimpses of the colorful figure behind the pine branches, he saw a sun priest in a cloak of feathers and a tall headdress, standing at the top of a great stone pyramid, in front of an altar where a young girl is bent back over the stone, her arms stretched behind her by attendants, as the priest plunges a sacrificial knife into her breasts, ripping out her heart and holding it, bloody, still pulsing erratically, frantically, toward the sun (*What a terrible waste,* George thought, *of pretty young girls, hundreds in a day, stacks of hearts, all those bodies, groan*)—he, still sitting, walked the chair on its rollers over to his filing cabinet and opened the center drawer, flipping through the folders until he found the one marked "New Home": the brochures and pamphlets and Chamber of Commerce flyers that he had collected when they first arrived.

He leafed through the stack of material—FLAGSTAFF: ARIZONA'S LAND OF SUPERLATIVES; FLAGSTAFF: CITY IN THE PINES; FLAGSTAFF: THE CITY OF SEVEN WONDERS—but aside from a lot of miscellaneous information—in 1978 there were 10,494 electric meters in town and the post office processed 26,950 pieces of mail; the name Flagstaff came from a pine tree that was stripped of its branches to serve, reasonably enough, as a flagstaff for the local celebration of the country's hundredth birthday in 1876 (reasonably enough; but somehow a dead, nude tree sticking out of the ground didn't sound like anything to be proud of); the Chamber of Commerce noted, under Business Opportunities, that "Anyone with sound ideas and adequate capital can make his own opportunity" (*Good thinking, men!*)—the only listing he found about the Hopi was that the reservation was listed among the local Scenic Attractions ("No cameras or tape recorders").

He rolled back to his desk and thought for a moment, about nothing really, then took the monocular again from the center drawer and went, tiptoed, back to the far window, humming to himself. In the instrument—it kept jiggling about; he was shaky this morning for some reason, he had to steady it with two hands; then his other eye kept fluttering open and he needed a spare finger to keep it closed—the kachina filled the small circle of the lens. The kachina had his back turned toward the house; George studied the figure painted on the back of the cape, the bird with the human head among the faded splotches of red and green and yellow. He clucked softly, cluck cluck; he had never been able to work up much reverence for the idea of a deity as a wafer of bread or The Great Bookkeeper, but he thought it would be sort of fun to believe in something with feathers and rattles and a big blue head. Just then, however, the kachina whirled around and faced George in the lens, looked right at him, glared back at him as if he heard him and was insulted. "Hello, George."

George jumped and poked himself in the eye with the monocular.

"Ouch! Don't do that!"

"I'm sorry, I didn't mean to catch you spying," Mary Olive said, leaning with her arms folded, watching him, against the door frame.

"You didn't catch me spying." George went back to his desk, holding his hand against his eye. "I was just checking to make sure the guy was still down there."

"And is he?"

"Yes," he said and sat down, still holding his eye.

"Let me see."

"You can't see anything. He's just there."

"I mean, let me see your eye."

"Oh."

She pressed his face between her hands as she gazed into his eyes, a smile on her face as if she knew something she shouldn't. *Is she laughing at me?* George squirmed uncomfortably; he had the sudden image of her giving his head a tug and pulling it off his shoulders like the end of a Tinkertoy. She tilted his head this way and that, then nodded and pulled her mouth, knowingly, and gave him a slap, harder than a love tap, on the cheek.

"Mary Olive!"

"There's nothing wrong with you, George."

"You hit me. That hurt."

"I just wanted to make sure you were alive."

"Of course I'm alive."

Mary Olive cocked her head dubiously at him.

George harrumphed. "I've got work to do," he said, laying his hands on the papers in front of him to affirm their presence.

"Of course you do, dear," Mary Olive said. She reached over him for the monocular and took it to the side window, training it at the Pikes' house. Usually gadgets or instruments of any kind stymied Mary Olive, but George noticed she handled the monocular as though she was familiar with it, as though she used it when he wasn't there; he decided he was going to have to start locking his desk whenever he went out. As she stood at the window, the light shone through her flimsy gown, revealing her body underneath. It was not a revelation that particularly thrilled him.

Her body was scrawny and, he thought, unlovely, the skin loose around her upper arms and thighs, her ass flat and almost non-existent. Her bare legs, below the bottom of the gown, were curveless, like twin white two-by-fours, the skin blotched and blue-veined; her ankles looked sharp enough to wound. George shuddered and busied himself looking through his papers.

"So Sally doesn't know if the doctors didn't find anything," he said absently, "or if Don just isn't telling."

"She said all Don did was mutter something about doctors charging too much to say the obvious, and went back outside to work."

"That sounds like Don. They could tell him he was dying and he'd go out and start digging his own grave. He'd say he'd want it done right."

"George, don't say things like that!" She looked at him but he didn't look at her.

"I was only kidding."

"Well, it's not funny. He might really be sick."

"I wouldn't have said it if I thought there was any chance it was true."

He was about to tell her what he had learned concerning the Hopi and kachinas from the dictionary when he noticed she was crying.

"Mary Olive, dear, what's wrong?" He got up quickly and went to her, put his arms around her.

"I'm scared, George. I don't like that thing down there. We don't know who he is and what he wants or what he's going to do next."

He patted her head against his chest. "Now now now. He's not going to hurt anybody. I'm sure there's some perfectly good reason why . . ."

"He's probably some crazy Indian who came back here to get even for Wounded Knee or something," she sniffled.

"I don't think so," he said, trying not to smile.

"You're laughing at me, George, but I don't think it's at all funny." She leaned back to glare at him.

George cradled her head back on his chest and rocked her slowly from side to side a couple of times; then the rock turned into a sway, and the sway turned into a dip, the dip turned into a bounce, and they began to two-step awkwardly around the room. She tried to continue to look sad and worried, her bottom lip stuck out like a child's, but he laughed at her and she laughed with him and he began to hum their accompaniment. He looked out the window and saw Don standing on the terrace, under the branches of the trees among the lawn furniture, looking up at them.

"Oh, there's Don."

"Don!" she said, and broke away from him and rushed out of the room. George looked after her, at the space where she had been, his arms still in the position to hold her. She was a strange woman. He waved to Don and held up a finger to say he'd be right down.

6

By the time George got downstairs and out the back door, Don stood at the end of the terrace, his hands wedged in his back pockets, his elbows winged out at his sides, as he picked at the loose stones on top of the wall with the toe of his boot. He was a small, wiry man, a few years older than George; he was dressed in work clothes, old Levi's and a blue work shirt, his clothes and white beard flecked with wood chips; when he took off his battered straw Resistol to wipe the sweatband, his scalp shone through his thin white hair, as pink as the underbelly of a hound. He was preoccupied, thinking about something, and hadn't noticed the kachina, bent over in the wash. George hurried over to him.

"Don, I really appreciate you coming like this," he said, pumping the man's hand, blinking once, closing his eyes for a second, then opening them abruptly, an exaggerated gesture, to show his pleasure, his sincerity.

"Sally said it was important." Don's voice was normally a resonant bass, but now it came out as little more than a whisper, barely audible.

"Don, your voice—"

"What voice, George? It sounds to me as though I don't have any voice at all."

"I didn't know it was this bad."

"Ignore it, George, like I do." Don tried to smile, but all he did was bare his teeth.

"But I feel bad now about calling you over."

"I'm okay, it's just that nobody can hear what I say now. Count your blessings. It doesn't hurt any more to talk than it does not to talk, it just hurts. I mean it, just try to ignore it."

Don looked away from him, down at the toe of his boot, as he picked again at the loose stones on top of the wall. His face was strained, his neck muscles taut.

George folded his hands in front of him, across the swell of his stomach, leaned forward a little, trying to see Don's face. "Who did you see, Doc Harvey?"

Don nodded, still not looking at him.

"Did he say it was all right to keep working?"

"One doctor tells you one thing, another tells you another. Just because a man's a doctor doesn't mean he always knows what he's talking about, you should know that."

"I thought you liked Doc Harvey. . . ."

"Of course I like Doc Harvey. I've known him as long as I've lived here."

"Then I don't understand—"

"Look, I didn't come over here to talk about this."

George pulled up his shoulders, coughed a little, blinked a couple of times. They stood side by side on top of the wall for a few moments, neither one saying anything, Don picking at the stones with his boot; when he succeeded in flipping one out of its socket, he tried to toe it back in place. The mid-morning sun was brilliant, the mountain air clear. At the end of the yard, the kachina was still bent over digging at something, his back mostly hidden by the fence so that he was barely noticeable. Then, as Don lifted his head to gaze off toward the hillside, the kachina suddenly stood upright and looked up toward the house, looked at them.

"What the hell!" Don croaked.

"That's what I wanted to show you."

Don looked back and forth between George and the kachina a couple of times, then headed down the steps and across the field toward it, George hurrying along behind. When they reached the fence, the kachina nodded his tall blue head once, *Hello.* With the sun higher in the sky, the feathers no longer glowed but the entire figure seemed more radiant.

"What do you think about that?" George beamed.

"What's going on here?" Don said, pushing his hat to the back of his head.

"I thought maybe you could tell me."

"Who is that?"

"It's a kachina."

The kachina cocked his head, as if interested to hear what they were saying; the cluster of red yarn at the tip of the mask slid from one side of the point to the other.

"I know it's a kachina," Don said. "I mean who is it? Who's wearing the mask?"

"I don't know," George said cautiously, folding his hands against his great tummy. "He wouldn't say who he is. But he seems friendly."

The kachina nodded slightly: *Thank you.*

"You talked to him?"

"Well, not really. I mean I tried, but he wouldn't say anything."

Don stared at the figure, anything but pleased. "How'd he get here?"

"I don't know, he just appeared." George shrugged. "Maybe he dropped from the sky, ha ha."

"George, don't be an ass."

"Don."

The kachina looked at George. *Is this guy a friend of yours?*

"Is this some kind of joke you dreamed up with Sally?" Don said, turning toward him, squaring off.

"Sally?"

The kachina looked around to see if he had missed someone.

"Because I don't think it's a damn bit funny."

"Don, wait a minute—"

Don turned to leave but hesitated when he saw Mary Olive hurrying down the yard to join them. In a few minutes' time she had changed into slacks and a blouse, adjusted her hair, and put on her makeup, things that usually took her an hour; she looked fresh and happy and ten years younger. George was amazed. She kissed Don on the cheek, smiled at him, took his arm. Don looked as though he wished he had left sooner.

"How's your throat?" she said.

"It hurts. What's this all about?"

"I don't know," she said, hunching her shoulders, her expression suddenly just as concerned as Don's. "We just looked out the window and here he was."

"Don, I—" George sputtered.

"Do you know anything about him?" Mary Olive asked Don.

Don looked at the kachina. The kachina leaned forward, resting on his staff, so he could hear better.

"I don't know for sure." Don cupped his white beard in his hand, pulled at it slowly a couple of times. "It's been a long time since I studied these things. But I think his name is Aholi."

The three of them looked at the kachina; the kachina gave a little bow. George waited a moment, then said, "A holy what?"

The kachina looked as though he wanted to groan.

"Not a holy anything," Don rasped. "Aholi. He's one of the chief kachinas, if he's who I think he is. They're very important figures."

The kachina wagged his head a little: *So-so.*

"What's he doing here?" Mary Olive said. She still held on to his arm, a two-handed grip, and looked intently into his face, her concern mirroring Don's concern, almost to the point of caricature.

43

"You really don't know anything about it?"

"We haven't the vaguest idea," George said, putting his hands in his pockets, rocking back on his heels.

"I don't know why he'd be here," Don said. "The kachinas are never seen off the reservation—well, I take that back. Once somebody convinced the Hopi to let the kachinas appear at the Grand Canyon, I think, but most of the Hopi thought it was a mistake. In the Rio Grande pueblos, over in New Mexico, whites never get to see the kachinas at all. These things are very sacred."

The Aholi looked at George. *What do you think about that?*

"But what do we do with him?" George said.

"Don't do anything with him," Don said quickly. "Just leave him alone. Let him do whatever it is he came to do and go back where he came from. You don't want to get involved with a thing like this."

"You mean you think he came here to do something?"

"There's shrines and holy places all over these slopes. These mountains are also sacred to the Hopi. The San Francisco peaks are supposed to be the home of the kachinas."

The three of them looked up at the peaks, rising above the forest on the other side of the wash and the tree-covered slopes of the foothills. The kachina turned around to look at the mountains too, then turned back to them, looked at George. *Be it ever so humble . . .*

Don sighed heavily, as if he didn't like talking about this; he took off his hat, held it down at his side. "The Hopi believe, or at least we think the Hopi believe, that everything that happens in the material world, the Upper World, has its counterpart in the spiritual world, the Lower World or the Under World. The material world is more or less the reverse image of the spiritual, and vice versa. When the sun shines in the Upper World, it's dark in the Under World; when it's summer in the Upper World, it's winter in the Lower World. The kachinas are the beings who can travel back and forth between the material and the spiritual worlds, and influence one or the other. Half the year they live in this world, and the other half they live in the spiritual world. And when they go to live in the spirit world, they enter the Under World through the San Francisco Mountains."

"Maybe this one took a wrong turn somewhere and missed the front door of the mountain." George smiled.

Don glowered at him, but before he could say anything the kachina stamped his foot, the turtle-shell rattle giving one loud *clack*. The three of them looked at him. *Now that I have your attention* . . . From the sack in his left hand the kachina took a handful of white meal and drew a design on the ground, a design that consisted of three half-circles, two side by side with the third sitting on top, a pyramid of sorts. The Aholi looked at his audience, to make sure they were paying attention; then he put the butt of his staff on the center of the design and swung the top in a slow, wide arc, a circle, as he sang in a high piercing voice, *"Ah-hol-li-i-i-i-i!"* When he was finished, he looked at them again, looked at George, and gave a sharp nod of his head. *So there.*

"Another country heard from," Mary Olive said.

"Amazing," George said, his eyes wide. "Simply amazing." He walked over to the fence for a closer look, then turned around to say something to Don, but Don was already walking back across the field toward the woods, back toward his house, carrying his hat in his hand.

"What's the matter with Don?" George said.

"You must have said something to upset him," Mary Olive said, looking reproachful.

"I didn't say anything." George headed up the field after him. "Don, wait a minute!"

"Don't leave me alone with this thing!" Mary Olive screamed and ran for the house.

As he hurried after Don, George glanced back over his shoulder: the kachina stood in the wash, looking around, looking after them, bewildered.

Where'd everybody go?

7

"Don, wait a minute. Wait a minute!"

Don stopped at the edge of the field, at the edge of the trees—he could already feel the coolness of the shadows, the slight breeze—his arms down at his sides, pressed against his body, his hat in his hand. It had been a mistake to come over; even though Mary Olive told Sally it was important, he should have known better. What was Mary Olive trying to do, snuggling up to him like that? Was it her way of trying to pretend there hadn't been anything going on between them? Or was it her way—more likely—to get back at him for telling her that he wasn't going to see her any more? *(Or, maybe, was she just that happy to see me?)* It was a mistake to come over, for any reason, wrong.

"Don, wait!"

I'm waiting, he said to himself, and turned around slowly.

George was puffing up the slight hill, his face flushed, his forehead broken out in sweat, his expression a mixture of concern and his own embarrassment at being winded so easily. Across the field, Mary Olive stood on the steps of the terrace, her arms wrapped about herself; when she saw Don look her direction, she waved. Don didn't wave back. In the wash, the kachina stood looking around as if wondering what to do next. Don felt woozy, exhausted; all he wanted to do was to get back home, back to his cabin, to lie down and rest awhile, to get out of the sun and heat. To get away from here, to get away from George. *This is wrong, wrong.*

"Don, what is it . . . what's the matter?" George said as he caught up to him, then leaned over, his hands braced on his thighs, wheezing, gulping air.

"I should be asking you," Don said. "You're the one who looks ready to collapse."

"I'm just . . . out of breath. Been meaning to lose some weight," he said, straightening up a little, patting his stomach, "but you know how it is."

"Yes, I know how it is." He waited while George recovered.

"I just wanted to ask you . . . what you're so angry about."

"I'm not angry, George."

"You certainly act like you're angry about something. Phewee!"

George exhaled sharply, blinked his eyes a couple of times, grinned tight-lipped in some attempt to be amusing and friendly. Don turned and walked on into the trees; it was impossible to try to explain to him. The small valley between their two homes was filled with second growth, young pines and groves of aspens, the branches overhead not yet thick enough to block the sun, so that grass still grew on the slopes of the hills, ankle-deep among the trees, and the trees, the pines and aspens, were still on equal footing, had not yet begun to struggle for the available light and space. It was cooler here in the leaf-filtered sunlight, and Don felt more relaxed the deeper he walked in among the trees. But George crashed after him, overtook him, and stood in front of him, blocking the path, looking very unhappy.

"Is it because we called you over to look at the kachina?"

"No, of course not," he said hoarsely, not wanting to look at him, wondering if it was worth it to walk around him or if he'd just come after him again. "I'm sorry I can't give you any more information about him."

"You told us quite a lot."

"Okay then, fine. Good. I'm glad." But George still didn't get out of his way.

"So what is it?"

Don sighed heavily; with each breath the air whistled in his throat—whistled, at least, to his ears; he wondered if anyone else could hear it—as much a pressure as a pain; the pain itself was as if he had swallowed a jagged piece of ice that was lodged halfway down, that he couldn't cough up or swallow. He thought of the Buddhist idea, taught during breathing exercises, that the breath is a fine silver cord that extends down the throat when you inhale, all the way to the base of the spine, and then out again on the exhale; except that in his case the silver cord must be resting against the inside of his throat, because every time he breathed, every time his breath traveled in and out, whether he was talking or not, the air felt as though it cut into his flesh.

"It has nothing to do with you," he said finally.

"It has to do with something."

Don closed his eyes for a long second and opened them again; he tapped his hat against his leg a couple of times. "I just don't think you realize what you're dealing with here. How serious that kachina could be. I don't think you realize what the implications could be of a thing like that. That is, assuming it is a real kachina and not just some fugitive from an institution."

"But that's why we called you. I want to know what to do about it."

"That's just my point, George. Why do you have to do anything about it? Just leave it alone. Don't even go near it. Don't muck around with something you don't understand."

"I want to understand."

"Then don't muck around with what you *can't* understand. That's what I'm telling you. You don't even know enough about this whole thing to know what you *can't* know." Don broke off, coughing hoarsely.

George watched him cough, blinking, each blink slow and determined, as if he was trying to register, print each word on his mind, what Don had just said. There were times Don wanted to hit him.

"George, there's a beautiful idea in this world that we're all basically the same, that all mankind is the same, that we're one people. That you and I are the same, that Americans and Russians and Saudis and Tanzanians are all the same kind of people deep down inside, and we can all understand each other if we just get deep enough. It's a bunch of crap. We're all different, that's the terrible part. And the sooner everybody understands that, the better off we'll all be. You have no more chance understanding a Hopi than if he came from a different planet. You'd have more chance understanding someone from a different planet, because you wouldn't be fooled by the superficial similarities."

"But we are all the same," George laughed, holding out his hands as if they displayed a self-evident truth. "Physically, the structure of the brain is essentially the same—"

"No, the brain is not essentially the same. Your brain and a Hopi's brain might look the same from the outside, but inside they're totally different. What an individual experiences changes the cell structure of the brain, and how impulses are transmitted and perceived—"

"Well, yes, of course—"

"And those changes accumulate and are passed along genetically—"

"Okay, but the basic structure is the same—"

"When psychologists try to give Hopi children some of the standard emotional tests, the results always come out as if the kids are crazy, but they're not, it's just that their concepts are different from ours."

"I don't see how that's possible. . . ."

"There's evidence that the ancestors of the Hopi were here in the Southwest ten thousand years ago; there's some evidence that says they were here sixty-five thousand years ago. There's even a theory that man developed in the Southwest and then spread to Asia and Africa, not the other way around. The whites and the Hopi might be all living here in Arizona in the late twentieth century A.D., but you and I got here by going around the world in one direction, and the Hopi got here by going around the world in the other direction. It's impossible for us to understand what they think or how they see the world."

"Aren't you exaggerating, just a little?"

Don's voice was getting weaker, barely a rasp, so that George, in order to hear him, had to bend forward, as if frozen in the middle of a bow. And Don thought: *Yes, the man is silly enough to do that, to go out of his way to listen to somebody tell him to his face that he's silly.*

"In the Hopi language, there is no past tense. Or rather, the past tense is the same as the present tense, so that everything that ever was, still is, still is now. Something that happened centuries ago is as much a part of the present as this very moment, and the future is only the past and the present getting later. That's not the same world we see, George. That's no exaggeration."

"No," George said, his eyes wide. "That's fascinating."

Don had the sinking feeling that, instead of discouraging George, he had only made him all the more interested. "George, the Indians guard their kachinas with their lives. In New Mexico there's stories about non-Indians being killed because they saw the kachinas when they shouldn't have. There's stories about Indians killing their own people when they gave forbidden information to anthropologists, not a long time ago but in the last fifty years. You don't know what the guy is doing down there. You don't know that somebody didn't steal that mask and costume and half the Hopi reservation is out looking for him."

"But they're liable to think I had something to do with it," George said, horrified.

It was hopeless; Don walked around him, into the trees.

"But you can't just leave me with it now," George said, hurrying after him.

"I told you what I'd do," he said without stopping. "Just lock your doors and leave him alone until he goes away."

"Isn't there somebody at Hopi I could call about this?"

"What are you going to say?" Don hacked. " 'Hello, there's a kachina in my back yard, I was wondering if it's one of yours'? Besides, each village in Hopi is totally separate; one doesn't necessarily know what's going on with any of the others. I don't even know if every village has an Aholi. That is, if that *is* an Aholi. You start calling around asking questions like that and you'll start all kinds of trouble, for everybody."

"What about the police?"

"There's BIA, Bureau of Indian Affairs, but most of the Hopi don't trust them." He stopped. "That's what I'm trying to tell you. This isn't like anything else you've ever dealt with. You have no business getting involved with it. Just consider it a gift, that you got the chance to look at it close up for a little while, and be thankful for it."

"A gift?" George said, and laughed.

Don looked away, at a single aspen a few yards away, its white slender trunk; in the sunlight that filtered down through the branches of the surrounding, taller ponderosas, the small triangular leaves of the aspen caught the slight breeze and the entire tree appeared to shimmer.

George steadied himself against the trunk of a pine, balancing on one leg as he raised the other to pick the blades of grass from the welt of his shoe.

"Try down at the museum," Don said finally. *If you have to do something, if you just can't leave it alone.* "They do a lot of research there about the Hopi. Talk to one of the curators. But be careful how you present it, you're liable to have all kinds of anthropologists tramping around your back yard wanting to interview it."

"I hadn't thought about the museum," George said. "And I hadn't thought about people wanting to bother it either. That's a good idea, thank you, I'll be careful." George considered something for a moment, considered how he wanted to say it. "I didn't know you were this interested in Indians. I thought it was mainly Sally."

"The Indian Lady of Flagstaff," Don whispered ruefully. "Most of what Sally knows about Indians she got from me. The trouble is she got it wrong."

"I thought she had some vision from a medicine man. . . ."

"She got that wrong too. It's a long story, George, one that isn't very pleasant to me, one that I don't want to go into now."

"But wouldn't she like to come over and see the kachina?"

"I want Sally kept out of it."

"But why?"

"I just do. Let the kachina go on its way before Sally knows about it. Do me that favor."

"Well, okay, Don," George said slowly. "If that's the way you want it. . . ."

"That's the way I want it."

8

He walked on through the trees a little ways, down the grassy slope, the shadows of the branches and leaves shifting slightly with the breeze in front of him, shifting as though the ground itself were shifting, as though the ground itself were moving, had a life of its own, and all he was doing was marking time and trying to keep his balance. He stopped and looked back. George was making his heavy way back through the trees, his bulk appearing to fill the spaces between the trees, zigzagging back up the slope, a great egg of a man; then he was beyond the woods and starting across the field, back toward his house, and Don watched as he slowly disappeared, in sections, piece by piece, first his feet, then ankles, knees, legs, buttocks, trunk, shoulders, the man walking beyond the rise at the edge of the woods, his head bobbing along the edge of the ground as it got smaller and smaller until it too was gone, swallowed up. The man was blind, a pompous fool, Don told himself, but he couldn't worry about that now; at this point it was every man for himself.

He looked down at his hand and discovered he was carrying his hat. When did he take it off? Why? I'm getting to be a forgetful old man, he thought. He walked on, on down the slope, down through the trees, still carrying the battered straw Resistol in his hand.

He noticed motion at the edge of his vision and looked up: above the branches of the ponderosas a crow soared toward the mountains, talking to itself about something. What did it mean to see a crow? Depends on who sees it, he smiled to himself. He had once started a list of Indian beliefs about the crow—some said it was a good omen, some said it was bad; some said it was good if it flew from left to right, some said it was good if it flew right to left, some said it was bad if it flew left to right—but had stopped the list when he got to twenty, most of his listings contradictory. Thirteen ways of looking at a blackbird: the blackbird is in the eyes of the beholder. He laughed out loud: what did it mean if his crow was actually a raven? Then he started coughing, rasping, again; the inside of his throat felt seared. His heart was pounding, he could feel it throughout his entire body, there was a high-pitched screaming in his ears. *Come on, heart, not you too.* Christ, one system went on the fritz and they all wanted to get their licks in. He sat down on the trunk of a fallen tree, stretched out his legs, put his straw hat over his knees.

A patch of sunlight glared in his eyes. He moved over to get away from it, then thought no, now that he was sitting down, now that he was out of the heat of the day, he wanted the sun, even if he had to squint: he wanted the warmth, he wanted the feel of it on his face. There would be time enough not to be able to feel such things, an eternity not to be able to feel, to have the sensation of, heat or cold or air. To his right was another stand of aspens. He loved the trees: the slender white trunks, these young trees with their trunks only as thick as a young girl's, a teenage girl's, leg, with the same grace and angularity, all beauty and awkwardness, the white bark scarred, like eyes, like mouths, where the branches fell off. The flat, thin, spadelike leaves caught the slightest wind and the trees appeared to tremble; in the fall, when the leaves changed, whole slopes of the foothills shimmered gold. Quaking aspens, they were called, but he used to think that was wrong, misleading: he used to think of quaking as in an earthquake, as if the trees were dangerous, threatening, until he realized that it might be the trees themselves that were afraid, trembling, shuddering. He could sit among them for hours.

He thought of the kachina, the Aholi in George and Mary Olive's back yard; of the kachinas he had seen at Hopi. While he taught at the University of New Mexico, in Albuquerque, he had traveled to Hopi a dozen times or more to see the dances, but he had rarely gone since they moved to Arizona (which was ironic, at best, because one of the reasons he had taken the job in Flagstaff—the university here was a good little school, for what it was, but the move was not what you would call a step up in his profession—was to be closer to the dances: he had found it difficult to live with the idea of taking a job in another part of the country and to think of himself walking down a sidewalk in Minnesota or Oregon or North Carolina and realizing, as he did so, that there might be Snow Kachinas dancing at Shipaulovi or Corn Dancers at Walpi, that they were dancing without his being there, without his being able to see them) and not at all since Sally had taken the Indians, and the Hopi in particular, to be her own special province. Now he couldn't stand to go to dances with her: her eyes glazed over, she jiggled along with the music, and from the expression on her face she appeared to be experiencing either a beatific vision or gas pains; it was embarrassing—she had become just another white woman who wanted, desperately, for who knows what reason, to be an Indian; she had become just another phony.

He remembered the first time he took her to see a dance, in New Mexico, while he was still teaching there (she was from Ohio; she had never known, never even imagined, such things existed), at Santo Domingo on Christmas Eve. They had only been dating a short time, he had only recently left his wife, the divorce hadn't even come through, and they spent the day together in the Travelodge in Santa Fe. He had planned to take her first to San Felipe for midnight mass and then to Santo Domingo, but it was nearly 1:00 A.M. by the time they got to San Felipe and they were too late—neither one of them had wanted to get up, get dressed, and go out in the near-zero weather, but he insisted, telling her that this was one thing she couldn't miss, the one time of the year when the Indians danced in the churches, danced before the altar of the Christian God, the Comanche dancers just coming out of the church as they arrived, the tall, feathered headdresses glowing in the streetlights of the pueblo. He decided it was just as well: he didn't particularly like the Comanche dancers, with their head-dresses and sun shields, their spears and war whoops and fur leggings, anyway. They were too much what everybody thought Indian dancers should be—when the men of the pueblo put on the trappings of the Comanches, became for a while raiders and killers to honor and celebrate all those things that they, the Pueblos, were not—they weren't what he wanted her to see first; he didn't want to reinforce her already Hollywood ideas of Indians.

So they drove back up the Rio Grande the fifteen miles to Santo Domingo, getting to the pueblo when it was almost two in the morning, though the pueblo was still wide awake, the night brittle cold, the temperature well below zero and the snow frozen to the ground, but the air filled with the smells of piñon smoke and coffee and fresh bread, the lights glowing in the windows of the small adobe houses, the narrow unpaved streets busy with men and women wrapped in blankets hurrying back and forth, the beehive ovens glowing and smoking in the yards, the children running around in the darkness, and the feeling of anticipation everywhere. The church was lighted but nearly empty; the pews had been removed and as yet there were only a few people inside, a few whites from Santa Fe or Albuquerque, sitting around on the floor against the side walls, and in front the old men, some of the elders of the pueblo (dressed as they usually did for ceremonies, in light-colored slacks with piping around the bottom of the legs, which were split to the ankle so they flopped around the men's moccasins, in loose-fitting, brightly colored shirts with the tails hanging out, and turquoise and squash-blossom necklaces), sitting on a line of straight chairs in front of the sanctuary, sitting with their backs toward the altar. As Don and Sally waited, finding a place to sit down on a small ledge against the wall, looking at the other whites on the other side of the church looking back at them, there was coffee and pueblo bread and apples served in a room off to the side, a squat old Indian woman came and told them they were welcome to help themselves, though Sally was too shy and Don was afraid they might lose their place, and one of the old men went around the room offering the steadily growing number of whites pieces of chocolate from a large box of candy (Don wanted to tell her the box of candy was a Whitman Sampler, but was afraid she'd giggle out loud, was afraid she wouldn't be able to maintain the right mood of reverence), thanking each person for coming. From the balcony came the sounds of birds, mechanical birds or bird whistles, like the plastic whistles his kids had that you could spit in and make warble, and some of the Indian children played up there too, making their own bird whistles and then giggling and ducking back out of sight. Through the night people continued to gather until by 4:00 A.M. the church was packed, jammed with Indian women with their shawls and blankets pulled up over their heads and teenagers looking around with a mixture of reproach and curiosity at the whites, Don and Sally included, who stood trying to press inconspicuously against the walls. The church became so hot that he had had to take off his overcoat and sweater, the air thick and full of unfamiliar smells, when they heard the beating of a distant drum and the sound of bells (before, he had thought of them as sleigh bells, ring-jing-jingling too, calling up images of horse-drawn sleighs pulling blanket-wrapped lovers through a snowy night, or over morning bridges to Grandmother's house we go, but now, having once heard them tied to the legs of dancing Indians, he associated the sound of the bells with something much, much different) and the men chanting as the dancers entered the church and walked in two lines down the center, where the aisle would normally have been, to the altar. There were fifty of them, maybe more, lined up as if for a corn dance, two men side by side, then two women, extending through the church past where the singers stood and the drummer and on out the door into the night: the men wore dance kilts and were bare-chested, with evergreen boughs strapped to their upper arms and holding evergreen boughs in their left hands and a dance rattle in their right; the women wore the traditional manta, the black dress with one shoulder exposed, and tablitas, sky altars, tall wooden tablets sticking up from the top of their heads. Then the drum, the deep-voiced drum called a belly-drum because that's where you felt it, the sound hit you straight in the stomach (sometimes after listening to it for a while you became physically ill, sick at your stomach, when it stopped again, a deep pit inside where something was suddenly gone, silent, again), began to pound, and the singers started the chant and the deep jingling of the bells tied to the dancers' legs filled the church as they danced the way they did for a corn dance, a dance almost like running in place, almost laughable in its simplicity when he first saw it until he had seen it enough to realize that it was as serious as anything in the world, the men's legs pumping up and down, the women's steps softer, their feet barely lifting, patting the floor, or, as the books about Indians like to put it, caressing the earth. (An Indian told him later that maybe the dance they did that night was the Plumed Serpent but the Indian wasn't sure or, and this was more likely, wasn't saying.) And there were dancers between the files of dancers, clowns, perhaps, though not painted in the black and white stripes of the koshares or the *chiffonetes*: there was one dancer holding the skin of what might have been a fox—it looked as if it had been flattened out on a highway and rotted for a month or two but maybe it was just ancient—holding it as though the animal were running or flying, motioning it toward the altar and then away; and there was an old man, maybe in his seventies, maybe older, dressed in white (it looked like his underwear, his long johns), his profile as sharp as a hawk's, his eyes glistening, his long gray hair bouncing on his shoulders as he danced. Holding Sally's hand, the dancers and the sounds of the singers and the drum and the bells filling him, Don thought he was as happy as he ever could be or ever had the right to be, though midway through the dance Sally had to sit down, on the floor among the people standing around them, afraid she was going to faint, not, as she liked to tell people later, when he heard her tell the story after they were married, because the experience was too overwhelming and she felt the dance had touched something deep inside her, but because they hadn't eaten anything for over sixteen hours except a piece of chocolate offered by an Indian and because they had killed a bottle of Jack Daniel's and two six-packs of Rainier Ale between them over the same length of time and because over the same length of time she had been plunked half a dozen times by her English professor.

He had wanted to be an old man like the one they had seen dancing in the church that night, maybe not with the long gray hair down his shoulders but maybe with that too, an energetic old man, aware of himself and of the world, nimble, alert, alive. Well, that didn't seem possible now. He got up from the fallen tree, put his hat back on his head, and started to walk—when a sharp pain cut through his body, a thin slicing thread of pain running from his bowels to his right shoulder, as if his bowels and his shoulder were somehow connected by pain. *Now, what the hell can that be?* He waited a moment and the pain went away again, but the ferocity with which it appeared, the suddenness, the finality, left him uneasy. What did they say? Death was always standing beside you, to your left, watching. Don looked to his left but all he saw among the trunks of ponderosas was a single young aspen, shimmering. *No, not yet.* He remembered the part in Castaneda where Don Juan tells Carlos that, when it's time to die, Death comes and takes you to a place that has been special to you in your lifetime, a place that is a place of power for you, and while Death watches and waits, you do the dance of your lifetime, the dance that expresses and sums up your time on earth, the steps it has taken a lifetime to learn, before Death nods to let you know it is time and leads you away, to the south. Don thought that, if he had a place of power in his life, it would probably be someplace in these foothills, someplace with a growth of aspen trees and the sun filtering down on the grass; and that, if he did the dance of his lifetime, of his life, it would be like the corn dance or the dance in the church on Christmas Eve at Santo Domingo, the dance that looked like running in place. He looked around to make sure no one was watching him—not Death: someone like George or Sally, someone who might laugh at him—then slowly, against the pain that came back in his shoulder and in his seared throat, he jogged a few steps in place. As he bounced up and down, his keys and change jingled in his pocket and he took out his key ring and held it in his hand, holding it so the keys jingled together almost like bells. He jogged for maybe thirty seconds, but then felt faint; his head was spinning, his legs ached, and there was a growing pressure in his chest. *No, not yet.* He leaned against the trunk of one of the pines until the pressure subsided and he could breathe easily again, then walked on down through the little valley and up the slope on the other side, keeping his left hand on his chest as if to keep his heart from pounding out through his ribs, thinking, *Thirty seconds: it's pretty fucking sad when you can do the dance of your lifetime in thirty seconds.*

When he emerged from the woods and started across the yard toward the house, the dogs on the back steps, half a dozen of them, setters and collies and mutts, stood up, wagged their tails, and whined, tongues hanging out *en masse,* looking around to see what to do next; only the old golden Labrador, Cable, came to greet him, walking slow. At the sound of the whining and stirring about, Sally appeared at the door.

"I was getting ready to phone over there," she smiled, a dim image behind the screen. "What was that all about?"

"Nothing," Don said, looking off toward the mountains, cupping the top of the old dog's head in his hand. "Nothing at all."

9

... *in a wash at the base of the San Francisco Mountains, a kachina by the name of Aholi pokes the butt of his feathered staff among some volcanic rocks, trying to remember the directions and recognize some of the landmarks, pokes his staff through a thin shell of earth and pine needles into a small hole in the bank, a small cave, and kneels down and enlarges the entrance with his hand, brushes the debris from the shelf of rock in front of the opening, and peers inside, into the little cave, which would be hard enough to do without trying to look through the eyeholes of a mask, to see if this is the right shrine and what the spirits have left there since the last time anyone or anything looked . . . while on the other side of Flagstaff, in another part of town, a Hopi Indian in his early thirties sits on a stool at his workbench in his workshop in what used to be a two-car garage when he first bought the house, sits under a bank of fluorescent lights behind an array of knives and paint and small brushes, pieces of cottonwood root gathered from all over the Southwest, and dolls, kachina dolls in various stages of completion—spare arms and legs, half of a body that split when it was almost done, a head with the imprint of a two-year-old's molars where his two-year-old son bit it—as he puts a drop of Elmer's glue on the tip of the blue cone-shaped head of the Aholi doll that he's almost finished and reaches for a couple bits of goose down—eagle feathers having been outlawed by the United States government, even for the adornment of a kachina doll—except that some of the glue is on the tips of his fingers so that the feathers stick to him instead of to the doll and when he tries to pick the feathers off with the other hand they stick to it too and he sits there, looking at his fluff-tipped fingers, and sighs . . . while on the edge of a mesa in the middle of northern Arizona, an old man, an Indian of indeterminate age, stands on the rim of the sandstone bluffs looking west, looking out across the desert floor far below, which extends a hundred miles to the peaks of the San Francisco Mountains, the mountains today a dull blue lump at the edge of a bright blue sky, muttering to himself about something, a prayer perhaps, then turns and walks away from the rim, back up the long natural steps cut into the sandstone by the erosion of the cliffs, the cliffs over the centuries sloughing away from the mesa from their own weight, the sandstone scarred and pitted by the rain and runoff, avoiding a cairn of stones put there by one of the other clans, and heads back across the top of the mesa, through the low juniper trees and the greasewood and clumps of scrub grass, past half a dozen old tires, scattered beer cans, the remains of a campfire, a condom rotting on a branch, back across the highway past the Government Health Center and a Craft Co-op where somebody is playing a Taos round dance on the stereo, the sound of the drum and the singing carried away by the passing tourist cars, through the campground and into the Hopi Cultural Center, where he brushes the dust from his summer-weight tweed suit pants and his Hush Puppies and adjusts the collar of his polyester white dress shirt before he enters the modern restaurant next to the motel, smiling as the first blast of air-conditioned air hits him, to count yesterday's receipts . . . while on the other side of the country, in New York City, a woman in her late thirties sits at her desk in her garret on Spring Street, listening to the sounds, outside her open window, of her Italian neighborhood cranking up for some festival or street fair, her bare feet tucked under her in the office chair, forgetting for a moment the article she's writing and hopes to sell to* Ms. *magazine as she stares up into the geometrical patterns of her angled, sloping, uneven ceiling, wondering if her lover got her latest letter and what he has to say about it . . . while in a small, trim white frame house outside of Flagstaff, Arizona, a man named George Binns stands at his window in his second-floor study peering through the small shaky tube of a monocular at a kachina by the name of Aholi who is poking around at the end of his back yard, who pokes the butt of his feathered staff among some volcanic rocks, in a wash at the base of the San Francisco Mountains. . . .*

George took one last look out the window: the kachina was still right where he had been, still doing whatever it was he had been doing. Satisfied, George put the monocular away and locked his desk, gathered up the letters he needed to mail, and went downstairs, his head up, his shoulders squared, appearing as businesslike as possible. In the dining room, however, he pulled up short: the Electrolux was gone, the space between the dining-room table and the Chinese vase empty. He had an uneasy feeling. He looked around, went across the hall, and stuck his head—carefully, slowly, as if ready for ambush—into the living room (*Nope, not here, hmm; now what's she up to?*), then went into the kitchen. The vacuum cleaner was beside Mary Olive, both of them on the floor, in front of the refrigerator.

"You'd think if it was so damn important to clean under this thing," she said, her bottom pointed his direction, "they'd make it easier to do."

She was kneeling in front of the refrigerator, bowed down in front of it; the bottom panel was off and she was probing around underneath the appliance with a long-handled brush. The Electrolux was beside her, like a curious puppy trying to see what she was doing. In addition to the attachments for the cleaner, there was an array of brooms and brushes spread out over half the floor.

"It seems to me you just cleaned under there a couple of months ago," George said. She had changed her clothes from when Don was here, changed into an old white blouse that she had made sleeveless by simply tearing off the sleeves, and old green slacks, her cleaning clothes. The bottom of her slacks hung in folds, as if they were pleated, as if she had no ass at all—George was uncomfortable looking at her.

"The serviceman told me that the reason the refrigerator didn't work right after we got it is because I didn't clean under it regularly," she said, reaching back to exchange a long narrow brush for a short fat one. "But he wouldn't define what was meant by 'regularly.' So I figure every two months is 'regularly.'"

"The serviceman told you that because he didn't want to honor the warranty on his product. We didn't have the refrigerator long enough for you to do anything with it 'regularly.'"

"The serviceman told me that the number-one cause of appliance failure is dirty bottoms."

"I had to pay two hundred dollars to have a new motor put in that thing, and we hadn't even paid for the whole refrigerator yet."

"That's why I'm cleaning under it. 'Regularly.'"

"I think you're being excessive," George said. "I'll bet there isn't another woman in Flagstaff who cleans under her refrigerator every two months. I'll bet there isn't another woman in the state of Arizona."

"Then their refrigerators have dirty bottoms. I'll believe what the serviceman said."

"The problem wasn't a dirty bottom," George said, becoming exasperated. "The problem was a bad refrigerator. The serviceman just fed you a line. I'll bet Sally doesn't clean under her refrigerator once a year."

"Sally is a slob," Mary Olive said, and wiggled her pleated bottom at him.

George clenched his teeth and growled in the back of his throat; he stepped over her, through the obstacle course of brushes and brooms and cleaner attachments, to the sink for a glass of water. There's dust on the dining-room table thick enough to write in, he thought, there's dust bunnies on the stairs, and the rugs haven't been vacuumed in a month, maybe two, maybe longer than the last time she vacuumed under the refrigerator. Don and Sally's house was usually messy, with things thrown here and there, and yet it seemed clean enough; while his house, on the other hand, his and Mary Olive's, was usually neat as a pin (except for the vacuum cleaner sitting out, of course; an accent piece?), and yet it seemed, well, less than clean—was, at the very least, dusty. He thought: I make forty-six thousand dollars a year, I am a respected professor of English, I am a published writer. After twenty-five years of marriage, I should be able to say, calmly and matter-of-factly, to my wife, that there's dust that needs to be taken care of, I should be able to say, without malice or fear, to my wife, that there's dust bunnies on the stairs.

"There's dust bunnies on the stairs."

Mary Olive rattled her brush under the refrigerator, making a dull ringing sound as it hit against the coils on the bottom, an off-key distant resonance, as if she hit the strings of a piano. "What?"

George cleared his throat, tried to speak distinctly. "There's dust bunnies on the stairs."

The rattling, the dull faraway ringing, stopped. She stayed where she was for a moment, still on her knees, still hunched over, resting her weight on her elbows, staring straight into the space underneath the refrigerator, side by side with the Electrolux; then she began to back up slowly, away from the front of the refrigerator, as if, slow and lethargic, she were backing out of a den after a long hibernation, a just-awakening and lugubrious bear, as if her skin as yet didn't fit quite right and she was only beginning to remember her strength, turning around slowly and sitting back on her heels as she brushed a wisp of hair, a fugitive strand of hair from her bun, away from her forehead, to look at him.

"There's dust bunnies on the stairs?" she said softly.

I make forty-six thousand dollars a year, George repeated to himself, I paid for this house, I pay the bills for this house, I should have the right to say such things, without malice or fear, with love and in keeping with the marital contract, to my wife. *Why did I get into this? I know better.* "I just thought I'd mention it."

"Oh, I'm glad you did, dear. I'm certainly glad you did," she said, getting up.

"I didn't mean you had to do anything about it right this minute. . . ."

"But George, if there's dust bunnies on the stairs we haven't got a moment to lose."

She walked out of the room with her legs wide apart and her stomach pushed out, her legs-astraddle walk, as he thought of it, a walk he had never seen her use until they came to Arizona, a walk she did, he was becoming convinced, to make herself look as unattractive as possible, just to bug him (or was she trying to make fun of him, mock him? He had watched himself in the mirror after he saw her walk that way, and he was pretty sure he didn't walk that way, at least not quite that way, though his stomach did stick out, he guessed, a little, and he had to walk, sort of, with his legs a bit far apart), as he stood there looking down at the Electrolux—*I should have known better, old-timer*—waiting for her to go through with it.

"My God, George, you're right!" her voice came from the hallway. "There's dust bunnies on the stairs! And it looks like they're headed our way!"

He leaned back against the drainboard, fitted the small of his back against the rolled edge of the counter, his head lowered, and, looking up under his eyebrows, looked at the Electrolux sitting amid the collection of brushes and attachments on the floor in front of the refrigerator; watched as his wife's bony, veined, and chapped ankles, her clunky, low-cut house shoes, came in the door and across the room, her legs astraddle; and after she grabbed the vacuum cleaner by its snout and hauled it out of the room—*Bye, old-timer*—continued to stare at the empty place amid the collection of brushes and attachments on the floor in front of the refrigerator where the vacuum cleaner had been. *I knew better.*

"I'm really glad you called my attention to them in time," she called from the hallway as she bumped around, getting the vacuum cleaner ready, plugging it in. "Another day and we might have been goners. They're as bad as gypsy moths or creeping socialism, you have to catch them in the early stages, stop them on every front, or else they'll take over the world." The Electrolux whirred into action; over the motor and the sound of her jamming the end of the hose attachment into the corners of the stairs, she kept talking, shouting to be heard. "Hear them, George? Hear them? That's the scream of dying dust bunnies! Take that, ye furry remnants of ages past! Dust you are, and to dust you shall return!"

Why did I ever marry her? I knew better.

In a few minutes she turned off the cleaner again. He continued to stand where he was, leaning against the drainboard, looking up under his eyebrows, as she came back into the room, legs-astraddle, dragging the Electrolux by its hose; he watched the little machine bump into the door frame and against the leg of a stool and get hung up on a bottle brush until she wrenched it free, wrenched it back into its spot in front of the refrigerator. Then he looked up at her. Mary Olive smiled, tight-lipped, at him.

"You're doing a fine job, dear," he said. "Goodbye."

"Goodbye? Where are you going?"

"I've got some errands to do."

"You can't do that." She wasn't smiling now, tight-lipped or otherwise.

"Of course I can," George said, smiling now himself. "There's some things I want to get in the mail today. I'll get something to eat while I'm out."

He went over and kissed her on the forehead, then patted her shoulders, patted her into place, and threaded his way through the paraphernalia on the floor into the hall.

"You can't just leave me alone here with that thing in the back yard," she said, following after him. She still had the hose of the vacuum cleaner in her hand; she started to drag the cleaner after her but the wheels jammed against an upholstery attachment and it wouldn't go any farther. She threw the hose down, the metal nozzle clattering on the tile floor.

George checked himself in the hall mirror. He was wearing his new burgundy-and-white sport shirt—he was proud of the tuft of chest hair, even if a lot of it was gray chest hair, sprouting out of his open collar; not bad for an old boy—and his new gray stretch-waist Levi's Action Slacks. Mary Olive joined his image in the glass. She no longer stood legs-astraddle, with her stomach sticking out; she stood with her arms wrapped around herself.

"You'll be perfectly safe," he said to her image in the mirror.

"How do you know I'll be perfectly safe?"

"Because I'm convinced the kachina or whatever it is down there doesn't mean any harm. He'll probably be gone before I get back." He gave one last nod of approval to himself, then turned around and bent over at the waist, keeping a distance between himself and Mary Olive, cupped her shoulders in his hands, and kissed her quickly on the lips. Both of them kept their eyes open during the kiss, such as it was, and for a second they stared at point-blank range into each other's eyes. George headed for the front door with Mary Olive at his heels.

"You're convinced? You're convinced?"

"That's right," George said, checking for his wallet. "I'm convinced."

"Well, suppose I'm not convinced?"

He would have made it too, all the way out the front door, except that the night latch was still on and he had forgotten his keys. He turned around, almost bumped into her, and doubled back to get his keys from the drawer of the hall table.

"George, you can't go now. What's so important that you have to go now? Why can't you go later? Or tomorrow?"

"I have to go now because I planned to go now. This is the time I set for myself to go. Therefore, I'm going to go now."

"I'll go with you."

"I have to go to my office."

"Why can't I go with you to your office?"

"Because you once said that you never wanted to set foot on that quote dinky unquote campus again."

"That was different."

"This is the same." He bent over again and held her arms close to her sides as he would a child's. "The only thing that's different is that now you think you're afraid of what's-his-name in the back yard."

"I don't think I'm afraid. I know I'm afraid."

"And I'm telling you, once and for all, that there's nothing to be afraid of."

"And I'm telling you, once and for all, that your telling me that there's nothing to be afraid of doesn't do a damn thing to make me less afraid."

"Then you see: it's your problem."

She started to say something but he waved his hands in front of him: enough; he wasn't going to listen to any more. He patted his pockets—right: keys, wallet, handkerchief; the letters he had in his hand; that's everything—and unlocked the front door.

"You're a heartless man, George Binns," she said behind him as he headed across the front yard to the car sitting in the driveway.

"If I thought you were in any danger, that would be different."

"If that thing so much as takes one step toward the house, I'm calling the police."

George stopped at the car door, speaking over the roof. "No, I don't want the police. If you have to call anybody, call Don. Besides, he's closer. The police might not even come all the way out here."

She stood in the doorway, glowering at him, as he started the car and backed down the drive. As he headed off, she said something to him but he couldn't hear what it was; he waved. Beyond the house, he smiled to himself: he imagined she'd spend the entire time he was gone looking out the kitchen window, watching the kachina, one hand on the phone, the other on her glass of wine. As he sailed up the hill, past Don and Sally's, he didn't see anyone about but he gave a little toot just in case they happened to look out and see him pass, to say hello, then kept on, going faster than he knew was safe but feeling happy and full of himself, the warm air whistling in the open window and up his shirtsleeve, a cloud of dust erasing the road behind him, the loose stones pinging merrily against the underbody, up the hill and around the bend and down the other side toward Fort Valley Road. He didn't even see the horse standing behind the fence with its head sticking over the top rail, Doc Harvey's horse, until he was almost beside it, until the horse, its teeth bared, raised back its head and screamed at him and surprised George so badly that he almost drove off the road into the ditch.

10

They lived ten miles north of town—"Flag," as the locals called it—off the windy two-lane highway that in the winter was busy with skiers going to and from the Arizona Snow Bowl and in the summer with tourists going to and from the Grand Canyon and all year round with Arizona drivers, sons of the Wild West, who seemed to take great delight in charging up behind him and chasing him around the curves. The museum was on the way into town; he had passed it every time he went back and forth to town since the day they arrived, but he had never stopped—another thing, add it to the list, he always meant to do. Now it was almost noon and he decided it would be wiser to wait until after lunch. In town he dropped his letters—a couple of bills; a letter of recommendation (with only guarded praise) for one of his students— at the post office, then, trying to avoid as much as possible the tangle of cars, tourists mainly, in the narrow downtown streets, drove to the university.

The school was only a few blocks from the center of town, a few blocks on the other side of the Santa Fe tracks that ran through the center of town. At the entrance a large electric sign, sponsored by a local bank, flashed HOME OF THE LUMBERJACKS—AW C'MON, SMILE! The campus was nearly deserted—it was between summer sessions—and he parked in an empty lot next to the gym that was usually restricted and walked across the street to the liberal-arts building. It was a newish, three-story red brick building, long and low, with trim white window frames; the one time Mary Olive had seen it (the same time she had called the campus quote dinky unquote) she said it looked like a high school, and George, unfortunately, had had trouble seeing it otherwise since. Beyond the front door, he stuck his head inside the English Department office: Becky, the secretary, was the only one there; she was on the phone and fluttered her fingers at him. He fluttered his fingers back, and went on down the hall to the mail room to collect his mail—it was distressingly little; he had even waited a couple of days for it to accumulate—then upstairs to his office.

The hallways were dark, the doors to the offices were closed, no one seemed to be around; the only light came from the end of the halls, from the windows in the stairwells, and from the small windows in the closed office doors, which showed up on the opposite walls as patches of institutional green. Down the freshly polished floor, the circles left by the buffing machine spread out in front of him as if he were walking on the surface of a quiet pond. In the distance, in another part of the building, someone was whistling; in still another part of the building, the buffing machine whirred. George unlocked his office door and left it standing open, though he didn't turn on the lights, preferring instead the glow of the closed venetian blinds beside his desk.

He shared the office with a man named Myers, the department's eighteenth-century man. Contrary to his title, Myers, a hangdog man in his mid-thirties from California, decorated his side of the office with posters of The Doors and The Grateful Dead; George's side contained only his desk and swivel chair, a straight chair for visitors, and a filing cabinet. He sat at his desk and flipped through the mail; there was a collection of university and departmental notices, a flyer advertising a film series, a card from a student visiting Crete, and a notice from the Patterson Book Search Service informing him that they still hadn't located a copy of a novel entitled *The Dreamer Dreamed* by George Binns (he never bought them when he advertised for one of his books; he was just curious whether there were any copies left floating around out there and what they were selling for these days). The brown manila envelope was the *Pawtucket Review* returning the poems he had submitted; he left it unopened. And there was an envelope from Sara.

Sara's sweeps and curlicues covered the front of the envelope. He wondered what Becky and the other secretaries thought when he got one of Sara's letters—surely they recognized them by now, it would be hard not to. Inside the envelope was a card and a folded sheet of yellow paper. The card showed the cartoon figure of a mouse, a surprisingly sexy-looking female mouse, standing upright in the open half of an oyster shell, the pose and background imitating Botticelli's Venus, one paw modestly covering her non-existent breasts, the other holding her tail. Sara had further decorated the cartoon by scribbling in a frizzy hairdo, a black curly perm like her own, and a great muff of pubic hair between the legs, also like her own. It was the most naked, most erotic-looking mouse he could imagine, and it bore an uncanny resemblance to Sara herself. Inside, the printed message said I'M YOURS!, to which Sara had added at the bottom:

Love on the half-shell . . . we'll cover ourselves with spinach
and cream sauce . . . don't forget the bacon bits . . . toast
ourselves by an open fire until we're plump . . . then take
turns . . . eating each other . . .

George's crotch squirmed. He opened her letter: the handwriting
was curlicued but frantic:

George,
I'm sorry this will be short but it will have to do for now. I
think the card will give you general idea anyway. I'm busy
busy busy. The job at Sarah Lawrence fell through, and Barnard isn't sure they'll ever give me tenure, so guess where
I'm thinking about? Chicago. Chicago! It would be small con-
solation to know I'd be closer to you geographically, if not
in body or spirit, but no more holidays when you come to
The Apple, dinners at the Algonquin and screwing in the
shade of Dorothy Parker. Shit shit shit. Such is the way it
seems to go with star-crossed lovers. Know that I love you,
know that I'm here for you, wherever here is, and how you
going to work this one, big fella?

                                                          S

He had started to read the note over again when he heard high
heels clicking down the hallway; maybe Becky the secretary was
coming to see him about something. He folded his hands over
Sara's note and sat up straight, looking expectant at the open door,
at the glimpse of dark hallway, but before she got to him she
turned down another corridor and her high heels clicked away
from him again and through another door and it was silent again.
George got up from his desk, feeling glum and disappointed, and
went over to the window, parting the closed slats with a finger:
on the front lawn, far enough away so that George couldn't hear
him, a workman rode a small tractor up and down the grass, a
gang of mowers bouncing along behind like devoted puppies. He
dropped the slat into place again and went back to his desk.

So Sara was thinking of moving to Chicago. He looked again at her card and letter, then locked them away in his desk: he wasn't sure how he felt about that bit of news. No question that it would change things between them; most likely it would end them. It had been difficult enough to think up reasons to get to New York a couple of times this past year; to think up reasons to get to Chicago would be impossible. And obvious. The thing that surprised him most, however, was that it didn't seem to mean more to him, the idea of her loss. Was he getting old? Perhaps there'd be another letter from Sara at the house tomorrow—she often wrote to the both of them, after she wrote to him at school (to appease her conscience?)—perhaps there'd be more information about her plans there. He stood up and gave his office a once-over, remembered the envelope from the *Pawtucket Review* and took it with him, and locked the door behind him. Back downstairs in the department office, Becky was busy typing; when she saw him, she looked up and smiled. George walked over to her desk and loomed over her. Her typewriter purred.

"I was just thinking that, the way you always have things so well organized around here, you're obviously a person who believes the shortest distance between two points is a straight line."

"That sounds like what they always tried to teach me in school," she laughed.

"Probably so. But I've been working on a better way. A shorter way."

"Really?" She cocked her head, unsure whether she was supposed to believe him or not.

"Yes. All you do is stay on one point and imagine you're at the other."

"Oh, you," she said and pretended to swat at him.

He left the office, his spirits up again, thinking himself a clever fellow (and not bad-looking either, in a heavy sort of way: a little handsome, maybe; distinguished, at least; a bit grand, even; he walked with a spring in his step, legs-astraddle, bouncing on his toes a little, a little like the college jocks did), and went to the library to pick up some books on Hopis and kachinas. When he got back to his car, sitting by itself in the restricted lot, there was a ticket on the windshield.

11

After treating himself to lunch at The Gables (the treat, besides the only decent Reuben sandwich in town, was sitting in the dark of a booth in the rear—the restaurant was decorated in the style of a Victorian bordello—and watching the college-age waitresses done up in ruffles and black velvet bustle back and forth, little maids all in a row), George headed out of town the other direction, toward the museum. It was a low stone building with a red tile roof, sitting like a mountain lodge among the heavy pines. George found a parking space in the shade and walked back through the gravel parking lot, reading out-of-state license plates. The idling tour buses filled the air with fumes; near the front steps a half-dozen women in sundresses and white sandals chattered happily among themselves about what all they had seen inside—*the women come and go,* George thought, *talking of Navajos*—while their husbands, looking pale and foolish in shorts and vacation clothes, stood around aimlessly, chewing toothpicks from lunch and jangling the change in their pockets, looking longingly in the direction of their cars. Children ran unchecked through the grounds, climbing among the volcanic rocks, yelling through the trees. George drew himself up to his full professorial height, adjusted his pants around his expanse of stomach, and entered the large front doors.

Inside, the main hall was confused with Japanese Boy Scouts, a tour of senior citizens (George shuddered), and families, all milling about; George decided to wait to ask for information until things cleared out a bit. He looked at the displays of books and publications for sale, then stood, out of the flow of things, at the rear of the hall, in front of some large glass windows, looking out into a central courtyard where there were flagstone walks and low shrubs and sunlight filtered down through the surrounding pines. He thought of Saturdays and going to the museums in New York, though, of course, the museums and the crowds there (the comparison made him smile: he thought of intense young people, artist- and student-types, the young men looking like a hybrid between Trotsky and Dylan, either Bob or Thomas—scarves, they always seemed to like to wear scarves—the girls with their hair long and their skirts loose and boots or sandals) were very different. Going to the Metropolitan had been one of his and Sara's special things to do, sitting in the restaurant by the fountain and reflecting pool, talking about the exhibitions and people-watching; or in the sculpture garden at the Modern, near the Henry Moore and the David Smith, holding hands and looking up at the towers of the city through the branches of the slender, fashionable trees, listening to the city's pulse and power (it was only traffic and air conditioners), feeling its magnificence, its promise. He turned away from the windows: thoughts like that, while standing in the middle of Arizona, would get him nothing except a straitjacket. The crowds in the hall, around the book counter and information desk, weren't getting any thinner; if anything, they were getting worse; a short little man, with hair sprouting from the sides of his bald head, like misplaced ear muffs, threaded his way back and forth across the hall, saying, not really shouting, "Janet? Janet?" George set out to find a curator on his own.

He wandered through the galleries, past display cases filled with Indian artifacts, potsherds and arrowheads, beads and the remains of early tools (as well as one very large and very dead spider). In several adjacent cases were scale models of different Indian villages of the Southwest, showing the evolution of their houses and their ways of life, but the only thing George really noticed was that, at least according to this model-maker, the women of the Pueblo II period had larger breasts than the women of Basketmaker I. He was joined in front of the case by a large potbellied Indian wearing a headband and long straight black hair, and a black T-shirt that said APACHE AND PROUD; George moved on.

In the next room there were displays of the Hopi way of life— how, for instance, they were able to be farmers while living in the middle of a desert—and a large glass case full of kachina dolls. George recognized the Aholi, with its blue cone-shaped head and spotted cape, and felt rather proud of himself, as if he actually knew about such things. Farther on was a life-sized replica of the inside of a Hopi ceremonial kiva, an underground chamber with stone benches along the walls, a loom with a half-finished dance kilt hanging from the vigas that supported the ceiling, and a ladder in the center climbing up to the opening—in this case, the opening in the ceiling where the lights were. (In the shadows under the benches, he noticed, cut into the wall, an electrical outlet; no doubt, he thought, for the museum's ceremonial floor polisher.) Beyond a room full of Navajo rugs, he found a door marked "Offices." He stepped inside, but there didn't seem to be anyone around; he walked down a short corridor, looking in the open office doors, but no one was at the desks. The last room appeared to be a storeroom for the gift shop; there were metal shelves full of kachina dolls, sand paintings, books. George stuck his head in the door, then stuck it in a little farther; a woman sat on the edge of a worktable, swinging her legs, a cup of coffee in her hand, looking back at him.

"Surprise," she said.

"Er, excuse me."

"You're excused. Are you looking for something special, or just generally nosing around?"

She was a short, lumpy woman with thick glasses and gray, bowl-shaped hair, wearing a purple jumpsuit. When she smiled her mouth tucked into itself, and her teeth were bad. George stepped into the room, so he could stand upright and regain some of his lost dignity, but his hair brushed against the exposed sprinkler pipes and he found it necessary to stand at a slight tilt.

"My name is Binns. George Binns. I teach at the university. I'm looking for someone to give me some information about kachinas."

She nodded, a bow of her head, still swinging her legs. "Well, George Binns, my name is Mrs. Jenkins, and maybe I can help you. What do you want to know?"

"Are you acquainted with the one named Aholi?"

"I've never been formally introduced to him, if that's what you mean."

George thought if he invited her out to his house he could change that. "I mean, you know the one I'm talking about."

"I think so, yes."

"Er, have you heard, uh, anything about him lately?"

"The last thing I heard, he was having a little trouble with his arthritis, but other than that he seemed to be doing just fine."

George wondered if he had missed something. *Is she laughing at me? Is she laughing at me too?*

"I'm sorry, that was a poor attempt at a joke," she said, and finished her coffee. "It's been a long day. Maybe you better tell me more about what you want to know."

"It's a little hard to explain," George said.

Mrs. Jenkins swung her legs for a moment, looking down at the floor, her arms braced on the edge of the table as if ready in case the table decided to pick up and fly away. Then she smiled at him—a thin, flat smile—hopped off the bench, and walked over to the shelves. "Then I guess we should take first things first." She came back with a wood carving of two figures, two kachinas, each nearly a foot tall, mounted on a common base. The figures were portrayed as walking, one in front of the other: the first kachina was dressed all in white with a white bullet-shaped head; the second kachina, walking a step behind the other, was Aholi. "Is this the fellow you're talking about?"

"That's the fellow."

"Well, now, at least we have a start. So, what did you want to know about him?"

"Anything I can, I'm afraid."

"You mean, like a basic introduction?"

George nodded.

Mrs. Jenkins looked up at him—she only came up to his chest—looking not especially pleased at what she'd gotten herself into; then her eyes rolled up into her head—for a second George was afraid what he said had made her faint—as if she were reading something written on the inside of her skull.

"Aholi is commonly referred to as Eototo's lieutenant—I might argue with that, but that's neither here nor there for what you want to know. That's Eototo in front; he's known as the chief of all the kachinas. He always walks in front, because he makes the road for Aholi; that is, he leaves a trail of sacred cornmeal for Aholi to follow and walk on. They're only seen on Third Mesa, though the other mesas are at least familiar with them, and except for one ceremony at the end of Niman where Eototo appears alone, they're always seen together."

George knew of one other instance when they weren't always seen together—at least so far: he wondered if the other one was going to turn up later. "Is there more than one Aholi?"

"There's only one Aholi, if you're talking about the kachina itself; he's not like a Hemis kachina, for instance, where you might see twenty or thirty at one time. But there may be more than one Aholi mask—several of the villages on Third Mesa might have an Aholi, I'm not sure. You see, Aholi is a chief kachina, which means he's a clan ancestor. The Hopi word is Wuya: The Old One. According to some of the stories, the chief kachinas came up from the Under World at the same time that the people came up, when everyone climbed up into the present world. As I remember, Aholi is the ancestor of the Pikyas Clan, and Eototo is the ancestor of the Bear Clan, but I'd have to look that up to be sure. Actually, the man who could tell you more about them is the carver who made this, Ernie Tewayumptewa." She rolled her eyes as she spelled the name for him. "He's in the phone book. Each carver has his specialties, the kachinas he's most familiar with, and these are some of Ernie's."

She looked fondly at the carving; the two kachinas—the Eototo, in a white tunic and white dance kilt, white leggings and its white bullet-shaped head, the only features on the mask the two small dots for eyes and a single dot for the mouth; the Aholi, in its colorful cape and tall blue head crowned with feathers and yarn— stood frozen in mid-step. Then Mrs. Jenkins returned to the shelves and brought back a third figure. This kachina was female: she wore a long white blanket trimmed in green and black, fastened about her shoulders and trailing down her back as a cape, over a black dress and tall white moccasins. In her arms she carried a sheaf of wands. The mask was blue, with the features portrayed by two large black inverted triangles, one on top of the other. Sticking out on either side of her head were large black wings.

"The Crow Mother," Mrs. Jenkins said. "Or the Crow Bride, depending on what time of day she appears and what the occasion is. At Powamu, she travels with Eototo and Aholi around the village, blessing it and performing ceremonies. But she also appears at other times and with other kachinas. Eototo and Aholi are a pair; they're the only ones who are like that, at least that I've ever heard of. Actually, there's a nice little story about the two of them: the Hopi traveled back and forth and up and down the entire continent during their migrations, in prehistoric times, after they climbed up into this world, and Eototo and Aholi traveled together with them. But one time, while they were in Mexico, the Hopi were attacked and Aholi stayed behind to hold off the Mexicans so his friend Eototo and the Hopi could escape. Well, the others escaped all right, but Aholi was killed in the process. But one of the handy things about being a kachina is that when you're killed it doesn't last very long, and when Aholi recovered he set out to find his friend again. He wandered after them for centuries, and didn't catch up with them again until the Hopi were living near the Colorado River, I think it was. When Eototo and Aholi saw each other again, they embraced and promised each other never to be separated again. It's sort of nice to think that spirits need friends too, isn't it? That's why I think Eototo always walks in front and makes the road for Aholi with cornmeal: they're best friends and he's honoring Aholi for giving up his life for him and the Hopi. But, like I said, that's just my own idea: I doubt if anyone else would agree with me, much less the Hopi."

George and Mrs. Jenkins stared at the carvings for a moment, as if giving the wood figures a chance to add something to what had been said. The Eototo and the Aholi walked on in silence; the Crow Mother held her sheaf of wands and kept her own council.

"So the masks for one of these fellows would be pretty important," George said finally.

Mrs. Jenkins leaned back to look down her nose at him and almost toppled over backward. "You're a fast learner, aren't you?"

George cleared his throat, stretched his neck. "I'm sorry. But I'm afraid I really don't know very much at all about these things."

"I'm becoming aware of that," Mrs. Jenkins said, flicking a dust speck off the small purple bulge of her bosom. "I'll try to explain it. Most of the kachinas that people see are dancers, and any of the men can impersonate them after they've been initiated into the cult or the tribe—which all children go through when they're about eleven or twelve. A man might own one or more masks, but basically the same mask is used over and over for whichever of the dancing kachinas he's going to impersonate—the mask is painted and decorated each time it's going to be used. But the chief kachinas are different. The right to impersonate a kachina like Aholi is handed down among the elders of the clan, and the masks never change, they're considered beings in themselves. They're kept in a special place in the home of the impersonator, and the matriarch of the clan takes care of it and feeds it."

"Feeds it?"

"With sacred cornmeal. And I guess with offerings of food too."

"So somebody's taking care of the mask all the time."

"Somebody's taking care of the mask all the time." She put the carvings back on the shelves. "The masks are very powerful; it would be like having a permanent fearful presence sitting in your back room. Personally, I'd think it would sort of get on your nerves. Sometimes the people who take care of the masks are so afraid of them that they won't even move them. They have to go get a village chief or an elder to come lift it so they can dust under it."

George laughed.

Mrs. Jenkins did not look kindly at him.

"The masks are powerful, and dangerous. If a mask is handled without the proper ceremony or respect, that person may die. And that's not just for the chief masks either; that's for any of the kachina masks. There's an entire ritual about how to take it off your head, I think it's with the left hand, and then you twirl it around your head or something. And if you try to put on a mask when you're not supposed to, well . . ."

"Well what?"

"I'm not sure exactly what the Hopi say will happen, but I do know that the Zuni believe the mask will stick to your face and suffocate you. I think there was a case like that recorded at Zuni sometime around the turn of the century—a mask suffocated a man who shouldn't have been wearing it, or maybe it was that he made love to a woman while he was wearing it or something. Anyway, it suffocated him, and when they tried to take it off, the mask stuck to the man's skin and pulled his own face off with it. Something like that. Gruesome, brrrr. The Hopi probably believe something of the same sort."

George stretched his neck, brushing a sprinkler pipe with his hair. "Then I guess it would be pretty difficult for somebody who wasn't supposed to have it to get hold of one of those masks."

"So that's what this is all about." She looked at him.

George blinked.

"What did you think you were going to do with it? Use it in one of your classes? Your own little example of primitive culture? Or are you some kind of collector?"

George blinked again. And sputtered.

"Were you going to hang it in your den?" Mrs. Jenkins advanced on him. Her face was the color of her jumpsuit. "Mount it on the wall like a hunting trophy? Or were you going to wear it to parties—'Great costume you got there, Professor.' I thought you looked like the type when you came snooping around in here."

"Mrs. Jenkins, I assure you I have no inten—"

"Well, you can just forget the whole idea. There's no way you or anybody else like you could get hold of a mask, a chief mask or any other kind of mask. And if you tried it, the mask wouldn't have to bother defending itself. The Hopi would skin you alive before you ever made it off the mesas. And I think it would be good enough for you." She took a finger and poked it, hard, into his stomach.

"Oof!"

"Now, if you'll excuse me," she said, and walked out of the room. Then she walked back in again. "No, I think you should be the one to leave, and I'll stay here."

"Mrs. Jenkins—"

"And if you don't do it right now, I'll call Security."

George ducked the sprinkler pipes and left the room, walked back down the corridor and into the galleries, holding his stomach where she had poked him. He was afraid she might get the idea to call Security anyway, and decided it would be better just to get out of there. As he passed the replica of the ceremonial kiva, a middle-aged couple in matching yellow shorts and white jerseys and jogging shoes stood at the railing, in front of the "Keep Out" sign, trying to coax their six-year-old to get down off the ladder and come back out of the display.

"Please, Jeffrey, don't climb up there; please don't do that; please come out of there; if you don't the Indians will get you."

Jeffrey just looked at them.

"Jeffrey, you get the hell out of there!" George bellowed.

Jeffrey looked at him wide-eyed and started to cry. His father turned on George. "Hey, fella—" His mother grabbed her purse, ready to swing it like a mace. George, smiling, walked on, feeling infinitely better.

12

Don Pike, in his old dusty cowboy boots, the pointed toes scuffed and starting to curl back on themselves, in his old torn Levi's and his blue Levi's work shirt with the Western yoke, waded through the dogs on the back steps and went on into the house, thinking:

Sweet Thames run softly, till I end my song.

Spenser. Of all things to have going through your mind, he thought, and at a time like this. What did Spenser, much less a bridal ode, have to do with anything in his life right now? *Upon your bridal day, which is not long: Sweet Thames run softly, till I end my song.* Christ: he hated Spenser. He was a Middle English man himself, yclept: if anything was going to run around in his brain, why wasn't it something from Chaucer, or from the *Pearl: I have been a joyless jeweler.* Well, no, that wasn't much better. Or Wyatt— *They flee from me, that sometime did me seek, With naked foot stalking in my chamber.* Oh, that naked foot—the nakedest foot in all literature! Why wasn't there a naked foot stalking through his thoughts? Spenser: it was as bad—he called it a fear, but if that's what it was, he had turned it into a party piece, a joke, something amusing he liked to trot out when he was holding forth at departmental picnics or graduate-student teas, to show the deadly workings of the world—as being in an auto wreck, lying on the pavement, watching your blood run out of you, feeling your life slipping away, and finding that, of all the beautiful, grand, inspiring things you had heard in your lifetime, the only thing you could think of was Wordsworth: *I wandered lonely as a cloud that floats on high, trala.* Graduate-student wives and new faculty members always howled at that. Is there no justice? Don would ask in his deepest bass, his eyes sparkling, and move off to get another drink.

The answer, of course, which he never stayed around to hear, was no.

He stood in his living room, looking around, feeling lost. Why had he come in here? What was he looking for? Then he remembered: a book. He took out his glasses and went over to the bookshelves to scan the titles first on one side of the stone fireplace and then on the other. Now all he had to do was remember the title of the book he was looking for.

On top of the shelves and on the mantel over the fireplace was their collection of kachina dolls, most of them old, from the turn of the century or before, when the style of carving was more abstract; as well as woven plaques from Hopi and Papago, pottery from Acoma and Jemez and San Ildefonso, fetishes from Zuni, a pair of Sioux beaded moccasins, an eagle-bone whistle and a metal drum from the Kiowa peyote cult, a child's bow and arrow given to him at the Home Dance at Shungopovi. There were Navajo blankets draped over the chairs, Navajo rugs on the floors; on the walls were a large Whirling Logs sand painting from the Navajo Night Chant ceremony, an Apache Mountain Spirit mask, a woman's tablita from the corn dance, and a lithograph of a drunk and damaged Indian by Fritz Scholder. It had taken them twenty years to collect it all.

The room itself was low, with vigas running across the ceiling, paneled walls, hardwood floors. He had built the room himself, just as he had built the fireplace and the bookcases, the end tables and coffee table, the second room he added on to the house after they moved in, the first being their bedroom. As it turned out, the bedroom was as light and airy as the living room was dark and closed; it had been a joke between them that maybe he got the plans turned around. But the truth was, he always liked the room, liked it for being the way it was, dark and closed—guests always said that the room was him, or he the room: that's right, brooding and sonorous, he'd reply, just like me, eyebrows pumping, in his deepest voice. The strange thing, now that he thought about it, was that, since he'd moved out to the cabin in the back yard, he hadn't seemed to miss the room at all.

Sweet Thames end softly till I run my song. Bah!

He had moved most of his books out to the cabin over the years—it was, after all, supposed to be his study, his workroom—the books of literature and philosophy, the books he taught from and used for research—but these in the living room had always been considered both his and Sally's, *their* books. Now he considered them all Sally's: the Indian books, the books about different tribes and ceremonies and crafts. From the rear of the house came the muffled sound of a drum, the sound of men chanting as they sat in a circle beating a drum (a bass drum, probably, lying on its side, the kind used by marching bands; how on earth did the Indians incorporate that into their customs?), the women standing behind them, their shawls and blankets pulled up over their heads, screeching the falsetto, trilling their tongues—a round-dance song: Sally played Indian records while she worked, she said it gave her inspiration. More than once he had looked in on her and found her with her smock tucked up over her head like a blanket, her eyes closed, holding a paintbrush like a prayer feather as she shuffled slowly around the room, shuffled in the steps of the dance. *Dance Hall of the Dead.* He remembered the title of the Indian mystery story by Tony Hillerman as soon as he saw it. He took the book and sat down in a leather chair, draped with a Two Grey Hills blanket, and turned on the lamp beside it; the parchment-colored shade made a yellow corner of light in the room. It had been his chair, his lamp, his corner; he had spent many hours reading here. Well, that was then, he reminded himself; this is now.

He hadn't thought about the mystery for a long time—he had known Hillerman, at least in passing, at UNM—but, after seeing the kachina in George's back yard, he remembered something about the story, something that bothered him. The episode he remembered took place when the high-school student who has been chosen to be the Fire God for the Zuni Shalako ceremony went out running through the hills at dusk, building up his endurance for the night of dancing. When he nears the end of his run, the boy, the Fire God, meets a kachina in the desert, a Salamobia. Don found the passage he was looking for at the end of the first chapter:

The figure which stepped from behind the boulders in the red darkness was not George. It was a Salamobia, its round yellow-circled eyes staring at him. The Fire God stopped, opened his mouth, and found nothing to say. This was the Salamobia of the mole kiva, its mask painted the color of darkness. And yet it was not. The Fire God stared at the figure, the muscular body in the dark shirt, the bristling ruff of turkey feathers surrounding the neck, the black and empty eyes, the fierce beak, the plumed feathered topknot. Black was the color of the Mole Salamobia, but this was not the mask. He knew that mask. His mother's uncle was the personifier of the Mole Salamobia and the mask lived at a shrine in his mother's uncle's home. But if it was not the mask . . .

The Fire God saw then that the wand rising in the hand of this Salamobia was not of woven yucca. It glittered in the red light of the twilight. And he remembered that Salamobia, like all of the ancestor spirits which lived at the Zuni masks, were visible only to members of the Sorcery Fraternity, and to those about to die.

Don put down the book. That was the only time he had heard of that: that ancestor spirits were visible to people about to die. Of course, in the novel the boy was killed, his throat slit, but not by the ancestor spirit of the Salamobia: it was slit by someone wearing a phony mask—an anthropologist, in fact, trying to protect his findings. Don didn't think the kachina in George's back yard was a tenure-crazed anthropologist looking for a new dig site, but he wouldn't be surprised if it was someone in a phony mask; on the other hand, he wouldn't be surprised if it was actually a kachina from the reservation, performing some sort of pilgrimage or ceremony, either. Whichever or whatever it was, it was certainly nothing to fool with, but that wasn't why he looked up the passage in Hillerman's novel. Sally, he knew, if she knew it was there, would take it for a sign, a vision, the ancestor spirit itself; he wasn't that naïve. But he thought that, if it really was Aholi standing down there in the wash behind George's house, it would be just his luck: a visitor, a message from the spirit world, and the spirit got the wrong house.

He took off his glasses and rubbed the bridge of his nose, thinking of George. He didn't like living this close to someone else from the department—the truth was, he didn't like living this close to anyone—but, when he had learned that a new professor was coming to the university and was looking for a place to live, Don had showed the house to George and Mary Olive, having heard, along with the fact that it was up for sale, the rumors of developers and subdivision. For a while the two couples had gotten along well, trading dinners, spending long leisurely evenings together, talking, reading plays. For a while it looked as though the four of them would be close friends; for a while they probably were. As he thought about it, he supposed that George was actually as close a friend as he had had, not only in the department, but since he came to Arizona. As he thought about it, that in itself seemed a sad commentary on something.

Sweet Thames. Sweet Jesus. Sweet shit.

The drums, the chant of the round dance swelled from the other end of the house as Sally opened her studio door. Don got up quickly to replace the book, but his elbow brushed the lampshade, nearly knocking the lamp off the table. He steadied the lamp and got the book back in its place on the shelf; he turned to leave but found Sally standing in the hallway, watching him.

"Hi."

He smiled, nodded, ran his hand down over his chin, pulled at his beard.

"Are you all right?"

"Yes, yes, I'm fine," he whispered.

"I thought you were out in the study."

"I was. I just came in to look up something."

The room was built two steps up from the hall; she stood in the hallway, in the light from the leaded windows near the front door, the light coming in from beside her so that her white peasant blouse, the left side of her face, glowed, her figure framed in the doorway, a study of chiaroscuro, the light against her as soft as in a Vermeer; he thought she could almost be a subject for a Vermeer too, this plumpish woman, her puffy white blouse, the fuzz on her cheek haloing her skin in the light, her wide-eyed, concerned expression frozen in mid-gesture, the glimpse behind her of the farther rooms—except that in this instance this plumpish woman wore an Apache headband, a long Indian-style braid draped down one shoulder, and an owl feather sticking up out of the top of her hair. Don shook his head; where had he gone wrong? He looked around the chair and end table for his glasses, then found them, already in their case, in his shirt pocket. Sally continued to watch him from the hall, her hands in front of her, fingertips barely touching, as if she held something very small and delicate.

"Don?"

"What?"

"You'd tell me if it was something serious, wouldn't you?"

"I'll say it's serious. I can't remember half the time where I leave things any more. They say that's the first to go, the memory." He looked into the shadows of the room for a moment. "No. That's not the first to go."

"You know that's not what I meant."

He touched his breast pocket again; his glasses were still there, in their case. Then he looked at her and slumped a little. "No, I know it's not."

"Would you tell me? If it was serious? If . . . what Doc Harvey said . . ."

"If Doc Harvey said I was going to die? Do you mean that kind of serious?"

"Don, don't even make jokes about that."

Don put his hands in the back pockets of his jeans; he touched the toe of his boot against the edge of a Navajo rug. "Yes, Sally, I'd tell you," he said hoarsely, then softer. "Yes, I'd tell you."

"I'm worried about you, that's all."

"I know you are and I know I'm not helping you any either. It's just so damned frustrating, to have your voice go. It makes you feel like a goddamn fool, going around croaking like a frog."

"Come here, frog," she said, smiling, her eyes moist, full of meaning, her mouth quivering, holding out her arms. "Let me make you a prince."

"No, Sally, not now," he said, unable to look at her, slamming his hand against the back of the rocking chair and almost knocking it over, heading out of the room toward the kitchen. "Not now. Not now."

13

The dogs heard him coming and scattered off the back steps before he flung the door open, all the dogs except Cable, who stayed where he was, lying in the shade of the house in the driveway; the dogs ran a few feet across the yard, then stopped, looking back, watching Don come out the door and down the steps, ready to take off again if they were the ones Don was mad at. As Don headed down the path toward the cabin, Cable got up stiffly and followed a few steps behind. The other dogs watched them go.

The cabin sat fifty yards from the house, at the edge of the woods. It was the last part of the house—he considered it part of the house then, just another extension of the house, another room, not a separate entity, as he did now—that he had built: he built it after Sally began to take up sculpture seriously and it was obvious that she needed someplace other than the kitchen table to work on, remodeling his study for her, adding a sink and more lights, enlarging the windows so that she had a better view of the mountains and more northern light, and after she decided she needed to play Indian records at full volume while she worked. At least those were the reasons he'd admit to. But an equal factor was a reason he wouldn't admit to, the hope that the cabin would be his inspiration to finish his book, a study of the *Pearl* poet. The book was to be the culmination of his work as a medieval scholar. He had been working on it—or not working on it—for twenty years.

As it turned out, the cabin was an inspiration, but not necessarily for writing. He had finished it a couple of years before, and outfitted it with a desk he made himself, with brass corners and recessed drawer-pulls in the style of a British campaign desk, architect's lamps, filing cabinets, an overstuffed chair to sit in, a couch to take a nap on, bookshelves from floor to ceiling. All of which was the way he imagined it, all of which was the way he planned it would be. The surprise came when it was time to hang some paintings, choose some objects to have around him as he worked, and when he discovered that, despite the way they had decorated the rest of the house, he wanted nothing to do with Indian things, with what he thought of (and this was the surprise) as Sally's Indians, Sally's ideas of Indians; instead, he chose reproductions of Impressionists, paintings he had loved early in his life, back in his student days at Chicago and Ann Arbor, paintings he had loved then though he didn't know yet what was important about them, what was important to him, paintings that he rediscovered at the same time he began to rediscover his body, to listen to his body, or, rather, listen to his body listen to itself as it said that something deep, very deep inside, was wrong, very wrong; paintings, he realized after he put them on the walls and sat back and looked at them for a while, that contained a quality he could only identify as a certain sweetness: there was a cheap reproduction of Cézanne's pine trees and boulders in the hills around Provence, done near the end of Cézanne's life, the trees and boulders looking surprisingly like the forests near the San Francisco Mountains (was that why, from the time he first moved here, he had felt at home here, felt he knew it already?), except that the colors in Cézanne's painting, even in the poor reproduction, were light and airy, and the colors of the forests he saw from his windows and walked in during the days seemed dark, mixed with darkness; and a couple of Renoirs, the full-cheeked, full-bodied nude bather who had filled his waking and sleeping dreams more than he ever realized, the plump young woman sitting on a rock, her voluptuous body radiant with life and health and sex, and the scene in the garden at Galette, the crowds of happy young people sitting in the garden under the trees, the beautiful young girl in the foreground in the striped dress leaning over the back of the bench talking to her suitor but turned slightly, turning as if to look at the viewer himself, look at him, and behind her the dancers, the couple locked in each other's arms in the blue-green shadows, the dappled light through the trees, holding each other under the branches of the trees and the globes and the strings of lanterns, swirling under the lights to the music, swirling and swirling.

He walked on, down the path toward the cabin, followed by the old dog. Across the small valley, above the growth of pines and aspens, George and Mary Olive's house sat on the opposite hill, the trim nondescript white frame house catching the afternoon sunlight, but he didn't see either of them in the yard, and the line of trees blocked his view of the wash—he hoped the kachina, if that's what it was, was gone by now. Closer to the cabin, closer to the edge of the woods, the trees blocked his view of the house as well. And he thought: Cézanne's career didn't blossom until he was an old man, he did his best work when he was in his sixties; and Renoir, crippled with old age, had his brushes tied to his hands and learned to refine his style, became an even greater artist because of it. He thought: There is still time, there is still the possibility to do something lasting, something . . . *No, there isn't. Stop kidding yourself. It's over now. Over.*

His jeep was parked on the grass near the front door of the cabin; Don walked around it, patting the spare tire sticking up from the back as if the vehicle were an old friend. Cable followed behind slowly, the old dog walking carefully, his tail neither up nor down, his expression neither happy nor unhappy, just concerned, concentrating on where he was going and what obstacles might be in the way, his legs spread as if he walked on a set of rails, making sure he got his paws down in the right order. Don left the cabin door open so the dog could come inside if he wanted to, but Cable took one look at the mess in the room and lay down in the doorway, half in and half out, keeping a worried eye on Don. The room looked as though it had been ransacked. The drawers of the desk and filing cabinets were open, cardboard boxes were sitting around on the floor, and everywhere were papers, stacks of papers. Don threaded a course through the boxes and papers to the center of the room and stood there looking around, his hands stuck in his back pockets.

"It's a mess, isn't it, old man?"

The dog swallowed, looked around.

"You know what this is?"

Cable was willing to listen.

"This is a lifetime of work. A man is what a man does. And what you see here is what I did, or tried to do."

The dog panted, smiled.

"And you know what it adds up to? Papers. Just a floor full of papers."

Cable looked around; it didn't seem so bad to him.

Don picked up a binder from the top of the pile; the title said *Retold Tales of the Hopi*. When he wrote it, ten years before—was it just another project to avoid working on the *Pearl*? *I have been a joyless jeweler*—he thought it would be a good idea to have a copy of the manuscript in a black snap-binder, in case somebody ever asked him to give a reading of it, but, of course, because he never tried to do anything with it after he finished it, never showed it to anyone or tried to get it published, nobody ever asked. He flipped through the manuscript, then, holding it at arm's length so he could see it without his glasses, he read out loud, addressing Cable:

Before there was anything else, at the time when the earth was covered with water, the Woman of Hard Things lived in the East, at one end of the world, and another Woman of Hard Things lived in the West, at the other end of the world. And every day Father Sun crossed the sky between them. The Woman of Hard Things of the East liked the arrangement, but the Woman of Hard Things of the West was dissatisfied.

"Big Daddy, I'm tired of you always getting up in the middle of the night and leaving me," she said, her eyes the color of turquoise, and just about as brittle.

Father Sun sat on the edge of the bed and yawned. "Isn't it enough that you're the one I come to at the end of the day?" he said, scratching his corona.

"But why can't I be the one you wake up with in the mornings?"

"Whoever heard of the sun rising in the West?"

"That's the trouble with you, you never want to try anything new. . . ."

Don looked at Cable. "What do you think?"

The dog smiled, licked his lips.

"Yeh, but you're prejudiced."

Cable rested his chin on his paws.

Don, the binder still in his hand, looked down at himself, looked around the room, at the piles of boxes and papers. "This is what it comes to. A man standing up to his knees in words, talking to a dog."

Cable didn't know what was wrong with that.

"What can you do when you know you should trust your instincts, and you've learned that your instincts can't be trusted? What can you do when you've learned that your instincts are against you?"

Cable didn't know.

"And when you've learned that, what else is there to do with this shit?"

Cable never said a word.

It was then that he heard the siren, or became aware of it: became aware that he had been hearing it for a while, and that it was getting closer. He went to the door, stepped over Cable, and stood on the front step. He wondered if it could be somebody down the road, down near Doc Harvey's, or Doc Harvey's itself, then wondered if it could be his own house, then watched as the police car, siren screaming, red and blue lights flashing, careened up the road past his house, followed by a cloud of dust, a large obtuse triangle of dust, as if the dust shoveled the car too fast in front of it so that the car slipped and skittered in the loose gravel, on down the road toward George and Mary Olive's. Don jumped in his jeep, only realizing as he went to turn on the ignition that he still carried the manuscript in his hand; he threw the binder on the floor and cursed himself and started the jeep, wheeled around on the grass, and charged across the yard toward the driveway, scattering the dogs, who were just now getting settled again around the back steps, the dogs low-tailing it for the woods as Don roared by, headed for the road.

14

When George drove up the road toward his house, he found a police car sitting in his driveway, its red and blue lights flashing, doors wide open, the radio crackling though no one was about—a woman's voice kept saying, "Where is he, where is he, over?" as though the car were talking to itself—and Don's jeep sitting at an angle in his front yard. His first thought was that Mrs. Jenkins had changed her mind and called the police on him after all—George Binns, that notorious thief of Indian masks—but he realized that was ridiculous. His second thought was more so-bering. He left his car sitting at the bottom of the driveway and ran for the house.

The front door was open; he ran through the house to the kitchen. Mary Olive stood at the counter, looking out the window, her arms around Don.

"What happened?" he said, out of breath.

Mary Olive jumped; Don spun around and turned away from her and crashed into the side of the counter, cracking his knee. He yelped hoarsely and grabbed his leg and hobbled around in a little circle, Mary Olive following behind, bent over, trying to rub it. George looked from one to the other.

"What happened?"

"He banged his knee," Mary Olive said.

"No, I mean why is that police car out front? You're all right."

"You don't have to sound disappointed."

George blinked. Don stopped hobbling around and braced him-self against the back of a chair. Mary Olive rubbed his leg for a moment—"It's all right, Mary Olive, it's all right," Don said—then straightened up, her hands on her hips, and glared at George.

"Leave me alone with a drunk Indian in the back yard."

"What did he do? Did he come up to the house? Did he try to break in? Did he . . . what?"

"No," Mary Olive said, and turned her back to him, looked out the window. "But he could have."

George looked at Don. Don straightened up and flexed his knee to see if it could still bend.

"I just heard the police car. . . ."

"You mean the kachina didn't do anything?" George said, his teeth clenched so tightly that he had trouble speaking. "He just stayed down there where he was?"

Mary Olive, her arms folded, tapped her fingers, beat out a little tattoo, on her elbows.

"And you called the police anyway?"

Mary Olive, her back still turned, shrugged a little.

"After I asked you, after I told you not to call them?"

Mary Olive looked at him over her shoulder, her top lip curled over the lower, trying to look cute.

George growled in the back of his throat, a growl that climbed like a siren; he clenched his fists and brought them up beside his head.

"Don't do that, George," Mary Olive said. "It makes you look undignified."

"No!" George stamped once, then stamped in a circle in the middle of the floor, then ran out the back door and down the yard. "No no no no no no no no no no no no . . ."

Two policemen—one in a white riot helmet, the visor up and sticking out in front of him like a clear plastic shelf—stood at the end of the yard, in front of the fence, crouched slightly, their hands near their holsters, flanking the kachina, watching it carefully, creeping forward.

"Okay, fella, put down the stick and come on out of there," the policeman in the white riot helmet said.

The other policeman, a kid with orange hair, orange complexion, who looked young enough to be George's grandson, feinted as if dodging blows. "Watch it, Charlie, watch it."

The kachina stayed where he was, in the wash, leaning on his staff, looking from one policeman to the other, looking rather bored. They all three stopped and turned to watch the roly-poly man who came running down the hill toward them, yelling.

". . . no no no no no no no no no no no no no no. . . ."

George collapsed on the fence, bracing himself against it as he gasped for breath, his chest pounding, waving feebly to the two policemen to wait a moment until he caught his breath. The two policemen looked uneasily at each other, uncertain whether to pay attention to the guy having a coronary on the fence or the guy with the blue head and the club in the wash.

"Just a minute . . ." George wheezed.

"You trying to tell us something, mister?" said the policeman in the white riot helmet.

The kachina nodded to George. *Hello, there. What's going on?*

"This is my place . . ." George said, still out of breath. "I own this. . . ."

"Is this thing yours?" said the orange policeman, motioning toward the kachina.

The Aholi looked at him. *Watch it, bub.*

It was then that George realized the orange policeman had his gun out.

"Put that thing away!" George bellowed at him.

The policeman looked at the gun, looked at his partner, and put it away. George straightened up.

The kachina nodded. *Good for you, George.*

"Look, mister," said the policeman in the white helmet. "Are you the owner of this property?"

"Yes, officer."

"Then that's your wife up there?"

George didn't quite like the way the officer said that. "Yes, of course."

"Well, she's the one who put the call in on this guy."

The kachina cocked his head.

"It's all a mistake, officer. She shouldn't have called you. She gets a little excited."

"She's not the only one," said the policeman.

"It's a little hard to explain." George smiled. He reminded himself: Policemen are our friends.

"Why don't you try," said the policeman, giving a little nod of his head, his visor rattling.

Why don't you try, the kachina looked at George, giving the same little nod of his head, a mimic.

George cleared his throat, stretched his neck. "Well, this kachina just sort of appeared here this morning."

"This kachina," the policeman said. "Do you happen to know his name?"

"It's Aholi."

George and the kachina looked at each other, waited, nodded to each other, as the orange policeman said, "A holy what?"

I get it all the time. The kachina shrugged.

"It's all one word," George said. "Aholi. It's Hopi."

"A Hopi kachina," the policeman in the riot helmet said to the orange policeman. Then to George: "Do you happen to know the name of the guy inside?"

"No, I'm afraid I don't." George smiled.

"Let me see if I got this right," the policeman in the riot helmet said. "You know the name of the kachina but you don't know the name of the guy who's dressed up like this; you know the kachina comes from Hopi but you don't know where this guy comes from or how he got here?"

Aholi looked at George. *That sounds about right, doesn't it?*

"That sounds about right, officer."

"Mr. Binns, it sounds to me like your wife was totally correct in calling us. It sounds to me like we better take this fellow with us until we can find out what this whole thing is about."

The policeman in the riot helmet turned back to the wash; the orange policeman reached for his gun again.

"Now, wait a minute, officer," George said. "There's been no law broken here, has there?"

"That's what we're trying to find out, Mr. Binns. We're just answering an intruder-on-the-premises call, put in by your wife. So I guess if nothing else, there's at least trespassing involved."

"But this is my property so I say he isn't trespassing," George said, hoping the policeman wouldn't start to check property lines. "And he can't be an intruder because I don't think he's intruding. He's just going about his business and when he's done he'll be on his way again."

Thank you, George.

"Then why'd your wife call us?"

"I'm afraid that was the result of a family argument."

The officers flinched at the words "family argument," as if George had taken a swing at them; they looked at each other as if they wanted to forget the whole thing.

"We'll have to speak to your wife about this. She's the one who put in the complaint."

"Certainly, officer, come on up and talk to her. You'll see everything's under control."

The kachina smiled at George. *Oh sure, you'll see.*

George led the way back up to the house, the two officers trailing along behind, their heads together, looking back over their shoulders at the guy in the blue mask in the wash, speaking in undertones—George was almost certain he heard one of them say "fucking weirdos." The kachina looked after them, as if sorry to see them go. The orange policeman headed around the side of the house, back toward the patrol car, while the officer in the riot helmet, guiding his upraised visor through the back door as if he were a great beaked bird, followed George inside.

In the kitchen, Don leaned against the sink, Mary Olive on her knees in front of him, her forehead resting on his stomach, as she rubbed his leg.

"Hi," Don rasped, his face red even through his white beard, his knobby cheeks burning, an embarrassed grin on his face. He tried to move Mary Olive away but she kept on rubbing.

"Knee," she said, looking up at the policeman.

"Oh," said the policeman.

"Banged it," Mary Olive said.

"Mmm," the officer said. He swept his visor around the room, to see if there was anything else going on that he should know about, then he pointed it back at Mary Olive. "I'm sorry to bother you, but your husband here says that you knew about the guy down there."

Mary Olive gave a few more rubs to Don's knee, then clapped him on the side of the butt—Don's face went bug-eyed—and got to her feet. She swaggered slowly across the room, her legs astraddle, her stomach pushed forward, over to her usual place at the counter, and tapped a cigarette out of the pack. She offered the pack to the officer, raising her eyebrows; the officer rattled his visor. Mary Olive lit the cigarette slowly, taking a long slow drag of smoke into her lungs, then blew it out just as slowly, a thin blue line, letting the cigarette dangle gangster-style from the edge of her lips.

George thought, Good luck, officer.

"So that's what my husband here says, huh, officer?"

"Yes, ma'am. And he says the reason you called us was the result of a family argument."

"That's what my husband here says?" she said, the cigarette flapping up and down as she spoke.

George thought, Good luck, George.

"And your husband here says that it's okay for that guy to be down there."

"My husband here says." An ash fell off the end of her cigarette, cascaded down the front of her sleeveless blouse, and powdered to the floor.

"Yes, ma'am."

George cleared his throat, blinked a couple of times. Don had developed a sudden interest in the floor tiles.

Mary Olive inhaled deeply, took the cigarette from her lips, and let the smoke trail out from her open mouth, a thin blue veil covering her face, as she looked at the officer. The officer pointed his visor from George to Don and back again, looking at them as if from underneath a shelf, trying to read what was going on.

"Well, if that's what my husband here says," Mary Olive said after a moment, "then that's the way it must be."

The three men sighed in relief. The policeman said that if that took care of it and if there wasn't anything else—he pointed his visor at each one of them: George blinked; Don looked away; Mary Olive waggled her cigarette at him—he'd be going, and George walked him to the front door. The orange policeman leaned on the roof of the patrol car, sighting down his finger at the house, firing off imaginary rounds; after George moved his car so they could get out, he waved goodbye to them, but neither of the policemen waved back. Don came out of the house and climbed in his jeep.

"Is your knee okay?" George said, going over to him.

"It'll be okay," he rasped. "Considering everything else that's wrong with me, it'll be splendid."

"Thanks for coming over—"

Don closed his eyes and waved him silent. "You don't have to."

"Well, I appreciate it. You're a good friend."

Don sat with his eyes closed, holding on to the steering wheel with two hands as if he thought it might fall off. When he opened his eyes again, he looked at the black binder on the floor of the jeep and, after thinking about it for a moment, reached down and picked it up.

"If you want to read something about Indians, maybe this'll interest you."

"What is it?"

"It's something I wrote a couple years ago. I guess it was about ten years ago now."

"Don, I'm flattered—"

"You don't have to be. There's a couple things in there about your friend Aholi, so maybe it'll give you some idea about how a Hopi thinks—no, I take that back, maybe it'll give some idea about how a white-eyes thinks a Hopi thinks."

"I'll treat it carefully."

"You don't need to do that either. When you get done with it, you can burn it."

"Ha ha," said George, but Don didn't look at him again; he started the jeep and backed down the yard, heading up the road again. George watched until the jeep disappeared in the dust, then walked around the side of the house, leafing through the binder. He walked across the back yard, under the trees, and stood on top of the terrace wall; the kachina looked up at him from the wash.

"Well, at least that's over with," George said to himself, out loud. "You owe me one."

The kachina looked at him across the field. *I owe you one.*

George went back in the house. Mary Olive was on the floor in the kitchen again, this time with her arm stuck halfway up the Electrolux, as if she were helping it to give birth, or the machine were trying to swallow her. She looked up at George and smiled. George set his jaw and kept walking.

15

He sat at his desk in his study. It was night now; George sat in the glow of the articulated lamp on his desk, a circle of light spread over his desk, looking through the books on the Hopi and kachinas he had picked up at the library. The furnishings in the room were spare, the room decorated that way on purpose, in keeping with what he considered the seriousness of his purpose. Beside his desk to the left, facing the wall, was a metal stand with his typewriter; behind his desk was a wood stand with his twelve-pound dictionary; to his right, on the other side of the door that led to the hall, were his filing cabinets. Under the row of windows, which ran the length of the converted sleeping porch, were bookshelves, with more bookshelves lining the wall across from the windows; sitting on top of the shelves under the windows, in the middle of the wall of windows, were his four books, the books that bore his name, each one specially bound in leather—*The Inner Cone of Silence, The Dreamer Dreamed, The Truth of the Matter, Love and After*—braced with a pair of sleeping-lion bookends. At the far end of the room, beside the window that looked toward the Pikes', was another lamp, this one with a warm-colored burlap shade, and another filing cabinet; on top of the cabinet, in the warm glow of the lamp, was a small photograph of a pair of hands of a migrant farm worker taken by Dorothea Lange, George's electric razor, and a human skull. The photograph and the razor were there because he couldn't think of any other place to put them; the skull was there to remind him of "last things." He used to keep the skull on his desk when he was writing—he had gotten it while he was at Berkeley, fifty dollars from a renegade medical student—but since they had moved to Arizona, having it across the room seemed close enough.

Outside, moths tapped at the windows like soft fingers; they skittered up and down the dark glass as if on tiny ladders, their eyes glowing. When George looked up, he saw himself sitting at his desk, portly and professorial, his murky reflection in the night-filled window beyond the blinds. The image pleased him—the writer at his desk—though he tried not to look at himself too often, he didn't want to be immodest. Beyond his image, if he looked hard enough, there was still a trace of light in the sky, a crack of blue twilight defining the peaks of the mountains, but the mountains themselves, the forests covering the slopes of the foothills, the pines in the back yard, were black, were not there at all. He wondered if the kachina was still in the wash or if it had left yet; he thought of taking a flashlight and walking down to see, but decided that wouldn't be very smart. Maybe Don was right, maybe it was nothing to fool with, especially at night. He could wait until morning easily enough.

If he leaned forward, he could see the lights from the kitchen windows spilling out into the back yard, the white wooden lawn furniture looking a bit ghostly. Mary Olive sat below him in the kitchen, almost directly below him, on her stool at the corner of the counter; sometimes he could see her shadow, depending on how she sat there, but tonight he couldn't. He knew she sometimes performed a complicated ritual of massaging her gums at night, complete with a series of different-sized rubber picks and rolls of dental floss; he knew she sometimes listened to all-night radio shows, the countdowns of Golden Oldies, the popular songs, often rock and roll, which she couldn't stand at the time the songs were popular, had used in discussions at cocktail parties and literary evenings in New York as examples of the degeneration of American culture, or the all-night talk shows, carrying on her own all-night talk show by talking back to the hosts and callers-in; he knew she sometimes brushed her hair, took down her loose bun and brushed each side conscientiously two hundred times, though no one except herself, including himself, had seen her with her hair down for—he thought it must be twenty years; he knew she sometimes read; he knew she usually drank. But exactly what she did down there in the kitchen at night, he wasn't sure. It was her time, the nights, when the house was hers, just as the mornings were his. He listened now, leaning toward the register, but he couldn't tell what she was doing, couldn't tell that she was there at all. He thought it was probably just as well. He smiled to himself, shook his head.

He had a moment's panic: Sara's card. He looked through the books he had brought home from the library, through the things he had brought home from the office, but it wasn't there; then he remembered locking the card in his desk drawer. He breathed a sigh of relief. He thought of the image on the card, the picture of the sexy mouse that looked—he wondered if she realized the resemblance when she sent it—like Sara; he put aside the book of kachinas he was looking through and wrote on a piece of scratch paper:

See Miss Mousy on a shell,
See the way her pubis swells.
Hear her laughter, smell her smells;
See Miss Mousy on a shell.

He considered sending it to her, writing a short letter to go with it, but decided to wait to see if there was a letter from her in tomorrow's mail; besides, he didn't know what to say to her, about her proposed move to Chicago, didn't know what he could say. He put the piece of scratch paper in his desk—that's all he'd need: for Mary Olive to find something like that lying around—and remembered the returned poems from the *Pawtucket Review*. He slit the envelope open with his letter knife; well, at least it was a handwritten note, not a printed rejection slip.

Dear George Binns,

Nice work, interesting ideas—but I'm afraid they just don't stay with me strongly enough. Close. Try us again sometime.

Regards,

D. J. Brown

Close, he thought, close: as if it were a race, a contest. In the late sixties, after a couple of his stories appeared in *Esquire,* the magazines—good ones too—used to contact him, asked him to contribute to them. The only reason he had sent these poems to an unknown magazine like the *Pawtucket Review* in the first place was that the magazine was just starting up; he thought they could probably use some name writers. (Was he a name writer? Well, he wasn't a big name, certainly. But there were people out there who would be interested in his work, he was sure. Who would still recognize his name.) *Close.* He looked through the sheets of paper to see how the poems fared, to see if the copies were reusable, could be sent out again to another magazine the way they were, or if they'd have to be retyped. They looked okay— no coffee stains, no signs that they'd been used to swat bugs or wipe shoes—except for the one on top. He read:

MAN IN A BOX

At first, it seems impossible to fit
A human being in a space this small;
Still you try, and find constriction
Seems to be a part of comfort.

You ease yourself further, tucking
Legs beneath your trunk, doubling
Over in a wrap of arms, and burying
Your head on a level with your feet.

There: you made it! And don't worry
If the fasteners are out of reach.
The fact that you are folded there,
Safe and snug, is lock enough.

Beside the second stanza was a penciled note, probably from
D. J. Brown: *You'd have to be double-jointed to do this!* Glib son of
a bitch. D. J. Brown was probably a graduate-student reader, what
would he (or she?) know about life? Now he'd have to type it
over again. He growled in the back of his throat, said out loud,
"The bastards."

"George?"

He looked at the register beside his shoe. *It's like being bugged.*
"Yes, dear?"

"I thought you said something. I hadn't heard you for a while."

"I'm still here. I'm working." He picked up the kachina book
again and turned a page, as if to prove it. "I haven't heard you
either."

"I'm still here too."

The register was silent for a moment.

"Was dinner all right tonight?"

"Yes, dear. It was fine."

"You didn't say anything. . . ."

"I should have. I thought it."

"And the salad?"

"Maybe there was a little too much garlic in the dressing. But
otherwise it was fine."

"I was afraid there was too much garlic."

"It was all very good." *For hash.*

The register was silent again. He looked at his image in the
glass in front of him, the image as murky as if he looked at himself
in black water. *Here sits George Binns the writer.* She needs me, he
thought, to help get her through the tragedies of every day, like
too much garlic in the salad dressing. He heard her place her
wineglass back on the counter.

"Are you mad at me?"

"What for?"

"For this afternoon. For calling the police."

He thought about it for a moment, trying to decide what was best to say; then he decided the silence was already pointed enough. "No, dear, I'm not mad."

"You didn't say very much at dinner. And you didn't stay down here very long afterward."

"I've been thinking about some other things." Well, it was true, in a way.

"I just got scared, that's all. That's why I called them."

"I understand, dear." Well, maybe that was true, in a way, too. He remembered Don's manuscript.

"George?"

"Yes, dear?"

The register was silent for a moment. "Would you like to come down here for a while? There's some cognac. And maybe we could listen to some music, *The Magic Flute* or something."

"I'm going to read a little more and then go to bed."

"Oh."

"Maybe some other night," he said in the direction of his shoe.

The register didn't say anything. He sighed; he knew he should go down, he knew she was trying to be friendly, but he didn't want to go down, he didn't want to sit with her. He looked out at the darkness, at the image of himself in the black window. The truth was, he didn't want to be with her. He cleared his neck away from his collar, opened Don's manuscript of *Retold Tales of the Hopi*—in the middle, where the manuscript more or less opened on its own, not really interested but curious, a courtesy to a colleague, a duty to a friend—and started to read.

16

THE UNDER WORLD

Things were looking bad for the Hopi in the Under World, the Third World. As bad as they had been back in the Second World. As bad as they had been back in the First World. But this time, in the Third World, the problem wasn't fire or flood or some natural disaster. In the Third World, the problem came from the Hopi themselves. The men neglected their ceremonies, the women neglected their children, everyone quarreled with everyone else.

Obviously, something had to be done.

Had to be done, if for no other reason than that the Under World was filling up with everyone's waste. There was only so much room. Everyone was slipping and sliding in everyone else's nose slime. Spittle ran in the streets. The urine and feces were . . . well, you get the picture.

Obviously, something had to be done.

Then somebody had an idea. Somebody had the idea that all the trouble came from sex . . . which, in one way of looking at it, probably wasn't too far wrong. The problem was that this somebody didn't think the idea through far enough. This somebody thought that, if the object of desire was taken away, then the desire itself would go away too. Accordingly, it made sense to this certain somebody that things would go better in the Third World if all the men lived on one side of the river and all the women lived on the other.

Sigh. Somebody's wonderfully brilliant bright idea. Of

course, when they tried it and everything went to hell, there wasn't anyone who could remember exactly who that certain somebody was. And nobody raised his hand.

But, obviously, something had to be done. So they tried it.

For a couple of years, the natural competition between the two sides of the river, the two sexes, kept things going along okay. But from the beginning the men had the advantage. The men and the women had divided up the available seed, but the men took along their weapons so they could hunt, and the men were more experienced in building houses. Also, the women were used to grinding corn, not growing it, so their crops did poorly. And the women not only lacked meat to eat, they didn't have any animal skins for clothes. In a few years they were definitely a ratty, mangy, miserable group of women.

But they sure looked awfully good to the men who stood on the opposite bank of the river.

As it turned out, the sexual desire hadn't gone away at all. As it turned out, the sexual desire seemed to grow even stronger. Sigh. And double sigh. Besides, a number of new problems had come up as a result of the separation. Problems that that certain somebody hadn't even thought of.

For one thing, the Hopi weren't getting any younger. Nobody died in the Third World, so a lack of people wasn't a problem. But the men and women kept getting older. And older. With no young strong healthy bodies coming along to help with all the hard work. And they noticed there was soon a lack of giggling, playful children running around too.

For another thing, there were the alternatives for their sexual desires that people kept coming up with. The men tried everything from the liver of a freshly killed deer to a gourd filled with warm rabbit's blood. Not to mention sheep, chickens, dogs, each other, and their ever-trusty hands. The women tried sticks covered with buckskin, or the stem of a cactus (peeled, needless to say). All of this was bad enough, of course—bad because the substitutes only served to remind everybody just how good the real thing was. But it was worse because the women, instead of giving birth to children, began to give birth to gods and monsters.

And it was not always easy to tell the difference.

One girl, a virgin, exposed her vulva to the sunlight, moving with the warmth and pleasure, and got herself impregnated by Father Sun. When she realized what had happened, she ran to a spring and tried to douche, but the water excited her all over again and she found herself impregnated a second time, this time by the Water Serpent. In nine months she gave birth to the Little War Twins, the Two. Another girl got herself off with an eagle feather. The eagle then carried her away to his nest in the San Francisco Mountains, where she gave birth to Kwatoko, the monster bird known as Knife-Wing.

Obviously, the idea of separating the sexes wasn't working out.

So finally the women swam over to the men, or the men swam over to the women—it depends on who tells the story—and life went back to normal. Normal, you know: rape, incest, fighting, laziness. A lot of nose slime and dung. Everyone hoped that somebody else would come up with a better idea. And that somebody would come up with an idea of what was making that sound that sometimes thundered overhead. A sound like footsteps, moving around in another, higher world . . .

17

He saw something; George looked up. He thought he saw a light, a flash of some kind, up on the hillside, up among the trees, but he didn't see anything now. He waited: nothing. He reached up and turned off the lamp over his desk, his image gone from the glass in front of him, the window in front of him black though the lamp was still on on the other side of the room, and looked out through the venetian blinds into the night. He waited. Then, for a few seconds, a small red light, a red glow, rolled across the darkness, up the slope in the woods, glided beyond the branches of the pine tree outside his window, then was gone again. He blinked, leaned forward over his typewriter for a better look, but it was too late; he opened his desk drawer and took out his monocular, holding it in his hand, ready to train it on the spot if the light appeared again. Who could be up in the woods at this time of night? Maybe it was hunters, out to jacklight a deer—Don said that happened sometimes—though he had never seen any deer around; maybe it was some campers lost on the fire trails, but there weren't supposed to be any campers in this area. Maybe it had something to do with the kachina—whoever it was going away, somebody come to meet him, the joke or ceremony or whatever it was over. George was glad he hadn't taken the flashlight and gone down to check on him—he didn't want to get mixed up with somebody in the middle of the night—though he felt a little sad, too: now he never would know what the whole thing was about.

He waited in the darkness. The moths yo-yoed up and down

the dark glass in front of him, gradually losing interest and drifting down toward the lighter end of the room; the sounds of Mary Olive's radio, some late-night music, came softly through the register. He waited another fifteen minutes, but the light never appeared again and he gave up.

"Good night, dear," he said to the register.

Maybe she didn't hear him, or maybe she didn't want to say anything, or maybe he didn't hear her reply. Whichever. He got up and went across the room to turn off the other lamp, then made his way back to the door, walking carefully, a man in the dark, upright and wary, his left hand extended slightly in front of him though he knew there shouldn't be anything in his path, experiencing a moment's panic when he missed the doorknob, groping frantically until he found it again, opened it, and walked down the hall, in the glow of the night light at the top of the stairs, to their bedroom. And went to bed, falling asleep immediately, as he usually did, a contented spirit, at peace with himself, or at least so he would say if anyone asked him (nobody did), sleeping soundly every night though he gnashed his teeth loud enough to be heard in the hall . . .

. . . while on the other side of Flagstaff, in the living room of the new modern house in a subdivision called Kachina Highlands, where she had moved a few years ago, after her husband died, Mrs. Jenkins sits stretched out on a Barcalounger, her stubby legs barely long enough for her feet to reach the end of the upraised platform, so that she feels like an astronaut in zero gravity, reaches for her gin and tonic as she looks through the pages of a fifty-dollar book of paintings of Hopi kachinas, looking for a picture of Aholi, wondering about the strange embarrassed man who talked to her at the museum today about wanting to buy a stolen kachina mask, and thinks, even though she knows she shouldn't, that such a mask would look nice sitting on her own mantel and wonders if she knows any way to get a hold of one, thinks it would be all right if she had one, because she would really appreciate it . . . while sitting alone in his dark living room, on the east side of town, his wife already gone to bed, Ernie Tewayumptewa watches the Tonight *show, where*

Johnny Carson is talking to a young fashion designer whose clothes feature the Southwestern look for fall, high-cheeked, blue-eyed girls wearing headbands and a two-hundred-fifty-dollar sweater woven in a pattern taken from Navajo rugs, long dangling turquoise earrings and a little black cocktail dress cut in the style of the traditional Pueblo Indian manta, beaded moccasins and old pawn concha belts with a hand-tailored, sandstone-colored Ultrasuede skirt, as he idly rubs his fingers together and finds, under his fingernails, bits of glue and feathers . . . while in a small trim white frame house ten miles north of town, Mary Olive Binns, having flossed and massaged and prodded her gums for the night, having taken down her hair and brushed it two hundred strokes on each side as she has every night since she was a child (pleased each time to rediscover just how long it is and pleased each time that she is the only one who knows it, that she is the only one who ever sees it down, a part of her nobody else knows, her secret), listens to an all-night talk show, tonight's topic "Whether the Meek Shall Inherit the Earth or Will the Poor Just End Up Eating the Rich," as she sits on her stool at the kitchen counter, comfortable with herself in the night, comfortable as long as she's up and dressed and moving around at night, as long as she's not lying in bed, where she still sees, when she closes her eyes, the baby girl, less than a year old, lying dead in her cradle, the eyes as blank as a doll's eyes, a crib death before they had a name for such a thing, the one time in the twenty-four-hour period when she feels in control of herself and her world (or maybe when she's just, finally, had enough to drink), so that she's not frightened or even taken aback much as she looks out the window and sees, coming toward her in the darkness outside, a face, a face that in the light spilling out the window seems pale and ghostly though not wholly unexpected, familiar, the white beard and knobby cheeks and watery blue eyes: Don's face; she eases off the stool, the room a little shaky from the wine, and goes and opens the back door for him, takes him by the hand, leads him into the room.

"You smell like pine trees."

They hold each other briefly, like old friends, for comfort, like brother and sister, then tighter, harder, clamp together.

"I went to the doctor," Don says into the side of her head, "I thought maybe you wanted to hear . . ."

She leans back, still in his arms, to look at him. "I don't care about any of that, I'm just glad you came back to me again" . . .

. . . waking only once, in the middle of the night, as he usually did: it was a little after 3:00 A.M. and Mary Olive still wasn't in bed, which was as usual too. On the way back from the bathroom, he thought he heard voices downstairs, but when he stopped to listen he didn't hear anything and decided it was only her radio or maybe she was talking to herself again—silly woman—and George padded back to their bedroom and fell right asleep again. As he usually did.

TWO

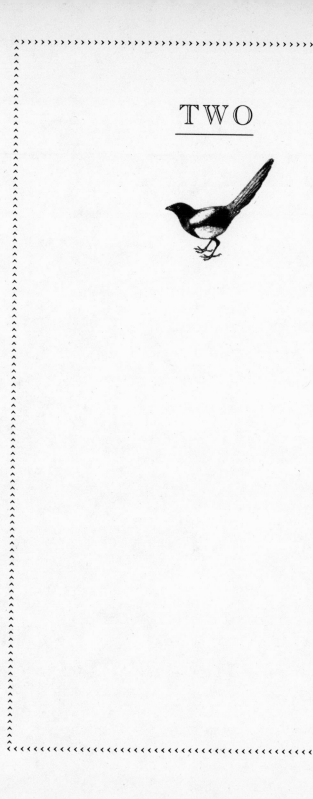

1

The next morning George woke at 7:10, his usual time, waking, as usual, without the alarm and, as usual, getting up immediately, at once wide awake and energetic and cheerful (Mary Olive called it despicably cheerful; she couldn't stand to be around him when he got up in the mornings, any more than he could stand to be around her when she got up because of her sourness; she said it, his cheerfulness when he woke up was the reason she stayed up so late at night, so she'd sleep late in the mornings and not have to be around him, and though anyone who knew them knew that that wasn't the reason, or at least wasn't the main reason, it made a good story; when she told the story, at parties or when they had guests, George just nodded and smiled, despicably cheerful), full of enthusiasm and anxious to start the day.

He stood up and swung his arms around a bit, loosening up, took some deep breaths, bent over to try to touch his toes a few times—he only got down as far as his knees but that was close enough: it was the intention that counted. Mary Olive lay flung out on her bed, her mouth open, as though someone had hit her with a club; George tiptoed into the bathroom, where he had laid out his clothes the night before. In the mirror above the sink he examined his color, the clearness of his eyes, made sure he was all still there—"Good morning, George." *Good morning, George*—stuck out his tongue. It was a sunny morning, but it sounded as if there was a wind. As he stood at the toilet bowl to urinate, he looked out the window, out the top half of the window, above the line of curtains that Mary Olive had put up to protect their privacy from the squirrels and magpies, at the branches of the pines stirring in the wind, and thought, Well, well. *Well well well.* Still dressed in his pale-blue pajamas, he went downstairs, stopping at the hall closet long enough to put on his black trench coat, the same black trench coat Mary Olive had used as a robe the day before, and padded on through the house, bouncing on the balls of his feet in his slippers.

When he stepped out the back door, the warm breeze pressed against him, then let him go; the air was full of dust. A long white cloud, the only cloud in the sky, clung to the top of the San Francisco peaks, trailing off like a scarf; on the slopes of the foothills, the groves of aspens shimmered. The magpies were back in force this morning, but they weren't saying much; a dozen of them stood around the lower yard, trying to face into the occasional breeze, the breeze otherwise getting up under their long tails and threatening to flip them over. As George padded down the yard, squinting to keep the dust from his eyes, the magpies skeetered off, only far enough to get out of his way, complaining briefly, *Rak rak rak rak rak,* at the disturbance. The kachina sat in the wash, on a rock on the bank, working at something in his hands. When the breeze came up, he dipped his head away from it; the feathers sticking up from the peak of the tall blue mask hummed.

"You're still here," George said, standing by the fence, blinking twice, three times to show his pleasure, smiling.

The kachina looked up at him. *That's very perceptive, George.* He went back to what he was doing, winding a length of string around the base of some feathers and sticks in his hand.

"The reason I'm surprised is because I saw some lights moving around up on the hill last night. I thought maybe it was you, er, going somewhere."

The Aholi stopped and looked up at the trees on the hillside—the breeze came up and blew aside the tufts of red yarn sprouting at his ears, exposing a rainbow design, a sudden flash of color, bands of red and blue and yellow, painted on the side of the mask—then looked back at George. *Nope, it wasn't me.* He went back to his work.

"Well, er, that's okay too."

The Aholi nodded.

"I mean that you're still here."

The Aholi kept on watching his hands.

"What are you making?"

The Aholi stopped and slumped a little, resting his elbows on his thighs as he stared off at the hillside.

"I'm sorry, I didn't mean to disturb you."

The kachina sighed and looked up at him again, *It's okay,* and held it up for George to see. George squinted at it, then climbed through the rails for a better look, this time sucking in his stomach and choosing his moves carefully so he wouldn't get stuck—the kachina looked away discreetly—making it all right this time except for one of his slippers that fell off, plop. George stood at the top of the bank, his hands in his raincoat pockets, pleased with himself, rocking back on his heels and craning his neck forward at the same time. In the kachina's hands were two blue sticks about as long as his fingers, one of the sticks notched at the top, which were tied at the base to a large feather, perhaps a turkey feather or that of a hawk. A tuft of white breast feathers dangled free from the bottom.

"A prayer stick," George announced. "You're making prayer sticks."

The Aholi cocked his head. *How did you know that?*

"I've been doing some reading."

Oh. The kachina went back to wrapping white string around the base of the feather and sticks.

"It's very pretty."

It's not supposed to be pretty.

"Well, I didn't mean pretty, exactly. I meant, well, interesting."

The Aholi gave him a sidelong glance and kept wrapping. When the prayer stick was finished, the length of string wound around the base, the kachina laid it on the ground beside him, along with several others he had already completed, then took two more sticks and a feather from the small pouch on his lap.

George thought a moment. "What I was reading said that making prayer sticks is one of the most important rituals for the Hopi."

That a fact? The kachina lined up the sticks and held the feather in place behind them.

"It said that making prayer sticks was one of the most important parts of the ceremonies in the kivas. It said the sticks are a sort of physical embodiment of a prayer."

If you say so. Aholi took another length of string from the pouch and began to wind it around the base.

"From what I was reading, I got the idea that the only time prayer sticks were made outside of a kiva was at a shrine or something."

The kachina sighed—a sound like a long hiss—and rested his elbows on his thighs again, looking off into space.

"Well, how would I know? I was only telling you what I read."

Yes. How would you know? The Aholi picked up the things from his lap and stood up, the turtle-shell rattle shifting noisily, the particolored cape ballooning out in the breeze; he walked a few steps down the bank and pointed.

All George saw was a few stones.

The kachina pointed again.

"It's a pile of stones. That's where you were digging."

The kachina stamped his foot—the rattle clacked—and looked stern. George walked over a little closer; obviously he was missing something. Then he noticed an opening among the rocks, a hole back into the slope of the bank. The hole—it was like a small cave—was only a foot or so deep, and inside there appeared to be a few bones and other debris. When George still didn't understand, the Aholi picked up one of the prayer sticks and put it in the dirt in front of the opening.

"It's a shrine?"

You got it.

"Oh, good heavens."

2

When he got back to the house, George put a kettle of water on the stove, fixed himself some toast with orange marmalade, then, while he waited for the water to boil, stood at Mary Olive's place at the counter so he could look out the window, so he could keep an eye on the kachina. (*An Indian shrine. In my back yard. Amazing. Now what am I supposed to do?*) Usually Mary Olive cleaned the counter before she went to bed, cleaned so that, when he came down in the mornings, the kitchen looked as though no one had been in it, ever, but this morning he found it in a mess: her empty wineglass, smeared with her fingerprints—two glasses, in fact; she must have forgotten she already had a glass and poured herself a second—an ashtray full of cigarette butts, bits of paper lying around that she had torn from something, a label, perhaps, and wadded up as she listened to the radio, her jar full of picks and probes for her gums, her comb and hairbrush. There was even a small nest of hair on the counter, pulled from the brush when she was through, that she had forgotten to throw away; it all made him uncomfortable. He pushed the things to one end of the counter and got out the phone book: there was an Ernie Tewayumptewa on Juniper Street, on the east side of town. As he wrote down the address on a piece of scratch paper, the phone rang.

"Yes?"

"Hello, love."

"Sara!"

"So how are you this morning?"

He looked around furtively, making sure the door to the dining room was closed, then turned toward the wall, his face a few inches from the corner of the cupboards, hunched over the receiver, and spoke softly. "Sara, what are you doing?"

"I'm calling you, George. To ask you how you are."

"I'm fine, but you shouldn't be calling now. It's prime phone rates."

She sighed. "Oh, George, that's so much like you. To be worried about prime phone rates when here I am, stretched out on my bed, without a stitch of clothes on, naked as the day I was born, nakeder, rubbing myself you know where while I listen to your voice. Oooooo."

"Sara!"

"George, say 'Let me tie you up' in your sexy voice," she giggled.

George cupped the phone, leaned his head into the corner of the cupboards and the wall. "Sara, don't talk that way. Suppose Mary Olive heard you."

"You know as well as I do that Mary Olive's asleep at this hour. She probably just got to bed. And besides, she's a friend of mine too. How would she know that I didn't call to talk to her?"

"She would if she heard the things you were saying."

"Ah. You mean like 'Cover me with egg whites and beat me, baby'?"

"Exactly like that."

"And if you're still worried about prime phone rates, it's my money, George, and I'd much rather spend it on this than anything else."

"I still don't think it's a good idea. . . ."

"George George George. You always worry about things so much. Actually, it's one of your endearing qualities, but sometimes you can be a real prude."

"Sara. . . ."

"I've told you where I am and what I'm doing; tell me where you are and what you're doing. Are you in your study?"

"No, I'm in the kitchen.. . . ."

"Ah. Fixing your Earl Grey tea with two slices of whole-wheat toast, cut diagonally, covered with Dundee orange marmalade."

George cleared his throat.

"You're so cute and predictable, George. What are you wearing today?"

"Actually, I haven't gotten dressed yet. I'm still in my pajamas." He realized he was also in his black trench coat, but he decided against telling her that; he promptly took it off.

"The pale-blue pajamas with the little crown over the heart?"

"Well, yes. . . ."

"Ah. I always liked those pajamas because it was so easy to slip my hand down inside the elastic—"

"Sara!"

"George George George."

"Besides the fact that I don't think we should be talking like this, I don't have time to talk very long right now. I've got a lot of things to take care of today."

"You always have a lot of things to take care of, George. Tell me what all you're going to take care of today."

"It's a little hard to explain."

"You're good at explanations, George. Or is it excuses. . . ."

"This is no excuse. We've got some kind of Indian spirit camped out in the back yard."

"Indian spirit."

"Well, it's not exactly a spirit, it's some guy dressed up like an Indian spirit. They call them kachinas; I guess they're something like Indian angels."

"George, that place out there is no good for you."

"I'm serious. This guy or kachina or whatever he is just showed up yesterday morning and he doesn't seem to want to go away. And this morning I just discovered he's got some kind of shrine out there."

"A shrine? Maybe he's a Shriner who lost his convention." Sara giggled.

"This is serious, Sara."

"Ah. Everything's serious, George."

"Anyway, I've got to try to find out what this whole thing is about."

"George, I think you need to see me. I think the altitude out there has made you philosophically lightheaded. You need me to ground you in reality."

"I'm not making any of this up."

"Or maybe grind you in reality. Bump and grind."

"Sara."

"George."

They were silent for a moment.

"Did you get my card? My letter? About Chicago?"

"Yes."

"So. What do you think?"

"About what?"

"About the possibility that I'm not going to be in New York any more. That it's going to seem more than a little strange that last year you came to New York for one thing or another, for conferences and seminars and to see some agents, and that all of a sudden, at the same time I move to Chicago, all the conferences and seminars and agents move to Chicago too. That, my sweet love, unless something drastic happens, we're not going to see each other any more."

"To tell you the truth, Sara, I haven't had much time to think about anything. Not with this guy in the back yard and all."

Sara was quiet. He hated that, when she did that, just kept quiet, didn't pick up her end of the conversation, just left him hanging there. He tried to wait her out, but he finally couldn't stand it any longer.

"Sara?"

"Yes, George?"

"I just wanted to make sure you were still there."

"I'm still here, George. I'm still, still here. Waiting."

"What does that mean?"

"I think you know."

"Look, I can't really talk now." He looked around, turned away from the corner of the cabinets, to see if Mary Olive had, somehow, magically appeared behind him. "I think it's really unwise, talking like this."

THERE'S SOMETHING IN THE BACK YARD

"Nothing we ever did was wise, George. It was just fun. And right. That was our strong suit. I think I was the first time you were ever unwise in your life. I think unwise becomes you, George."

"Sara, I think we better hang up."

"George, I think you better wake up."

The phone clicked dead. He held the receiver for a moment, wondering whether he should call her back. No, he didn't want to have to explain to Mary Olive, if the question came up, what he was doing calling Sara at this hour of the morning; besides, it was already after eight, the rates had gone up (that made sense, despite Sara's sarcasm: it was a legitimate, intelligent consideration). He hung up the receiver and looked out the window, at the splotch of color, the figure in the tall blue mask, the tropical-colored cape, sitting at the end of his yard. What could he say to her anyway? He had wondered, for some time, how he could ever break it off with her, how he could ever tell her; there were parts of their relationship—how he hated that word, it was too clinical, too trendy: "affair" was more like it, he liked the ring of it too—that he'd hate to let go. He could think of a couple of her parts—her body, small, compact, just slightly muscular, like a peasant's maybe, though soft, white as a glob of pastry dough—that he wished he had hold of right now.

("Sexist," she would say; "Sexy," he would reply; "Male Chauvinist," she would giggle; "Female Delicacy," he would say, lick his lips, and bury his nose in her wiry muff.)

He had forgotten his tea; the water had almost boiled away. He poured what water there was left into his cup, dunked the strainer for a minute, and sipped it and ate his toast while looking out the window, remembering. Then he washed his dishes—he left Mary Olive's—and carried the piece of paper with Ernie Tewayump-tewa's address back through the house and upstairs, to get dressed, feeling enthusiastic, ready to get things settled, cheerful, hopeful, proud of himself for being such a well-controlled, well-ordered, basically reasonable and likable fellow.

3

After he showered and shaved and dressed, he went into his study and, while he waited for it to get a little later before he went to see Ernie Tewayumptewa, he looked in the books from the library to find out more about prayer sticks. Except that now, as he read more carefully, he realized each book seemed to say something different. The books couldn't even agree on the Hopi name for the sticks: some called them *pahos,* some called them *bahos.* (And were prayer sticks the same as prayer feathers?) He found the passage he had read the night before that said the making of prayer sticks was at the heart of the different rituals; but another book said that making prayer sticks was only a preparation for the main rituals. One book said they were made with eagle feathers, and gave a long explanation of the symbolism of the eagle, lord of the sky; another gave a list of the different kinds of feathers that could be used, including turkey, duck, eagle, hawk, flicker, jay, bluebird, oriole, towhee, warbler, and even cowbird; one book said the feathers were tied to willow sticks; another book said the sticks were of cottonwood and likened the *pahos* (or *bahos*) to kachina dolls. Some books said that only wing feathers were used, or tail feathers, or just the tips of the feathers, or only downy breast feathers; some said the breast feathers were like the clouds, or maybe like the breath, or maybe the breath was like a cloud. . . .

Nor could different books agree on how the prayer sticks (or were they prayer feathers? he still didn't know) were used, what the Hopis did with them once they were made. One book said they were planted in the fields with the crops, another said they were given to the kachinas to take back to the Under World, another said they were placed in the springs or at the water holes; one book said the prayer sticks were left standing up, another said they were placed lying down, another said they were covered over, another said they were left exposed; one book said they were placed among the rafters of the house so they would be closer to the clouds, another book said they were buried in the corners of the house, or buried in the corners of the entire village, in order to root the house, or the village, with the earth. One book said the prayer sticks were offerings, one said they were reminders, one said they were a summons, one said they were a payment, one said, or at least implied, that kachinas just liked to have a lot of feathers lying around. . . .

George was confused.

This time when the phone rang, he caught it before the first ring was finished.

"Yes?"

"That must be very uncomfortable, George."

"Sara!" He looked around to make sure the study door was closed, then huddled over the receiver and spoke in little more than a whisper. "Sara, I—"

"I mean sitting on top of the phone like that. I don't think I've ever known anyone before who could catch the phone before it stopped ringing on the first ring. Do you practice that, George? Is that a spiritual discipline of some sort?"

"Sara, what is it?"

"What is what?"

"Why are you calling again?"

"Were you really worried about my last call because it was during prime rates?"

"Sara. . . ."

"Ah. You're sputtering, George. But that's not really why I called. This isn't really why I called either, but it just dawned on me that I'm the one who always calls you. You never call me. Well, actually, it didn't just dawn on me, I've been thinking about it for a long time. But I just thought about it again, after we hung up. Why is that, George?"

"I don't really think this is the time to discuss it."

"I think it's a splendid time. Seeing as how I just called you again to find out why it is I'm the one who usually calls you. God, do you believe this? I just did it again, I called you. Why do I keep doing that?"

Because you're not very smart. "You know as well as I do that the reason I don't call you is because Mary Olive would wonder about it."

"But Mary Olive calls me sometimes."

"Well, that's different."

"What's different about it? You're both supposed to be my friends."

"Because you're not sleeping with Mary Olive, that's what's different," he hissed.

"How do you know that? And besides, the way things are going, I'm not sleeping with you either. And besides again, you're the one who pays the bills, so she wouldn't know about it anyway."

"Sara."

"George George George."

He wondered, could Mary Olive and Sara have slept together? But the idea was so preposterous, the idea of Mary Olive sleeping with anybody else, he quickly put it out of his mind.

"But that wasn't why I called you back either. I called to tell you that the Chicago thing isn't definite."

"What do you mean it isn't definite?"

"I mean it isn't irreparable. That I can still change it. Well, that, actually, I haven't made the decision yet."

"I thought you said the Sarah Lawrence job fell through."

"It did. At least as far as tenure is concerned. They won't give me tenure, and neither will Barnard, but I can still go on at both places part-time, like I have been."

"So what's the problem?"

"The problem is that Chicago offered me tenure. It's a permanent position."

"Then it doesn't seem to me there's any decision to be made. You have to go where the better job is."

"But that means leaving New York."

"People have been known to leave New York and survive."

"But we won't," she said in a small voice.

"Sara, I don't think you're being very responsible about this. I don't think you're keeping your eye on the ball."

"I'm trying to keep my eye on your balls, George."

"When you decided to get out of publishing and get into teaching, you made a commitment for a new career, and it only stands to reason that—"

"Reason, my ass. You're talking to me like you think I'm a little child or something."

"Sara!" He was genuinely shocked.

It was Sara who hissed now, though not because she was afraid someone might overhear her. "You still don't know what I'm telling you, do you, George? You still don't understand what it is I've been offering you."

"What? What are you talking about?" Despite himself, he found that he was smiling, that he was almost laughing.

"Or maybe you do. Maybe you do. . . . Maybe I'm the one who's never understood what you've been telling me."

He sat there with a huge grin on his face—he couldn't help it; he didn't know what caused it or where it came from; he felt terrible that he would feel this way, this wasn't funny—afraid to speak for fear of laughing out loud, the laughter bubbling out of him, uncontrollably.

"Goodbye, George. You're right. It's prime rates."

As soon as she hung up, however, he was no longer smiling, no longer felt as though he wanted to laugh. He sat staring at the phone for several minutes, solemn, morose, his hands folded across his stomach. Women. Then he got up, stuck the paper with Ernie Tewayumptewa's address in his shirt pocket, snapped his teeth once, biting air; he couldn't let himself think about it any more, he couldn't let it bother him. There were things to do, he had things to take care of.

4
—

*R*ak rak rak rak rak rak rak rak rak rak rak rak rak.

The breeze was gone, the day had settled down, but there was still dust in the air—as he walked down the back yard, under the pine trees and down the terrace steps and out across the field, he could feel it, the dust, the grit, on the insides of his elbows, in the creases of his neck. The magpies were gone except for one who sat in a tree on the other side of the wash, close to the kachina, watching him, talking about something.

Rak rak rak rak rak rak rak rak rak rak rak rak rak.

George leaned against the fence, rested his tummy against the top rail, bounced a little good-naturedly against it, watching the kachina work. The Aholi was having trouble lining up a new pair of sticks (willow? cottonwood?) with the feather (turkey? hawk?); the sticks kept rolling off center before he could tie them securely, and the feather wasn't cooperating either. The magpie flew down a little closer, from one tree to another, the black and white of its wings and belly flashing between the pine branches.

Rak rak rak rak rak rak rak rak. Rak rak rak rak rak.

The kachina looked up disgustedly at the bird, then noticed George on the other side of the fence. The Aholi nodded *Oh, hello again* and went back to getting the sticks lined up.

"Uh, I thought I'd tell you that I'm going on a little errand. I won't be gone very long."

The kachina glanced sideways at George *And you don't want me to get into any trouble while you're gone* still fumbling with the sticks and feather.

"I didn't mean that the way it sounded. What I meant was, I'm going to be away from the house a little bit and . . . uh, you know my wife tends to get a little excited sometimes."

Sometimes.

"But I think everything will be okay if, well, you know, if you stay down here and, er, keep on doing what you're doing."

Should be okay.

"I mean I don't think it would be a very good idea to go roaming around or anything."

George smiled uneasily. Aholi stopped fumbling with the sticks and feathers, rested his elbows on his thighs, and looked at George.

What are you trying to say, George?

"What I'm trying to say is—"

George closed his eyes for a second, to collect himself *I'm not doing this well* to start over, then looked at the kachina again. And saw, this time, not the blue pointed mask with the red yarn and feathers, the painted slashes for eyes, the inverted triangular mouth, the mouth at once quizzical and slightly bemused, whimsical, but the eyeholes, the eyes inside the mask; as the kachina sat on the rock, his head turned toward him, the sun struck the side of the mask, the light washed across the face of the mask, so that for the first time George thought he saw, for a brief instant, the eyes of a person inside, large brown-black eyes, like smooth wet stones, the whites glistening, the eyes set well back inside the mask, not close to the openings but deep inside, as if whoever it was looked at George from inside a cave, though when he looked for them again, tried to get a better look at them, the light didn't seem to be quite right.

"—er, nothing. I think you know what I'm getting at."

I think I know what you're getting at.

"Just—" He cleared his throat, his throat felt gritty too; he stretched his neck, removed his paunch from against the rail. "I'll be back in a little while."

Goodbye, George.

Rak rak rak rak rak rak rak rak rak rak rak rak rak, said the magpie from a nearby branch, bending forward, flicking its tail. The kachina looked up at it.

And that's enough out of you too, bird.

5
—

Ernie Tewayumptewa's house was in a rundown neighborhood on the far side of town, a section where George had never been before—it wasn't that he was afraid, really, it was just that he was, well, uneasy—where the streets were oiled instead of paved and the sidewalks were just paths among the uncut grass and weeds; it was a one-story stucco house, on a street of one-story stucco houses, all of which appeared to have been built during or right after World War II, a development or tract that didn't work out, all the houses deteriorating at the same rate and in the same ways, Ernie Tewayumptewa's house distinguished from the others on the block only by a low cyclone fence out front. Inside the fence, the yard was bare, there was no grass, not even a few clumps of weeds, only the same brownish-red earth that showed through the oiled streets and marked the footpaths, though next to the house was a border made of bricks to show where a flower bed had been; a broken plastic tricycle, a big-wheel, sat upended beside the depression in the dirt yard that served as the front walk. In the yard next door, three tough-looking young men—Indians, George thought, from the long black hair and headbands, though he wouldn't have known the difference if they were Spanish—stood, their hands wedged in their jeans, in front of the open hood of an old car up on blocks; they watched George as he got out of his car and walked across the street. George wanted to go back and make sure he had locked the doors but he didn't dare; he walked, businesslike, his shoulders back, head high, stretching his neck, conscious of the swell of his chest and stomach in front of him, moving his bulk, directing it, as if it were a separate entity, a buffer, through the unlocked gate and across the dirt yard.

When he rang the bell, a plump, bashful Indian (or at least red-skinned) woman in her thirties, wearing a house dress and large fluffy blue slippers, came to the screen and, giggling about something, directed him to go around to a two-car garage behind the house. Parked in front of the closed doors of the garage, in the dirt driveway, was a late-model pickup truck, dust-covered but still shiny, with huge off-the-road tires and the body raised high off the chassis, so high that George thought you'd need a ladder to get up into it; there was gold pinstriping on the fenders, a black Naugahyde tarp over the bed, and chrome exhaust pipes sticking up on either side of the cab. A bumper sticker said INDIAN POWER with a clenched fist. George circled the truck carefully—as if he thought it could bite—and knocked on the side door of the garage; when nobody answered, he tried the door and stepped inside.

The near side of the interior was dark, the floor crowded with cottonwood stumps and sections of tree roots lying around, with more stumps and roots stacked up along the walls, but the far side of the garage was brightly lit from rows of fluorescent lights hanging from the ceiling; under the lights there were band saws and table saws and jigsaws, workbenches, and pegboard on the walls with rows of woodworking tools. Against one wall was a set of metal shelves with dozens of completed kachina dolls, carvings of whipper kachinas and clowns and monsters. A large orange cat, a real one, curled on top of a metal filing cabinet, kept a sleepy eye on things. On the large worktable in the center of the area were more kachina dolls, most of them unfinished, and some of them little more than blocks of wood; small arms and legs, an occasional head, lay around. A dark, potbellied man sat on a stool at the table, a pair of magnifiers over his eyes, painting details on a figure with bulging eyes and a terrible scowl. George waited in the dark end of the garage until the man raised the magnifiers and looked in his direction, squinting.

"What can I do for you?"

"There's a kachina in my back yard," George blurted out, feeling suddenly giddy.

Ernie Tewayumptewa was in his early thirties, with short black carefully combed hair and a broad, soft face, the skin dimpled in unexpected places; his muscular arms in a white T-shirt were heavily tattooed with dragons and flowers and a Liberty Bell; his eyes were moist and black and noncommittal.

"I know it sounds crazy." George tried to laugh, walking closer to him, coming out of the shadows to stand on the other side of the table. "But the guy just appeared in my back yard yesterday."

Ernie continued to look at him without expression. The orange cat on top of the filing cabinet got up, stretched, and jumped lazily to the floor, ignoring George as it walked past. George smiled feebly and, when Ernie still didn't say anything, pumped his shoulders.

"What do you mean, a kachina?" Ernie said after a few moments, taking the magnifiers from his forehead and laying them on the table.

"I mean a real one. I mean a guy in a mask."

"You don't mean a carving?"

"No, I mean a real full-sized man, wearing a mask and costume. I think he came out of the woods." George wished he could start the entire conversation over again. Why had he acted so flip? "It's Aholi. Or an Aholi. However you say it."

"Aholi?"

"Eototo's lieutenant." George looked over at the shelf of finished kachina carvings and pointed to an Aholi.

Ernie sat hunched over on his stool, his elbows resting on the workbench. He picked up an X-acto knife and began turning it end over end, first the point then the butt resting on the table, in his fingers. He stared absently at the knife, watching it without paying any attention to it.

"I think he's found a shrine of some kind."

Ernie looked at him slowly.

"I mean I think it's a shrine. There's a hole in the bank of the wash, among some rocks, in back of our house. He poked around with his staff until he found it. That was yesterday. And today he's making prayer sticks."

After a long silence, Ernie said, quietly, "I think you better go now." When George showed no signs of leaving, Ernie looked him squarely in the eyes. "I don't know who you are or what you're trying to pull but you better get out of here."

"Look, I know I've explained this poorly," George said, seeing the headlines: MAN SCALPED WITH X-ACTO KNIFE. "But I don't know who else to ask. Mrs. Jenkins at the museum gave me your name. I know this all sounds crazy, but I'm serious about this."

"You told Mrs. Jenkins about . . . this kachina?"

"No. I only told her I wanted to find out more about Aholi." From the expression on Ernie's face, it appeared to be the first right thing George had said to him. "I didn't think too many people should know about it until I found out what was going on."

"Does anybody else know?"

"My wife called the police."

"The Flagstaff police?"

"Yes. I told her not to, but while I was gone—"

"What did they say?"

"They wanted to take him in, but I talked them out of it. The guy, the kachina, hasn't done anything wrong that I know of."

Ernie thought a while, watching the knife wheel slowly in his fingers. "Do you think it's real?"

"I don't know. I've never seen a real kachina before. But he looks like all the pictures I've seen, and like your carvings."

"So why did you come to see me?"

"Well, I thought maybe you'd have some idea of what is going on."

Ernie smiled ruefully at that.

"I thought maybe you'd know if this is some kind of ceremony or ritual or something. Or maybe you had heard if the mask and costume were stolen."

"It doesn't sound like any ceremony that I've ever heard of. And as for if the stuff was stolen or not, I wouldn't know a thing about it."

"I meant, because you're Hopi, I thought maybe you'd hear—" Ernie's smile turned bitter. "I'm not the best example of a Hopi. You probably know more about what's going on at the res than I do." He thought about something for a moment, turning the knife slowly end over end, then tired of it and tossed it down. "There are a lot of people who would say I'm Kahopi."

"I don't know what that means."

"Hopis don't really have words for 'right' and 'wrong' like you do. If you live the way you're supposed to and keep to the Hopi Way of Life, then you're Hopi. If you don't, you're Kahopi, not Hopi. It covers a lot of ground."

The door opened behind George and two children came into the garage, a little girl of perhaps eight, holding the hand of a little boy who was barely old enough to walk. The children walked past George and went to Ernie; the little boy grabbed his father's leg and gurgled something and Ernie lifted him up on his lap. The little boy clapped his hands, missing the first time, gurgled some more, picked up the doll Ernie had been working on, and waved it in the air, smearing the paint. Ernie took the doll away and wiped the child's hands on a cloth; then he bounced him on his knee until the boy gurgled some more, kissed him on the cheek, and put him back on the floor.

"Crystal, take him outside and play."

"He wanted to play in here."

"Not now. I'm talking to the man."

"The Bahana?" the little girl said, eyeing George suspiciously.

"Yes, the Bahana. Now, take him outside."

"Okay."

"I'm the Bahana?" George said, after the children had left.

"Yes. It means 'white man.' "

"Is that good or bad?"

Ernie shrugged, then grinned on one side of his mouth. "Well, originally it meant 'white brother,' but nowadays I guess it's something like 'nigger' or 'honky,' or 'cocksucker,' you know?"

George cleared his throat. "Does anybody ever get hold of a kachina mask who shouldn't?"

Ernie thought for a while. "How much do you know about the Hopi?"

"Well, I've been reading—" Then George thought better of it. "Very little. Next to nothing."

"You must understand that the pressures on the Hopi, the people in the villages, are very great. It's hard enough to try to live as farmers in the middle of the desert, using only the old ways. But the Navajo have encroached on the little land that we have, and your government doesn't honor its treaties with us. The tourists come in and treat the sacred ceremonies like they were part of Disneyland. The coal companies are digging up the sacred lands of Black Mesa, and they use the underground water to pump the coal to Nevada. They've already lowered the water table several inches for the entire region; if they lower the water table one foot, then the corn cannot grow and the Hopi Way of Life will die. You must understand that the way the Hopi live is sacred, that it is the way we were told to live when we came into this world. And if the Hopi stop, the world stops. You must understand that the people up there on the mesas believe that the ceremonies and their way of life is what's holding the world together, not just for the Hopi, but for all people, that they were instructed to live like that when the Guardian allowed them to come into this world.

"So the pressures are very great. And some of the Hopi can't take it. They say that not very long ago some of the men of Moenkopi burned their kachina masks on the main street of the village. Many years ago a man dragged the Bear Clan altar and the sacred mongkos out in front of Hubbell's Trading Post, so that everybody, even the whites, could see them, and then burned them. So now Oraibi doesn't have its ceremony any more."

"Do you think this Aholi in my back yard is something like that?"

"I don't know. Maybe. The Hopi have many prophecies that they, that we, brought with us from the last world. One of the prophecies says that if the Hopi don't live good lives, if they don't live as Hopi and keep to the Hopi Way, the Hopi will lose their ceremonies and their way of life to the Bahana, the white man. Then the Hopi Way of Life will disappear and the time of Purification will come."

"Purification for the Hopi?"

Ernie shook his head. "Purification for everyone, for the world. There's supposed to be earthquakes, fire storms, a holocaust. They say the morning the elders saw the flash of the first atomic-bomb test across the desert, without even knowing what it was, they knew the time of Purification was coming." He picked up the knife again, turning it slowly over and over in his fingers. "A lot of the Hopi can't take all the pressures of the different ways of life. Some crack up. Some become drunks. Some go away to school or to the army and then go back and try to forget the white man's world." He thought a moment. "Some even move off the mesas and end up carving kachina dolls to sell to the turquoise ladies of Scottsdale."

He looked at George. George tried to smile but couldn't.

"Would you come over to my house and take a look at it?"

"Why would I do that?"

"Well, maybe you can find out what he's doing there. Maybe he'll talk to you. Maybe you can tell him to go back to the reservation."

"There's nothing I can do about it." Ernie shook his head. "It's up to him what he does."

"But at least you could tell me if it's real or not."

"It doesn't matter whether it's real or not. Whoever is wearing the mask has to decide what he's going to do. If the mask is real, then it is very sacred to the Hopi. If it's not real—well, there are many witches around."

"Witches?" George blinked three times.

"The people with two hearts: one heart is human, and one heart is animal. The Hopi are very afraid of witches. A witch is only supposed to hurt one of its own relatives; it has to kill someone else so it can stay alive itself. But there are other witches that cause famines or stop the rain from coming. Maybe this is something like that. I don't know."

"You're afraid it's a witch?"

"I don't care if it's a witch or not. I don't care if it's a kachina or not. I don't want to have any part of it, either way. I told you, there's nothing I can do about it."

They were silent for several minutes; George didn't mind a titular deity in his yard, but a titular witch was a different matter— that made him a little uneasy. Ernie watched his knife.

"It just seems to me," George said finally, pounding his fist softly—a pretend pounding, really—on the edge of the table, "that that mask and that costume and all must be important to somebody in Hopi. And it just doesn't seem right to me to try to ignore this guy, whoever or whatever it is. Maybe it's somebody who needs help. Maybe it's something awful that could be averted or corrected before it's too late. Maybe—oh, I don't know. It just doesn't seem right. You must know somebody in Hopi that we could talk to to find out what's going on."

"There's a lot of people in Hopi," Ernie smiled sarcastically, "who think I'm a witch. It's not a good thing for a Hopi to get too well known or make too much money."

"Then I'll talk to them, I'll even go over there if it will help, I don't care."

"Why do you want to do all this?"

"I don't know," George said, thinking. "I guess maybe it's because he ended up in my back yard. I guess it makes me feel responsible."

Ernie shook his head slowly, as if such an idea were beyond his comprehension. Then he looked at George a long moment. "The only person I know to ask is David Lomanongye."

George repeated the name several times, with Ernie's help, until he got it right and thought he could remember it. "Is he a chief?"

"No." Ernie smiled. "He's not a chief. He's an old man; well, maybe not so old either. But he usually knows what's going on. He would probably know if the mask was taken."

"Where does he live?"

"In Old Oraibi, but that won't help you much. Whites aren't allowed to go in there now. But there's a dance at Mishongnovi tomorrow. David will probably be there sometime during the day."

"Mishon . . . ?" George repeated it, again with Ernie's help, until he could pronounce it.

"It's on Second Mesa. It's the only Home Dance on the mesa this weekend, you can't miss it. You'll see the cars."

"And how do I find David Lomanongye?"

"You'll just have to ask around for him. When you find him you can tell him you talked to me."

George thanked him, then wrote his name and address on a sheet of paper and gave it to Ernie. "Just in case you change your mind about coming over to look at the kachina."

They shook hands—Ernie barely grasped the ends of three of George's fingers, barely shook them at all—and George made his way back through the dark end of the garage. As he opened the door he looked back to wave, but Ernie didn't see him; Ernie sat at his bench, under the rows of fluorescent lights, staring at the knife as he turned it end over end in his fingers, looking very unhappy . . .

. . . while in the yard next door, three young Navajo men standing in front of a twelve-year-old Chevrolet that refuses to run no matter what they do to it watch George leave Ernie Tewayumptewa's place, watch him carefully close the gate to the small cyclone fence behind him and walk, head up, shoulders back, bouncing slightly on the balls of his feet, across the street to his car and get into it and think, respectively, There goes: a bill collector; a plainclothes cop; a white rich fat-assed son of a bitch; and think, respectively: I hope he nailed that fucking Hopi; I hope he's not looking for me; I hope he gets the hell out of here before I do something I'll wish I hadn't . . . while in her bedroom Mary Olive wakens suddenly, decidedly, as if she's been struck in the face but

it's only the sunlight coming in through the blinds and she lies there, her mouth feeling like something that has lain out on a highway for a couple of days and maybe tastes something like it too, trying to remember if it was something George said to her the night before that makes her feel so bad this morning, that hangs over her, threatening, terrifying, but decides no, it isn't that, and wonders if it's that thing of George's that was in the back yard yesterday and wouldn't surprise her at all if it was still there today, but decides no, it isn't that either, and wonders if it was something she dreamed, some nightmare she just can't put her finger on, but decides no, it isn't that either, as she suddenly does remember, remember all too clearly: Don—and feels the sinking in her stomach again, the nausea and the loss and the injustice and, yes, even betrayal (There won't be anybody worth talking to in this whole god-forsaken state; oh, that's a terrible thing to say, that's a terrible thing to feel), and gets up then, and without bothering with her slippers or robe or anything else over her nightgown goes downstairs to the kitchen for a glass of wine, hoping there's enough to get her through this day and knowing there couldn't be enough in the world to get her through this one . . . while at the base of the foothills of the San Francisco Mountains, someone or something wearing a tall blue pointed kachina mask stands in a wash bashing himself on the side of his head with his hand, whacking himself in the face, trying to kill the fly or bee or whatever the hell kind of bug it is that's just flown in through the mouth hole of the mask and is buzzing furiously, deafeningly inside . . . while in a car on a highway north of Flagstaff, Arizona, a family in a late-model station wagon drives slowly along the winding road, the man, the driver, an insurance agent from West Mifflin, Pennsylvania, sulking, still angry at his wife for not letting him buy the silver wrist band inlaid with turquoise that they saw back at the Silver Kachina Art Gallery in Flagstaff ("You wouldn't wear it, you'd look silly in West Mifflin wearing a thing like that," she said; "That's for me to decide," he said, but didn't buy it anyway), ignoring his wife, who looks out the window at the trees and the mountains, pointing out things of interest to the children in the back seat, who ride in the flat area behind the back seat, the four girls and the one small boy who are only interested in waving to the fat man driving the car behind them, the fat man who is obviously bothered by the fact that their own car is going so slowly and by the fact that the five children are all looking at him and waving at him, talking about him and giggling, until they all duck down out of sight and take off their shoes and socks and on the count of three, one, two, three! all stick their feet up in the air and present the fat man with a forest of prepubescent legs and feet and toes all waving and wiggling at him, the children looking up in time to see him, eyes locked on the road, jaw set, pass them much too fast and on a curve, their father cursing at him and honking his horn and shouting after another goddamned Arizona cowboy. . . .

6

Geoge passed the car, going much too fast, going much faster than he should, and passed on a bad, dangerous stretch of road as well, but he couldn't stand poking along behind the tourist car any longer. *Goddamn rubberneckers, why don't they go back where they came from?* He looked in the rearview mirror, trying to see the expression on the driver's face, *Eat my dust* laughing to himself *Eat it.*

The warm wind whipped up the sleeve of his shirt, down across his chest; he beat time with the clunky, tick-tock rhythm of the song on the radio, beating with his left hand against the rim of the steering wheel, singing along silently with "Minute by Minute" by the Doobie Brothers. He didn't listen to popular radio that much—or, rather, he listened to it all the time, every time he got in the car, but rarely heard it, rarely paid attention to it, though occasionally he tried to make it a point to pay attention to it, to learn what his students were interested in these days, sitting in his parked car, his head cocked, his eyes closed, concentrating earnestly on the rhythmic structure, the lyric lines of the Grateful Dead or the Rolling Stones. But he remembered the Doobies, remembered this album, it was one of Sara's favorites: she had insisted he sit on the floor, in her garret, to listen to it, listening to it until she leaned over and pushed him down on his back and she mounted him, both of them still in their clothes, in the middle of this song, he thought, yes, he was sure of it, sat on top of him, looking down at him, the playful, mischievous smile on her face, her face soft and handsome in the dim light of the room, working her hips on him in the rhythm of the song, until they took off their clothes and she started the song over again and they repeated the scene, this time for real: she was lovely in the soft light, riding above him, lady in ecstasy, rampant. . . .

He kept driving fast, along the winding road that, by now, after a year of traveling back and forth once or twice or three times a day, he knew as well as he had ever known any stretch of road, feeling happy and pleased with himself (and pleased with the memory of Sara), feeling as if he'd accomplished something by going to see Ernie, and was maybe on the way to finding out something about this character in his back yard, had the name of someone in Hopi who might know what was going on. As he drove along, the sunlight glinted off the hood of his car, the oncoming cars and trucks passing him in whooshes, the sun too bright, then flickering as he passed a grove of trees close to the road, flickering as though he were driving through the shadow of a set of enormous venetian blinds.

And he thought: Sara was the most loving, the most playful woman he had ever been with; she liked sex play, liked to be adventurous, to try new things, liked to please him for the sake of pleasing him, and liked to get something out of it too, and cared for him, really cared for him. And now she was moving to Chicago. . . .

"—*Else!*" he sang, out loud, one word from the lyrics of the song, the sound of his own voice startling him so badly that he kept on going straight even though the road didn't, cutting across the opposite lane (how did he know there weren't any cars coming?

Did he know?) and into a turnout, skidding and sliding in the loose dirt amid clouds of dust and pinging stones until he got the car under control again, coming to a stop a few feet in front of a tree. He turned off the engine and got out, carefully, shaken. A horn sounded from the highway: he looked around in time to see the station wagon from Pennsylvania sail by, around the curve, the driver honking and waving, waving his middle finger above the roof of the car so his wife and children wouldn't see it, while, as the car disappeared around the bend, the rear window was filled with a small forest of upturned legs and feet.

Then it was silent, the sound of the car trailing off, and George became aware of the silence around him, behind him, almost like a presence, and he turned and looked into the woods for a moment, looked around. But there was nothing, no one here, only the trees; he waited a few moments, just to make sure, then walked a little ways until he was among the trees. He was still short of breath, still quivery. The ground was soft under his feet, noticeably soft, from the carpet of pine needles, a carpet inches thick, springy though it still crunched under his weight, each step bringing with it the smell of the needles, of the trees; nearest the road was a stand of older ponderosas, at eye level an irregular colonnade of several dozen trunks, the branches thirty and forty feet overhead, the sunlight muted and soft underneath, though beyond was newer growth, clusters of low trees as thick as bushes, the branches starting at knee level, with an occasional thick tall fifty- or maybe hundred-year-old ponderosa standing in the midst of the new trees, in a circle of young trees, a clearing, like a totem pole, a monument. George looked back, making sure that he could still see his car, the road.

He stood for a while near the new growth, letting the woods settle down again around him, letting himself quiet down after losing control of himself, after losing control of the car. He felt peaceful now among the trees, but he didn't care to go in among them any farther. He felt no great love of wilderness, no great love for nature, even (maybe the idea of it, of growing things, but no love for the actual experience of it, the actual trees and earth and rocks themselves). It was a misconception—an idea started while he was living among the totally manmade concrete-and-steel-and-glass world of New York that he did love and need nature, did need to be around trees and mountains and earth (he knew he was sensitive; he knew he was supposed to love and need such things)—that had been dispelled only by actually coming here and living for a while among trees and mountains and earth. He was a small-town boy, not a country boy—and especially not a mountain man—a difference that had neither been explicit nor understood until now. Wilderness made him uncomfortable, in fact; he saw people here, or the possibility, the threat of people, people in isolation without the restraints of other people and law and custom, without civilization: a man stepping out from behind a rock, holding a gun; a gang of young men, looking at him, grinning, worse, saying, "Yo, fat man, come over here, yeah, come over here. . . ." The mountains were fine, seen from a small-town street; the trees were lovely, viewed from a study window.

He had gone far enough; he turned and kept walking, though now in an arc, a semicircle, keeping the car, the road, just within sight.

He smiled a little to himself as he remembered the memory of listening to the record with Sara, remembered singing out loud in the car, surprising himself. He was pretty sure, now that he thought about it, that the *else* had been his own invention—was that what surprised him so badly?—he was pretty sure the lyrics of the song just said, *You could spend your life with someone.* He thought the next time he was in New York he'd ask Sara to play the record again, and he would tell her the story of hearing the song on the radio and thinking about their making love to it and driving himself off the road; it would make a good story, one to impress upon her how much he cared for her. Except that there might not be a next time in New York, might not be a next time with Sara, ever. He stepped over a fallen tree trunk, watched a chipmunk dive for cover. "You still don't know what I'm telling you, do you, George?" she said. "You still don't understand what it is I've been offering you"; "What?" he said. "What are you talking about?" and sat there holding the phone, grinning like a fool. But he knew. He was going to lose her if he didn't do something; she all but came out and said it for him, begged him to convince her not to take the job in Chicago, to convince her to stay in New York. And for that matter, why didn't he? For that matter, maybe he should. He didn't want to lose a good thing (that sounded callous, cold; *I don't want a good thing to get away, no. . . . I don't want to lose, no*). He was getting older; there weren't going to be many more opportunities to meet a woman like Sara, a younger, attractive, intelligent woman—a woman like Sara. This was different from playing around, sleeping around with the coeds of the world. There weren't going to be many more opportunities to meet a woman like Sara, one he could love, be with, live with.

He walked on. Through the trees, the patches of sunlight, dragging his feet a little, kicking at the stones.

I could spend my life with someone: else.

He had never considered such a thing. He had never known it was possible for him to consider such a thing. He had never considered such a thing possible.

Beyond another grove of young trees, the trees growing closely together, too close to walk through except on the already established path, the trees too close together for all of them to survive, their branches interlaced, touching each other, reaching through each other like green lace, green mesh, he came to another stand of older ponderosas, still circling, of course, still walking so that his car was just in or just out of view. At the base of the trees, in the open area between the trunks of the trees, the carpet of pine needles had been swept aside and there were the remains of a campfire—a ring of stones, charred, half-burned logs, ashes. There was the spot where the sleeping bags had been laid out, the mattress of pine needles, a fire-blackened tin can, some chicken bones, several cigarette butts. George looked around, he half expected, was half afraid to find a hand sticking out of a shallow grave, a body thrown underneath some bushes. He kicked at the blackened earth; the place depressed him. He shuddered. He walked on, still circling.

He thought of Mary Olive. She was the most bitter, the most sarcastic woman he had ever known. *Why did I ever marry her?* And thought, as he usually did, as if part of the same question, *And how many times have I asked myself that question?* A litany of a kind. *Why do I put up with her?* Well, that was another question he asked himself from time to time, though not as often as the others, it was nothing new; he kept on walking, his head down, watching the floor of pine needles sag beneath his weight. *Why do I continue to put up with her?* He stopped walking at that: now, that was a different question, a new question. *Why do I stay married to her?* His head snapped upright, as if reined back: in twenty-five years of marriage, that was one question that had never really occurred to him. Before.

He stood there, among the trunks of the pines, blinking three, four, five times, slowly, not to be amusing or good-natured now, not even to himself, but questioning. Why did he stay married to her? The question had, of course, been floating around somewhere in his mind before, especially at the time he thought Mary Olive might stay in New York when he decided to come to Arizona, but it had never been formed into words before so he could look at the idea, weigh it properly, see that it was real (he needed that to happen, he needed to see it printed out in his mind's eye, so he could say the words, if only to himself; how else could he sort out the jumble of the world?); he had never considered it a serious possibility. A man wasn't supposed to feel that way, to think such things about his wife, so George had always been very careful not to. But now the words and feelings came clicking along as if on a ticker tape. He didn't, in fact, have to stay married to her, he didn't have to put up with her. He could, in fact, change it, leave, break it off: end it. Other people, other men, did such things all the time. It was a real possibility, something he could do. And what's more, in considering such a possibility, he felt as though he had already, in some way, taken the first step away from her, had opened his life to other, new possibilities. He stood there, among the trunks of the trees, blinking three, four, five times, grinning, amazed.

He walked on, through another thicket of young trees, though he felt lighter now, a bit tentative, wondering, as if exploring a new world, then stood in a small grove of aspens. These were thick, older trees, comfortable trees, their bark as fine as parchment, and he wandered among them, touching them, as if he had just discovered trees, reading the initials carved in the bark, imagining faces and eyes in the scars where the lower branches had fallen off. Then he laughed out loud, howled with delight: in front of him was another scar, this one vertical, the bark peeled back and bulged like a pair of lips, shaped like a woman's vulva. He shook his head, marveling at the irony, the appropriateness of the scar. Oh, he did love women—the trappings, the movements, the smells of women! (The only smells he associated with Mary Olive were of old wine and cigarettes; he could smell cigarettes on his clothes, in his hair, just from being in the same room with her; he longed for the smell of powders and perfumes.) When he was younger, a teenager and into his twenties, a woman, a girl, was a presence, almost too good to be true, a golden moment come to life; later he realized he thought of a woman as a prize too, something to be won, a mark of achievement. But he thought now, he supposed with the perspective of age, that, whatever else a woman was—and as he got older, there came a further appreciation of their other parts too: the structure of a face (he was glad Mary Olive had a good face: high cheekbones, a strong jaw, a face, if not lovely, at least handsome), the unspeakable curves of a woman's body, the marvel of thighs—a woman was this: this organ, these folds of flesh, that hole. He became giddy, standing there in the aspen grove, looking at the vulva-shaped scar on the tree in front of him, thinking of women, thinking of all the women of the world who at that very moment were walking down sidewalks and along corridors, their vulvas, cunts, cuts, pussies, quiffs, quims, gashes, slits underneath their skirts, rubbing between their thighs, being squeezed as they sat down, opened as they spread their legs—thinking of all the women who might still open their legs for him. He leaned forward and kissed the vulva scar on the tree— and tasted dust and dirt and flakes of bark. He spit and sputtered, and headed back toward his car, wiping his mouth on the backs of his hands, trying to get the taste of dirt off his lips; he looked around to make sure no one had seen him; he felt a little silly— but happy, happy.

7
—

When he got home, George left the car in front of the garage and walked back down the lawn to the mailbox, but there were only bills, a circular for a sweepstakes, and the latest copy of *The Little Review*—no letter from Sara. He stood on the lawn awhile, leafing through the magazine, stalling, not wanting to go inside—he didn't want to see Mary Olive, feeling as he did, happy, he didn't want to spoil his good mood, to get embroiled in any of her foolishness. But he couldn't very well stand on the front lawn the rest of the afternoon either. He made up his mind to go through the house as quickly as possible, just to say hello to her if she was around and get it over with and go on upstairs, up to his study, and close the door behind him. Taking a deep breath, drawing himself up, he walked toward the house, walking quickly, businesslike, officious, eyes alert, shoulders back—Charge!

Mary Olive stood at the kitchen table, her arms spread as she leaned over the table, spread like a tripod over an open book, a glass of wine in front of her; her head pivoted upward, slowly, mechanically, to look at him (She's taking a bead on me, he thought) as he entered. George hustled across the room, holding up the mail like a white flag, waving it a little, gaily, to show her why he was there. He put the mail on the corner of the table; her head swiveled, tracking his movements.

"Hello, dear. Mail," he said, leaning over to give her a quick kiss on the cheek, as quick as though he had just lit a fuse, and turned to run.

"*Beignets de maïs,*" she replied.

George stopped in mid-turn, mid-step. *Don't ask.* "What?"

"*Beignets de maïs,*" she said quietly, matter-of-factly, her eyes without malice or mischief, or particular friendliness either, heavy-lidded. "Corn fritters."

"What?" Thinking: Corn fritters? Thinking: As in bullshit? as in goddamn? *Don't ask.*

"Or *maïs en suso aux abitis de poulet.*"

George blinked twice, three times. *Leave.*

"Corn with chicken giblets."

"Mary Olive, what are you talking about?" *Run.*

"I decided to fix something to eat for your fine feathered friend down there," she said, straightening up, taking a long slow drag on her cigarette. "So I was looking up recipes. Indians are supposed to like corn, aren't they?"

"Technically, he's a spirit," George said, thinking, I'll make a little joke. *You'll be sorry.* He went to the sink for a glass of water, let the water run, stuck his finger in and out of the stream until it got as cold as it was going to get. "Technically, he doesn't eat food. He just eats the spirit of food."

"I don't care what he does with it or how he eats it, I just got to thinking he's probably hungry."

"I was just trying to point out something to you that I read. Something I thought you might find interesting." *You asked for it.*

"Technically, then," she said, crushing out the cigarette, her eyes still heavy-lidded, matter-of-fact, without mischief or malice or particular friendliness either, "does that mean he only takes spiritual bowel movements too?"

That made him blink again; he hadn't thought about that before—just what was the kachina doing about such things? The idea of a guy down there shitting and pissing in his back yard made George a little queasy, indignant. *Told ya so.* He wouldn't think about it. He finished his glass of water quickly.

"Actually, I think I'll just fix him your basic *maïs frais au beurre.*"

"Shh!"

"Fresh corn in butter."

"Be quiet!"

"What's wrong with fresh corn in butter—"

George waved angrily at her to be quiet as he walked over to the open window, his head bent. There was a clacking sound, like a loose link on a set of tire chains, only this was the middle of July, a rhythmic *clack, clack, clack, clack, clack* then a pause then it started again—and a low moan along with it, as if the wind had come up again, blowing hard through the trees up on the side of the mountain, though he could see for himself that the day was still. The sound came from the back yard, from the wash. George leaned on the windowsill, his face close to the screen, and peered out. The kachina was standing up in the wash, kicking at something, kicking or stomping. . . .

"Fire!" George yelled and ran across the room and out the back door, running all the way down the back yard, down the terrace steps and across the field, getting all the way to the fence before he realized he hadn't brought anything with him to fight the fire, a shovel or a rake or even a broom to help put it out. Then he realized there wasn't a fire either. George rested his stomach against the top rail, wheezing, gasping for breath, his temples thumping as if ready to burst out of the side of his head. *I've got to slow down, I've got to stop running down this hill, I'm going to kill myself.* The kachina stopped his stomping and singing and looked at him.

What're you up to, George?

George tried to speak but he was panting too hard.

The Aholi shrugged and went back to stomping. The prayer sticks, some standing upright, some lying down, were in front of the opening between the rocks, in front of the shrine. The kachina stood a few feet away from the shrine and began to sing again, a low guttural moan, the strange words muffled by the mask, his voice distant, hollow, the song with eccentric pauses and progressions that George couldn't follow. As he sang, the kachina stomped with his right foot, stomping time to the broken rhythms of the song, pistonlike, the turtle-shell rattle flapping against the calf of his leg *clack, clack, clack* . . . *clack, clack* . . . facing one direction for a while, then revolving slowly to face the opposite direction, then turning back again.

"Is he okay?" Mary Olive said from George's elbow.

"I guess."

"I thought you said there was a fire."

George looked at her; she was holding a box of salt.

"I guess he's only dancing," he said.

"That's dancing?"

"I guess that's the way they dance."

As they watched, the Aholi turned slowly to face the opposite direction and back again, still stomping, stomping.

"Vo-do-de-o-do," Mary Olive said, waving her index finger in a circle.

"These dances are sacred," George hissed.

She sucked in her lips, pretending to be sorry. They watched for several minutes.

"It seems to me the Indian dancers I've seen in pictures always had a rattle in their hand," she said.

"Well, he doesn't have one."

"I'm sure that's the way I've always seen them."

"Maybe he forgot it. Maybe he lost it. Maybe he never had one, I don't know. All we know is that he doesn't have one now."

They watched a moment longer.

"I think he's supposed to have a rattle," she said, loud enough for the kachina to hear her, and turned and walked back toward the house.

George growled in the back of his throat. The kachina stopped singing and looked at him, but kept dancing, kept stomping. *It doesn't matter.*

"She does those things, says things like that just to bug me."

It's not important. It's not what's important.

The kachina stared at him a moment longer, then turned back, still dancing, picking up the song again, at once absorbed in it again. George leaned against the fence, watching him, trying to anticipate the pauses in the rhythm but always missing them. Ten minutes later Mary Olive came back down the yard again, carrying something in her hand. She had taken the metal filter from the percolator and jammed it on the end of a long wooden spoon, taping the lid on top. Around the outside of the metal cylinder she had drawn some stick figures with a Magic Marker, and fastened a couple of red and green ribbons, part of some gift wrapping, to the top. She shook it in George's face: the cylinder rattled.

"Rice," she said. "Long-grain rice. Sounds pretty good, doesn't it?"

Before George could say anything, she slipped through the rails of the fence and walked down the bank of the wash to the kachina. The kachina had his back toward them, having just started one of his turnarounds; as he slowly turned back again, he came face to face with Mary Olive. The Aholi stopped singing and dancing. Mary Olive held up the homemade rattle, then shook it in his face, in front of the eyeholes.

The kachina just looked at her.

"It's a rattle," Mary Olive said, shaking it again at him. "I made it for you."

The kachina looked at her.

George could see the headlines: BIZARRE MURDER IN THE SOUTHWEST.

"Go on, take it," she said, pushing it in his hand.

The kachina shifted his staff to his left hand along with his sacred bundle and took the rattle. Mary Olive nodded once, satisfied, and climbed back through the fence, nudging George softly in the stomach with her elbow as she passed, a playful poke.

"It's the spirit that counts," she said, and walked on up the hill, back toward the house, weaving slightly.

The kachina held the rattle up in front of his eyes so he could see it, stared dumbly at it, then shook it a couple of times. Then he shrugged and started dancing again, shaking the rattle, stomping, glancing over at George before he started to sing again.

Well, why not?

"Yes, I guess so. Well, why not?"

George turned and walked back to the house.

8
—

I can be nice to her, that's the least I can do. It'll be easier for everyone if I'm at least nice to her.

George sat at his desk in his study, afternoon sunlight slanting through the windows, looking through the pages of a book on Hopi ceremonials, as he listened to the sounds of Mary Olive working below in the kitchen. When things settled down, when he heard her sit down at the counter, he leaned over a little in the direction of his shoe, addressing the register.

"You know, dear, that was a very thoughtful thing to do."

"What was that?" came her voice.

"To make that rattle for the kachina. It was, you know, considerate."

"You sound surprised, George."

"Well, I was afraid at first you were making some kind of a joke or something."

"I have been known to do a few nice things in my life, you know."

"Oh, I know, dear. I didn't mean—"

"Wait a minute."

He heard her get up off the stool, heard her turn on the water in the sink; George continued paging through the book on Hopi ceremonies. Out the window, through the branches of the pines, he caught glimpses of the kachina still stomping away in the wash. He heard the water turn off, heard a cupboard door slam, a drawer slide open and close. In a few minutes the legs of the stool clattered a little against the side of the counter; it sounded as though she banged her knee sitting down.

"I'm back," came her voice from the register.

He sat for a few minutes, reading over a passage, thinking about whether he should or not; then he leaned to the side of his chair, still holding the book on the desk, and spoke into the space between his arm and his lap. "Would you like to hear something I found out about our friend?"

"More than anything in the world."

"I mean I thought you might be interested to hear something about his background. I found it in one of the books I got from the library."

"Of course, George. Read to me."

George stretched his neck away from his collar, cleared his throat, sat up a little straighter in preparation for his reading. He put his hand on his stomach, to make sure he was breathing correctly, from the diaphragm, full deep breaths for projection.

"Well, this is a description of part of the Powamu ceremony, which takes place in February. It's supposed to be one of the most important kachina ceremonies, and it says it's for purification and fertility."

"Isn't everything?"

George shifted his neck again, adjusted his glasses. "The ceremony, as I understand it, lasts somewhere between twelve and sixteen days, and some years it includes the initiation of the children into the kachina cult. But this is what happens when our friend gets into the act."

"Your friend, George. Let's keep him as your friend."

"Ahem."

THE NINTH DAY

Preparation for this day starts very early in the morning, long before sunrise, because there is much to do. The beans that have been forced-grown in the sweltering kivas must be harvested and tied into small bundles, and the dirt that was used for the growing must be hidden so that the children who have not yet been initiated into the kachina cult won't see it. Presents of kachina dolls or small bows and arrows are tied to these bundles, which will be given to the children later on in the day. And everything must be in readiness, for at dawn three of the most important kachinas make their appearance in the village.

The first of these kachinas is Angwusnasomtaqa, or the Crow Mother Kachina, who lives with her brother at The Spring in the Shadows, forty miles north of the village. This kachina is also known as the Crow Bride, because legend has it that, after her wedding to another kachina, her brother, in accordance with custom, was bringing her back from the groom's family's home at the base of the San Francisco Mountains to her own family's home when she received an urgent prayer from the Hopi to aid them in the Powamu ceremony. Because she would never fail to help them, she came immediately, without waiting to change her wedding garments. Among the gifts she carries are bean sprouts, corn, and boughs of spruce, though she also carries strips of bayonet yucca to whip offenders if the ceremony does not go well.

The Crow Mother is an imposing figure. She wears a black woven dress with a long white-fringed wedding belt at her waist, knee-high bridal moccasins of white buckskin, and a beautifully embroidered bride's blanket draped around her shoulders and down her back. Around her throat is a ruff of spruce. The mask is a beautiful turquoise blue, with face markings of two black inverted triangles, one on top of the other. But by far her most distinguishing features are the two large black crow's wings that extend from either side of the mask.

The Crow Mother enters the village at dawn with great dignity, looking straight ahead and moving very slowly, singing a song to herself that recounts the migrations of the Hopi. Periodically she gives her call, a long-drawn-out cry: *Huuu-hu-hu-hu-hu-hu!* As she proceeds through the streets of the village, women and children reverently approach the kachina, sprinkle her with sacred cornmeal, and take a shoot of corn or a sprig of spruce from the woven plaque she carries in front of her. After passing through the village, she recites a long prayer at the Powamu kiva, then stands majestically as she awaits the appearance of the two other kachinas who are performing their ceremonies in the village.

Eototo and Aholi have left the Kwan, or One Horn, kiva at about the same time the Crow Mother entered the village, and the two kachinas make their own way through the streets, stopping at various places. Eototo walks in front; he is known as the father of all kachinas, for he is the one who knows all the kachina ceremonies, and is therefore among the most powerful of all the spirits. Like most of the chief kachinas, or "ancient ones," he wears a rather plain mask. It is a domelike mask of white buckskin, with only three small dots to mark the mouth and eyes; it is crowned on top by a small cluster of eagle or sparrow-hawk feathers. Around his neck he wears an old fox skin. He wears the usual white woven dance kilt and sash, with an old white shirt of native cloth or buckskin, and a white ceremonial blanket and a bandolier of dark-blue yarn over the right shoulder. His legs are covered with knitted cotton leggings—the effect being of a figure almost entirely in white. In his hands he carries a mongko, or chief's stick, which is both the symbol of his office and a sacred object, and a sack of sacred cornmeal.

Aholi, who always accompanies Eototo and walks a step or two behind, is among the most beautiful of all the ka-chinas. . . .

"That's your guy, right, George?" came the voice from the register. He heard her working at something.

"Yes, dear."

"Just wanted to make sure. Sometimes it's hard to tell the horses from the jockeys without a scorecard."

"Ahem."

His body is bare to the waist, with one half painted turquoise and the other half painted squash-yellow; he wears a woman's sash in addition to the traditional dance kilt and sash, and around his shoulders is a cape made from an old blanket splotched with variegated colors. On the back of the blanket-cape is the image of a winged figure with a human head. Aholi's mask is one of the most unusual of all the kachinas'. It is a tall blue cone with tufts of red hair and macaw feathers at the very peak, and red tufts or blossom symbols projecting from the sides. An old fox skin is tied around his neck, and another fox skin is tied at the waist and trails behind him, reaching almost to the ground. In his left hand he carries his own mongko, and in his right hand he carries a staff tipped with feathers and seven perfect ears of corn, known as Corn Mothers, tied to the top.

As the two kachinas move through the village, Eototo "makes the road" for Aholi by sprinkling a trail of sacred cornmeal on the ground. At various places along their route they stop and Eototo uses the sacred meal to draw a cloud symbol on the ground. Then Aholi places the butt of his staff on the cloud symbol and rotates the top of it in a circle, first in one direction and then the other, giving his peculiar, high-pitched cry: *Ah-hol-li-i-i-i-i!* Then he faces the opposite direction and repeats the action, or stamps his right foot and hits the butt of his staff on the ground a number of times. Earlier, a hole had been dug in the plaza near the Powamu kiva and a prayer stick and sacred corn meal placed in it; now Eototo and Aholi proceed to that hole, and Eototo draws a line with cornmeal and sprinkles water into it for each of the six directions—north, south, east, west, nadir, and zenith. Aholi does the same. Then they join the Crow Mother at the Powamu kiva.

Eototo and Aholi stand beside the Crow Mother in front of the kiva; then Eototo draws a line with sacred meal and sprinkles water from each of the six directions into the hatchway of the kiva, and Aholi does likewise. The chiefs of the kiva emerge and bless the kachinas with smoke, water, and sacred meal. The tray is taken from the Crow Mother and she is given prayer sticks, which she takes out of the village to a shrine on the mesa. This concludes her appearance. Eototo and Aholi, however, proceed to various houses in the village, including those of important chiefs and the houses of the Bear and Pikyas clans, where the Eototo and Aholi impersonators were born and where the sacred masks are kept during the year. The two kachinas bless these houses, with Eototo drawing a cloud symbol on the ground with sacred meal and Aholi revolving his staff while he sings his high-pitched cry; in return they receive prayer sticks from the occupants of the houses. Meanwhile, a number of other kachinas have appeared in the village, such as the Hemis, Koyemsi, Tassap, Huuve, Anga, Hehea, and others. These kachinas run about distributing the gifts of kachina dolls and bows and arrows which were prepared earlier for the children. Throughout the rest of the day the children are seen running around with their special presents, which, along with the magical appearance of fresh bean sprouts in the middle of winter, show the children the power and the good will of the kachinas. . . .

"In other words, they trick them," Mary Olive's voice said from the register.

"No, I wouldn't say they trick them, exactly. . . ."

"What would you say, exactly?"

"Well, I mean they sort of trick them, but they don't do it maliciously."

"I didn't say they did it maliciously. I just said they trick them. I'll be back in a minute. I'm going to take this corn down to Big Bird."

The screen door slammed, and he watched her walk out into the yard, carrying a plate of freshly cooked corn, half a dozen ears piled up and steaming. When she got as far as the lawn furniture under the pine trees, she turned and presented the plate to him, raised it up a little so he could be sure to see it from the window—her head cocked, the same noncommittal, matter-of-fact expression on her face as she had had earlier, as if to say, *So there, what do you think of that?*—then carried it on down the terrace steps and across the field to the wash. She leaned through the fence and slid the plate toward the edge of the bank. The Aholi kept dancing; from the window, through the branches of the trees, George couldn't tell whether the kachina acknowledged either Mary Olive or the corn. As Mary Olive came back up the yard, appeared underneath the branches of the trees, she looked up at George and raised her index finger (at least it isn't her middle finger, he thought), revolving it in a little circle as she mouthed *Vo-do-de-o-do* before she disappeared below the edge of the window. The screen door slammed again.

He waited several minutes, heard her sit down again at the counter, heard what he took to be the jug of wine being pulled from its place on the bottom shelf. And he thought: It was considerate of Mary Olive to fix the corn for the kachina too. What was going on? What was she up to? Her expression as she showed him the corn, standing under the trees, the noncommittal, matter-of-fact expression on her face, the smile that wasn't quite a smile, reminded him of the expression she got sometimes at cocktail parties or dinners, when she listened to somebody, a young poet or know-it-all critic, shoot his mouth off about something of which it was obvious he knew very little, interested, apparently agreeing with him, drawing him out, smiling her not-quite smile encouragingly—"Oh, really? Is that right? That's very interesting"—until he had gone too far, said too much, become too full of himself, then *Whammo!* she'd turn his words back on him, pinpoint his absurdities, turn his arguments against him, make a fool out of him—she had a gift for it, a talent; McCann would sometimes set her up, set her after people he wanted to humiliate. George shook his head, smiled; she was an original, all right, there was nobody else like her. And she was no one to have against you. He waited another minute. When she still didn't say anything, he spoke into the space between his arm and lap: "That seems to be all in this book about Aholi. What I read to you."

Still no answer. What was she doing now? Drinking? Smoking? Sitting there smiling to herself, knowing that her silence would bug him? Finally she said, "I don't see what any of that has to do with initiating the children into the tribe."

"Oh, that happens on an earlier day. I'll read that to you too," he said, flipping back through the book. When she didn't say anything, didn't object, he cleared his throat, sat up straight, checked his breathing again.

Then overhead, from outside the dark kiva, come the sounds they have awaited and feared from the time they were old enough to understand. There is the sound of tramping feet, the click of turtle-shell rattles and the jingling of bells, the dreaded howl of the Hu Kachinas, the Whipper Kachinas: *U'huhuhuhuhu!* The whippers run around the outside of the kiva four times, lashing the ladder poles in seemingly uncontrollable fury and beating on the roof, grunting and howling, then enter the kiva quickly without invitation, hurrying down the ladder. The children to be initiated are trembling, and some begin to cry.

There are two of the terrifying Hu Kachinas. Their bodies are naked except for red horsehair kilts; their bodies are painted black with white dots to which small white eagle feathers are attached, their forearms and calves painted white. The masks are black with bulging eyes, huge mouths with bared teeth, and long black-and-white-striped horsehair beards; at the top of the mask is a spray of eagle feathers pointing toward the back, and eagle feathers dangle from the tips of the horns. In each hand the Hu Kachinas carry long yucca whips. Following the whippers down the ladder into the kiva is Angwushahai'i, the Whipper Mother, who carries more yucca whips. She is another manifestation of the Crow Mother, Angwusnasomtaqa, and their costumes and masks are almost identical, particularly the extended crow wings tied to either side of the mask (see the Ninth Day Ceremony for full description). The main difference is that, when the Crow Mother appears at the Powamu ceremony, her face is portrayed by two black inverted triangles, one on top of the other, both of which are blank; whereas when she appears as the mother of the Whipper Kachinas, there are two small white dots in the top triangle for the eyes, and one small white dot in the bottom triangle for the mouth.

The Hu Kachinas continue their howling, beating the air with their yucca whips, stamping around with their rattles and bells. The Whipper Mother stands nearby, impassive and with great dignity. The boys who are to be initiated are naked, the girls are allowed to wear their dresses; the sponsors are nude or wear a small breechcloth. A sponsor then leads the first child out into the center of the floor, holding the child's arms above the head while positioning the child in the center of the sand painting in front of the altar. It is traditional that the whippers administer four lashes with the yucca whips, but this is not always the case; occasionally they will only lightly touch a particularly terrified child, or the sponsor may take pity on his ward and after one or two lashes substitute his own thigh for the whipping. But most of the time all four lashes are administered, and with particular fury to those children who are known to misbehave or show disrespect to their elders or the Hopi Way.

After one of the whippers administers the lashes to a child, he alternates with his partner for the next, the worn yucca whips given to the Whipper Mother in exchange for new ones. Added to the commotion of the Whipper Kachinas are the cries of the Whipper Mother to lash harder, the protests or cries of favoritism from parents or relatives, and the screams of the children in fear and pain. Many of the children and sponsors are bloodied, and some children micturate and defecate with terror. . . .

"Wait a minute, George," said the register. "How old are these children?"

"I think around nine or ten, maybe twelve."

"And this is something that used to go on?"

"No, no, they still do it. This is the way all the Hopi are still initiated into the tribe—"

"This is the tribe whose name means 'People of Peace,' isn't that what Sally told us once?"

"You think that's something, later on it gets even wilder. The whippers start whipping each other, let me find that. . . ."

"No thanks, George, I've heard enough. That's sick."

"No, it isn't, it's just their way."

"Then their way is sick."

"Wait a minute; here it is."

"I said I've heard enough, George."

" 'The scene lasts half an hour—' "

"I don't want to hear it, George."

" '—or longer. Then after the last child is whipped—' "

"Shut up, George!" she screamed, and something slammed against the register.

He sat for several minutes, still holding the book of Hopi ceremonies, conscious of his breath, conscious of the set of his mouth, his jaw, as if his whole being had been drawn to the lower part of his face, was focused there. *See? I told you so. I told you she was acting funny. That's what I get for trying to be nice. I don't have to put up with her any more.* Then he put the book down and got up from his desk and left the room, walked down the hallway and down the stairs, being careful to look straight ahead, being careful especially not to look into the kitchen—then he stopped; and walked back and stood in the doorway to the kitchen: Mary Olive stood with her back to him at the counter, leaning against the wall, holding a cookbook (*Joy of Cooking*) against the air vent, leaning against it with both hands, braced, pressing the book against the grate, as if either keeping something in or holding something out, staring at it—and he walked on through the hall and out the front door to his car and drove away, not fast or recklessly, just drove, holding the steering wheel with both clenched hands.

9

He drove for several hours, just drove, up and around the mountains and back again, taking the dirt roads to Hart Prairie and Saddle Mountain, Deadman Flat and Schultz Pass, never really knowing where he was going or where he would come out, and never really caring, just wanting to drive; he decided to head back when the sun was low enough to glare in his eyes through the windshield. As he drove back up the road toward home, he turned in at Don and Sally's, up the long driveway, and parked beside the house and got out—and was immediately knee-deep in dogs, milling about him, wagging their tails, nuzzling up against his hands.

"Hello hello, yes hello, go back, go away. . . ."

The dogs panted happily *Hi George hi hi I remember you George here we all are George* pressing against his legs. He waved his arms, trying to shoosh them away; an Irish setter named Goofy looked up at him with big friendly eyes, wiggled its back end, and bopped him in the crotch with its tail, a blow as if from a billy club. George doubled over and a wet tongue slid in his ear; he almost fell over sideways. The dogs were in a frenzy of friendliness now: as George straightened up, his hands over his balls, a collie-mix jumped up and put his front paws on his chest and panted at him nose to nose while another one got behind George's knees and the two of them together almost knocked him over backward—the dogs agreed among themselves that that was a pretty good one—while a beagle ran through the taller dogs' legs to claim the cuff of his pants, and all George could do was holler, "Help! Somebody!"

"You've got a lot of friends, George," Sally laughed from the screen door.

"Just get them away, Sally, please."

"Bart, Mala, Goofy, Apples, Bully, Vic—all you guys, leave George alone."

"Yes, leave George alone!" he said, and kicked at them, not nearly as hard as he wanted to. Sally was still laughing as she held the door open for him, waving the dogs back with a dish towel as George came inside. As he lifted his leg up the last step he felt a decided nip at his ankle. He whirled around; at the bottom of the steps half a dozen furry faces looked up at him, all grinning. *Hi George hi hi when you coming back George. . . .*

"Grrrrrrr," George said.

The dogs were not impressed.

"Poor George," Sally said, stretching up to give him a kiss on the mouth, then patting the side of his tummy. "Everybody loves George."

"Those dogs could love somebody to death."

"It's just that we never get a chance to see you around here." She looked at him, her eyes teary as if she had just thought of something sad, and hugged him awkwardly, holding on to his stomach as if it were a separate entity between them. Then she leaned back and gazed at him, patting his stomach, plumping him up.

"Oof," said George.

Sally beamed, her eyes still teary.

She had a round, pretty face, though her mouth slanted down to one side so that her words at times seemed to spill out of the corner, and her eyes were usually moist, brimming over, as if she were just about to cry or had just finished. She was wearing a lime-colored cowboy shirt, splattered with paint and dirt and open four buttons down from the top so that her ample bosom had trouble staying in bounds, a long black peasant skirt, and tall fringed moccasins; her hair hung down over her left shoulder in a long black braid, thick as the handle of a whip, and she wore a headband decorated with Indian signs pressing down her bangs. From the rear of the house came the sound of Indian chanting and drums.

"I'm so glad you stopped over," she said, still beaming at him, still looking as though she was about to cry. "We never get to see you any more, at least I don't get to. I guess you and Don see each other at school. Sometimes I think he's trying to keep you away from me, ha ha."

"Ha ha, nothing like that," George said, remembering Don had asked him not to tell her about the kachina.

"I was telling Don we had to have you and Mary Olive over soon—no, that's a lie, George. I didn't tell Don anything like that. The truth is, I hardly ever see him myself any more. The truth is, we hardly ever talk at all."

She walked in to him, against him, to be held, so that either he had to put his arms around her for balance or she might knock him over. She rested her head on his chest; they met like two reversed parentheses; he put his arms around her as far as he could and patted her on the back. *I don't need this.* After a moment she leaned back and looked up at him, her mouth crinkly, her eyes moist.

"Thank you."

"For what?"

"For being here. For being a special friend."

She said it with such intensity he felt himself blush. *On the other hand.* She caught him looking down her shirt front, into her cleavage, and grinned.

"Come on," she said, clamping his hand in hers, looking meaningfully into his eyes. "I want to show you something."

She led him out of the kitchen and through the house, through the step-ups and step-downs of the different-level rooms, the narrow odd-shaped corridors—where was she taking him, to the bedroom? could he really think of such a thing, going to bed with his best friend's wife? well, yes, as matter of fact he could, the idea had occurred to him before, he had always liked Sally—to her studio at the rear of the house. *I must be an animal.* The sound of the Indian music coming from the stereo was deafening. It was a large, bright room with a picture window looking out toward the mountains—the mountains already turning rosy in the late-afternoon light, purplish—and skylights between the vigas, though the room itself was a mess, a jumble of worktables piled with cans of paint and old cloths and brushes; there were stools, light stands, an upturned wheelbarrow, a pile of sand, bags of cement and plaster, a cement mixer, several easels, the walls crowded with taped-up sketches, color charts, and feathers (Mary Olive called Sally a slob; looking around the room, George was afraid Mary Olive was right). She led him through a path into the room—he stepped on a coil of water hose and jumped, afraid it was alive—and positioned him in front of what appeared to be a mound of crinkled-up plastic sheets. It took her a minute to find what was underneath the sheets, to unwrap what she wanted to show him. Then she stood back, proud.

"Well, what do you think?" she shouted over the music.

"It's . . . ah . . . er," he said, and shook his head in amazement. It appeared to be, sitting on a wooden pedestal, a large flat black rock.

Sally beamed, her eyes brimming. "I call it either *The Turtle Mother,* or *The Emergence,*" she shouted. "I haven't decided which."

She said something else, but it was lost in the sound of the Indian singing and drums. As he studied it longer, he realized, indeed, that the large flat black rock was in the shape of a turtle, and that the turtle had an old woman's face. On the side, underneath the lip of the shell, was a model of some cliff dwellings, the white house at Canyon de Chelly, and below that, emerging out of the stone, still part of the stone, were the heads of two Indians, a man and a woman, their long hair cascading down over the modeled rocks like waterfalls, their mouths open, screaming.

The record of the Indian music ended. Sally watched him carefully. The abrupt silence made him uncomfortable. She closed her eyes and sang a few bars of the song that had been playing, moving her hands in front of her as if she held something in each one, doing a few shuffling steps. Then she looked at him again.

"I'm embarrassing you," she said.

"No, no, it's just that I don't know very much about Indians. . . ."

"It's okay, George. I understand. It makes me happy to know that you're that close a friend, that you would tell me if I embarrass you or not. That's what good friends are for."

George blinked twice, smiled, tight-lipped, tucking the ends of his smile up into his cheeks—it was better not to argue, she was going to think what she wanted to anyway. Sally looked out the window.

"I embarrass Don too, but he can't say things like that to me, he can't open up. It's sad, because our love of Indians used to be one of the things we shared together."

"Well, Don's been sick. He's probably not himself because of the pain."

"No, I know what it is," she said, thinking of something. She looked back at George and smiled sadly. "Did he ever tell you how this throat trouble started?"

"No, I had the idea it was some kind of an infection."

She rolled something over on the tips of her fingers, watched the tips of her fingers. "When we went over to Albuquerque last winter, for his daughter's wedding, his ex-wife, Julia, was there, along with her husband. And Don and Julia started talking, and I can understand how it happened, the chemistry that brought them together in the first place was still there. Anyway, Don started flirting with her and they danced a lot together, and her husband didn't like it. So he and Don had some words, and you know how Don is when he's been drinking, or how he used to be. And somebody said something and I guess Don took a swing at him and the guy hit Don in the Adam's apple."

"He could have killed him," George said. "No, Don never said anything about it."

"I didn't think he would; he was very ashamed of himself afterward. And as I said, I can understand how it happened with Julia; I never held that against him. But things have never been the same between us since. It was a little after that that he began

to take most of his things out to the cabin. You know he more
or less lives out there now, by himself, not in the house?"

"I thought it was something like that, but I didn't know for sure.
He never said anything about that either."

Her eyes overflowed; two channels of tears ran down her cheeks.
"His throat started to give him trouble after the fight, and he said
he moved out to the cabin because he was having trouble sleeping
and didn't want to disturb me. But I think he's still ashamed of
himself. He's a very unforgiving person, of other people and of
himself. I think he's ashamed for getting into a fight at his daughter's wedding, and for flirting with Julia and letting the whole thing
get out of hand. I think he's ashamed of himself for carrying on
that way in front of me. But that's not what's important to me. I
know he didn't mean anything by it. Don is what's important
to me."

She cried without effort or sobs, the tears simply pouring out
of her eyes, following the channels down her cheeks. She walked
back into his arms and he held her as she dampened the front of
his shirt. He thought Don must be crazy to treat her the way he
did—this loving, affectionate, attractive woman. She was everything Mary Olive wasn't; he thought she must be marvelous in
bed, inventive, giving. . . . *I must be an animal. Thy neighbor's wife.*
George stretched his neck, cleared his throat.

"Would you like me to try to talk to him?"

"Would you, George?" she said, looking up at him, smiling,
blinking back the tears, taking his hand again in hers. "Try to find
out what's wrong with him, find out what the doctor said about
his throat. He won't tell me, and I can help him. I know people
over at Hopi, medicine men, men of power. They can help him,
I can help him, if he'll let me."

"Well, his throat may be pretty serious, he may need more than
a medicine man."

"Oh no, George, that's where you're wrong." She held his hand
down in front of her, fitting his arm neatly between her breasts.
"The Hopi are very powerful people. That's what my sculpture is

about. They live at the electromagnetic center of the universe, they're the keepers of Mother Earth. All the other Indian tribes know that about the Hopi. There are strong powers over there."

She held his hand, pressed his hand against her skirt, against her crotch.

"I, er, just thought Don probably needs something a bit more scientific. . . ."

"What could be more scientific than electromagnetism? George, I could tell you stories you wouldn't believe."

He believed it.

Her eyes were getting misty again, now as if she was going to cry for joy; she pressed his hand deeper into her crotch, held his arm tighter against her breasts, stroked it. His penis stirred. *An animal.*

"I met a man at Hopi, an elder of the tribe, who told me there was a white aura all around me, and that the top of my head was open to the sky. They can see things like that, George; the Indians are so wonderful, so vital, so close to the powers of the earth!"

"Maybe a second opinion wouldn't hurt."

"He performed a ceremony over me, George. He welcomed me into the tribe, so that I can see things too. I am a Hopi."

She rubbed his arm, pressed it into her breasts, as if she thought it could ejaculate. His penis was beginning to get tangled in his underpants.

Thy neighbor's wife. She's a goddamned animal.

And then she let him go, dropped his hand, stepped away from him; she looked at him, her down-slanted mouth quivering, her eyes brimming over again with tears, a look of martyrdom and triumph on her face. "Go to him, George. Tell him I can help. Tell him for me."

"Ahem. Yes. Well."

George bit air, mumbled goodbye, and turned around and walked back through the room, back through the house, careening softly against the walls and door frames as he maneuvered his stomach through the narrow hallways, walking rather stiff-legged until the lump in his pants went down. Before he reached the kitchen, the Indian chant, the beating drums started again behind him, coming from the studio; he hurried out the back door and found the dogs waiting for him, panting, grinning, milling about his legs as soon as he stepped off the steps. He walked quickly then began to run, along the path toward Don's cabin, covering his vitals with both hands as the dogs' tails whipped about his legs, the dogs bouncing and leaping around him until he got to the cabin and found Don wasn't there, and he went on toward the sound of the jeep, toward the woods. The dogs stood on the slope near the cabin, looking after him *Where you going George hurry back George we'll be around George* watching him walk on toward the woods, grinning, panting; they watched him for a moment, then looked at each other and turned around and ran back toward the house, raced each other back to the steps to wait for Sally or somebody else . . .

. . . while half a mile away, in the trim white frame house sitting on the other side of the shallow valley that separates the two houses, Mary Olive stands in the window of George's study, looking through George's monocular at the Pikes' house for some sign of Don, wondering what he's doing and how he's feeling today, how he's holding up, wondering if there isn't some way to get a hold of him, contact him, to say hello and let him know that he has a friend in this world (and maybe find that out for herself, that she has a friend in this world too), and sees instead, in the small shaky circle of the precision instrument, her husband trotting across the Pikes' back yard, down the path from the house toward Don's cabin, a balloon of a man, his hands cupped over his balls, surrounded by the Pikes' collection of jumping leaping bounding dogs, across the yard and out of sight beyond the line of trees, and she goes back to the desk and puts the monocular back in the center drawer where he keeps it and locks the desk again with her own key and goes back downstairs to the kitchen, saying softly to herself, "George George George. . . ."

10

The jeep was digging itself deeper into the ground; the winch line was attached to the stump of a pine tree and the wheels of the vehicle were spinning, sinking into the forest floor, into the covering of pine needles and rotting leaves and pieces of wood and on into the dark earth underneath, sinking almost to the hubs, the engine screaming, sending up great clouds of dust and dirt and pine needles. Through it all, Don sat calmly in the open jeep, his eyes fixed on the winch line, determined apparently either to pull the stump from the ground or to let the jeep dig its way down to the floorboards, it didn't seem to matter which. George stayed back, among the trees, a safe distance away, away from the dust and debris or the line if it snapped, watching the jeep buck and shimmy, tugging against the line like a dog or a bull maybe, braced, frantic. Finally Don eased off the accelerator; he pushed his battered straw Resistol to the back of his head, rested his arms on the steering wheel, rested his head on his arms. When the dust had settled a bit, George walked over to him; Don watched him approach, looked at him sideways without raising his head.

"Looks like it just doesn't want to come out."

"Looks like it's going to take a while," Don rasped.

"You look tired."

"I'll be okay."

Don took a deep breath and straightened up again, turning off the engine. Dust and wood chips flecked his cheeks and stuck to his beard and work shirt; his blue eyes, under the chewed brim of the hat, looked drained. He reached over on the seat beside him for a half-empty bottle of vodka and took a swig, then offered it to George; George shook his head. Don took another mouthful, gargled it deep in the back of his throat, and spit it out; he kept the bottle between his legs.

"You trying to take down the whole forest?" George said, looking around.

"Sometimes it feels like it." Don looked for a while through the dust- and mud-splattered windshield, looked up at the branches of the aspens overhead; though there didn't seem to be any breeze, the leaves flickered. "I'm just trying to take out a few of these pines. The aspens protect the young pines because the aspens grow faster, but as they get older the pines overtake the aspens and choke them out. I guess I'm just trying to even up the odds a little. This stand of aspens is one of my favorites."

"It all sounds rather godlike," George smiled.

"Yes. Maybe it does." Don looked at George, sized him up, deciding how to take the remark. Then he took another long swig from the bottle of vodka, gargling with it again before swallowing it. "But then we all tend to play god once in a while, I guess. Like the way you're looking at me drinking from this bottle."

"I didn't mean to. I'm just surprised you're drinking so much."

"I don't usually. Not any more. But today it seems to be the only thing that makes my throat feel better. And my mind. Maybe I should do it more often. Even gods need a little comfort now and then, don't they, George?"

He leaned over toward George, as if sharing a friendly secret, but there was nothing particularly friendly in his smile; his teeth showed yellow in his white, dust-flecked beard. He thumped the rim of the steering wheel several times with the flat of his hand. "Is your kachina still there?"

"Yes. In fact, he seems to have found a shrine down there. I guess that's what he was digging around for."

"A shrine." Don shook his head. "A little piece of Indian holy ground right there in your own back yard and you didn't even know it."

"And today he made some prayer sticks and was doing some kind of a dance."

Don looked far away, past the shimmering aspens; then he shook his head again, making a clicking sound with his cheek like a restless piñon jay.

"I've got the name of a man over in Hopi who might know something about what's going on. If the kachina isn't gone by tomorrow, I think I'll go over and see what I can find out. In fact, I think I'll go over anyway, whether the kachina's still there or not—there's a dance over at Second Mesa, I'd like to see that. I'm getting interested in all of this. That's one of the reasons I stopped over: I wanted to ask you if you could keep an eye on Mary Olive again if she has any trouble."

Don looked at him for a long moment, then took another mouthful from the bottle and put it back on the seat beside him. "The next thing you know you'll start wearing moccasins and head-bands and squash-blossom necklaces, like my Indian princess up there. Did you stop at the house?"

George nodded. "Sally showed me the sculpture she's been working on. It's very interesting."

"The Turtle Mother?" Don smiled sarcastically and shook his head; he coughed, deep and raspy, into the inside of his elbow. "I don't know where she gets those ideas. I guess she just makes them up as she goes along."

"I don't know what you mean."

"There's no Turtle Mother legend in Hopi, at least that I've ever heard of, and I think I know one hell of a lot more about it than Sally. But you can't tell her anything. She has her own ideas about Indians, and that's that."

"She seems sincere about it."

"Oh, she is, no question about it. Unbalanced people are usually the most sincere people you'll ever meet."

"Come on, Don, I don't think you're being very fair to her. She told me about some of her experiences—"

"Her experiences," Don laughed, which started him coughing again. He wiped the corners of his mouth on the side of his wrist, readjusted his hat on the back of his head. "I suppose she told you about meeting a Hopi elder?"

"Well, yes."

"First of all he isn't an elder, he's a jewelry maker. She met him one time when she went over to buy some jewelry. And she probably also didn't tell you that after he supposedly read her aura and told her she had an opening in the top of her head so that she was open to the sky he also found out that she had an opening between her legs and helped himself to her goodies. That's the ceremony he performed over her, to welcome her into the tribe. And then he turned around and sold her a twenty-five-hundred-dollar bracelet on top of everything else. I'm afraid the only opening Sally has in her head is the one that lets the wind whistle between her ears."

"Don! She's your wife!"

"I'm well aware of that, George, and isn't it a fine thing? Here I am, I'm supposed to be an intelligent man, a man of letters, a teacher of other human beings, for Chrissake. And my wife thinks that every man with red skin is the embodiment of natural wisdom and the inheritor of all the secrets of the universe. Five thousand years of Western civilization thrown away in favor of dark skin, drums, and feathered loincloths. What makes it even worse, you can find the same story all over Scottsdale and Santa Fe, it's not even original. Excuse me."

He climbed out of the seat, past George, without looking at him, and went around to the front of the jeep to check the cable and the winch. When he came back, he plopped wearily behind the steering wheel.

"She's very concerned about you," George offered.

"In her way, I'm sure she is. Don't tell me: she wants me to go see a medicine man."

George stretched his neck.

"George, the Hopi attract every insecure and unhappy person who stumbles across them. They're in the same unfortunate league as Zen monks, Tibetan monasteries, and primal-scream therapy. I'm not exactly thrilled that my wife has become just another Indian groupie."

"But I've heard you say the Hopi are special."

"I'm not putting down the Hopi, or Zen monks or Tibetan monasteries or anything else, for that matter. What I'm talking about are all the non-Hopi who think they see something in the Hopi that isn't there, and therefore can't see what actually is there."

Don started coughing again, into the crook of his arm, hacking at something in his throat that wouldn't come out, which sounded as though it couldn't come out. He started to reach for the vodka again, then decided against it.

"So why care so much about it?" George said. "You can only see the world the way you see the world. We're each locked into our own perceptions."

"Because maybe the Hopi are right," Don said, leaning toward him. "Because maybe their language structure enables them to see things about the world that are mysteries to us. Maybe the reason we can't understand some of the basic mysteries about existence is only because we don't have the language to describe it."

"But that's no reason to get mad at Sally because she likes them. She's seeing them the only way she can."

"No, she's seeing them only from sentimentality, from what she wants the world to be, not from anything that's there. She's reduced the Hopi down to the level of greeting cards and cute puppies. These things are too important to be gushed over, to be treated that way."

"But who are you to say who sees them properly or not? It doesn't seem that what you know about it has made you any happier. You don't even want Sally to see that kachina or whatever it is in my back yard, and you know how much it would mean to her. She'd love to see it."

"You're right about that. She'd love it to death."

"Who are you to say that she shouldn't see it?"

"Because I'm the one who's going to die."

"Don't be ridiculous," George laughed. "We're all going to die."

"No, George. Not you, not Sally, not anybody else. Just me," Don hissed as he started the engine again, glaring at George as he raced the engine, raced it until George stepped back from the

side of the jeep and Don ground it into gear, the jeep shuddering
as it pulled taut again against the winch line, Don looking at him
as he mouthed the words against the roar of the engine, *Just me.*

11

THE HOLE IN THE SKY

The Little War Twins talked it over with Spider Grandmother
and decided that, if the Hopi really wanted to climb up into
the Fourth World, they would help by punching a hole in the
roof of the Under World, the Third World. But as for figuring
out how to get up there, the Hopi would have to do that for
themselves.

"Snot-nosed brats," the Chief muttered. "A lot of good a
hole in the sky does if there's no way to get up to it."

"What about asking one of the Two-Hearts?" said Mockingbird. "Maybe a witch would know how to get up there."

The Chief bopped him on the head with a piece of piki
bread. "A lot of help you are too. Here we are trying to get
away from the Two-Hearts, and you want to ask them how
to do it."

"Well, you've got to admit that sometimes they have some
pretty clever ideas," said Mockingbird, in the Chief's exact
tone of voice. "That trick of being able to turn themselves
into an animal ain't bad."

"The Two-Hearts are also the ones who are causing all the
trouble down here. Use your head, bird brain."

"Yes sir yes sir Chief," Mockingbird said like a parrot. The

Chief threw another piece of piki bread at him, but this time the bird caught it and ate it. "Squawk. Polly wants a cracker. The Chief is always right. Squawk."

The Chief was getting discouraged. Things were going from bad to worse. The Under World was overflowing with mother-jumpers and sister-diddlers. That was the bad part; the worse part was that the mothers and sisters loved it. The only thing people wanted to do was party, morning, noon, and night. The witches, the people with two hearts, were thriving. And his best friend was a bird with visions of being a stand-up comedian. The Chief didn't know what to do.

In his despair, the Chief had asked for divine guidance, but the only gods who responded were a couple of tattered twelve-year-old boys with runny noses, the Little War Twins, who spent most of their time playing ball. Things did not look good for the Hopi. There were times when the Chief thought of chucking the whole idea of finding a better world and settling down to a career of deflowering virgins like all the other elders. But then he'd hear those footsteps overhead again, clomping around the sky. . . .

"*Oy vey,* Chief," said Mockingbird in the voice of a Jewish tailor. "Have I got a deal for you!"

"Bird, I'm in no mood to listen to you do impressions."

"Seriously, Chief. I think I know a guy who can fly up to the hole in the sky and look around. That way you'll at least know if the Fourth World looks like someplace you'd want to be. The guy's name is Eagle."

The Chief had run out of ideas of his own, so he agreed, and Mockingbird sang his eagle-calling song. When Eagle appeared, the Chief explained the problem.

Eagle listened impatiently, whistling tunelessly under his breath and patting his bald spot. "Okay, okay, I got it. You want me to fly up there and have a look-see, right?"

"That's right," said the Chief. "We want to know—"

"Okay, okay. I got it, I got it."

Before the Chief could say anything more, Eagle flapped his great wings and took off. They watched him circle higher and higher, whipping the air, until he was out of sight; then they sat down and waited. Eagle was gone a long time, so long that they began to wonder if he had decided to stay up there. But finally he reappeared, a speck high up in the clouds, coming down fast. Coming down too fast.

"Damned show-off," muttered the Chief. "That's the trouble with this world, you can't get any decent help. . . ."

"That's a negative, Chief," said Mockingbird in the voice of Mission Control. "This bird is coming in on a wing and a prayer."

It was true. Eagle was in a power dive and looked as though he would crash, but at the last minute he was able to pull up his beak and land in the Chief's pile of prayer feathers.

"The eagle has landed," intoned Mockingbird.

"Cut that out and give me a hand," said the Chief.

They dug Eagle out of the prayer feathers and propped him up against a tree. When the bird recovered, the Chief asked him, "Did you see the hole in the sky?"

Eagle had trouble talking; he was still out of breath, and his beak had been pushed slightly off center from the force of the dive. "Yeh, it's up there, all right. But I didn't see anything else. By the time I got all the way up there, I was worn out."

"Well, thanks anyway," said the Chief. He sat down again, under the shade of a piñon tree, more discouraged than ever. But Mockingbird paced back and forth, his wings folded behind his back.

"Basically, it's a problem of what will someday be known as aerodynamics," he said professorially. "Eagle did the best he could, of course, but he's just not built for the job. Instead of a big bird with big wings, we need a little bird with little wings. Wind resistance and all that."

"And you just happen to know someone," said the Chief.

"As a matter of fact, I do," said Mockingbird.

So, after Mockingbird summoned Hummingbird, the Chief explained the situation. "Any questions?"

"Hmmmmmmmmmmmm," said Hummingbird.

"Do you think you can make it?" said the Chief.

"Mmmmmmmm-hmmmmmmmm," said Hummingbird.

"Now, what's that supposed to mean?" the Chief asked Mockingbird and Eagle. But the little bird was already airborne, his wings whirling. The three of them watched him fly out of sight, then sat down to wait.

Hummingbird was gone as long as Eagle. And when he appeared again, they could all see that he was in trouble too. He was coming in tail first, his tiny wings crossed over his breast, spinning out of control and looking rather green. Fortunately, Eagle had recovered enough to fly up and catch him in mid-air.

"Thank you, Eagle," said Hummingbird when they were back on the ground. "Mm-mm, I thought I was a goner."

"That's okay, okay," said Eagle, clacking when he talked, because the top half of his beak still didn't meet with the bottom. "That's my thing, you know, snatching things out of the air." He still held Hummingbird in his talon, and he looked at the little bird with new interest.

"Er, look, Eagle, if you're hungry, there's some lamb stew over there in that pot," said the Chief.

"Yeh, sure, okay, okay," Eagle said, remembering himself and laughing a little. "Sorry 'bout that. I guess I still don't have my head on straight."

When Hummingbird had recovered, the Chief asked him what he had seen.

"Mm, mm, mm, sure is purty up there. Blue as turquoise."

"Did you see the hole in the sky?"

"Mm-mmm. It's purty too."

"What's it look like!? What's it look like!?" the Chief said, picking up the little bird and shaking him like a dance rattle.

"You'll have to excuse the Chief," Mockingbird said to

Hummingbird. "He's been under a lot of pressure lately."

Hummingbird's eyes rolled around in his head like beans in a gourd. "I mm only mm saw mm it mm, I was mm too mm tired to mm go through mm. . . ."

The Chief dropped Hummingbird in a heap and went back to sit down. But Mockingbird had that gleam in his eye.

"Soaring," said Mockingbird.

"Soaring?" said the Chief.

"Soaring!" said Mockingbird, with an edge to his voice like a gypsy. "Big wings can't do it, little wings can't do it. So you want wings that can soar."

"Like a hawk?" said the Chief.

"Like a hawk," said Mockingbird.

"I don't know," the Chief said uneasily. "To tell you the truth, that guy always scares me a little. He always looks so, you know, fierce."

"Determined, Chief," said Mockingbird. "Try to think of him as determined."

The Chief wasn't going to argue the point, but, just the same, he sat near Eagle and Hummingbird while Mockingbird did all the talking to Hawk. Hawk listened, staring open-mouthed at the Chief as if he'd never heard of such a preposterous thing, looking at him with first one side of his head and then the other. The Chief was getting uncomfortable. Finally Hawk gave a couple of last indignant, mouth-open jerks of his head, opened his great wings, and rose like a kite, riding the air currents up into the clouds. The Chief wasn't altogether sure he wanted this scout to return.

Hawk did return, though, in about the same length of time as the others, gliding back into sight and settling down in front of them. He seemed more indignant than ever.

"And now I suppose you want me to give you some kind of a report, right?" said Hawk to the Chief, his mouth open, jerking his head for emphasis.

"Well, yes, that is what I, er, we had in mind."

"You want me to tell you all about the hole in the sky and

where it leads to and what's up there, right?" He looked at the Chief with first one unblinking eye, then the other.

"Well, you see, er, that is why . . ."

"And while I'm up there battling one-hundred-mile-an-hour tail winds and trying to chip the ice off my wings, you're just sitting down here passing the time of day, waiting to take all the glory, right?"

"In other words," said the Chief, "you didn't make it."

Hawk suddenly became very interested in an itch in his tail feathers. "Well, you see, there was this downdraft. . . ."

The Chief went off to sit by himself again. When Mockingbird finally came over and sat across from him, the Chief stared at him stonily.

"Go on. Who is it?"

"Shrike."

"The butcher-bird."

"Shrike," said Mockingbird.

"The most obnoxious bird I know."

Mockingbird shrugged.

"Do you want to tell me why?"

"There's several reasons, actually," said Mockingbird, shooting an imaginary set of cuffs and speaking in his best salesman's voice. "The main reason, of course, is precisely because he is so obnoxious."

"Of course," said the Chief.

"Because what kind of bird, human or otherwise, always gets the furthest in this world?"

"The obnoxious one," said the Chief.

"You bet your life," said Mockingbird, working his eyebrows up and down and flicking the end of an imaginary cigar.

"That's one reason," said the Chief. "You said there were several."

"Because he's a strong middleweight, he's got good moves, quick wings, a real contender, he can go the distance. . . ."

"And?"

"And because this is the fourth time we've sent a bird up

there, and the fourth time is a charm for the Hopi. Of course, if you're Bahana, the white man, three is a charm; I guess there's some Indians that consider five a charm, and I've even heard of a sect in the Far East that thinks that seven—"

"Stop!" The Chief supposed it was what he deserved, hanging around with birds. While he waited for Mockingbird to summon their latest candidate, the Chief busied himself by scraping the continually rising muck of the Under World from his moccasins.

"They tell me you got yourself a little problem, Chiefie," Shrike said when he arrived, leaning into the Chief's face. The Chief turned away: Shrike's breath smelled of blood. Shrike nodded to the other birds, blinking at them behind his black eye-mask.

"A little problem, yes," said Mockingbird, in the Chief's voice. "We've been trying to fly up and find a hole in the sky for the Hopi."

"A hole in the sky." Shrike laughed. "Well, what's wrong with these other guys? Why can't they do it?"

"Because it's not as easy as it looks, butcher boy," said Hawk.

Shrike picked at his notched beak with a dusty gray pinion feather. "Then you must have been going about it the wrong way. You birds got to remember that, if you're going to work for the Hopi, you got to do things the Hopi Way. Everybody should be of one heart and thinking good thoughts, even those who are just watching. That way everybody adds good energy to the project."

Shrike looked over the group and clacked his strong, hooked beak once.

Maybe I'm in the wrong line of work, the Chief thought. Maybe I'm not cut out for this. If those kachinas weren't so weird-looking, I could carve some copies of them and start a line of dolls. . . .

Mockingbird mirrored Shrike's matter-of-fact expression. "Sometimes it's hard to keep a pure heart, Brother Shrike, when you're up to your pinfeathers in everyone else's toe jam and belly-button goo."

"But we have to try," Shrike said, leaning into him and nudging him in the ribs. "That's what it's about, right, Mugsy?"

Or weaving, thought the Chief. I could start a line of dance kilts and sashes . . . no, that's no good, somebody has to discover cotton first. . . .

"All right, youse boids," Shrike said, flexing his pinions. "Stand back, give me some room here. And start generating those good thoughts. We got to make this baby fly. Up, up, and awa-a-a-a-ay!"

He took off in slow, determined circles, dipping the ends of his wings at them and grinning before he climbed up out of sight.

"It'll be just our luck that that silly son of an egg makes it," grumbled Eagle.

"Mmm-mmm," said Hummingbird.

"Now I'm sorry I didn't look him up for lunch last week, like I was going to," said Hawk. "I ate a chipmunk instead."

"But maybe he does have a point," said Mockingbird. "About thinking good thoughts and all. It's worth a try."

The birds mumbled to themselves, then settled down to sing their prayer songs, trying their best to think pure thoughts and keep sincere, meaningful expressions on their beaks. The Chief smoked his ceremonial pipe, thinking that few things are as silly as a bunch of birds trying to look sincere.

Shrike was gone for days. The other birds got hoarse from singing prayer songs, and the Chief's tongue was about to fall out of his mouth from smoker's bite. Finally Shrike appeared again, floating slowly back to earth. When the bird landed, the Chief ran over to him.

"Whatdidyousee? Whatdidyousee?"

The other birds all grouped around, wanting to hear about the hole in the sky. Shrike fluttered his eyes behind his mask, put a wing on his hip, and preened his tail feathers, shamelessly proud of himself.

"Well, I found the hole all right. At first it was a little narrow, but higher up there were some overhanging rocks, so I could rest before climbing all the way through. Actually, the opening looks a lot like the opening of a kiva."

"What's it like in the Fourth World?" Mockingbird said.

"It was dark most of the time I was there, but I did see your basic trees and grass and water."

The birds and the Chief all clapped each other on the back. Shrike accepted their congratulations as a matter of course.

"And there's birds and animals and bugs," Shrike chirped on. "In fact, there seems to be everything up there except people."

"Sounds like heaven," the Chief said, all smiles. "And what about the footsteps? Did you find out who's making those footsteps?"

Shrike looked troubled for the first time. "Chief, maybe you better sit down again."

12

George reached up and turned the light off over his desk and sat in the dark for a while, the darkness outside the window, on the other side of the blinds, as deep as on the inside, on this side of the blinds, thinking about what he had just read—*Why hasn't Don tried to get it published? It's good. He's a better writer than I am. That son of a bitch*—and burped, a loud and resounding *Baroop!* carrying with it the taste of guacamole and sour cream, memories of the three Burrito Supremes he had eaten for dinner. He cocked his head in the direction of the register, listening to see if Mary Olive had some comment to make, to see if she had even heard him at all—*Bring it up again, George, we'll vote on it. Class always shows, George*—but the register remained silent. A bad sign, he thought. *Right Turn Only. No Shoulder. Bridge Out Ahead.* He patted his stomach with two hands, like comforting an old friend, and wished he had another Burrito Supreme.

When he had left Don, sitting in his jeep in the woods, the jeep bucking and whining against the winch line, the clouds of dust and debris billowing up into the branches of the trees—and in the midst of it Don sitting there, the small, determined man with his cowboy hat pulled down over his forehead, his white beard filled with dust and his face sunken, hollow, staring straight ahead at the line as if daring, just daring it to break, watching, maybe waiting too, to see what would give first, the line, the stump, or the jeep—George had intended to come home, it was getting on toward dinnertime, but he found he was restless, as restless as before he had left the house; he was angry. So he drove back into Flagstaff and stopped at The Gables for a couple of bourbons and water—Don's vodka hadn't given him a buzz, it only made him want one—then, still restless, or, if not restless now, because he did feel calmer after the drinks, at least still just not wanting to go home, unable to face the idea of another night of hash, no matter how fine the ingredients were or how expensive the skillet it was cooked in, he went to the local Taco Bell and sat outside on the patio, at a table that reminded him of a large concrete mushroom—and didn't that make him the caterpillar? what he needed now was a hookah; he sat sucking on the straw of his large Coke, thinking, *Who are all these people?* (those bourbons must have been stronger than he thought)—watching the teenagers and the families carrying their bags of fast-food treasures back to their cars while he stuffed himself with Burrito Supremes and enchiladas and tacos. It was after nine when he got home.

He had wondered if Mary Olive would still be standing in the kitchen, holding *Joy of Cooking* against the register; he had wondered, somewhat facetiously, of course, somewhat sarcastically, but only somewhat—with Mary Olive a lot of things were possible.

But she was only sitting at the counter, a stack of the bound back issues of *The Little Review* beside her, reading; she didn't look up as he came into the house and stood in the doorway to the kitchen for a moment, and he came on up to his study without speaking to her. He didn't want to speak to her now either (*Detour. Men Working. Watch Out for Trucks*) but he thought he better.

"Mary Olive?"

Nothing.

Oh, how I wish.

"Mary Olive?"

"Yes, George?"

She didn't sound particularly drunk, just distant, away.

"I thought I better tell you. I'm going over to Hopi tomorrow. To see somebody about the kachina."

"All right."

No, she didn't sound drunk at all. She sounded sober, as a matter of fact. Very sober. For some reason, that made him all the more uneasy.

"I don't know how long it will take. I suppose I'll be back sometime late in the evening."

He listened, but he couldn't tell what she was doing. *Merging Traffic. Yield.*

"So you don't have to worry about fixing me anything for dinner. I'll get something while I'm out."

"All right, George."

He waited again.

Blind Crossing. Slow Children. This isn't funny, he told himself, don't play around. This is the way trouble starts; just get your business over with. *Blasting Zone.*

"And I'm sorry about dinner tonight. I hope you didn't go to any trouble."

"It's still here if you want it."

He wondered if it was. He pictured a congealed mass sitting in a Le Creuset skillet, a small hillock of *hash mystérieux* piled at his place at the table. He shuddered.

"No, thank you."

It was then that he looked up and saw the light on the hillside again, through the branches of the trees, a small red glow (a lantern? a torch of some kind? no, he didn't think so), rolling across the darkness, gliding, slower than the night before, and more shakily too, flickering as it passed behind the trees on the hill, disappearing for a few seconds, then appearing again before it disappeared for good. Who could be up there at this time of night? What was going on around here lately?

"You broke my heart," Mary Olive's voice said from the register, barely audible.

"I what?" He laughed. Uneasily. Just because I didn't want to eat hash? *Caution. Merge.*

"You broke my heart the first time I met you, the first day I talked to you. Do you remember that day, George?"

"Of course. It was after that Shakespeare class."

"You talked to me on the steps."

"I had been trying to figure out some way to talk to you for a year," George said, thinking back. *Lane Narrows. No Passing.*

"Do you remember what I said?" she said, her voice still small, far away.

"No, not offhand, but it was probably something about the class—"

"I insulted you. I told you I thought you were staid. I told you you were stiff and staid and I thought what you said in that Shakespeare class was stupid. I insulted you but you didn't go away. You broke my heart because you didn't go away, you just stood there and smiled and took what I had to say, and the next day you tried to talk to me again as if nothing had happened, and you kept wanting to talk to me no matter what I said to you, no matter how I insulted you, and then you married me and made me happy for a couple of years at least and I know I'll never be happy that way again. You broke my heart because you didn't go away, just like you break my heart now because you keep on writing and trying to write even though you haven't been successful and you're not even that good at it, just like you'll keep teaching at this dinky university or some other dinky university just like it, trying to find some place where they'll respect you even though they never will, just like you stay with me even though I'm not really the kind of woman you want and I can't treat you any other way no matter how much I want to and I'll never be able to give you half of what you want or need or what you deserve, I'll never even be able to tell you whether I love you or not. You break my heart because you never know when to leave things alone, you never know when to quit."

Falling Rocks. Hospital Zone.

George stretched his neck away from his collar—No, this isn't funny, he thought—looked in the darkness at his folded hands.

She didn't know what she was talking about, of course; even though she didn't sound drunk, it was the alcohol talking, she must be bombed out of her mind. It didn't even warrant a reply. He stood up and took one last look out the windows, looking for the lights on the hillside again—he remembered, in one of the books he got from the library, somewhere he had read that Masau'u, the Hopi god of the earth, of fire, and of death, walked around the earth at night, all the way around the earth, in fact, carrying a torch, looking after the world, and showing the dead the path to the Under World; maybe that's who it was; maybe it was Masau'u up there on the mountain, prowling around, checking up on things—but there was nothing there now. George clucked softly to himself, *cluck cluck,* shook his head, and left the room, heading down the dark hallway; he had to get to bed, he was beginning to sound as loony as Don or Mary Olive . . .

. . . and George goes to bed, goes to sleep, as usual, at peace, content, sleeping the sleep of the righteous and the blessed, mindful that he needs a good night's sleep because of his trip the next day, only later beginning his nightly grinding of teeth, a clicking, scraping sound like some small animal, or maybe not so small either, digging at the foundations of the house or chewing within the walls, trying to get in or trying to get out, accompanied by a low, mournful groan that isn't animal at all but all too human . . . while downstairs in the kitchen, Mary Olive sits at the counter, at her usual place, not massaging her gums tonight, not talking back to the talk-show hosts or callers-in or trying to guess the Golden Oldie from 1962, not drinking or crying, not doing anything except looking out the window hoping for Don's face to appear as it did the night before, as it used to, knowing already that it won't, knowing already that he may have gone back one night on his resolve not to see her any more but he won't allow himself to go back on his resolve two nights in a row, that he'll wait another day, another night before he comes back to see her again, thinking, *He just went to bed. I told him the most important thing in my life—well, the most important thing in my life about him—and he just went to bed. Damn his eyes* . . . while across the shallow valley that separates their two homes, on the opposite hillside, Don stands in the moonlight, midway between the dark jumbled form of the house he built (or at least built over, added onto) and the dark trim form of the cabin he built later, midway between the light coming from the house, the light in Sally's bedroom, what used to be their bedroom, where he can see a glimpse of the curtains and the wood paneling and the top of the bedstead, where she lies, probably reading, and the light from the open door of the cabin, a slit in the darkness, against the darkness of the woods, showing his desk and the edge of his chair and a bookcase, the Renoir reproduction on the wall and the piles of his manuscripts and papers on the floor (and in the darkness, midway between himself and the cabin, Cable, the coat of the old golden Labrador glowing in the moonlight, a luminous dog, sitting there watching him), while he looks at the square of light on the opposite hill, above the black shape of the trees, the sawtooth edge of the tops of the pine trees all the blacker because of the rich blue of the moonlit sky, the small frame of light that must be the kitchen window, must be the window where Mary Olive sits at night, thinking, *No, I won't, I can't. I don't care if you've got dry rot or a case of terminal static cling, you can't go see her again tonight. Your neighbor's wife. Christ* and turns and walks back to the cabin, followed slowly, carefully, by the old glowing dog . . . while on the Hopi Indian reservation, in an underground kiva on Second Mesa, a teenage boy, tall for his age, having gone a few years ago through his initiation into the kachina cult during the Powamu ceremony, having been whipped by the Hu Kachinas while the Crow Mother screamed, takes his place at the end of the line of men, dressed like the other men in a loincloth and moccasins, the line that is supposed to be straight but because of the cramped quarters in the kiva is more of a spiral, curled in upon itself near the ladder, and like the other men begins to sing the low rhythmic chant, practicing the songs composed for the Home Dance tomorrow, the first time he will dance in the plaza, stamping the rhythm of the chant with his right foot, stamping and singing while the elders sit along the sides of the kiva smoking their ceremonial pipes, and the kachina masks, his mask among the row of masks, a row of heads, sit along the benches waiting to have their collars of fresh spruce boughs attached, the row of masks watching the row of men who will become the kachinas tomorrow, as the boy thinks, *This is harder than it looks. My left leg feels like it's going to cramp already and I've only started. When am I supposed to turn around— oops, here we go* . . . while in his bed in his home in the foothills outside of Flagstaff, Arizona, in view of the sacred peaks of the San Francisco Mountains, George Binns lies in his bed, asleep, the sheet pulled loose from the bottom to expose his toes and the top wrapped around his head like a turban, his teeth-grinding over for the night, peaceful and content, dreaming that he stands naked in a forest, the ground covered with pine needles as soft between his toes as a shag bathroom carpet, walking naked among the trees, his skin slightly blue in the moonlight, his body, the great swell of his stomach, luminous among the trunks of the dark trees, walking among the dark trees into a clearing in the forest where there stands a large white rock, as tall as or taller than a man, a stele, glowing the color of the moon; the rock shudders, bristles as he approaches, stone chips ripple across its surface like a ruffling of feathers as the top of the great stone swivels around to face him, and it is the head of a great white owl, blinking at him, its eyes like pools of oil, saying to him, *Who are you, George?* and George says, *I thought that was the caterpillar's line. Are you sure this is right?* and the Owl says, *It depends on what you're looking for,* and George says, *That's what I was afraid of,* and the Owl extends its wing toward him and George takes it in his hand, the pinion feathers fitting in his hand like fingers, the feathers stiff and, well, feathery; the Owl looks at him and nods *Are you ready?* and George says, *As ready as I'll ever be*; then the two of them, man and bird, hand in wing, on cue, each extends his right foot and taps once and brings it back, then each extends his left foot and taps once and brings it back as the Owl shouts *Oopah!* and George sings *Who?* and they dance on in the small clearing, under the moonlight, dance in a small circle to the song of the crickets in the underbrush and the song of the night wind in the tall trees, the naked, heavy-bellied man and the great snow-white Owl, together, glowing in the dark forest, dancing and dancing. . . .

THREE

1

In the morning he drove into town to pick up Route 89, then followed it north, circling the base of the San Francisco Mountains, to the east of them now, the gray volcanic peaks (with a cloud, there always seemed to be at least one cloud hovering nearby) and the miles of pine forests etched in the strong morning sunlight. It was a little after eight. The day was clear, crystalline, though within the space of a few miles the air whipping through his ventilator windows and up the sleeves of his short-sleeved shirt went from cool to warm to hot as he began to leave the mountains, as the highway descended from the high mountain air and the smells of the pine forests, the rich green of the forests and the highway laced with shadows and the outcroppings of rock, the reminders of the mountain way of life around Flagstaff, the lumber trucks and the service stations and motels built to look like log cabins and restaurants advertising lumberjack breakfasts, and into the high-plains country, lush meadows dotted with piñon and juniper and scrub cedar, the land rolling away unimpeded toward the horizon. He noticed it had been a bad night for critters; the crows were out, perched on fence posts or walking along the shoulders, pacing with their wings folded back like worrisome morticians, waiting for the cars to clear so they'd have their chance at the squashed and bloody things left on the highway. George tried the radio, but all he could find was Western music or rock and roll, and even they soon dissolved into static. He drove on in silence, trying to find a cool spot on the windowsill for his elbow, his left hand propping up his head.

Beyond the town of Gray Mountain, a collection of cheap motels, gas stations, and trailers, a sign informed him that he was entering the Navajo reservation—a police car passed that said "Navajo Nation" on the door; the two brown-faced policemen in their Smokey Bear hats and dark sunglasses looked over at him, their faces, what he could see of them, without expression—and he started down a straight, miles-long grade into the Painted Desert, into a mineral landscape, the earth the color of minerals, a barren land with sparse sage or greasewood, high-tension wires stretching off in several directions, the giant spidery towers walking off over the edge of the earth toward distant cities, and an occasional fenced-off substation, clusters of low, windowless buildings like bunkers. On the other side of Buck Rogers and Cameron, along the side of the highway, there were lean-tos and roadside stands pieced together from scraps of wood, and parked cars with their doors standing open and pickup trucks with their tailgates down; hand-lettered, hand-painted signs said NAVAJO JEWELRY, TURQUOISE, CEDAR BEADS. The Navajo women wore long black skirts and red or blue or purple velveteen blouses, with squash-blossom necklaces and silver wristlets; the men wore silver concha belts with their torn Levi's, and tall, round-topped, flat-brimmed hats, a few of the men had braids dangling down the front of their shirts. A girl in a sweatshirt with NORTHERN ARIZONA UNIVERSITY stenciled across the front sat on an empty counter, swinging her legs, watching the cars go by; George waved but the girl just looked at him. As he turned east, past the turnoff for Dinosaur Tracks, the world turned red: red earth, red hills, a landscape without life that he could see, a landscape of red slag.

Tuba City was a bit greener, but not much. He turned at the Navajo Trail Shopping Center and the Nava-Hopi Kitchen restaurant, following the signs for the Hopi reservation, and within a few miles passed Moenkopi, a Hopi farming community built outside the rest of the reservation, a small village off to the right of the highway, in a depression filled with trees, cottonwoods and a few cedars, and orchards of apple and peach trees. Near the highway there were tract-style homes on dirt yards, dirt streets, though farther back was a glimpse of some older stone buildings grouped around a plaza; behind the village there were fields carefully laid out in what appeared to be a dry riverbed, at the base of some red-earth bluffs. Beyond Moenkopi, for the next thirty miles or so, the land opened out, as flat as a desert was supposed to be, though here the land was green, or at least appeared green as seen from the highway, a dusty green, the earth covered with sage and rough desert grass; overhead the sky was hazy blue, becoming milky toward the horizon—the color, it occurred to George, of semen. He wished he had some coffee.

Then the horizon became broken and craggy. The mesas rose up in front of him before he realized that's what they were, and by the time he realized that's what they were, the road gained elevation and he was on top of them, driving across Third Mesa, past a few scattered homes among the junipers and greasewood and pine scrub. They were new homes, ranch-style homes (he thought, *American-style homes*), with picture windows and insulated siding and TV antennas on the roof, with a late-model car or two or a fancy pickup truck in the driveway, with flower beds and lawn decorations. (He thought, *Maybe they aren't Indians.*) He laughed out loud: well, what did he expect? What he expected was something a bit more mystical, something with the feeling of El Greco's painting of Toledo, perhaps, a white-walled citadel sitting on a mesa top, glowing under a dark and significant sky; or tipis, even, at least something Indian, although he knew tipis belonged to another kind of Indian. (He thought: *I could be anywhere.*)

In a few miles he passed Bakavia on one side of the road and Hotevilla on the other, but they looked like any Western or even Midwestern town that was too small to have a main street. As the highway curved down off the other side of the mesa, Oraibi, the town that the tourist folders always referred to as the oldest continuously inhabited village in the continental United States, sat off to his right, a collection of small flat houses scattered off toward the tip of the mesa, the shell of a burned-out church sitting by itself off to one side, looking as though it were sliding off the edge—if there was a pueblo, if any of the oldest continuously inhabited buildings were still there, George couldn't see them from the road. Tucked away in the washes and gullies along the side of the mesa were gardens, rows of beans and corn, carefully laid out in pockets that reminded him of sand traps on a golf course. George drove on.

On the desert floor, between the mesas, he passed the crossroads at New Oraibi, a service station or two, a market, a couple of buildings that appeared boarded up; then, in a few miles, Second Mesa rose ahead of him like a wall. The lower elevation was dotted with small, low trees and boulders that, over the centuries, had tumbled from the cliffs, but the cliffs themselves looked like battlements: the strata of sandstone along the top were broken up like courses of masonry, only in this case the masonry was done with boulders each weighing tons. The road swept up along the face of the cliffs, climbed through the boulders and outcroppings along the heights; then he was traveling across a table of land, flat prairie land. There were no modern ranch-style houses here; in fact, he didn't see any houses at all. An old man walked along the side of the road, bowlegged, his face the color of a well-worn catcher's mitt, his hands curled at his side as he walked, simianlike, scuffling along, ignoring the two young white men who approached him, jogging, wearing expensive running suits and white terry-cloth sweatbands. In a mile or so, George passed the Government Health Center and the Craft Co-op; in the campground between the Co-op and the Hopi Cultural Center, a dozen Winnebagos and camper trucks were drawn up in a circle like a wagon train. George pulled into the parking lot in front of the Cultural Center, got out, and stretched. The sun, the heat in the still air, clutched him like a hand.

The Cultural Center was a complex of windowless concrete buildings, an architect's adaptation of the classic pueblo style, squares piled on squares, with blank exterior walls and flat roofs. The museum and the information center were still closed, but he walked across the compound, the courtyard of the Cultural Center Motel, to the coffee shop. The coffee shop looked the same to him as the coffee shop in any other modern motel—muted carpets and low, soundproofed ceiling, room dividers and decorator plants (plastic?) and indirect lighting—with the exception of the kachina dolls hanging from the exposed roof timbers and the menu that said "Welcome to Hopi Land, The Center of the Universe." The waitresses, all teenage Indian girls, wore the traditional black cotton dress cut to expose one shoulder, only in this case the dress exposed not reddish-brown skin but a white waitress's uniform underneath. There were only a few people at the tables, all whites, tourists, from the looks of them; George took a place at the empty counter, barely able to fit his stomach between the stool and countertop, his knees wedged hard against the side.

The four or five waitresses were huddled at the far end of the counter, looking through an Avon catalogue, while the cook leaned through the window of the pickup station, a young man with a broad face and NAM tattooed on his burly arm and a mane of black hair like that of a lion—a friendly lion, but a lion nonetheless; the girls and the cook were discussing something in Hopi—at least George supposed it was Hopi—the only words of which he recognized were *Charlie's Angels*. When the busboy came through the kitchen doors, George caught a glimpse of a fat Hopi woman in restaurant whites, patting dough, flipping it back and forth from hand to hand, patty-cake patty-cake, at a stainless-steel table. The radio beside her played Fleetwood Mac's "Go Your Own Way."

George ordered coffee and the specialty of the house, blue-corn pancakes. He was slightly disconcerted when the pancakes arrived and they actually were blue, but he ate every bite—every gritty bite—cleaned his plate and smiled to the waitress, to show that he had a good heart and was a friend of Indians and agreed that Custer had it coming. The waitress, a round-cheeked, acne-scarred girl with hair as black and curly as a shampoo advertisement, gave him directions to the dance and agreed it was a nice day for it. But when he asked if she knew how he could find a man named David Lomanongye, she looked out the window and shrugged her shoulders and didn't speak to him again.

2

George eased his car into a space between a pickup truck and a VW van, and held his breath: the edge of the mesa slipped out of view beyond the end of the hood, and even though he felt the front tires come to rest against the stop, a log staked to the rocks, the car seemed to hang out over the edge of the mesa, suspended, teetering above the desert floor hundreds of feet below, as if he were positioned on a launching pad. He opened the door and peered out carefully; two Indian boys, standing on the edge of the mesa, watched him and laughed. George got out, stepping gingerly, uneasy at the prospect from such height even though he was back at least ten feet from the edge, unsure that he wasn't going to fall or leap or fly off, and locked the door.

"Do cars ever roll over the edge?" he asked the boys, staying where he was beside the door.

"Oh sure," said the larger of the two boys.

"Really? What happens to them?"

"They crash at the bottom and somebody comes and hauls them away." The boy took a wind-up and arced a stone high out over the desert.

The smaller boy looked at George, as if to say, *What else did you think would happen to them?*

George moved a little closer to the boys; he eased his stomach through the narrow space between the truck and the car, going as far as the front fenders but no farther, at least not until he got used to being up this high in the air, and smiled at them, a rather forced, queasy smile, trying to appear friendly, harmless. He leaned his paunch against the fender of the truck to steady himself—the edge of the mesa, where the boys stood, simply dropped away—then yelped and jumped back when the metal was hot. The larger boy looked at George then arced another stone out over the desert; the smaller boy just looked at George.

The larger boy—he was maybe eleven or twelve—wore a football-style jersey with a picture of a rock group on the front and the word KISS in stylized letters; the smaller boy, a few years younger than his friend, wore a dirty yellow T-shirt with a picture like a color snapshot of a sailboat tacking through rough water. Their black hair was long over their ears and they had bangs across their foreheads. The smaller boy's left eye was crossed, giving him a forever dubious expression; he was holding a package of orange Kool-Aid, into which he dipped his grimy index finger and then licked it off, leaving an orange ring around his mouth.

George stepped around the front of his car, one hand reaching back toward the fender to steady himself. By leaning forward he could see, over the rim of the rocks, a garbage dump, a crevice decades full of tin cans, broken bottles, broken furniture, stove ashes, corn shucks, plastic garbage bags. To his left, along the edge of the mesa, George recognized, from the books he got from the library, the sacred Corn Rocks, two large upright boulders that the Hopi thought looked like two large upright ears of corn; to George they looked like two large upright boulders. Beyond, the desert floor stretched away for miles. The larger boy was giving the smaller boy instructions on the art of stoning a rabbit that was hiding somewhere down the slope.

"If you get him from this high, you'll splatter his brains. Powee!"

The stone arced out, hitting something metal; the larger boy frowned. The smaller boy wasn't watching anyway; he licked his orange finger with his orange tongue and watched George.

"Where's the dance going to be today?" George said.

The smaller boy pointed his orange finger up in the air in the direction behind George; the larger boy said, "Up there," and looked for another stone.

George turned around. On the other side of the road, rising above the few houses built along the foot of the slope, was a bluff a hundred feet or so high with a ridge of buildings along the top, low stone buildings the same color as the sandstone bluff, so that, if he didn't know they were there, if they hadn't just been pointed out to him, he might have missed them. Crisscrossing the face of the bluff were several trails, leading up to a couple of openings, spaces between the walls of the buildings. For a moment, peering up at the village, which looked like a fortress on top of the rocks, he thought he heard the beating of drums and the growl of male voices, hundreds of men, braves chanting—he thought of the scene in *Zulu* where the old warriors chanted and danced and waved their spears in front of the bare-breasted, incredibly nubile teenage girls—he thought of the scene in *The Naked Prey* where the women of the tribe took the captured white man and stuck a couple of straws up his nose and rolled him up into a ball of mud and roasted him on a spit, alive—he thought maybe he didn't hear anything after all.

Something poked him in the ribs.

"Ouch! Hey!" George jumped. The two boys stood beside him, looking up at him. He looked down at the side of his white shirt: there was a dirty orange smudge, the exact size and shape of the end of a ten-year-old boy's index finger.

"You have anything to eat?" the larger boy said.

"Harrumph." George stretched his neck. "Well, I did bring along some granola bars."

"Yay!" said the larger boy. "Granola bars!"

"Yay!" said the smaller boy. "What are granola bars?"

"I don't know," said the larger boy.

The smaller boy bent over to examine George's shoe and touched the toe of the cordovan with his index finger, giving it a poke. When the boy straightened up again, there was a dirty orange smudge, the exact size and shape of the end of a ten-year-old boy's index finger, on it too. George envisioned himself polka-dotted with dirty orange smudges. He unlocked the car door and opened the box of granola bars, giving each boy one of the sealed foil packages. The boys grabbed them and started to run off.

"Hey, wait a minute," George called after them. "How do I get up to the village?"

The boys slid to a stop.

"The trails," the larger boy said, pointing.

The smaller boy looked at him. *How else would you get up there?*

"It's okay for me to just walk up there?" George said. "I mean, the people in those houses won't mind?"

"Sure, why not?" said the larger boy. He said something in Hopi to his friend and they both giggled.

"Bye, Bahana," said the smaller boy, waving his orange finger at him, and they ran down the road.

3

The houses along the road, at the base of the bluff, were one-story stone buildings, some of them surprisingly new, the others of indeterminate age, perhaps ten years old, perhaps a century or two, the houses sitting on the bare earth that was the color of the sandstone mesa that was the color of the houses too, each house surrounded with what looked to George to be mostly junk: steel drums, parts of machines, tires, propane tanks, piles of stone or cement blocks, the remains of a room taken off one of the houses or perhaps the start of a new room going up, cartons of toilet tissue, piles of firewood, sacks of cement, used Pampers, plastic garbage bags. George walked between the houses, afraid with every step that someone would yell at him, and started up one of the crisscross paths toward the top of the bluff, already breathing heavily.

As he climbed higher, halfway up the slope, a dust devil appeared on the trail in front of him; the knee-high cyclone of dust skirted along a little ways, then picked up an empty 7-Up can and rolled it along; the can bounced merrily up the trail a step or two in front of him, defying the laws of gravity, ringing like a bell to announce his coming. George stepped on the can to silence it; the can wrapped itself around his instep, a sudden hand, an aluminum jaw, and almost toppled him off the path and down the face of the bluff. George kicked at it, doing a one-legged dance, trying to get it off, but the can held on, taking on a life of its own. George looked around, looked up at the top of the bluff: along the edge of the wall, half a dozen Indian girls, teenagers in jeans and T-shirts, sat swinging their legs, watching him. George sighed—sometimes it seemed the world worked awfully hard to make him look foolish—and limped over to a rock to sit down.

He pried the can off the bottom of his shoe, then continued to sit there while he caught his breath, looking at the world below. The height didn't bother him now; in fact, he sort of liked it, liked the view from up here. The rears of the houses along the foot of the bluff were crowded with old appliances, gas and electric stoves, refrigerators, freezers, cookers of one kind or another; the appliances looked abandoned, inoperative, but on the back porch of one of the houses, a handful of women were hacking up the body of a small animal—it was probably a sheep or a goat—giggling and chattering among themselves as they tended a couple of large stew pots on top of an ancient porcelain stove. Through the screen door of another house, in the dark interior, he could see the flicker of a television set.

Along the road, more cars and trucks were arriving, looking for places to park. From a couple of converted school buses, the tops of which were loaded down with makeshift luggage, cardboard boxes, and duffel bags, and the sides decorated with matching tie-dyed flags, a group of a dozen or so hippies—the young men in long beards and long flowing hair, in billowy homemade shirts and pants of white muslin with hunting knives stuck in their belts, the young women in long homemade dresses of the same white muslin, their heads covered with sunbonnets, some carrying children papoose-style—started up another trail of the slope, attacking it as if they were assaulting a stronghold. A white family stood in the road behind their RV; the two boys ran among the parked cars, shooting each other with fingers in a quick game of cowboys and Indians, while the little girl, in a pink dress and a headband with a few plastic feathers sticking up around the top, stayed close to her parents. The parents, a couple in their mid-thirties, dressed in tennis whites and thongs, looked around, confused, shielding their eyes from the sun, as they tried to figure out what was going on and where they were supposed to go. George got up from the rock and resumed his climb, puffing himself on with new resolve and determination, carrying the squashed 7-Up can with his fingertips.

At the top of the bluff a few steps were cut into the rock, leading up to an opening into the village. The girls sat on the wall beside the opening, still swinging their legs, watching him occasionally, talking among themselves and looking out across the desert. He climbed the last few feet into the village thinking his legs were going to buckle out from under him, his pulse pounding in his temples and his lungs gasping for air. He was greeted with the smell of old urine and feces, not an unpleasant smell, just strong, like opening the door of a desert outhouse. The girls watched him; a couple of them almost smiled.

"Where can I put this?" George said, gasped, holding up the squashed can.

"Just toss it," one girl said, in a singsong accent that trailed away.

"Here," another girl said, holding out her hand. George gave her the can and she winged it, out over the edge of the bluff; the can sailed briefly, then nose-dived into the slope, skating into a crevice near the bottom. The white family George had noticed earlier, standing now at the bottom of one of the trails, looked up at the girls, wondering if the missile had been aimed at them. The girls laughed among themselves.

George blinked, stretched his neck. "Er, which way do I go?" he said, looking through the opening into the streets of the village.

"You can go that way," said one girl, pointing left.

"Or you can go that way," said another, pointing right.

"Just don't fall over the edge," said the girl who had disposed of the can. The girls giggled.

George decided to try left.

The houses of the village were much the same as the houses at the foot of the bluff along the road, one-story stone buildings, only here the houses were pressed together, jammed against one another, fitting together at different elevations and angles depending upon the topography along the narrow dirt streets—some of the walls were of fitted stone, ancient walls built without mortar, others were of stone in neat cemented rows and courses like ready-made siding, still others were of cement blocks or stucco. Along the façades, the vigas, the roof-support timbers, stuck out below the roof lines, the ends of the unfinished timbers as weathered as if they'd been chewed. A few of the houses had porches, with low stone walls under a corrugated metal roof, but they were more outdoor storage sheds than anything else, crowded with more fifty-gallon drums, cartons of laundry detergent, stacks of firewood. He stopped in front of a window, a new aluminum-frame window with sliding screens and insulated glass, where a parakeet in a cage sat on the sill along with a bottle of Joy, a vase of plastic flowers, a postcard from San Francisco, a room deodorizer in a Disneyesque ceramic skunk; then something moved behind the still life, coming closer, moving over it: a woman's face, broad, red-skinned, with black hair black eyes, looked back at him, saying something that he couldn't hear. George walked on.

The narrow streets were deeply gouged and rutted from the runoff, the ridges of dirt worn shiny from centuries of feet; the streets climbed in and around the village like a puzzle, he couldn't imagine a car trying to use them—how did cars get up here, any-way? there had to be a back road—yet a few cars and pickups were parked here and there, at improbable angles, nose or tail pitched skyward. He had walked only about the length of a city block when he found himself back at the edge of the mesa, having walked through the village on one side, this time with a new vista of the desert floor. Below the edge of the mesa, a dozen or so outhouses teetered precariously on the slope, looking as though each one could tip over if a person inside made the slightest wrong move, while, farther down, the rocks were covered with refuse, paper sacks and garbage bags and garbage just heaved. George turned around and tried to find another opening into the village, walking down a narrow passageway between two buildings; he turned a corner into another street and the two boys from the parking lot ran at him from a doorway, heads down, arms extended—"Ya-a-a-a-a-ay!" They grabbed him, one on each side, nearly knocking him over, together holding him captive, looking up at him with large black eyes.

"Give us some more granola bars!" the larger boy said.

"Yeh, or we'll scalp you," said the smaller boy, laying his chin against George's stomach and grinning up at him over his belt. The orange outline around his mouth was now itself outlined in dirt.

"I left them in the car," George said.

"Oh," the boys said, and that seemed to settle it. But they continued to hold on to him, giggling back and forth.

"My name's Jerry," said the larger boy. "And that's Jimmy."

"I'm Jimmy," said the smaller boy, his crossed eyes gazing up at George with unabashed affection. George stretched his neck and looked around to see if anyone was watching them; he tried to move but it was no go.

"Where's the dance supposed to be?"

"The kachinas are resting now," Jerry said. "But come on, we'll show you where to watch."

They each took a hand and led George through another narrow passageway, around the back of the village, then let go of him and climbed up a ladder to the roof of one of the houses.

"Can I do that?"

"Why not?" Jerry looked back down at him.

"You're not too fat," Jimmy said earnestly.

"I mean, are you sure I'm allowed to climb up there?"

"You worry a lot, Bahana," Jimmy said.

"Come on," Jerry said, and the boys disappeared beyond the

edge of the roof. George stood there a moment, wondering what to do, looking around, looking up at the roof, then slowly, very carefully, hugging his body close to the ladder, one step at a time, bumping his stomach on each rung, he climbed up after them.

4

The boys sat at the front of the roof, dangling their legs over the edge. George hunched over as if he were dodging bullets, afraid with each step that he was going to crash through the tarpaper into the house below, and went over to sit behind them, keeping a few feet back from the edge. The building was at the narrow end of a long plaza. The plaza was empty except for what appeared to be a pile of old mattresses in the center and a small pine tree stuck in the ground at the far end; around the perimeter, a few people, whites and Indians, sat on the benches and on rows of kitchen chairs in front of the houses. The bright mid-morning sunlight divided the plaza into deep shadow on one side and intense light on the other. The sunlight hurt George's eyes, and the tarpaper was too hot for him to rest his hand on; there were a couple of pieces of wood behind him and he sat on one and used the other to lean on. He was just about settled, almost comfortable, when he noticed movement out of the corner of his eye. He looked beside him: sitting on the parapet of the second-story porch of the building next door, six feet away from him, was an eagle.

The bird sat as tall as George and was watching him, the black liquid eye staring at him, unblinking; then the head swiveled and the other eye took its turn. The eagle was chained to a post, with a tin of water and the remains of some raw meat sitting on the parapet wall in front of it; a smaller eagle, its feathers matted and uncared-for, huddled sickly near the end of the open sleeping porch, close to the house. George looked around; there were a dozen or more eagles, as well as a few hawks, sitting chained on the rooftops, singly or sometimes two or three together, like living gargoyles. The eagle beside him twisted its head again, shifted its perch, the talons scraping on the wood; the great eye blinked. George edged a little away from it. The boys giggled.

"Don't be afraid," Jerry said. "The eagles are going home tomorrow."

"They let them go?" George said.

"Nah, they kill them," Jerry said. "Somebody strangles them."

"No, they don't," Jimmy said. "They smother them."

"Strangle them," Jerry said, and punched the smaller boy in the arm. Jimmy pushed him back and they began to wrestle—George was afraid they'd fall off the roof.

"Settle down, settle down," he said. He took a package of granola bars from his pants pocket, the package he'd brought along for a snack, and held it out to them. "You guys want this?"

The boys grabbed the package and opened it and divided it up.

"I thought you said you left them in the car," Jimmy said.

"I forgot," George said.

The boys looked at him as they munched on the bars, seeing through his lie. Jerry patted all George's pockets to see if there were any more. The eagle looked sternly at George: *Where's mine?*

"What kind of kachinas dance today?" George said, trying to change the subject.

"Home Dancers," Jerry said. With his finger he drew the image of a mask on the tarpaper, a tall mask with stepped edges.

"Did they start already?"

"They came at sunrise," Jerry said.

"They came first in the middle of the night," Jimmy said.

"But nobody's allowed to see them then," Jerry said.

"I heard them," Jimmy said.

"You did not, you were asleep," Jerry said. "They'll be back again pretty soon."

"The kachinas bring presents today," Jimmy said.

"Yeh," Jerry said. "A new truck, a dirt bike, a color TV . . ."

"Maybe the kachinas will bring us a black girl," Jimmy said. The boys giggled. George wondered if they meant what he thought they meant.

He shifted on his wood cushions. From where he sat he had an unobstructed view not only of the plaza and other rooftops around the village but of the surrounding country too, sitting, as it were, on top of the world, a sidesaddle Buddha on a prayer platform, a wide-angle panorama spread out below him. The village sat at the tip of the long finger of the mesa, on a cone of rock, and the desert, the dusty green plain, extended twenty miles or more in three directions. A road curved through the plain, a defining gash stretching away toward a low range of mountains to the south, toward Winslow; to the west, barely visible in the haze, he could make out the San Francisco Mountains along the horizon, blue on blue. It seemed impossible that he had been there just this morning, that he lived on the other side of those mountains and had never realized any of this existed.

And he thought: *This is a really strange thing to be doing, this is really strange to be here,* and felt exhilarated, giddy, proud of himself. The boys, one on either side of him, stretched out along the edge of the roof, each one resting his head on George's legs, their eyes closed, talking back and forth about something in Hopi. Thinking: *This is wonderful. Today I'm really doing something. Today I'm really happy.* On the far side of the village, to the east, an eagle, chained to a rooftop, spread its wings and started to fly, reaching a foot or so into the air before the chain ran out and snapped the bird back to the roof, the bird continuing to flap terribly against the hold on its leg, calling, screaming, a few of the other birds taking up the cry, the air filled with cries and whistles. George looked at the bird beside him; its eye went suddenly white as it blinked, then returned again. *I'm alive. I'm really alive.* Then, as the birds began to settle down, George heard, in the distance, coming from somewhere outside the village, a swishing sound, like wind stirring leaves, and a measured *clack clack clack clack clack,* a faint sound coming closer, the sound of dozens of turtle-shell rattles beating against dozens of legs.

5
—

They appeared over the top of a large outcropping of rock at the far edge of the mesa, a knoll a hundred yards east of the village, walking one by one over the top of the knoll, each one silhouetted for a brief second against the sky, twenty or more of them—*They're like cornstalks,* he thought, *they're like a row of giant walking cornstalks*—coming single file down the knoll toward the village. The kachinas wore blue-and-red masks with tall blue tablets sticking up from the top, the steps of the tablets—the steps that Jerry had drawn on the tarpaper with his finger—decorated with upright feathers and tall stalks of grass. Around their throats were evergreen ruffs, and there were evergreen boughs sticking out of their armbands and hanging down from the sashes tied around the tops of their dance kilts; in his left hand each carried a sprig of evergreen, in his right a dance rattle. Leading the file of kachinas were three men dressed only in white kilts and moccasins, the kachina fathers, one of them a very frail old man who was bent over like a question mark; coming behind the kachinas were the kachina manas, the kachina women, dressed in black cotton dresses and red-and-white blankets fastened around their shoulders for capes, with white leather moccasins wrapped up around their legs. As the kachinas approached the village, the only sound was the clack of the turtle-shell rattles against their legs, the swish of the evergreen boughs like sheets of rain through the trees.

George's hair bristled against the back of his neck.

The boys blinked up at him, two inverted faces against his legs, then they heard the kachinas too and rolled over lazily, propping themselves up against him to be comfortable. Without looking at him, Jimmy said in his trail-away voice, "Don't worry, Bahana. We won't let the kachinas get you."

The line of kachinas disappeared from view for a moment behind the buildings as they entered the village, then reappeared again at the far end of the plaza, coming into the plaza single file through a passageway between the buildings, the kachina fathers in their white kilts leading the way for them, sprinkling a trail of cornmeal in front of them, making the road for them. As they entered, the people of the village came out of their houses and took their places on the chairs and benches around the perimeter of the plaza; the rooftops along the sides of the plaza filled with spectators, though George and the two boys were alone at the one end; George still waited for someone to tell him to get down. The kachinas took up a position on the east side of the plaza, facing him, still in single file, with the kachina manas in a shorter line beside them; the kachina fathers stood near the center of the plaza, facing the kachinas, directing them into position, correcting the space between them, their alignment, making sure they were in the right place—How nice, George thought, even the messengers to the gods have to be kept in line—shouting encouragements to them.

Then the kachinas began to dance. In the middle of the line, a few of the kachinas began to sing, a low, deep, muffled chant, a sound like a strong wind blowing far away in the mountains, and the other voices picked up the song until the entire line was singing, stamping their right legs to the song, the same way the kachina in his back yard, the Aholi, danced, the clack of the turtle-shell rattles driving the song. Then the first kachina at this end of the line, the smallest kachina at this end, a teenage boy perhaps, began to turn around slowly, still stamping, to face the opposite direction, while midway through his turn the next kachina in line began to turn around too, and then the next kachina, and the next kachina, one by one turning around to face the opposite direction, the kachinas turning inward toward the kachina women as the kachina women turned inward toward the kachina men, so that the two lines appeared to mesh like a set of gears, turning each other around, as if a wave swept down the two lines, spinning the kachinas in its wake. The kachinas faced the other direction for a while, as the kachina fathers circled them, sprinkled them with cornmeal, and spoke to them in low voices, then took their places in the center of the plaza again, watching the kachinas, watching as the first kachina at the far end of the line, the smallest kachina at that end, began to turn around slowly as the next kachina began to turn and the next kachina and the next, the wave sweeping back down the lines of kachinas until they were all facing George again, still singing in the low, deep, muffled voices, still stamping.

When the song was finished, the line of kachinas all turned to face the center of the plaza, the ends of the line curved inward to form a crescent. The kachina fathers took the old mattresses that had been left in the center of the plaza and placed them in front of the kachina men, and the kachina manas knelt on them, in front of the kachinas, facing them. In their hands the kachina manas carried large hollow gourds that they set upside down on the ground; the gourd acted as a resonator for a notched stick that each kachina mana placed on the gourd, over which she dragged a bone to produce a sound like the croak of a giant bullfrog. The deep scraping, the chorus of giant frogs, started slowly, seemingly at random, then picked up in tempo, together, and the kachinas began to sing again, a different song this time, each one stamping his right foot again, driving the song, but this time they shook the rattles in their hands in double time, the sound like some great determined machine. Toward the end of the song, the kachina manas stopped their scraping and stood up, the kachina fathers hurrying to get the line of mattresses out of their way, and finished the song by joining the kachinas in stamping their right feet. When the song was over, the kachina fathers led the kachinas to a new position at the end of the plaza, in front of George and the boys, and the dance started all over again, the kachinas in a line, all facing one direction, the kachina manas beside them, stamping and singing, until the slow wave started down the lines again.

The face of the kachina masks was smooth, curved, of course, as if the mask were made from a bucket mold, but without external features, the markings painted on; the face was divided down the center with a panel-like design on each side, like a small door on each side of the face that could be opened, so you could open it up and look in at the person inside, the panel on one side of the face painted coral on a turquoise background, the panel on the other side painted turquoise on a coral background. The eyes were long black slits painted near the top of each panel. On the brim of the mask, between the face and the tall tablet superstructure, white breast feathers hung out over the forehead like a fluffy white eyeshade, a layer of white clouds. The manas' masks covered only the face, not the entire head, a yellow mask with a thin veil of red hair covering the eyes; the manas' hair was done up in squash-blossom whorls, each mana having a tall white feather sticking up from the top of the mask and a rough dirty beard dangling down from the bottom.

The line of kachinas was directly below George; if he had leaned forward—something that George, of course, would never have done—he could have almost brushed his hand through the tall grass and feathers sticking up from the tablet superstructure on top of the nearest kachina. But something was wrong. *Here I am. Here is George Binns, the professor, the writer, watching a kachina dance. What's wrong with me?* What he was looking at didn't seem to be getting through to him, or seemed to be following the wrong circuitry, so that even though he was looking at it he didn't seem to be seeing it, as if the visual impressions were hitting his eyes all right but were rerouted so that the information, instead of going to his brain, was ending up in his right elbow, or, more likely, in the knot of muscles developing behind his neck. *Overload. In Case of Fire Break Glass. Eject.* He told himself to cut it out, this was no time for jokes. *Panic Button.* He tried to look harder. *Look at this. This is important. I've never seen anything like this in my life.* But instead of looking at the kachinas, he found himself scanning the crowds of spectators, the whites and Indians crowded around the plaza and along the rooftops, reading the legends on the T-shirts of the teenage girls: HANDLE WITH CARE. DO YA THINK I'M SEXY? DALLAS COWBOYS.

He shifted his position, moved his legs, adopted what he thought was a good professorial pose, his head cocked slightly, a meditative finger placed lengthwise against his lips; his shifting around disturbed the boys, who looked up at him, questioning him with their eyes; then they sat up, moved a little ways away from him, so they were no longer resting against him. *This is really happening. I'm really here. I'm really seeing this. Why aren't I really seeing this?* He forced himself to stare at the dance, repeated the details of what he was looking at to himself, tried to etch what he saw on his mind. *There's phallic symbols painted on the tablets sticking up from the top of the masks, phallic symbols, hell, those are penises, big black cocks with white heads, they're parading around with paintings of cocks on their heads, there's fox tails hanging down the back from their waists, like the Aholi in my back yard, are they supposed to be tails? Look at the way the tails wiggle, it's like the foxes were alive, it's like a line of very tall thin foxes, it's like a line of foxes all standing on their hind legs doing their own dance, how can those fat guys keep dancing like this and in all this heat too, they're fatter than I am, well not quite ha ha, I'd be ready to drop, who wants a god with a beer belly?* It was no good. He shook his head, trying to clear it, blinked four times. One of the kachina fathers, standing below him, standing in the arc of the kachinas, a hatchet-faced man about George's age, looked up at him, looked without expression, or with a severe blank expression, then looked away. *What's wrong with me? Why isn't this registering? I'll never see anything like this again. This'll make a great story to tell at parties. This'll make a great story.* George watched a vapor trail slice the sky toward the San Francisco Mountains, watched the trail blur and broaden and turn to gauze.

The kachinas moved to a third position, across the plaza from where they had started, and began to sing again. The boys sang along with them, tapping their feet to the rhythm, never missing any of the eccentric pauses. George cleared his throat, blinked, yawned, rubbed the ache in the back of his shoulders, shifted his legs around the other direction. Again the kachina father looked up at him, turned his head to look at him from the other end of the plaza, with the same blank hatchet-faced expression. George wondered if the man was David Lomanongye or if he divined why he was there; he wondered if the man thought he was a child molester. George had to go to the bathroom. On the far roof the eagle that had tried earlier to fly tried now to take a walk, out along the length of its perch, but it came again to the end of the rope and fell heavily on its chest; the bird flopped against the board half a dozen times, flapping its wings, screaming, until it backed up a ways and could stand up again, its wings extended, staring down open-mouthed at the knot around its legs. The eagle beside George winked at him, like a fellow conspirator, the white lid trailing slowly up the black jewel of the eye: *What do you think of that?*

Then the dance was over. The fathers led the kachinas from the plaza, and George waited to see them walk back up the trail outside the village, back up over the knoll, telling himself to watch carefully so he wouldn't miss any part of it, so that he'd have at least one clear-cut image to take back with him to tell people about—"When the kachinas walk over the top of the knoll outside the village, they look just a row of giant cornstalks"—but they didn't appear on the trail again. *They disappeared. They walked out of the village and stepped through a trap door in the rocks. They walked off the end of the mesa and rode away on a cloud. Maybe they weren't here in the first place. Maybe I'm not here. Don't be ridiculous.*

Then he heard them singing again and dancing again, from somewhere else in the village, but he was too tired, too worn out, to get up and climb down off the roof and find out where they were and what they were doing. He turned sideways to the edge of the roof and moved back a little and stretched out his legs, leaned back, propped himself up on his arms, then gave in to the tiredness, gave in to the weight of his body and lay back, lay down, folded his arms across his chest, enjoyed the heat of the tarpaper through his shirt on his aching back. He closed his eyes. He heard, far away, from someplace else in the village, the scraping of the hollow gourds, the rasp of the giant bullfrogs as the kachinas began the second figure of their dance; he heard, closer to him, the boys saying something to each other in Hopi, and then the sound of moving about. He opened his eyes: all he saw was murky blue, the limitless sky above him, then he raised his head. The two boys were on their knees peering over his stomach, over his folded arms, peering down at him, their eyes wide, inquisitive.

"Hey, Bahana, did you ever see *Star Wars?*"

6

The boys left; from his perch on the roof, George caught glimpses of them occasionally around the village, running between the houses, playing with their friends. For a while they disappeared into one of the houses, and Jimmy appeared later, sweeping the dirt in front of the house with an old broom. George stayed on the roof while the kachinas went back to the knoll and waited until they appeared again, over an hour later, and repeated the series of dances in the plaza, the songs and dances the same as the first time, returning to the knoll when they were through. But George had seen enough, he couldn't sit there any longer; it was nearly two o'clock, he had stayed through the heat of the noon-time; his skin was sunburned, his eyes were little more than slits from all his squinting, and he still had to go to the bathroom. He climbed down off the roof—when he tried to stand up, he found he could hardly move; his legs were so sore he was momentarily afraid that he wouldn't be able to negotiate the ladder ("Hey, Mom, there's a fat man stuck on the roof!")—and walked through

the narrow streets, circling the village, looking for shade; he asked
the few people he met if they knew a man named David Lomanongye—he only remembered after the boys had disappeared that
he hadn't asked them—but they lowered their eyes and shook
their heads and moved away. Once, when he rounded a corner,
he came upon Jerry and Jimmy with a group of other children,
but when he spoke to them and started to ask them about Lomanongye, the children all ran away.

Then the wind came up, strong and sudden, the eagles and hawks
on the rooftops shifting their positions, all at the same time, like
weather vanes, to face into it; and the dust, waves of dust and dust
devils, swept down the streets—it got into his eyes, stuck to the
sweat on his skin, crunched between his teeth. The Indian women
pulled their shawls up over their heads, huddling along like ghosts;
a chair scuttled on its own down a narrow alley between two
buildings. The light turned brown, then gray, though far to the
west, out of the range of the approaching rain, the desert and the
San Francisco peaks were still in sunlight. Veils of rain drifted
across the desert—he could see each storm, see where the rain
began and ended—the black curtains flashing with lightning. The
village grew dark, the air cool, cold even, against his skin, and
there didn't seem to be anyone left, the streets and plazas were
empty. He stayed close to the sides of the buildings and found
his way back to the opening in the wall, the stairway down to the
trails across the face of the bluff, where the other whites were
already hurrying back to their cars and trucks, stumbling and sliding on the trails. The wind snapped his sleeves and pant legs as if
they were wings; he was afraid the buffeting wind would knock
him off his feet, that he'd slip and lose his footing and fall, kill
himself on the rocks. The rain started when he was halfway down
the slope, hitting the dust around him like bullets, pockmarking
the loose earth, and he was soaked by the time he reached his car.
He was in the car before he looked back up the hill and saw,
dimly, through the rain-soaked windows and the steam covering
the inside of the glass, Jerry and Jimmy and their friends, sitting

on the wall in the driving rain, talking and swinging their legs, watching the tourist cars drive away.

And just as quickly as it arrived, the rain was gone; in fifteen minutes the sun was shining on the mesa again, though he could still see the storm, the drifting curtain of rain and lightning, making its way across the desert floor toward the mountains. As he backed out of the parking space and headed up the road, something, a stone, then another, hit his car. Were the boys throwing things at him? He kept on going. Back at the Cultural Center, he joined the lines of tourists waiting to use the rest rooms, then sat at the counter of the coffee shop again, this time to have a Hopi taco— a piece of fry bread covered with chili and lettuce and onions— for his late lunch.

After he ate, he felt better and walked across the parking lot into the picnic area beside the complex of buildings; the campers and Winnebagos that had been there in the morning were gone, and the shelters were empty except for one where an old Indian sat at the wooden table, tying feathers to a child-sized set of arrows. George considered going over to talk to him, to ask him if he knew Lomanongye, but decided against it; at this point he didn't care if he talked to Lomanongye or not. He sat at a shelter across the area from the old man, tucked away among some thick juniper trees so he could hardly see the Cultural Center or the road. It was getting close to five o'clock. He thought he'd lie down for just a few moments, to rest up before starting back to Flagstaff, and stretched out beside the table, balancing himself on the narrow bench. He fell asleep almost immediately.

He woke once, abruptly, to the sound of laughter, and turned his head to look across the way: the old man tying feathers to the arrows had been joined by another old Indian, this one with his arm around a plump young girl one-third his age, kissing her on the cheek as he talked to his friend, his hand draped over her shoulder and touching her breast. George adjusted his position on the bench. In another shelter, in another part of the picnic area, a family was cooking dinner—hamburgers, from the smell—

speaking French. To the west the sky showed the first signs of red, layers of red on red; overhead, from somewhere above the corrugated metal roof of his shelter, George heard a cry, the whistle of a nighthawk. He closed his eyes again, just for another moment, before getting up. When he woke again, it was dark, though the lights of the Cultural Center and parking lot beyond the trees provided some illumination, lit up the sky above the junipers. He looked over, but the old men were gone from the opposite shelter; he listened, but he couldn't hear the French family. As he turned his head, however, he noticed, under the edge of the table beside him, a pair of legs, someone sitting at the other bench across from him. George raised his head carefully. A small older man sat at the table, his hands folded in front of him, smiling at him, his white dress shirt glowing in the half-light.

7

"Good evening," the man said. "Did you know you grind your teeth in your sleep?"

"What?" George was so stiff he could hardly move; when he tried, he lost his balance on the bench and toppled off the side, landing on his hands and knees in the sandy dirt. The old man leaned forward to see him better, his smile unchanged.

"You grind your teeth in your sleep," the man went on as if nothing had happened. "I've always heard about people who did that, but I've never heard anyone do it before. It's very interesting. But I'd think it would hurt your jaw."

George, still on his hands and knees, felt his jaw; it was, in fact, sore, as if someone had hit him. Slowly, awkwardly, he got himself up, in stages, using the bench and table as props, and sat down, sidesaddle, across from his visitor. The man appeared to be in his sixties, though he might have been older, a small, diminutive man, almost a scaled-down version. George assumed he was an Indian, but his delicate features and round face, his small mouth and chin, his light complexion, seemed almost Oriental. His thin black hair was combed straight back over his head. In the darkness it was hard to see his eyes—his rimless glasses, like an accountant's, caught the glow from the Cultural Center and, with certain turns of his head, flashed—though he seemed friendly, almost jovial. The long sleeves of his dress shirt were rolled up past his forearms; the pants George had seen under the table looked as if they belonged to an old suit. The man studied George. George rubbed his eyes, trying to get awake.

"So. You came all this way to see an Indian dance. And then you left before it was over."

"It started to rain," George said groggily.

"Oh," the man said. "Well, that was one of the reasons for the dance, you know. The snake dance is even worse. It almost always rains during the snake dance, just like it's supposed to. It makes the Christians very unhappy."

"You mean they went on ahead and danced anyway? I thought maybe they called it off."

"You mean like a baseball game? No, I'm afraid not. You know what the BIA police say: the Sioux have enough sense to come in out of the rain, but not the Hopi. But then a lot of the BIA police here are Sioux, so they're prejudiced. You have to remember the Hopi are desert people, and desert people spend most of their lives trying to find water, not get away from it."

"I guess I never thought about it. . . ."

"And why should you? You probably live in a nice modern house with sprinklers all over the lawn, so all you have to do is go out and turn on a key and you get all the rain you want."

"Well, the sprinklers are only around the back terrace. . . ."

"There, you see?" the man said pleasantly. "So it's a different point of view when you have to go out and turn on the whole sky instead. Of course you wouldn't think about rain the same way the Hopi do, I wouldn't feel bad about that at all. Is that your car over in the parking lot?"

"I guess so; I mean I left it over there. It better still be over there. What—"

"That's what I figured. Yes, it's still over there. So tell me, how did you like the dance, what you saw of it? Is that your first one?"

"Well, yes. I liked it, it was . . . very impressive."

"Very impressive," the man smiled. "A dance is a strange thing. There are always some dancers who aren't dancing. There are always some dancers who aren't even watchers. And there are always some watchers who are actually dancing."

"It sounds like a riddle."

"Maybe you're right," the man laughed. "What I mean is, there are always some dancers who are only dancing because they want to use the dance, the power of the dance, to help them get something, a new car or a better job or a prettier girl, something like that. So they aren't really dancing. They're like the people watching who might as well be watching television or a movie; they're not really watching either. But there are always some people who are watching with the same spirit as the dancers who are dancing, so they're dancing too."

"Hmm," said George.

"You don't believe me," said the man.

"I'm not sure I understand it."

"I guess it does sound a little confusing. But the chiefs understand the difference, that's the important thing, and they always allow for it."

"How do they do that?"

"Let's say they keep it in mind. They know it all adds up, some way or other, dancers and not-dancers, watchers and not-watchers. That's why all people should be welcome to see the dances. A Hopi—a good Hopi, I mean—somebody who follows the Hopi Way, doesn't try to judge who's participating more. Only the dancer or the watcher knows that. Maybe, when you were asleep here in this shelter, you were dancing more than some of the dancers in the village." The old man opened his hands on the table, cupped his hands as if holding a globe to show George, but his palms were empty.

"Are you a Hopi?" George asked.

The old man laughed softly. "I was afraid you were going to ask me if I was a dancer. Yes, I'm Hopi."

A pickup truck drove into the picnic area and parked at the shelter across from them; a young Indian couple, college-age, got out. They looked around a moment, then spread a tablecloth over the wooden table and unpacked a picnic dinner from a wicker hamper, complete with long-stemmed wineglasses, china dishware, and a tape deck playing chamber music. The couple lit some candles and made a toast.

"Very romantic," George said.

"Just hope the police don't come along. They're not allowed to have spirits on the reservation, at least not that kind of spirits, no matter if that's Hearty Burgundy or Châteauneuf du Pape."

George looked at him.

"Surprised? I was in Europe during the war. Personally, I came to like the Bordeaux best, but everyone to his own taste. In Winslow or Flag, the choice usually comes down to Gallo or Thunderbird. My name is David Lomanongye; I heard you were looking for me."

"Yes, I was, I mean I am." George stretched his neck, tried to laugh. "How did you find me?"

"It's not a very big reservation, unfortunately. There's not too many places to go. The boys told me what kind of a car you were driving."

"Ernie Tewayumptewa, in Flagstaff, gave me your name. He's the one who suggested I talk to you."

"How is Ernie? I haven't seen him for a while."

"I don't really know him that well, I just went to see him about . . . some information."

"And he was the one who told you about the Home Dance today?"

"Yes."

"Well, it's good to know that Ernie still thinks of us up here on the mesas. What did Ernie tell you to see me about?"

George took a deep breath, thinking ahead what he wanted to say, wanting to get the tone of voice right. "There's a kachina in my back yard, not a carving, a real kachina, a man, I'm pretty sure he's an Indian, in a mask and costume. He showed up there a couple days ago."

"What kind of kachina is it, do you know?" He didn't seem surprised, he didn't seem anything at all.

"Aholi. The one with the tall blue pointed head and a cape."

"How did he get there?"

"I think he just came out of the woods. You see, we live on the other side of the San Francisco Mountains and—"

"And you think it's real?"

"Well, yes. Yes I do."

"Has anybody else see him?"

"Do you mean, am I hallucinating it?"

"The idea did cross my mind."

"Yes, other people have seen it. And he was still there when I left this morning. He seems to have dug up a shrine of some kind, and was doing some kind of a dance in front of it."

"Aholi doesn't usually dance. No one that I know of has ever seen him dance."

"Well, he's dancing now."

"Of course, we only see him when he comes to the villages for the ceremonies. Who knows what he does on his time off?" David Lomanongye smiled, proud of himself. "Did Ernie say it was Aholi?"

"He wouldn't come out to look at it. He said he was afraid it was a witch."

David Lomanongye nodded and puckered his mouth, as if that was a possibility.

"I asked Ernie who I could talk to up here about it, I wanted to find out if the mask and things were stolen."

"What if they are?"

"Well, I thought you'd want to know about it. I thought some-body would want to come down and get the stuff."

"And that's why you came all the way over here?"

"I didn't know what else to do. From what I've been able to find out, I thought these kachinas are pretty important to you people."

"It's interesting that you'd be so concerned," David Lomanongye said.

"Whether it's a witch or not, I thought somebody up here should know what's going on."

"Of course, it could be something else besides a witch."

"It didn't sound like any ceremony I've heard of, but I've only been reading—"

"No, it doesn't sound that way to me either. But then Aholi is the Old One of the Pikyas Clan, and I'm Coyote Clan."

George shook his head to show he didn't know what that meant.

"Each clan has its own rituals and duties. Most of the time they include the other clans and the entire village, at least some of the time, but once in a while they don't. On the migrations, the Coyote Clan always came last along the trail, to close the door. So far I've found that's pretty much the story of my life."

"So it could be a ceremony or something that only the Pikyas Clan knows about."

"It could be. Or maybe it really is a kachina, a real kachina, and only the gods know what he's doing there."

"Ha ha," said George. But David Lomanongye didn't laugh; he was smiling, but he always seemed to smile. "You're joking, of course."

"Why would I joke about a kachina?"

"But I mean, you don't really think . . . I mean kachinas are spirits. . . ."

"Yes."

"And this one is in the flesh."

"Did you touch him?"

"Well, er, no."

"So how do you know?"

"Ha ha," said George. "Well, because I know. This guy is real."

"So are spirits. Real."

"But not like this guy's real."

"What's real?"

"Ha ha," said George. "I think you're pulling my leg."

"You know, Christ at one point says an interesting thing about all this," David Lomanongye said, leaning forward, rubbing his hands together a little bit, his smile broader than ever. "I don't remember the exact wording, so I can't quote it to you, but he says something to the effect that, if the body came into being because of the spirit, then that's a wonder. But if the spirit came into being because of the body, then that's the wonder of wonder. That has some pretty far-reaching implications, if you think about it, particularly in regard to evolution."

"Which Christ are you talking about?"

"Jesus Christ."

"I'm sorry, but I've taught classes on the Bible as literature, and I've never read anything like that."

"Oh, this is in the Gospel of Thomas."

"Who?"

"Thomas. It's part of the Gnostic tradition of the early church. I guess most Bibles don't include that, do they?"

"No, er . . ."

"That's a pity. It was back in the early centuries of Christianity, when no one could make up their minds what kind of church they were going to have, much less what kind of Christ. Eventually, of course, the church as a political power won out over the more mystical forms, but there're a lot of interesting ideas in the things that got repressed."

"Well, I've heard of the Gnostics, of course; I've always meant to read—"

"There's another part, where Christ is telling the disciples the things they have to do to save their souls, and he tells them to 'become passers-by.' That's nice, isn't it? It's like the Gospel written by Camus. And there's another part that sounds like the Gospel according to Freud: 'If you bring out what is inside you, what is inside you will save you; but if you don't bring out what is inside you, what you don't bring out will destroy you.' You should read up on the early church some time; it's almost as weird as the Hopis."

David Lomanongye leaned back, watching George, his eyebrows arced above the top of his glasses; in the shadows, with his glasses catching the glow of the lights of the Cultural Center—the lenses murky, blanked out—George still couldn't see the man's eyes, to see if he was making fun of him or not, but David Lomanongye's smile seemed playful.

"Don't you think this is just a little peculiar?" George asked.

"How is that?"

"I come over here to learn about Indians, and you end up telling me about the history of Christianity."

"Ah, I'm sorry. I've made you uncomfortable."

"No, I didn't mean it that way. . . ."

"You'll have to forgive me. There's always some denomination or other trying to convert us, so I thought I better find out what the competition was talking about. I've also done a lot of reading about the Navajos, for that matter—what would you like to know about Monster-Slayer or the Changing Woman?"

"Have you read Freud and Camus too?"

"It was called the GI Bill. The government is always trying to give us things we don't want and take away the things we do. I thought I might as well get an education out of it. Sometimes I think I might have helped my village more if I'd taken another water pump instead."

George cleared his throat, stretched his neck away from his prickly collar. "Getting back to this kachina, what am I supposed to do with it?"

"Nothing, as far as I can see. You've got a kachina in your back yard. Very well. There's really nothing to be done about it."

"But somebody should do something, shouldn't they?"

"I suppose you could invite him indoors, if you wanted to. But it seems to me, if you feel strange about him being in your back yard, you'll feel even stranger with him sitting in your living room."

George strained in the darkness to read the man's face. "Look, I'm very serious about this."

"I am too," smiled David. "I'll be damned if I'd want to mess around with a kachina if I found him in my back yard. Those spirits are supposed to be incredibly strong, like Jacob wrestling with the angel." He pretended to be a wrestler, looking for an opening.

"Goddamn it!" George yelled, slamming his fist down on the table. "I'm trying to do what's right!"

The young couple at the other shelter stopped eating to look over at them.

"Then you've got yourself a real problem, don't you?" David Lomanongye said calmly.

They sat in silence for a couple of minutes, staring at one another across the dark table.

"The thing is," David Lomanongye said finally, "it's up to you what you do about it. And it's up to Aholi why he's there and what he's going to do. You say he's there, so he's there. He must have a reason for it. So that's up to him. That's the Hopi Way. I'd just leave him alone."

"Well, that's all very well and good if you live up here on this reservation, but it's a little bit different down there in the world. Suppose a television station gets hold of this story, or a newspaper—they could, you know. You mean to tell me you wouldn't care if pictures of the kachina got splattered all over the six o'clock news? Whether the kachina's real or not, whether somebody's supposed to have the mask or not, you mean to tell me that you wouldn't care if carloads of tourists started poking around it? I find that very hard to believe. And here I am, trying to help you people out, and all I'm getting is the runaround."

David Lomanongye looked at him for a while; his smile was a little more serious, but not much. "You really are concerned about it, aren't you?"

"Maybe I just want to get him out of my back yard. For your sake, for my sake. Look, can't you do something to help me with this, please?"

"Shit. You must have read that somewhere."

"What?"

David Lomanongye got up from the bench; he was shorter, no, slighter than George expected. "You must have read that: if you ask a Hopi to help you, a Hopi can't say no."

He shook George's hand, grasping only the fingers, his smile as pleasant and intractable as before. Then he turned around and was gone, into the darkness of the juniper trees.

George continued to sit there awhile, staring off into the darkness as if he expected David Lomanongye to return again, more puzzled than ever. Across the picnic area, the young couple blew out their candles and, taking the tape deck with them, climbed into the bed of the pickup truck; the boy and girl sat there a moment, talking about something, then they pulled their jerseys up over their heads and disappeared. George got up heavily and walked back through the junipers to the parking lot. There were only a few cars left in the lot, the floodlights from the Cultural Center and on the light poles overhead still burning, the acres of lighted, empty pavement stretching away into the desert night. In the hot night air, the only sounds were the hum of the lights and the air conditioners at the motel, and the beating of wings: a dozen nighthawks, nightjars, circled over the parking lot, an aerial circus, circled out of the darkness canopied right above the light poles and into the clouds of insects that danced around the globes, then swerved away again, the birds whistling, flying across the parking lot at times only a few feet above the ground before they banked and climbed again, flying—George stood there, alone under the lights, entranced, alone on the concrete expanse—only a few feet away from him, accepting him after a while as not a danger but only as another object not to fly into, flapping sweeping whistling around him, the wide black button eyes fixed on him nonetheless as they passed.

8

It was after midnight when he got back to Flagstaff, back home. The front of the house was dark, as he expected it to be; he sat in the car for a few moments after turning off the engine and the lights, listening to the car tick in the silence, holding on to the wheel as if he were still driving, still feeling the drive in his shoulders and neck. Then he got out, stretched, rubbed the back of his neck as he walked wearily around the side of the house. The lights from the kitchen spilled out across the back yard, the glow ending just beyond the dropoff of the terrace wall; in the kitchen window, Mary Olive was perched on her stool at the counter, talking away, to herself or to the radio or maybe to the register—maybe she had forgotten he wasn't there, maybe she was talking away at him, had been talking away at him for hours, thinking he was upstairs in his study and just not answering; maybe she was that drunk— holding forth in one of her monologues. George shook his head, sighed, and walked to the end of the terrace.

At the end of the field, in the moonlight—the field blue in the light, lighter than the sky, against the black of the hillside and the trees—he could make out the dim figure of the kachina, the dim glow of its head and cape, huddled on the bank of the wash beyond the fence. That at least made him feel a little better: after driving all the way to Hopi, after talking to David Lomanongye, he would have felt foolish if he had come home and found that the kachina had already gone away on its own. Not that anything was apparently going to come from all his efforts. He turned around and looked at the house, the black pine trees looming in front of it, at Mary Olive, underneath the lower branches, sitting in the kitchen window. And he felt a sudden, surprising wave of affection for her. Affection, or maybe it was sympathy. She was an intelligent, thoughtful woman, he had always respected her for that, it had been one of the things, her intelligence, maybe the main thing, that attracted him to her in the first place. He thought of what she had said the night before, that he had broken her heart. He clucked softly—*cluck cluck cluck.* Still, it couldn't have been easy for her, this last year, coming here, leaving New York and her friends and her job, her career. He was sure that's what was bothering her. *Cluck.* As he watched she held up her wineglass, making a toast about something, laughing; a wisp of hair had escaped from her bun and fallen across her forehead and she brushed it back, lifted it back into place, a gesture he had seen her perform a thousand, ten thousand times. He smiled to himself. *Cluck cluck.* She would get a kick out of hearing about his adventures with the Indians; of all the people he knew, or had ever known, for that matter, she would understand how he felt about it, the incongruity of his being there in the first place, his awkwardness and uneasiness. He walked toward the house—*cluck cluck cluck*—and as he watched she got up off her stool and turned around and Don walked into her arms.

"Well, here's Leatherstocking back from the Indian wars," Mary Olive said as George walked in the back door. She stepped away from Don, reached for her wineglass, and raised it in a little toast.

Don stood with his arms out, around the space where she had just been, looking dumbfounded at George.

"Is everything all right?" George said quickly. "Hello, Don."

"Everything is wonderful," Mary Olive said. "Why wouldn't it be?"

"Don's here. I thought maybe there had been some trouble."

"You mean maybe I called the police again, or attacked the kachina?" Mary Olive said. "No, O mighty Leatherstocking, there's no trouble, no trouble at all. The fort is secure, the watch is set, and the fires are banked for the night. But I think I'm going to have to get you a better name than Leatherstocking, somehow it doesn't fit."

She drained her glass, looked in turn at George, then Don, then back at George, worked her shoulders, wiggled her hips, and refilled her glass from the jug of Mountain Red; she sat again on her stool, crossed her legs and folded her arms, and watched them, as if ready to see what would happen next. Don stood where he was, beside the sink, his arms only gradually returning, lowering, together, as if they were in a fixed position like those of a mechanical man, to his sides. George blinked three times, gave an exaggerated smile, and went over to the sink to wash his hands.

"Excuse me, Don."

Don didn't move, didn't seem to hear him; he was staring at Mary Olive.

"Excuse me?"

"Yes, sure, of course," Don croaked finally and stepped aside.

George washed his hands, rubbed some cold water on his face and the back of his neck—his skin, on his arms, the back of his hands and neck, his face, was tightening up with sunburn; he needed to get some lotion on it soon. He dried himself carefully, patting his sore skin, on the towel beside the cabinet and turned around again, blinked again, smiling, ready to join the conversation.

"Leatherfoot," Mary Olive said. "No, that sounds like a skin disease."

"Are you drinking, Don?" George said, getting a glass from the cupboard and filling it with ice from the freezer tray.

"Where were you?" Don rasped as he shook his head, his voice barely audible.

"At Hopi. I told you I was going yesterday." He poured himself a glass of bourbon from the bottle beneath the counter and sat at the kitchen table, on the other side of the counter from Mary Olive, poking the ice in his drink with his middle finger. He looked at Don and blinked, smiled. "It was very interesting."

"And you're just getting home now?"

"Just now. It's about a two- or three-hour drive over there, by the time you get up on the mesas and all." He judged his drink was cold enough and raised his glass. "Cheers."

"Hooray," Mary Olive said from her perch above and behind him, on the other side of the counter.

"To a good friend," George said, "who would even come over in the middle of the night to make sure things were all right while I'm gone."

"Leatherpants," Mary Olive said, taking out a cigarette. "No, that makes you sound like one of the gay boys from Frisco."

A cloud of blue smoke descended around him as Mary Olive lit the cigarette. He sat, watching his finger poke at the ice cubes, then looked at Don.

"Are you feeling all right?"

"Yes, I'm all right," Don said, barely a whisper.

"You look a little upset or something."

"I was surprised to see you come walking in the back door, that's all." Don looked at Mary Olive.

"Oh, I walked around the house to see if the kachina was still down there. And he is." He smiled, blinked. "Wait till I tell you about—"

"You've also been known to come in the side door too," Mary Olive said.

"Well, yes," George said. "What difference does it make?"

"I was just surprised to see you come in any door," Don said.

"You would have been more surprised to see him come in a window," Mary Olive said.

"Not by much," Don said.

"What is all this fuss about how I came in the house?" George said, laughing, waving his hands beside his head, pretending to get mad. "This is a boring conversation. Grrrr. I want to tell you what all I saw today."

"I'm surprised because I thought you were back already." Don looked at Mary Olive again. "I thought you were upstairs asleep."

"Oh," George said. "Then I guess that would surprise you." A blue cloud descended on him again; he waved his hand.

" 'Surprise' is not the word," Don said.

"Leatherbritches," Mary Olive said, slapping the flat of her hand on the counter. "That's it! The brave Indian fighter Leather-britches. That has just the right amount of panache and paunch for you, George."

"If you say so," George said.

"I say so," Mary Olive said.

"Here's to it, then." George raised his glass. "Here's to good friends."

"Here's to the human heart," Mary Olive said.

"You two deserve each other," Don said and walked across the room and out the back door.

Mary Olive, still perched on her stool, tried to curtsy as he passed, spreading her arms and bending forward, but she lost her balance and almost fell headfirst across the room. George got up and followed Don to the door, watched his friend walking across the back yard, his figure disappearing into the darkness, out of the glow from the windows, toward the woods, called after him, "Hey, Don, come on back, I didn't tell you what I saw in Hopi!" But Don kept on going . . .

. . . *while on a warm, clear, moonlit night outside of Flagstaff, Arizona, in the small valley separating his house from that of George and Mary Olive, Don Pike stands in a grove of young aspen trees, their trunks glowing white in the shadows of the surrounding taller pines, their leaves shimmering silver against the stiff black branches of the ponderosas, stands pulling at the trunk of a small four-foot-tall pon-derosa that grows among the grove of aspens, pulls at it, gets it down to a thirty-degree angle and stomps on the trunk trying to break it or pull the roots from the ground, something, the branches shuddering like the sound of a dozen dance rattles, the noise and violence sending dozens of small creatures scurrying through the underbrush and waking the magpies in the branches overhead, his hands burning from the coarse bark and sticky with sap, the smell of pine all around him like a scream, hacking and coughing and barely able to breathe from the pain in his throat, clenching and unclenching his teeth She did that on purpose,*

*she knew he'd be coming home then, she set me up that fucking bitch
. . . while on the other side of the valley, in her bedroom, which used to
be their bedroom, in the bed her husband made from slabs of cherrywood,
Sally Pike puts down a copy of* New Perspectives on the Pueblos *and
thinks about Michelangelo's statue of David, of African chiefs
with sticks of bamboo tied up in front of their stomachs like twelve-
inch erections, of peasants in the paintings of Brueghel with their
codpieces sticking out, of Don, thinking, How did that Indian girl in
the myth ever masturbate with a feather and give birth to a monster?
A feather wouldn't rub hard enough . . . while on a mesa top in the
center of Arizona, David Lomanongye stands on the roof of a kiva,
looking up at the moon through the twin poles of the end of the ladder
sticking up against the sky, looks out over the edge of the mesa at the
blue-gray desert spread below him in the moonlight, at the twin dots
moving across the desert floor, headlights going someplace, wondering
what else is out there moving around in the blue-black night, then looks
down through the opening into the kiva, into the underground room
lit only by a few candles, where a group of old men sit around the room
on the stone banquettes, a few smoking ceremonial pipes, a few tying
prayer sticks, but most of them just sitting, looking off into the shadows,
waiting for him to arrive to tell them what the fat Bahana told him,
and sighs and takes a deep breath and starts down the ladder, thinking,
White Man speaks with forked tongue, as they say in the movies, but
no, that white man was too naïve to be making it up . . . while in her
kitchen, perched on her stool, Mary Olive Binns stares at the blank
window in front of her, her shoulders sagging, her forehead so heavy
with wine she can hardly hold her head up, thinking about the time
she went to John Updike's house for dinner when she was editor of* The
Little Review, *and she didn't remember what she said, didn't think
she had said anything special, and Updike leaned over to her and said,
"You're a writer, aren't you? And if you're not, you should be. You
have a writer's way of saying what needs saying," the happiest evening
of her life, thinking, The look on Don's face when George came in, he
knew, he's not dumb, he was never dumb. He only came over in the first
place because he couldn't sleep; he only came over, ever, because I was
the only one around. Why can't they see me for what I am? Why can't*

anyone see I'm special? . . . while upstairs in their bedroom, George Binns, in his blue pajamas with the small crown on the pocket over his heart, lies in bed, reading, waiting for the alcohol to wear off a little so he can get to sleep, his mind a kaleidoscope of images, a row of fox skins all in a row, standing on their hind legs dancing in the dust, a row of cornstalks coming over a distant knoll—I forgot to tell Mary Olive, my best line and I forgot it—sitting in the shadows of the picnic shelter, in the darkness, across from David Lomanongye, his glasses picking up the glow of the distant lights, the lenses flashing, blank, thinking, I told him "This guy is real" and he said "So are spirits real" and I said "But not like this guy's real" and he said "What's real" and I laughed and he said "Did you touch him?" and I said "I think you're pulling my leg," thinking, That was really strange today, I'll bet I can get a poem out of it

> *The row of fox skins shuffled in the dust*
> *As the cornstalks sang their—*

Oh well I'll try tomorrow morning, I'm too tired now, and plumps up the pillow under his head, adjusts his glasses midway down his nose so he can see lying down, and reads. . . .

9
—

WHAT THE SHRIKE SAW

When Shrike flew up through the hole in the sky, through the *sipapu* from the Under World into the present world, he didn't think this new place was anything special, and certainly nothing to write home about. There were hills and trees and animals, just as there were down below in the Third World—though up here there didn't seem to be a waste-disposal problem, at least not yet. But this Fourth World was dark and murky, and there was an unpleasant sulphurous smell that hung over everything. All in all, it didn't seem a particularly hospitable or agreeable place to live, especially considering all the trouble it took to get up here. But maybe the Hopi would like it. One thing he had learned a long time ago—about the time he thought he had discovered shish kebab by learning how to skewer a chipmunk or a sparrow on a twig, only to find out that people called him the butcher-bird on account of it—was that there's no accounting for taste.

When he thought he had seen enough, he turned around and headed back toward the *sipapu*. But as he flew through the gloom, he noticed some footprints on the ground, some very strange footprints. They were shaped like a human being's but they were much larger and disproportionately long, almost as if someone was walking around on boards. He decided he better investigate to find out just who this Big Foot was.

Shrike followed the footprints across a vast dark plain until he saw a glow on the horizon. As he got closer, he saw that the glow came from a ring of fire that surrounded some fields of corn, beans, watermelon, and squash. The air was heavy with smoke, and the flames sparked and flared up into the black sky, almost singeing his tail feathers as Shrike flew over. In the center of the ring was a huge bonfire, along with a supply of wood and coal; a man, the keeper of the fire, sat nearby on a rock. Shrike flew around the fire a couple of times, trying to get a look at the man's face, but the man kept his back turned and his shoulders hunched up to hide his head, so that he appeared not to have a head at all. The only thing Shrike could tell about him was that the man was very large. Then Shrike realized that it wasn't a rock the man was sitting on; the man had apparently taken his head from his shoulders and was sitting on that.

Shrike didn't like the looks of this.

Finally the man said, "Hey, you there, bird. What's all this fluttering about? Settle down."

Shrike flew down and sat on the edge of a piñon log, but kept his distance just in case.

"I didn't mean to disturb you," Shrike said. "I was just wondering what was going on with all these fires."

"You must be new around here," the man said, his back still turned.

"Well, yes, actually. It's a little hard to explain. You see, I'm from the Under World. . . ."

The man turned around then, and Shrike saw that his head was on his shoulders after all. In fact, the man was exceptionally handsome. His face was painted on both sides with two lines of specular iron from the bridge of his nose to his cheeks; he wore four strands of turquoise around his neck, and large turquoise ear pendants. What he was sitting on was a mask, a very hideous mask. It was made from rabbit skins, with large eyes and a gaping mouth; the entire mask was covered with blood. Shrike tried to appear nonchalant, as if he saw such things every day.

"You're the first one ever to see me without my mask," said the man. "You caught me at an awkward moment."

"Sorry 'bout that," said Shrike, wondering if words were sufficient at this point. He wished he had remembered to bring some prayer feathers.

"Just what are you doing up here anyway?"

"Well, things aren't going so well down below. You know, your basic problems: crime, waste, pollution. And the Hopi were wondering if they could come up here to live."

The man sighed, as if he expected the neighborhood to go to hell sooner or later. But he seemed resigned.

"You can see for yourself how I live up here," the man said, looking away from the fire into the gloom. "I don't have very much, only my digging stick and a few odds and ends, and there's not much to do except a lot of hard work. But living this way is good for the spirit—builds character and all that. If your friends the Hopi wouldn't mind living like this, they're welcome to come up and join me."

"I'll tell them," Shrike said, thinking the Hopi might just be crazy enough to do it. The man stood up and put on his mask.

"Now, if you'll excuse me, there's work to do. Got to keep the home fires burning, you know."

"What's your name, masked man?"

"They call me Masau'u. This is my world up here—or at least I'm in charge of it. The Caretaker, you might say. The Guardian."

"Any charge for living up here? You know what I mean: hidden expenses, surprise taxes, that sort of thing?"

Masau'u tilted his head and thought a moment; drops of blood fell from the mask and hissed in the fire. "No, none that I can think of. I guess the only thing that's different up here is that everybody has to die at some time or other. Everybody, that is, except me. That's part of my job too. I tell you when that time comes."

"Okay, great, I'll tell them. And thanks again."

Masau'u gave a little wave and went off to tend his fires. Shrike noticed that at times the man looked like a glowing skeleton, at times like a burning bush. Odd fellow, he thought as he flew back to the *sipapu,* anxious to tell the Hopi the news. Now all they had to do was find out what "to die" meant.

10

George put the manuscript down on the floor beside the bed and swung his legs over the side and sat for a moment, a brief, exaggerated (he was trying to be comical, amusing, but only for himself, there was nobody else there) look of disgust on his face, disgusted with himself for not taking care of these things before he got settled; then he patted his knees three times, pat pat pat, priming himself, to get himself rolling, and got up, slipped his feet into his slippers, and went into the bathroom. Standing in front of the sink, in front of the mirror on the medicine chest, he rolled his pajama sleeves up his arms and got the Caladryl lotion out of the medicine chest—third shelf, in the back corner, behind the VapoRub and Sayman Salve—and covered his arms and the backs of his hands, the back of his neck and his face, remembering, with the smell, the way it tightened against his skin as it dried, his skin feeling as if someone were taking a tuck in his loose edges, the sunburns when he was a boy. He padded back to the bedroom and sat on the edge of the bed again, waiting for the lotion to dry completely, his skin becoming hard as if he were encased in or growing a pink shell—*One night Gregor Binns sat on the edge of his bed and found himself transformed into an enormous bug*—still in his slippers, staring down at Don's manuscript on the floor, his hands on his knees, patrician, thinking it over, then nodded to himself, once, having made up his mind, and padded back out of the bedroom and down the hall, down the stairs, as quietly as possible. He peeked around the doorway to the kitchen: Mary Olive sat at the counter, her head drooping as if she were asleep. George tiptoed down the hall and out the front door, then walked around the side of the house, making a wide circle to avoid the kitchen windows, down the field toward the wash. As he approached the fence, the kachina stirred, turned his head toward him, stood up. On the bank was the plate of corn Mary Olive had brought down the day before; the ears were scattered around the plate; one ear lay on the ground nearby, as if picked at by birds or small animals. In the moonlight, the Aholi's tall blue head was ghostly, and the same color as George's pajamas.

"I didn't mean to disturb you," George said softly. "I didn't know if you'd be asleep or not."

The kachina looked at him curiously, a bit sideways. *No, I'm not asleep. What happened to you?*

"Oh." George looked down at his hands; the Caladryl lotion on the back of his hands and arms glowed purple; he could imagine how his face looked. He laughed. "I got sunburned. I . . . took a little trip."

I was wondering where you were today.

"I had some things to take care of." He thought of telling the kachina where he'd been, of telling him about the Home Dance and his talk with David Lomanongye, but thought better of it. "It's a beautiful night, isn't it?"

The kachina looked around stiffly, having to turn his entire body, then looked back at George, the two black lines of the eyes focused on him. The feathers on the peak of the mask stirred in the breeze, a slight breeze that George didn't feel. *What is it, George? What do you want?*

"Ahem. Well, I know this is going to sound a little strange," George said, stretching his neck. Then he hitched up his pajama pants around his stomach and climbed through the rails of the fence; the kachina backed up a few steps down the edge of the wash to give him room, the turtle-shell rattle on his leg clacking softly. Once he was on the other side, George worked the loose pajama bottoms into their proper position again, straightening the inseam of the crotch away from his genitals; he felt the breeze for a second, like a whisper against his skin, reminding him just how flimsy the pajamas were. "There's something I'd like to do, just to prove a point. Okay?"

I guess.

"Would you mind holding still, for just a moment?"

The kachina cocked his head.

George laughed uneasily, coughed, then walked over to the edge of the bank and stood in front of the Aholi, the closest he had been to him (thinking: *Christ, this guy is big*). Up close, the kachina smelled musky. Slowly, carefully, George reached out and, slowly, carefully, with one purple finger, touched the kachina's arm beneath the cloak, felt the solid muscle of his upper arm underneath the blanket-cape. Aholi watched him, watched the slow, careful purple finger touch him and move away again.

"That's all," George said, smiling, feeling foolish. "That's all I wanted to do. Ha ha. Thank you."

He turned around to go back through the fence but froze as the kachina stamped his foot, one loud hard crack; he remembered, only then, something that Mrs. Jenkins had told him, something about people who died because they touched a kachina when they weren't supposed to. He turned around. Aholi walked up the edge of the wash and stood in front of him, towered over him, the kachina nearly eight feet tall, the ghostly head looking at him against the blue-black sky.

"I didn't mean anything," George said meekly.

The kachina stared at him for a moment. Then he shifted his staff to his left hand and, the kachina's own hands painted white with rows of wavelike designs across the backs, slowly, carefully, reached out with one white glowing finger and, in the same place on the upper arm where George had poked the kachina, the kachina poked George. Aholi nodded once. *How do you like that?*

As Aholi turned around and went back down the bank to his rock, George erupted with laughter, only to stop just as quickly when he noticed, far up on the hillside, a light, a small burst of flames.

"Look at that!"

The kachina looked at him, then shifted around so he could see where George was pointing. The flames, the size perhaps of a small bush, flared up and then died down again, becoming just a faint glow among the darkness of the trees; in a few seconds it was gone completely.

"What the hell is that?" George said. "That's the third night in a row somebody's been up there."

George walked over to the edge of the bank for a better look, took a step or two down the bank, looking up at the woods, but the Aholi moved in front of him, held his staff in front of him, blocking George's way, shaking his head.

No.

"What's wrong?"

The kachina stared at him fiercely. *Just no.*

"I wasn't going up there."

The kachina continued to stare at him, his staff raised in front of him, until George went back up the wash, went away from the edge; then he relaxed a little.

"What's going on around here?"

Just go to bed, George.

George laughed a little, adjusted his pajama bottoms around his stomach, harrumphed. But the kachina didn't go back to sit on his rock beside the shrine until after George climbed through the fence again and started up the hill toward the house.

FOUR

1

When he woke the next morning, his hands were raw and sore—and smelled of pine; he rolled over on his back, wondering where in the hell that came from. Then he remembered standing in the woods in the middle of the night, after he had left George and Mary Olive's, trying to pull up the small pine tree. Don looked up, above the bed, at the ceiling of the cabin, the underside of the roof; the morning sunlight came in through the windows and the screen door, the light golden on the undersides of the vigas, highlighting the round shaved timber above his head. And for a moment he was on the ceiling of the room, as if he were tied to the viga or perhaps the viga himself, looking down, looking down on the morning sunlight falling across a blond girl's leg, looking down at the room and the stacks of manuscripts and piles of boxes around the floor until he was once again lying on the bed, blinking, trying to get awake.

My life is a dream, he thought: not an original thought, that. We are the dreams that stuff is made of, and our sleeps are rounded with a little life.

I am an old man, a teacher, taking solace in other men's words. I am a dying man.

Maybe he should cut his hair and go begging, he thought: that was what the old men of India did, those who were searching for spiritual enlightenment in the face of death, those who had come to believe, for whatever reasons, that the riches and pleasures and beauties of this world are all illusions, all a dream, who had come to believe that the substance of the world is somewhere else: they cut their hair, shaved their heads and their beards, and set out to live on the road, to spend their few remaining years begging, with only a robe and a staff (and maybe a tin cup? did the robe have pockets?) as they held out their hands to this world of dreams to see if the dream world would give them enough hard reality to live on another day. It was supposed to be, in India, a respected and honored way to finish one's life. But it wouldn't work in America: the cops would arrest him for vagrancy, and high-school kids would beat him up for being a hippie. For a moment he pictured himself, sitting on a guard rail beside a highway, outside a Midwestern town at dusk, with a full white beard and long white hair, wearing three or four overcoats, one on top of another, looking at a scrap of newspaper as he tried to figure out which town he was coming to next or which town he had just left, a shopping bag with all his earthly possessions beside his worn-down boots, waiting for his next ride to anywhere. No, that wouldn't work: he wouldn't be able to decide which books to take with him. Maybe he could pull a little red wagon behind him, filled with books, so that he could sit on the guard rails and read Chaucer, Shakespeare, Wyatt—no, he was dreaming again.

I am a silly old man.

I am a silly dying man.

I am a silly dead man—if I keep on thinking like this.

He swung his feet over the side and sat on the edge of the bed. The bare wood floor was cool beneath his feet even though the room was hot, the air hot against his body. He was naked. It's a pleasure, a privilege to feel such things—heat, cold, air, floor— he told himself; there's going to be an eternity without them; as long as I can feel them I'm not dead yet. He danced a little pretend-jig as he sat there, lifting his legs, heel and toe, heel and toe. He could still smile.

Lord Krishna says a man dances four times in his life, he re- membered. As a boy he dances at the wonder of the world; as a youth he dances for love; in middle age he dances in the search for the meaning of his life; in old age he dances to show his courage in the face of death. Or something like that; that was close enough. Or there was Shiva, god as destroyer and restorer too, whose dance

itself is the world. The cosmos as discothèque. The only pictures
he had ever seen of Hindus dancing were the yogis, who hotfooted
it across a bed of coals, and that was more of a run than a dance.
He thought of George, at the kachina dance over at Hopi: he
hadn't listened when George wanted to tell him about it, and he
probably should have. He pictured George, large and ponderous,
standing by the stone wall of one of the houses, in a crush of
Indians, nodding his head in time with what he thought was the
rhythm of the dance. George tried; George was very trying. He
thought of George, hotfooting it across a bed of hot coals—"Oo,
ee, yikes!"

Yes, he could still smile.

George didn't need a bed of coals: he had Mary Olive.

That was no way to talk about a friend. Or a friend's wife.

A friend's wife, who also happened to be your ex-lover.

Ex-lover; it sounded so much better than it was.

Didn't everything?

I am a dying man. I am a dead man. I am trying the words on
for size, the idea, to see how they fit.

Don't kid yourself, old son: there ain't no way on earth you're
going to know how it feels not to feel. No way in hell, hah!

"You might feel different about it in a few days," Doc Harvey
had said, leaning back in his big leather chair.

"No," Don said, putting his shirt back on.

"I'd like to try the radiation first, but if you're opposed to that,
we could go on ahead with chemotherapy."

"I told you I don't want any of it."

"Will you tell me why?"

"Because what difference will it make? I mean as far as time."

Doc Harvey put his fingertips together, resting them against his
mouth. "As your doctor or your friend?"

"Both."

"Maybe a couple years. Maybe."

"And without it?"

"It's hard to say. I don't know how strong you are, or how
ornery."

"Like it is, Doc." Don buttoned his cuffs, still standing.

"Maybe six months. Maybe a year. Maybe less, I don't know."

"That bad."

"It just started hurting in your throat. Probably because of the blow. But I'm afraid it's pretty much all through you."

"Ravaged."

"What?"

"Nothing." Don turned away from him, to tuck his shirttail in his pants, then turned back, sat down across from him. "I'd much rather spend six months with the pain I've got than doped up on drugs. I don't want to be one of those guys whose hair starts falling out, who wastes away to a skeleton while trying to pretend everything's going to get better. Hubert Humphrey—Christ! I don't want to spend my last days on earth feeling like I'm going to throw up all the time."

"The pain's going to get worse. A lot worse. And it's going to hurt more places."

"If it gets too bad toward the end, maybe then you can give me something to help it. It's the knowledge of it, what's happening to me, that's going to be hard to live with. But I don't want to kid myself about it. And I don't want to have what's happening to me hidden from me by drugs. I want to go out with a little dignity. I want to know what's happening, all the way to the end."

Doc Harvey swiveled away from him a little, looked away from him, thinking, his fingertips a small chapel in front of his face. "What's happening to you now is just the extreme of what's been happening to you, to everybody, all along. Death is part of the normal course of events, part of the process of being alive. A building could fall on you tomorrow, a car wreck, a heart attack. A lot of people, probably most people, don't prepare themselves for it, because no one ever thinks it can happen to them. What's happening to you is terrible, I say that as your friend, there's no question of that. But if there can be a plus side to such a disease—I'm inclined to think everything has a plus and a minus side in this world, though I'll admit sometimes it's hard to see it—at least a person has the knowledge beforehand of what's going to happen, you can prepare yourself, put things in order, make your peace. I've seen some patients reach a degree of serenity, almost joy, knowing they were going to die soon, every moment they were alive a jewel. I've seen others go crazy with frustration and rage."

"I think we spend our entire lives trying to keep from going crazy, from all the disappointments at all the things that don't work out the way we want them to. And I think we spend our entire lives trying to hide from ourselves what the organism, just like any other organism, any living thing, knows all along, that we're terrified of dying, that we're frantic to keep from ceasing to be. I don't want to take any make-believe cures. I don't want to hide anything from myself."

"I understand that." Doc Harvey swiveled back. "And I respect that. But, as I say, it might look a little different to you in a couple days. After you talk it over with Sally and think about it some more. . . ."

"I'm not going to talk it over with Sally."

"She has a right to know."

"I don't want her to know, at least not yet. I don't want her fussing, I don't want her tears, I don't want . . . I just don't want to go through all that, not yet."

Doc Harvey looked at him for a moment, studied him over the spire of his fingertips. "Well, whatever your situation is with Sally, I think it's one of the first things you'll want to put in order."

2

His hands were so sore it was difficult to close them; he flexed them several times, then got up and went into the bathroom, still naked, walking like a hunter, a small lean wiry man, his pubic hair as white as his beard, to wash and run cold water over his hands. He thought again of pulling at the pine tree, trying to uproot it. And thought of Taos. Of the clowns at Taos Pueblo, the *chiffonetes,* on San Geronimo Day, the saint's feast day, dressed only in loincloths and moccasins, their hair tied up in corn husks, their bodies painted in broad black and white stripes, their faces in black and white stripes, with white radiating lines and black raccoonlike masks around the eyes, the Black Eyes, they called them, the time he took Sally there while they still lived in New Mexico, while they (go on ahead, say it:) were still in love (he had been showing off when they first got to the pueblo for the feast day: he had called the clowns koshares because that's what they were called at the other Rio Grande pueblos, until Sally said something about koshares and a boy, an Indian boy, beside her sneered, "They're not koshares, they're *chiffonetes,*" and Sally looked at him, at Don, bewildered and almost scared until he explained it to her—"It's a generic term," he said; the Indian boy looked at him as if he had just blasphemed—and Sally nodded and smiled and was reassured again); of the fat clown who sat at the base straddling the pole, the forty-foot pine log that had been stripped and shaved until it was almost white, shiny, his legs on either side of it, the pole sprouting out of his crotch as if it were the largest erection in the world, the base so wide that he couldn't get his arms around it though it tapered down as it neared the top, staring up at the height of the pole, at the body of the deer and the sacks of groceries and bread tied at the top, waiting at the top for him or someone to climb up and distribute the goods for the feast. Don thought of the teenage boy who finally succeeded in climbing to the top of the forty-foot pole; now there was somebody whose hands had a right to be sore.

He put his hands under the cold water and held them there, looking out the window. At the edge of the woods, a squirrel hugged the trunk of one of the ponderosas, holding on with all four feet, clicking about something, bottom side up. Don splashed some of the cold water on his face and through his beard, then wiped his hands and face as he walked back into the main room of the cabin, taking the towel with him, wiping his hands absently, wiping the then damp towel behind his neck and down over his naked body, as he looked around the room for a few moments, his eyes coming to rest on the Cézanne reproduction on the wall, the painting, done by Cézanne when he was an old man, of the pines at Aix. Don threw the towel down on the unmade bed and got dressed.

She had called him her teacher then—he was her teacher, of course, her professor, but she didn't mean it that way, or, rather, she meant it differently, she meant it as more than just a teacher; she took special pride in the term, as if she thought of him as her teacher ("master" would seem to have been a better word) before anything else, before either professor or lover or husband or just Don. At the time he was flattered. At the time it seemed enough, it seemed more than enough: a self-proclaimed disciple, and a pretty one at that, made him feel godlike. Made him feel loved. He remembered walking in the plaza at Taos, the plaza filled with booths of Indians selling jewelry and pottery and kachina dolls; and holding hands with Sally, walking hand in hand, as he pointed out the differences between the pots of San Ildefonso and those of Acoma, the differences between Navajo silverwork and that of Zuni (he didn't know that much about it, he could admit that to himself now, he made up most of what he said as he went along, but it had been enough to impress her, to make her happy), Sally skipping about him like a child, pleased, she said, because he took time to tell her these things, pleased, she said, because it showed how much he loved her.

Then, it was close to noon, there were shrieks from the top of the pueblo and everyone in the plaza froze: at the top of the pueblo, standing on top of the highest room, five stories in the air, were the *chiffonetes,* six or eight of them, Black Eyes, screaming and calling, taunting the people below, warning them. In a few minutes, after dancing and waving their asses at the crowd, lifting their loincloths, they began to descend, climbing down the face of the pueblo, jumping from level to level (one of them fell trying to ease himself down over a parapet and he got up and brushed himself off and fell down to the next level as well), as the crowds panicked and ran away from them and the owners of the booths frantically tried to cover their displays.

"Why are they covering everything up?" she said, clutching his arm tightly, staying close to him.

"Because the Black Eyes are allowed to take anything that isn't covered up."

"Why are they allowed to do that?"

"Because nobody can stop them. The clowns are sacred and above the law. They're like children, like crazies. Like death."

Where did those feelings go? The joy? Why did they have to go away?

Then he remembered too what she had said to him that day as she turned her head and stretched up to whisper in his ear: "You've taught me how to see all this. Thank you."

He pulled at his beard. And why did her saying things like that, even the memory of them now, drive him up a wall?

His clothes, his Levi's, his work shirt, smelled of smoke. He finished getting dressed, then stepped out the front steps of the cabin. Cable, lying under the back end of the jeep, got up, stretched, and came over to him, fitting the top of his head into Don's hand; the dogs on the back steps of the house stirred, raised their heads, kept an eye on him across the yard to make sure they weren't missing out on something. The shades in Sally's, their, bedroom were still drawn; the house looked quiet, still. Sally was probably still in bed; he could just walk in, walk into the bedroom, climb into bed beside her.

"Stay here, Cable."

Cable smiled, sat down.

Don patted the dog again and headed into the woods. Thinking of Mary Olive.

It had started in the spring, after he began sleeping in the cabin— he told Sally it was just a temporary thing, that because of his throat he found it hard to sleep, he was restless and coughed a lot and he didn't want to disturb her (all of which was true, but they weren't all the reasons)—after he had been to see Doc Harvey the first time about his throat, though he already knew before he went that there was more wrong with him than just a gravelly voice and a sore Adam's apple. One night when he couldn't sleep, after midnight, he was out slogging around the mud-locked fields for a breath of air, he and Cable, the old cream-colored dog behind him glowing in the moonlight, when he noticed, on the other side of the black valley, the lights on in George and Mary Olive's kitchen. He knew Mary Olive stayed up most of the night; the subject had come up several times during their get-togethers, and when he saw the lights on again the following night (he knew the second night he went out to look for them on purpose), he thought it might be an amusing, an offbeat thing to do to walk over and say hello to a fellow night owl. He told Cable to go back to the cabin, and sludged off into the woods.

He approached the house carefully and peeked in the window. Mary Olive was dancing around the kitchen, her arms outstretched, a wineglass in one hand and a cigarette in the other, gliding and dipping and swaying gracefully about, not so much like Ginger Rogers but more like Fred Astaire, approximately in time with the rock-and-roll music coming from the radio. Don watched for several minutes, too embarrassed to interrupt and too fascinated to move away, until she happened to see him at the window. Without missing a beat, she motioned him to come in.

"You caught me," she said as she greeted him at the back door. "You found out my secret."

"What secret?"

"That I listen to Golden Oldies on the radio, though I must admit most of them are new to me. That I dance around here in the wee, small hours. I don't like the dances these kids do nowadays—have you ever heard of one called the Philadelphia Chicken? I can't imagine what that's like. So I sort of make up my own." She held out her arms again and glided around the kitchen, then went over to the cupboard and got another long-stemmed wineglass and poured him some Mountain Red.

Don made a production of holding the glass of cheap wine to the light, swirling it around, and testing its bouquet. "Personally,

I've always preferred the Stones and Creedence Clearwater Revival."

Mary Olive raised her eyebrows; she stood beside the counter, feet apart, flat-footed, facing him head on, squinting a little as she studied him closely, a playful smile on her lips, as if ready for a challenge. "I didn't know you were an aficionado. I thought I was alone in the wilds of the San Francisco Mountains. Or at least among the wilds of the local academic community."

"I'm afraid anyone with a car radio in this society is an aficionado of pop music, whether they know it or not. Though I admit it still surprises me to see little old ladies listening to 'Satisfaction' without so much as batting an eye."

"Little old ladies need satisfaction too," she said coyly, and chucked him under his beard.

"So do little old men," he said, equally coy. "What does George make of all this?"

"George doesn't know or care what I do down here at night. George thinks I'm a kook, and maybe I am, at least to his standards. George is just glad I'm awake at this time of night and not during the day, or at least during the mornings, when he wants to work. It's a funny thing, if your sense of humor has that kind of bent to it. We started this schedule when we lived in New York, when we were both busy working, George on a novel and I was editing. At least that was the theory, that we were both working on our own things. The truth was, I opted for the night shift because I knew he wanted the apartment for himself in the mornings, that it made him nervous to have me around when he was trying to work. He didn't consider editing as quote serious unquote as writing. But then I got to love the nights. And I also felt better being up when he got home from his little escapades with his students or whomever."

"He was having . . . an affair?"

"Affairs. Plural. I always preferred the term 'fooling around' myself, but I suppose I was biased. Of course I knew; I may be a kook, but I'm not stupid, though I guess George thought I was stupid, because I don't think he ever knew I knew. The amazing thing to me now was that I didn't seem to mind all that much; I knew the girls and most of the time I approved of them, I even liked them. Most of them I would have picked out for him myself, if the choice had been mine. But I still liked to be up when he came in, to make sure he hadn't collapsed with a heart attack in bed, or got run over by a subway on the way home. And I must confess I always liked to put him on the spot a bit, make him sweat. He flusters so easily."

"George was the one who was crazy," he said, "for not realizing what he had at home."

She looked grateful. She was wearing a man's V-neck sweater, the sleeves pushed up past her elbows, and a pair of men's baggy, pleated tweed pants, but rather than sloppy she looked stylish, full of energy and with a hard sensuality; her face was still sweaty from her workout, a small row of beads across her upper lip, and her skin was moist and gleaming, her eyes bright and mischievous. He leaned over and kissed her.

They kissed again, put down their wineglasses, and embraced, fumbled with each other's clothes. She led him by the hand into the dark living room and they lay on the couch, their clothes pushed up or down. Her body was athletic, muscular—that surprised him, he expected her to be only thin, scrawny even, but her body was full, her breasts small and full, as present when she lay on her back as when she was standing up (he thought of Sally's breasts, whole handfuls when she was upright but only puddles when she lay down), her thighs long and muscular, like a runner's. He sucked on her breasts for a few moments, she rolled his balls around in their sack and pulled on his penis as if shucking an ear of corn. Then he noticed she was staring at him, a bemused expression on her face.

"Are you enjoying this?" she said.

"Not really," he said, their faces inches away. "How about you?"

"No, but then I never do all that much. It's one of those things that always sounds better to me than it actually is. I like the rolling-around part, but I never like all the mess afterward. It's sort of like baking: you spend all that time mixing and stirring and heating up the oven, but then you have all those dishes to do afterward and all you've got to show for it is a plateful of cookies."

Don felt more relief, more release than if he had ejaculated: the truth was, he didn't want a lover, he needed a friend.

It was the only time they made love, or tried to. He planned not to see her again, he told himself it was best just to stay away, but the next night, standing out in his yard again, when he saw her lights on in the kitchen, he sludged back through the woods to the opposite hill. He found her sitting in the window, sitting at her place at the counter, staring out the window, waiting for him, a glass of wine poured and waiting for him; and on the counter beside the glass of wine, a plate of store-bought cookies.

3

There was a bug in his beard. He scratched at it and it flew onto his lips, into his mouth—briny. He stopped and spit, sputtered, again and again, trying to get the taste out of his mouth, off his lips. He walked on.

The woods were busy with magpies. Strange. Some years there were hardly any, this year they were all over the place. The sun flashed at him, between the branches of the trees, marking his progress as the pines wheeled at his pace past the sun. Cézanne's pines, only here the colors were dark, the branches not green but blue-black green, the shadows as much a part of the colors as the colors themselves, even, perhaps especially, in the sunlight, where Cézanne's pines, even, perhaps especially, in shadow, were filled with light. The difference between Life and Art.

Or maybe the difference between Flagstaff and Provence.

Whatever the difference, it wasn't enough to excuse what he

had done, the way he had acted. Destroying the pines. Mucking around with the natural order. Stupid. He knew better. He walked on.

The heels of his cowboy boots sank into the floor of pine needles, giving him the sensation almost of walking uphill even though he was walking down, down the slope of the valley. The difference between Life and Art. It's not nice to fool Mother Nature. Where does love go, where does it run, why does it always leave just when it should be fun?

It sounded like a song lyric. A soul song. Soul is right. Soul is white? Sole is wight.

A magpie on a branch thought something was funny. *Rak rak rak rak rak rak rak rak rak.* Then it flew away. The wings, the white crescent when the wings unfolded, the white underbelly, flashed through the blue-black green of the branches. Quick, as a gunshot. Something inside Don flinched. He could still smile.

He reached for his hat to push it back on his head at the same time he realized he had forgotten to wear it. He walked on.

He thought the story was from Taos. Lived at Taos, as the Indians would say: the story as a living thing, an entity, a continuing presence that the teller taps into briefly. In this case, the story of Magpie.

Magpie is known as the bird of wisdom, and the bird of the east; she is sister to the morning star. Her only duty is to stand each morning between night and day, darkness and light, and protect Father Sun as he arrives from the Under World, because the Sun, like anyone else, is very vulnerable when he's just getting up. And each morning, as she stands on the edge of the world, holding her wings like a cape, shielding the Sun until he is strong enough, old wily Coyote comes over and lies down, a little ways away, panting, smiling, watching what's going on.

"Hey, Maggie," Coyote says. "Why don'cha come over to my place? I got a lot of things I could show a girl like you."

"No thanks, Wily," says Magpie. "You know I've got things to do."

"Ah, come on, my little chickadee, don't be that way. Why

259

don'cha come over for breakfast as soon as you get off? I could fix us some nice *huevos rancheros* or something. Or we could go out somewhere. What'cha say?"

"You're barking at the moon. You know that's not my style."

"All right, then, sweetie-pie. Come on over and let me show you some jewelry. I have some real nice turquoise stuff, nothing from Taiwan, that would look great with that black-and-white outfit you're wearing."

"Forget it, Coyote. You'll never be the light of my life."

Each morning Coyote tries to trick her away, because he knows he's clever, but that's all, and he thinks if he can get Magpie then he'll have wisdom too. But Maggie doesn't listen to him; she's heard it all before. She waits until Father Sun has collected himself, until he's strong and warm and has started on his journey up across the sky; then she flies off, going on about her own business, looking for garbage and squashed dogs.

What was wrong with him? It was a good thing the Hopi had never seen the way he treated their sacred myths; they would never understand why. (Why did he?) They would only see it as an insult. (Was it?) They would never understand that he was really on their side. (Was he?) A war party standing on his front lawn, if the myths were ever published. A scalp dance. With his scalp.

Now he wished he hadn't given the manuscript to George; he wished he had just burned it. What was wrong with him? Hadn't he given up any hopes for it, long ago? George wouldn't understand it either; if he liked it, it would be for all the wrong reasons. He could see George, hands folded across his stomach, blinking, mugging, running through his repertoire of sincere faces—"I really do think you should do something with it, Don"—George raises a professorial finger—"Morally, I think a work of art itself is a sacred thing, a manifestation of the spirit of mankind. . . ."

George. Or George George George, as Mary Olive would say.

Mary Olive. A merry olive? As opposed to a black olive?

My mind's not right, said Robert Lowell, and everyone loved him for it: Nobody's here. Only the skunks.

Rak rak rak rak rak rak rak rak rak rak rak rak.

In this case, flying skunks. Skunks with wings. The myth of the Magpie made them sound so good, so mystical. A lie there too. They were nasty birds, worse than nasty. Carrion birds, not always willing to wait until the meal was off the hoof. He had seen them back a squirrel off the end of a branch, chase it backward step by step until the squirrel either jumped or fell, apparently just for fun. He had seen them attack Cable, for no reason, diving for his eyes. Where did he hear the story, just recently: a boy had a pet magpie in a cage and one day a flock of wild magpies, a dozen or so, settled in the tree outside the window where the boy kept his pet, calling to the caged bird. The boy began to feel guilty about keeping the bird caged up, so he opened the cage and let his magpie fly out the window. And the wild birds immediately attacked the just-freed bird and pecked it to death as the boy watched.

Birds were as bad as people.

Don walked on.

Betrayal. It had never been a big word in his lexicon. He had never even thought about it much, it seemed a word from a different era, from a different set of values. A different time. Until recently. Betrayer. As you betray, so shall you be betrayed. *Rak rak rak rak rak, rak rak rak rak rak rak rak rak rak rak.* It takes one to tell one. Go to hell, magpie.

We are not amused. The kingly we, the editorial we, the wee we. Me.

So nothing had happened, actually, unless you could call sitting, nightly, around a kitchen table—or, rather, he sat at the kitchen table; she maintained her place at the counter—drinking wine and eating cookies while her husband was upstairs asleep, talking about supply-side economics and pre-emptive nuclear strikes, the use of onomatopoeia in the metaphysical poets of the seventeenth century and whether or not the use of the wah-wah pedal was critical to the development of heavy-metal rock, nothing. (Actually, the nights were something to him: no, stronger than that: the nights, their nightly discussions, were almost everything to him; he felt more alive talking to her than he had in years, an irony that was not lost to him, seeing as how he was already pretty sure he was dying, that it was only up to Doc Harvey to decide exactly the reason and where the disease was located and how long it was going to take; they meant enough to him that he stopped sleeping in his bed, with his wife, altogether, moved more or less completely out to the cabin, even eating his meals there, as a middle-aged man would if he went bonkers over a teenage lover except that all Don wanted to do was to be able to walk over to his neighbor's kitchen for another discussion in the middle of the night without his wife asking where he was going.) So he couldn't blame Mary Olive. Oh, he could, and he did, but he knew he had no claim to her, no rights. If she had set him up to make George jealous or to hurt him in some way, get even with him for something—was that what she was doing all along? All those nights? Waiting for George to come downstairs and find him there? Waiting for the scene? It seemed par for the course, it seemed in keeping with the workings of the human animal, as he understood them at least, in an uncaring, self-centered universe. It seemed in keeping with a world where people spent their lives ripping out each other's hearts on the altar of their own desires. He would, of course, be married to an overzealous woman who idolized him and whom he could no longer stand for that very reason; Mary Olive would, of course, be married to a man so sure of his own bluster that he couldn't see his hand in front of his face. "Here's to the human heart," Mary Olive would make her toast; well, it might be human, and it might have a heart, but it didn't seem to have much to do with humanity. Or was it love?

And what of himself? *Rak rak rak, rak rak.*

What of George? George George George. Why was he so mad at George? Why did the very sight of the man infuriate him? Poor George, poor sightless blob. He owed George an apology for the way he'd been acting, for the way he'd treated him. He owed him some kind of explanation, though he wasn't sure any explanation he could give would do very much to make George feel better. I hate you, George, because I love talking to your wife in the middle of the night. I hate you, George, because I prize your wife's sarcasm and wit and at times nastiness, her cold clear appraising eye, her calculating intelligence, her refusal to put up with bullshit; I hate you, George, because who she is, what makes her who she is, scares you and drains you and tears you down, just as it excites me and energizes me and builds me up. I hate you, George, because you got the one woman I've ever met whom I could have lived with and been happy with. Who would have pushed me, helped me to be all the things I could have been. No, that wouldn't do much to set George's mind at ease.

And what of Sally? He had hurt her so much lately he could barely stand to think of it.

Doc Harvey sat in his leather chair, aiming at him down the notch of his fingertips: "This is a time to put your life in order. This is a time to find peace."

Doc Harvey was right. He'd go over to George's and make some kind of an apology, try to give some explanation; and if the kachina was still there, he'd come back to the house and get Sally. They'd walk through the woods, these woods, hand in hand, the way they used to, the way they used to go to Indian dances, to Taos; he'd take her to see the kachina, to watch the kachina dance. Maybe it wasn't too late for them. Maybe he could get the feelings for her back again, maybe they could get back to the way things used to be.

Rak rak rak rak rak rak rak rak rak rak. The magpie flashed through the branches, off to the side, keeping an eye on him.

He found the grove of aspens where he had been the night before, found the small pine tree that he had tried to pull out of the ground. The tree was bent over, almost touching the ground, nearly half its branches torn off, its trunk torn where he had stepped on it trying to break it, an open green wound. Don felt sick at his stomach. He straightened up the tree as best he could, tamped the earth firmly around its base to help hold it up. He looked at it for a moment. The tree listed badly to one side. He wished he had some way to brace it, wished he had something with which to close and seal the wound. He touched the branches.

"I'm sorry," he said out loud.

"That's okay, Don."

He jumped back, stumbled backward, and lost his balance, fell. He hit the ground hard, knocking the air out of him; he felt dizzy, the world was spinning, he started coughing, there was a figure standing over him, a man, a large man wearing a loose blue shirt, a powder-blue pajama top with a little crown embroidered over the heart, grinning down at him, his face painted a dull, streaked fuchsia.

Rak rak rak rak rak rak rak rak rak rak rak rak, sang the magpie, and flew away through the trees.

$$4$$

"George."

"I didn't mean to scare you."

"What's that on your face?"

"Do I still have that on?" George touched his cheek with his fingertips, examined the backs of his hands. He laughed. "It's Caladryl lotion, I got sunburned yesterday. No wonder I scared you."

George helped him get to his feet and brush himself off. He was wearing a pair of trousers pulled over his pajama bottoms, and shoes without socks. He seemed amused about something.

"What are you doing running around the woods in your pajamas?"

"I was in a hurry. There's something I want to show you; I was just on my way over to get you."

"Is the kachina still there?"

"I want you to see for yourself." George grinned, his eyes popping. He charged off, up the hill, then stopped and turned around to make sure Don was coming. "I was going to drive over but I didn't want the car to disturb Mary Olive. I think she's going to be disturbed enough as it is."

"About what?"

"You'll see, you'll see."

"I hate games, George."

"This isn't a game," George said over his shoulder, puffing, leading the way up through the pines. "And I would have called but I didn't think you had a phone out there in the cabin and I didn't want to have to lie to Sally about the kachina."

"I wanted to talk to you about that," Don rasped. George's pace—how did a fat man move so fast?—wasn't making it any easier on his throat. "I know I've acted badly about all this. . . ."

"I'll say." George looked back at him.

Their eyes met briefly and George grinned over his shoulder but he kept stumbling on.

"No, I mean it, George."

"I mean it too. I think you've been acting very badly lately. This business about keeping Sally in the dark about the kachina . . ."

"I know, I know," Don said, waving his hand, motioning him to stop. He leaned against a tree to catch his breath. George stopped, puffing, a few steps farther up the slope, looking down at him; his pajama top hung loose over his belly like a maternity blouse. After a minute or so, they went on.

"I don't think you've been at all fair to her," George said, picking it up again as soon as they were moving, glancing back over his shoulder. "Sally's a wonderful girl; you should hear the way she talks about you. She's still crazy about you. And you take her for granted."

"I don't think you know the whole story," Don said, watching the ground, not looking at him.

"I think I know enough of it."

"Spare me, George, your moral superiority."

"I think I have a moral obligation to tell a friend if I think he's behaving badly."

" 'Behaving badly.' One of my least favorite post-Freudian expressions. It's presumptuous, it always makes the other person sound like a naughty child, and the speaker sound like a parent. Let's just say that, whatever my problems are with Sally, they're as real to me as your problems are with Mary Olive."

"What problems do I have with Mary Olive?"

"Oh, come on, George."

"No, I'm serious," George puffed, laughed, looking back. "Mary Olive and I don't have any problems."

"George, how can you say that?"

Don stopped; they had just come out of the woods, into George's back yard, near the house.

"Because it's true," George said. He hunched his shoulders once, opened his hands as if it were all right there for anyone to see. "We get along beautifully. What's wrong?"

"Who are all these people? What's going on here?"

"Oh, that."

The back yard was full of Indians—at least that's the way it appeared to him at first. There were a dozen or so pickup trucks and cars and vans parked in the driveway and on the grass beside the house, and down in the field a group of twenty-five or thirty Indians, old men for the most part, some in tunics and silver necklaces and beads around their necks, others in work clothes as if they'd just come from the fields—in tall cowboy hats or headbands, a cloth knotted around the head—sat in a semicircle in front of the fence. A few smoked stubby ceremonial pipes, but most of them just sat there, looking at the kachina on the other side of the fence, who sat on his rock on the bank of the wash, looking back at them.

" 'Oh, that?' " said Don. "That's all you can say? 'Oh, that?' "

"Isn't this something? This is what I wanted to show you. I just woke up this morning and here they all were. I didn't even hear them drive up. What do you think I should do now?"

George hiked up his pajama bottoms beneath his trousers and snapped the elastic against his tummy, a large grin on his face, as if he had conjured up the scene in front of them himself, blinking slowly with the wonder of it all.

Don turned around and walked back into the woods.

5

George stared at the circle of Indians, the old men, sitting in his field, an uneasy smile on his face, blinking, still unable quite to believe his own eyes, still unable to fathom how they all got here without his hearing them or what they intended to do now that they were here, unsure whether he should feel honored or imposed upon or what.

"What do you think I should do now?" he repeated, turned to ask Don again, but Don was already walking away, heading back into the woods.

George started to call after him, then stopped. *I've had just about enough of that. I've had just about enough of him turning around and walking away from me. Just about enough of people not taking me seriously, of people giving me the runaround, of people taking advantage of me. I've had just about enough.*

At the end of the yard, the group of Indians took turns, one by one, climbing through the fence, each with a small white sack in his hands, to sprinkle cornmeal over the kachina. The cornmeal covered the Aholi's shoulders, dribbled down the folds of his cloak, collected in small piles on his lap; the kachina shifted his position and the cornmeal sprinkled off him like snow. Aholi looked at George across the yard, over the heads of the old men seated in front of him, a blank, forbearing expression on his face—mask. *What are these guys doing here? Was this one of your ideas?*

George harrumphed; he hitched up his pajama bottoms underneath his trousers—this time he hitched them up too far and caught himself in the balls with the inseam—pointed his stomach toward the end of the field, and rumbled forward. David Lomanongye saw him coming—George hadn't noticed him, singled him out of the crowd before—and got up to meet him, heading him off before George reached the group. He was wearing the same clothes as the evening before, the sleeves of his sweat-stained white shirt rolled up past his elbows, the same baggy suit pants—or clothes just like them—as if he'd been up all night. His eyes were puffy behind the rimless glasses, but he smiled merrily at George and shook his hand, gathering George's fingers all in a clump.

"Some people wanted to come down and have a look at Grandfather here," David Lomanongye said.

"Who are they? How did you find out where I live?"

"Oh, just some people. I called Ernie Tewayumptewa, he had your address."

"Then you must think it's real."

"Real? Well, there certainly seems to be something sitting on the other side of the fence, doesn't there?" David Lomanongye said cheerily.

I've had just about enough.

George decided he didn't like David Lomanongye; he wasn't sure he liked Indians at all. The Aholi looked at him over the rows of headbands and cowboy hats. *Easy, George.*

"What?" George said.

David Lomanongye was looking at him funny.

"It's Caladryl lotion," George said. "I got sunburned. . . ."

"That's what I assumed, I didn't think you were into body decoration. No, what I was curious about . . . Are those pajamas?"

"Ahem, well, yes, they are." George stood a little taller; the pajama top draped out over his stomach, ski-jumped over the edge. "I was in a hurry to find out what was going on out here. . . ."

"I've never understood why they always put a little crest over the pocket. Sears Roebuck has pages of pajamas with little crests or initials or leaping lions on them. I've never understood what it's supposed to mean. But I guess I've never understood the whole business about pajamas either. You people certainly have some strange customs." David Lomanongye smiled at him.

"There's nothing out of the ordinary about me wearing pajamas around my own back yard—I've got my pants on. Though I'll admit I didn't expect to be the host of a powwow. . . ."

"Oh, no offense, Mr. Binns. I didn't mean to imply I thought there was anything wrong or improper about it. I just thought you might want to put on something a little more, how can I say it, substantial, if you're going to stay outside here."

"Substantial?"

"Of course, it would be best if you'd just stay in your house, at least for the time being. That goes for your wife too."

"You want me to stay up in the house?"

"I didn't think you'd like that idea."

"Mr. Lomanongye, I'd like to remind you just whose land you're standing on. . . ."

"That's funny, I was thinking of reminding you of the same thing." David Lomanongye smiled again, tight-lipped, his eyes jolly and good-natured behind his glasses. "But you do whatever you think best. I only thought I'd mention it."

He nodded and went back to sit down. George sputtered a moment. *Just about enough.* The Aholi looked at him again, over the heads and hats; an old man stood beside the kachina, puffing on a short stubby pipe and blowing clouds of smoke against the side of the kachina's blue pointed head. *You're not the only one with problems, George.* George turned around, pointed his belly at the house, and rumbled back up the hill.

6

Mary Olive stood beside the top of the terrace steps, her arms folded about herself. She was fully dressed, in a red turtleneck and old slacks; her face was drawn and sallow, her shoulders turned in upon herself.

"Don't say it," George said as he walked past her, up the steps. "Don't say a word, I don't want to hear it."

"What do they want?" she said quietly.

He stopped and looked at her. "What they want is for me to get dressed and stay up here at the house."

"They both sound like fairly reasonable requests," she said, still almost whispering, rubbing her upper arms as if she was chilled. "Why are you still wearing your pajamas?"

"Why is everybody so concerned about my pajamas?" George said, waving his clenched fists beside his head.

"I thought I saw Don," Mary Olive said.

"You did, but you had to look fast. A fine friend he turned out to be. He took one look and turned around and walked away. That's the last time I'm going to ask him for anything."

"Did he say anything about last night?"

"No, why should he? What about last night?"

Mary Olive shook her head, looked away.

"I found him out in the woods talking to pine trees."

"After last night, I wouldn't think he'd want to talk to either one of us." She looked off at the mountains.

George had no idea what she was talking about; he followed her eyes, saw only mountains, and headed on toward the house.

"I'm in no mood today, Mary Olive. No mood for anything."

"I'm not either," she said, following a little ways behind him, her head down.

"So it'd be best just to stay out of my way. Just leave everything alone."

"I only came out to tell you your girlfriend called."

"My girlfriend?" he said, stopping halfway through the back door, thinking, Sally? A student?

Mary Olive closed her eyes, shook her head. "I shouldn't have said that. I mean Sara. Sara called."

"Why did you call her my girlfriend? She's your friend too."

"That's right, George. You're right."

"I don't think you should make jokes about a thing like that."

Mary Olive looked exhausted; her cheekbones appeared to have collapsed into her face, leaving the skin under her eyes loose. "I told her you'd call her back as soon as you finished the Indian question. Let's just leave it at that."

"Leave what at that?" George said, still halfway through the door.

"George," Mary Olive sighed. "Nothing, George. Really nothing. We don't want to get into this now."

"Get into what now? I don't know what you're talking about."

"George George George."

"What are you talking about?"

"I'm afraid you're going to have to finally decide, George, which one of us it's going to be, Sara or me."

"Are you giving me an ultimatum? How dare you talk to me that way. And who said there was anything going on between me and Sara? There's nothing going on—"

"No, I'm not giving you an ultimatum, George. I think she is. And I'm sorry for you, George. I truly am."

"Sorry for me? Why are you sorry for me? What are you talking about? What's going on around here?"

Mary Olive closed her eyes again and didn't open them; her arms were locked across her chest. "Go call Sara, George."

George stretched his neck so hard it hurt.

7

"Hello, George."

"Sara, how did you know it was me?"

"Maybe after all this time I can recognize your ring. Even if I am the one who usually calls you. Are you going to give me a lecture on correct phone etiquette too?"

"No, of course not. And I wasn't going to say a thing about prime phone rates."

"That's because it's Sunday, George."

From the register beside his foot came the sound of paper crinkling. As though Mary Olive were trying to imitate the sound of a fire. Then it occurred to him: maybe it actually was a fire. Maybe she was trying to burn down the kitchen, the house. He stood up and leaned close to the windows, looking down the side of the house, but he couldn't see anything, he couldn't smell any smoke. What was she doing down there?

"George?" Sara said.

George eyed the register suspiciously; he turned away from it, hunched over the receiver close to the wall, his hand cupped around his mouth, trying to shield his voice. "Sara, I think Mary Olive knows about us."

"Well, of course she knows about us. She always knew about us. Don't try to tell me you didn't know that."

"I didn't."

"Of course you knew, George. I knew. How could you not know?"

How could he not know? It didn't sound possible, hearing her say it, even to him, that he couldn't have known, but it seemed true. He tried again but the words sounded even more feeble. "I didn't know."

"Whether you admitted it to yourself or not, that's a different matter. Or maybe you just didn't care. But you knew. Every time we saw each other while you were still here in New York, every time you came back last year to see me, it was with Mary Olive's blessing, her silent agreement, and you're insulting your intelligence as well as mine if you pretend differently."

"What is this? The world is going crazy today. My back yard is full of Indians. My best friend talks to pine trees but he won't talk to me. My wife and my, er . . ."

"Lover, George," Sara said. "Try lover. Or mistress. Or paramour. Sweetheart. Lady love. Girlfriend. Main squeeze. Or how about this one: The Best Thing That Ever Happened to You."

George curled himself more around the phone, cupped his hand tighter around the receiver. "Sara, I need to see you." His voice sounded hollow even to him.

"You sound like you're speaking through a vacuum cleaner, George."

"I don't want Mary Olive to hear. She's downstairs."

"You just got through telling me that Mary Olive knows about us. What difference does it make whether she hears you talking to me now? Besides, I told her all about my job in Chicago when I talked to her earlier. I'm sure she's smart enough to figure out what that means in regard to you and me, even if you aren't."

"I've been thinking about that, Sara. Maybe it wouldn't be such a good idea for you to take that job in Chicago. Maybe you would be better off to stay in New York."

Sara didn't say anything for a while; and when she spoke, finally, she didn't sound jolly. "The last time we talked, you told me it was irresponsible for me to stay in New York. That I wasn't, I believe your term was, keeping my eye on the ball."

"Well, I've thought some more about it."

"Ah. You have."

"Yes, and I think you might be better off to stay in New York. I mean, you love it there, all your friends and all are there, everything you care about is there. I'm sure you can find some teaching jobs, and you can always get free-lance work. And maybe a tenure job will come along. . . ."

"And you'll still be able to finagle a couple trips here a year?"

"Yes, I'm pretty sure. . . ." He peeked under his arm at the register; it had been a while since he had heard Mary Olive; somehow that bothered him more than if he could hear her moving around.

"Well, I've thought some more about it too. And what I've got to tell you isn't based on a young woman's fantasies but on a forty-year-old woman's realities. If you really want to be with me, you pick the place and I'll be there. Not just for a weekend but for good, you and me. It can't be New York, and it can't be the Southwest—I want us both to start over fresh. But you get a teaching job at a school where you think you'll be happy, and I'll come be with you—like you said, I can always make it free-lancing, it doesn't matter where I am for that. What matters to me is that I am where you are. Instead of talking about being together, we'll do it, we'll make it real, we'll make the big gesture, take the big chance. I want to do that, George, I want to do that with you. Otherwise I'm afraid I just can't sit here the rest of my life waiting for you to fly in for these little parcels of time."

"It sounds like you're giving me an ultimatum."

"No, George. I'm just telling you that the ball, to continue your metaphor, is on your side of the court. How you play it now is up to you. So far in this game, all either one of us has on the board is love, and I think it's time to score some points."

"After all the time we've been together, I think I deserve to be treated better than this."

"That's funny, George, I've been thinking the same thing. And in case you haven't noticed, you're still treating me like a child."

"Sara, Sara . . ."

"George George George. Let me know what you decide, dear heart. I won't be calling any more."

Click.

He sat for several minutes holding the phone, listening to the dial tone, staring into the branches of the pine trees outside the window—there seemed to be more activity in the yard, the men down by the fence were moving around, though he wasn't really paying attention to them—until the receiver screeched at him and he put it back on the cradle. He looked down at the register.

"I suppose you heard all that.",

"Wog mozzle weople toom tamle pip," came the muffled reply.

"What?"

"Mizzle crak wopple seng torng graggle zzizz."

She's laughing at me, she's always laughed at me, she's laughing at me again.

"Wuzzle eep dackle bop?" said the register.

He lifted his fists to his head again, started to growl in the back of his throat—his mock growl, his pretend growl, his game of anger he started years ago because he thought it was healthy to make a joke of getting mad and it was funny and dumb and good for a laugh—then he stopped. *No, that's enough of that. It's no time for that.* He sat for a moment longer, staring out the window, at the branches of the pines, the glimpses of the old men moving around at the end of the yard, exhaling sharply, blowing the air out his nostrils (thinking: *I sound like a whale blowing air; I suppose that's funny too*), then pushed himself back from the desk—he wasn't trying to be noisy, wasn't trying for sound effects, he didn't care, he didn't even notice when the chair banged against the dictionary stand behind him—and trudged through the upstairs of the house, clomped down the stairs and into the kitchen. He wasn't even that surprised when he found Mary Olive, sitting at her usual place at the counter, with a brown paper bag over her head.

8

The eyes were cut out into rough, elongated pentangles, the right slightly larger than the left; the mouth was a small down-turned oval, slightly off center and too far to the left, a shape like a small fish, a mouth that was formed into a forever disappointed "Oh." The bottom of the bag was rolled up into a small ruff around the neck of her red turtleneck sweater, resting on her shoulders; the surface of the paper was crinkled and creased, aged; the sides were indented and there was a slight bulge where the nose, her nose, would be. Her face sat far back inside the bag, out of the direct light, so that the eyes and mouth appeared only as blank, black spaces, empty. She cocked her head, the mask, slightly in his direction, studying him.

"What's this supposed to be, Mary Olive?"

"This is Mary Olive wearing a bag over her head."

"What's it for?"

"For a little while. For now and for forever, for the time being. I don't know, George."

"I mean, what's it supposed to mean?"

"Oh, mean?" The blank face straightened up and looked around, looked toward the window. The mouth was cut too low to match her own, so that when she talked, turned now a little more toward the light, he could dimly see her bottom lip flicking up and down, but with no apparent relation to what she said. "Actually, it doesn't mean anything. No hidden meanings. No symbolism intended. It just is."

"I've had enough, Mary Olive."

"I admit I thought of putting it on in the first place as a little joke, because you said you didn't want to be bothered today. I thought it probably looked the way you wanted me to be, just a blank. But after I put the eyes in it it sort of got a life of its own. You'd be amazed if you knew just how little this has to do with you."

"I'm not going to play any more games."

"The point is, this isn't a game."

"Then what would you call it?"

"This is me, George. This is the real me. I didn't put on a mask, I took one off, and this is what I found inside. This is what I feel like, a plain brown face, recyclable, as the label says, heavy-duty, no double-bagging necessary. I'm not wearing this on account of you, I'm wearing it on account of me."

"I don't care why you're wearing it. Take it off now, or else I'll take it off for you."

She turned toward him, her shoulders, to look at him straight on, the blank black eyes staring at him.

"*U'huhuhuhuhu!*"

"What did you say?" George said.

"I thought you said something," Mary Olive said.

"*U'huhuhuhuhu!*"

The sound came from outside, from beside the house. There was the sound of bells, a deep jangle like sleigh bells. He thought, *A Good Humor man; the Indians have brought their own refreshments; they're going to sell ice cream in my back yard.* George and Mary Olive looked out the windows—Mary Olive still with the bag over her head—but it wasn't a man in a white dairyman's suit pushing a cart who came around the side of the house. Dancing into the back yard were two whipper kachinas, stomping up and down, calling to each other, "*U'huhuhuhuhu! U'huhuhuhuhu!*" and brandishing yucca whips in their hands. They were naked except for flimsy skirts made of long red hair and breechcloths, with bells and rattles tied to their bare legs; their bodies were painted black with large white blotches, their forearms and calves painted white. The masks were black, with horns sticking out at the sides, bulging eyes, and large hideous mouths, grinning, their teeth bared. A

long black-and-white beard draped down each kachina's chest, and
eagle feathers bounced from the top of the masks, dangled from
the tips of the horns.

"Huuu-hu-hu-hu-hu-hu!"

The Indians at the far end of the yard turned to look at the
kachinas. Behind the two whippers came the Crow Mother, the
Whipper Mother, dressed in a white blanket-cape, the large black
crow wings sprouting out from the sides of her blue mask, walking
stately, slowly, taking a step, then pausing as she gave her own
cry. *"Huuu-hu-hu-hu-hu-hu!"* In her arms she carried bundles of
more yucca whips. The presence of the Crow Mother seemed to
drive the whippers into a frenzy; they danced harder, snapped
their heads back and forth as they stamped the earth, out into the
back yard under the two pine trees, lifting their knees higher,
whipping the air with the bayonet yucca, at times whipping each
other until there were welts and blood on their arms and torsos.
As they danced toward the field, the kachinas began to whip the
lawn chairs, the chaise longue.

"They got all dressed up just to attack our lawn furniture?"
Mary Olive said, shifting the paper bag for a better view out the
eyeholes.

"They must be going to whip the old men, and the kachina.
That's why David Lomanongye wanted us to stay in the house.
Do you know what that means?"

"Somebody's going to get hurt."

"This must be a ceremony or something. This is fantastic, I'll
bet Don's never seen anything like this!"

"U'huhuhuhuhu!"

"Huuu-hu-hu-hu-hu-hu!"

"U'huhuhuhuhu!"

George pressed his face to the screen, blinking. He didn't even
know Mary Olive was gone until he heard the screen door slam,
and then saw her hurrying out across the back yard toward the
kachinas, the paper bag still on her head and a broom cocked on
her shoulder.

"U'huhuhuhuhu!"

"Huuu-hu-hu-hu-hu-hu!"

"Who-who-who-who-who-yourself," Mary Olive said, and blocked their way to the terrace steps.

The whippers stopped dancing. They looked at the woman in the red sweater with the broom on her shoulder and her head in a paper bag, then looked at each other. Then they looked at the Crow Mother, standing a little ways behind them. The Crow Mother shrugged.

George, blinking at the window, said under his breath, "Mary Olivvvvvvve . . ."

"Huuu-hu-hu-hu-hu-hu!" said the Crow Mother.

"I don't care who you are," Mary Olive said from her paper bag. "You leave our kachina alone and get out of here!"

The whippers looked at each other again. The Crow Mother nodded angrily, urging them forward. The whippers started to dance again, jogging up and down, tentatively at first, then harder, working themselves up, rabid again, the bells on their legs jangling, twisting back and forth, shaking their bodies, whipping the air. One of the whippers moved toward Mary Olive, crying *"U'huhuhuhuhu!,"* his whip cocked in her direction. Mary Olive lifted the broom from her shoulder, ready to swing. The whipper stopped dancing again; then the other one stopped too. The whipper slashed the air in front of Mary Olive with the yucca wand, missing her by a foot. Mary Olive teed off at his head, a roundhouse swing, missing him by inches—the whipper ducked and stumbled and careened into the other, knocking his head askew.

"Fuck this shit!" came a voice from the lopsided mask. "Get me out of here, this woman's crazy!"

9

*H*e *would take me on stakeouts. What a crazy thing to do. Sitting on a stakeout in Cleveland.*

> Southward we came.
> We traveled a road marked
> With beautiful kernels of corn.
> Then we saw the house
> Of Eototo and Aholi.
> A white mist enveloped the house.
> Then we entered.
> The Eototo was there,
> The Aholi was there.
> They had beautiful corn of
> All different colors, they had
> Watermelon and muskmelon and beans.
> That is the way they lived.

Sally Pike stopped her recitation of the chant from Powamu, cocked her head, and listened. There had been traffic on the road all day, pickup trucks and vans, cars full of people, heading up toward the mountain. At least that's where she guessed they were going. The only thing she could figure was that somebody must be having a picnic, somebody must have found a spot up one of the fire trails, up on government land, and was having a get-together of some sort—the only other thing, farther up the road, was George and Mary Olive's house, and she was sure all these cars and trucks couldn't be going there. Still, just to be on the safe side, just to make sure he knew about it and everything was all right, she thought she better check it with Don.

Sitting in a car, together, on a stakeout in Cleveland.

She left her studio and walked through the house, up this step and down that, through the different levels of the rooms and hallways, the different levels of the house. Today she was wearing her buckskin skirt, her favorite, with the long fringe that cascaded from the waist down her legs, below the tops of her tall moccasins, and as she walked through the dark, quiet house, the morning sunlight from the windows lost in the dark wood paneling, absorbed into the bare wood floors, she swayed along, swung her arms like a dancer, to set the fringe in counterpoint against her, the fringe swaying against her, brushing her like children's fingers, as she finished the prayer, completed the recitation to each of the four directions. It was the speech of the God of Germination to the children who were about to be initiated into the tribe; Sally said it to herself once a day, and sometimes more, not because the prayer had any direct meaning for her (it wasn't even a prayer, for that matter, it was just a talk, a chant, but that was close enough for her) or because the Powamu ceremony had any importance to her life, but because it was the only Hopi prayer or chant she knew and because she thought it was pretty and because, as she recited it, it reminded her of rows of masked dancers and the look of brown-eyed wonder on the faces of Hopi children and the feelings she got of reverence and awe and happiness every time she visited the mesas, every time she heard the voices of the kachinas singing and the sounds of the drums and the bells.

> Now is the time for
> The chiefs to gather
> Your people around you
> And hold your children
> On your laps, protect them.
> Now is the time for
> You to open your hands
> To these boys and girls,

That the yucca suds
To wash their heads
And the strokes of
The yucca whips
Will open their hearts.

Then follow the road
Marked with cornmeal
To the white dawn
And the yellow dawn,
The road of the four staffs,
The four stages of life.
Lean on the four staffs
As you travel the road,
And, finally, braced against
The shortest staff of all,
May you fall asleep as
Old men and old women;
May you find a peaceful death
On the road
Marked with cornmeal
To the white dawn
To the yellow dawn.

Sitting bundled up in a car, together, in Cleveland, watching for numbers runners.

She stood at the screen door. On the back steps, the dogs looked up at her, got to their feet, as they did each time she came to the door—how many times today? a dozen? two dozen? But she didn't open the door, didn't look at them; she leaned against the door, pressed her nose against the screen, against the smell of the dirty metal, the tiny grid flattening her nose, the door giving slightly with her weight. Across the yard, Don's jeep was parked in front of the cabin; Cable, the old Labrador, lay flat out in the dust beside it, catching what little shade he could find, asleep. Sally assumed Don was out in the cabin, but she wasn't sure; she listened, but she couldn't hear the chain saw in the woods, couldn't hear him chopping wood somewhere. She thought again of going out to ask him—how many times today? a dozen? two dozen?—where all the cars and trucks were going on the road, but again decided against it. If he was busy, if he wanted to be alone, she didn't want to disturb him; she didn't want to make him any angrier with her than he already was, than he already must be. She turned around and started back through the house again, back through the different levels of the rooms and hallways.

He would take me on stakeouts. He would set me in the car beside him because he said it was safer that way, it was safer for him if I was there, no one would suspect him with a little girl. And maybe we looked like a couple too, not a married couple, I guess, but maybe that too, to somebody, harmless. I was his cover, I helped him, protected him. He would bundle me up in blankets and scarves and a pillow for me to sit on, to boost me up so I would look taller and older or maybe not, maybe it was just to make me high enough so anyone could see I was only a little girl, and we'd sit there together for hours watching a car or a pool hall or that rib house on the east side. When the man came out and the car moved, I would keep track of the car in traffic and tell him which way to go though he must have known all that himself, and then we would park again and sit for hours eating hamburgers and drinking milkshakes and sometimes the other men, his friends, the other policemen would stop by the car and say something to him, and look over at me and maybe tip their hat and say, "Hey, Harry, who's your girlfriend?" sitting on stakeout in Cleveland.

In the living room she paused, then sat down, in the chair in the corner, the brown leather chair draped with a Two Grey Hills Navajo rug, Don's chair; she patted the arms of the chair, thumped them affectionately: an old friend. She looked around the room, dark even at midday, at their collection of Indian things—dolls and pottery and prints: things they had bought together. When they first started living together, even before they were married, they said they didn't want anything of their past lives around them, they didn't want one item of furniture or decoration or even clothing to remind them of their lives before they knew each other. Of course the pact, the gesture, applied more to Don than it did to herself: What did she have of a past life? What was she going to bring, a stuffed teddy bear or one of her dolls from Cleveland? Sitting in the room now, however, with Don living out in the cabin—they had bought that eagle dancer at San Ildefonso, where the young girl with the big black eyes looked at them and smiled shyly and asked Don, "Is this for your daughter?" meaning Sally; they had bought that Scholder print at Tally Richards's Gallery in Taos, where they sat in the white gallery long after it had closed, drinking wine and looking at prints as Tally told them what it was like to be a beauty queen and after; they bought this Two Grey Hills rug in Santa Fe at that gallery near the plaza where the saleswoman had been a student of Don's at UNM and she looked at Don and she looked at Sally and Sally could tell she was jealous—it was like sitting in a room full of recriminations and lost dreams. She pushed herself up out of the chair and continued back toward the end of the house, toward her studio glowing through the open door at the end of the narrow, stepped hallway.

When he came home he took off his sport coat and took off the shoulder holster with his gun and laid out his wallet with the badge. Then he'd look at me but he wouldn't have to say anything; he'd just go down in the basement to the place where he kept the record player and his collection of records; he'd put on a record of Heifetz or Menuhin and take out his old violin from its case and put it under his chin, sticking out from his neck like a wooden shelf—he always put a handkerchief on his shoulder too, like we saw them do at the symphony. He'd tune the violin to the record and then he'd stand in the center of the floor under the spotlight of the bare bulb hanging from the ceiling, still dressed in his baggy white shirt and the red suspenders and his red bow tie with white polka dots and he'd scratch and screech along with Heifetz or Kreisler while upstairs Mom banged her cupboard doors. I would sit on the steps with my knees drawn up, touching my not-quite breasts, my skirt wrapped around my ankles. And sometimes I'd get up and dance pirouettes in the shadows, waving my arms in time with the music, spinning and turning, and when the record was over he'd look at me and bow and I'd look at him and curtsy.

Her studio window looked out toward the San Francisco Mountains; she leaned on the windowsill, her palms forward, hands reversed, let the sill take her weight, leaned forward until her nose touched the glass: she kissed the image of the mountains, home of the kachinas, the peaks draped now with a wispy mantle of clouds in the otherwise blue sky, then laughed at herself, cleaned the smudge of her lips off the peaks. *Sally, there's a right way to do things and there's a wrong way to do things. It's as simple as that.*

"I think it's time I got some air," she said out loud. She pushed herself away from the window, patting her thighs, her saddlebags, and made her way through her cluttered studio back into the house. So as not to disturb the dogs on the back steps, so they wouldn't follow her and turn her little walk into a parade, she slipped out the front door, out across the front yard to the road.

Rak rak rak rak rak rak rak rak rak rak rak rak rak, sang the magpie in the tree beside her.

"Wrak wrak wrak wrak wrak wrak wrak wrak wrak wrak," sang Sally in return. The magpie looked at her and flew away.

"I hope it wasn't something I said," Sally called after it. She scuffled on down the dirt road, swinging her arms, swaying with the motion of the fringe on her skirt, toward George and Mary Olive's, kicking up little clouds of dust with her moccasins.

He had his workshop, his tools, out in the garage. He made lamps and tables and that chair that never sat straight and Mom eventually burned. On the weekends the garage was full of the smells of cut wood and burned wood and wood shavings and paint. Sometimes he let me put on the shellac or the varnish; he taught me how to prepare the surface and clean the brushes afterward and how to use the grinder and the planes. He always said, "Sally, there's a right way to do things and a wrong way to do things. It's as simple as that." He loved me.

A grasshopper landed in a puff of dust on the road in front of her, adjusted its trajectory, and rattled off again; a yellow-and-black butterfly fluttered along beside her, danced around her, keeping her company. Sally opened her arms to the day, felt the air in the dampness under her arms. High above the trees, a hawk hung motionless on the air, riding a current of air she couldn't feel, then plunged headlong out of sight into the forest. She thrilled to be alive. It was the kind of day when she felt she could just keep walking, it didn't matter where she'd end up. It was the kind of day she wished she could show her father, take him for a walk down this road, show him the forests, the mountains, talk to him, show him what had become of his daughter, what had become of his little girl. *A right way, Sally, and a wrong way.* She had never had the chance to tell him, to thank him for all he had done to make her life better. He died, victim of a heart attack, while she was still in school in New Mexico, while she was with Don one day, watching the feast day, the buffalo dance at San Juan Pueblo.

He had chest pains when he came off the night shift, Mom said he said it was like some guy putting a bear hug on him only worse, a big guy who didn't know when to stop, and pains down his arm, enough pain that he knew what was happening to him, he knew; he told Mom about it but even then she didn't take him seriously, nobody ever took him seriously (that's what I wanted to tell him, one of the things, I took him seriously, he meant everything to me), she sent him on to the hospital but didn't go with him, she told him she'd meet him there later, she went to church, she didn't want to miss mass. And I can still see him sometimes, though I didn't see him then, lying on a gurney in the corridor of the hospital, still in his salt-and-pepper tweed suit (I don't know if that's what he was wearing or not) and his red bow tie with the white polka dots, lying there staring up at the top of the white walls and the white ceiling, listening to the voices coming from the emergency room down the hall, the bong of the call buttons and the pages on the intercom, the footsteps of the people walking past, the doctors and the nurses who walked right past and ignored him, let him just die, slip away, because somebody at the desk put his form on the wrong pile so—"I thought you were taking care of him," "No, I thought you were"—there was no one to help him, no one to talk to, no one to hold his hand and tell him that it was going to be all right (it wasn't) (nothing was ever going to be all right ever again) (for him or for me), no one with him, and I can see him sometimes, he gets up and sits on the edge of the gurney for a minute and looks around, straightens his bow tie, smooths down his hair with both hands just like he did every time in the hall mirror before he left the house, before he gets up, slowly, and walks down the corridors, his arms outstretched, looking for me, his face the color of a slug, his face already collapsed in upon itself, his mouth stretched open, hideous, his eyes blank, wandering down the corridors dark and empty and endless, saying, "It's the wrong way, Sally, I'm lonely."

There were times when she could still hear the bells, or thought she could hear them, the straps of sleigh bells tied to the legs of the dancers, hear them in the wind through the trees or in running water or even in the ticking of her watch, a slight tinkle concealed somewhere deep inside the tiny mechanism when she took it off and put it on the windowsill when she did dishes. She thought she could hear the bells now, faint, distant, coming from somewhere in the woods, though she knew it was impossible, that it was only her imagination—or maybe a gift, a reminder from some higher power. She stopped in the middle of the dusty road and listened: it *did* sound like bells. She tried to do the steps of the buffalo dance in time with them, bouncing her right leg up and down, scuffling her left foot back and forth in the dust of the road, but she couldn't get the steps started so they worked together, she couldn't get them coordinated, and she walked on, pulling her thick braid back into place, draped over her right shoulder and down her breast.

The driveway and side yard of George and Mary Olive's were filled with cars and vans and pickups, parked every which way— Sally was hurt: George and Mary Olive must be having a party and hadn't invited them. Then she wondered if something was wrong. Then she heard them, for certain: bells. She walked up the driveway, she was just going to take a quick peek around the side of the house, to see what was going on—the bells seemed to be coming closer—when she met two broad-faced kachinas, whippers, their mouths in hideous grins, their eyes bulging, coming toward her between the parked cars and trucks. She fell to her knees and crossed herself and buried her head against the side of a fender *Bless me, Father, for I have oh my God* expecting to feel the lash of the whips any second, but the kachinas brushed right past her as if she weren't there.

"I told them the kachinas shouldn't leave the reservation," said one muffled voice. "I was afraid something like this would happen."

"Just help me get out of tis," said the second. He was tagging along behind the first, holding on to the other's horsehair kilt, his head wrenched off center. "I tink I broke my gnose."

"I only said I'd do it in the first place because I owed Fred a favor. . . ."

I'm dreaming, Sally told herself, I'm dreaming or hallucinating or I'm finally having a vision. She crawled a couple of steps, still on her knees, watching the two kachinas thread their way between the parked vehicles; she had started to get up to run after them when she heard something behind her and looked around to see the Crow Mother, her great black wings on the side of the mask barely able to clear between the side mirrors, standing over her, glaring down at her. Sally screamed.

"Get out of the way, you silly bitch," said the Crow Mother, kicking at her.

Sally huddled against the side of the truck again until the kachina was past, then slowly, looking around to make sure no more were coming, got to her feet. At the end of the driveway the kachinas piled into a white van—it had spoked wheels and chrome exhaust pipes sticking up by the doors, and the side was painted with a mural of a desert scene, a mesa at twilight with an Indian on horseback holding a spear—and sped away. Then she heard them behind her, more footsteps, and turned and found a mob coming toward her between the cars and trucks, dozens of old Indian men, stone-faced and sad, coming to tear her apart—she covered her head and screamed again and pressed against the truck beside her but the men passed by her too, got into their cars and trucks—an old man in a cap that said RAINBIRD SPRINKLERS stared at her from the door of the truck beside her, stared until she moved away—and started to leave. Sally walked in a daze among the revving vehicles, around to the back of the house. George stood on the terrace wall, looking down at the end of the field, where another kachina, this one with a tall blue pointed head, wearing a beautiful tropical-colored cape and carrying a staff, stood at the fence along the wash, looking back at him, the two of them, the man and the kachina, shaking their heads at each other, as if equally bewildered by it all, as if they were having a silent conversation. She ran to George.

"Sally!"

"Oh, George, George." She ran into his arms, holding on to him, draping herself over his tummy. "I'm so scared."

"Don't be scared, it's all over now."

"Don't leave him alone, please don't, please. . . ."

"You don't have to worry," George said, looking off toward the house, toward the kitchen windows. "I think Mary Olive took care of all that. . . ."

"I would have been with him if I could," she sobbed.

George looked at her. "But you didn't know it was even here. . . ."

"I never meant to hurt anybody, I never meant to do anything wrong. . . ."

"What? Who are you talking about?"

But Sally was crying, spasms running through her body uncontrollably, hysterical.

10

After George helped her home, after he got her in the car and drove her home and helped Don get her into the house and into bed; after Doc Harvey came over (on horseback, yet, dressed in his riding clothes, an old flannel shirt and chaps, from the middle of teaching one of his daughters how to barrel-race, looking like a white-haired trail boss: "This isn't a house call," he said, a sun-blistered Santa Claus, "this is a horse call") and gave her a shot to help her relax and stop crying and shaking so she could get some rest (he held her knee for a moment, before he left, looked down at her with unabashed affection, and said, smiling, "There you go, young lady, that'll fix you up, good as new; as soon as that shot hits you, you'll sleep till tomorrow noon and wake up wondering what all the fuss was about," then turned around and looked at them, Don and George, looked for a long moment at Don); after Doc Harvey left and Don went over to the bed and kissed her on the forehead and squeezed her hand and told her he'd stay close by just in case she needed anything, that if she needed anything all she had to do was whistle, "You know how to whistle, don't you?" Don said as he and George went to the door, Sally mouthing the words along with him to the old Lauren Bacall line, a shared joke, "All you do is put your lips together and blow"; after Don walked him back through the house and out to his car, already, as soon as he was away from Sally, distant and abstracted, thinking of something far away, hardly saying thank you before he turned and left him there and walked back toward the house, George drove home and went right up, without speaking, without even looking to see where Mary Olive was or what she was doing, to his study (. . . as Sally lies in her bed, stretches, sits up long enough to throw off the light spread, then lies down and stretches again, beginning to feel sleepy, lifts the sheet from her body and watches it drift down again around the mound of her toes, the mid-afternoon sunlight from the window falling across the foot of the bed, falling across her legs under the sheet in a small warm rectangle, and looks out the window at the rectangle of blue sky, remembering the sky over Tesuque, the small abrupt hills covered with piñon right outside the pueblo, which protected and sheltered the pueblo, and the day she and Don went there to watch the eagle dance: the dancer with great feathered wings attached to his arms as he steps and circles and dips, the motions of an eagle in flight, then turns to face her, his wings outstretched, enormous, the white eagle's head with its hooked yellow beak sitting on top of the dancer's head, the dancer's face visible below the face of the eagle, and it is her father, covered with feathers and straps of bells tied to his legs and he's wearing his red bow tie with white polka dots as he says, *The steps go like this, Sally. You see, there's a right way to fly and a wrong way to fly. It's as simple as that,* and she looks down at herself and there are bells strapped to her legs so that every movement she makes jingles and she is covered with feathers so that her body ripples with the slightest wind and her arms are great feathered wings that take the air as she follows her father out across the dust of the plaza, follows him in the dance as she flexes her wings and steps, circles, flies . . . as Don, after making sure that Sally is asleep and comfortable and won't be needing anything for a while, leaves the house and walks back across the yard, through the late afternoon sunlight, to the cabin, where he sits again on his desk chair in the middle of the room and packs the last of his papers into the last of the cardboard boxes, to get it over with, to be free of them once and for all—a freshman paper he saved from his first year of teaching, written by one Paul Schmitt, entitled "My Wonderful Head"; a proposal from a graduate student for a dissertation entitled "The Use of the Implied Narrator in an Age of Doubt" with Don's handwritten note in the margin *Bullshit;* a rough draft for an essay of his own entitled "The Symbolic Use of Foliage in Middle English Lyrics" (he looks for a pen to write *Bullshit* in the margin of it too but his pen is across the room on the desk and he is too weary to get up and get it and simply dumps the manuscript in the box with the others)—and thinks, *A lifetime of scholarship and study and this is what I've got to show for it,* thinks, *I gave up my career for her, I buried myself at the foot of these mountains for her because she wanted to stay out West, because she said that's where our life was, our life together, and she wanted to stay near the Indians so we could have a simpler, more spiritual way of life, live close to the birds and the animals and the trees and the mountains, I built this house for her in the shadow of these mountains, I stayed at this go-nowhere school and nobody ever heard from me again and nobody ever will now,* as he remembers Sally as she walked toward him down the corridor after they first met, while they were still in New Mexico and she had changed her major from anthropology to English, clutching her books to her breasts like a high-school girl (*I thought I was something, I thought I was something special to get a girl that pretty, to get a pretty girl that young*), with the smile on her face whenever she saw him, the bounce in her step, the lines of her thighs in her tight skirts, the eagerness in her face just to be with him, remembers making small talk with her, trying to appear casual, talking to her about her other classes as they walked to his office to make love—"I know what the man is saying rationally, but the rational mind doesn't interest me very much," she said (he could laugh at such statements then, think her naïveté somehow cute, charming: proof of how much she needed him to guide her), and he said, "How can a rational being not be interested in the rational mind?" (he couldn't laugh at such statements now, he didn't think her naïveté charming or cute or even naïve, just dumb; why did he always have to be so hard on her? why was he so angry at her?) —and when they were in the office and the door was locked she walked into his arms, he felt her give her weight to him, at peace, as she said, softly, laughing a little to herself, at her weakness, at her dependence on him, "Because I'm not a rational being, I'm a noodle . . ." and thinks, *She was like a child when I met her—she was a child. She needed me to establish the boundaries, to tell her what was right and wrong in the world. My word was law for her, how could you ever trust anyone like that? How could you ever believe her? She had no thoughts of her own, she depended on me to show her the world. How could I ever believe her when she said she loved me? . . .* as Mary Olive sits, at dusk, in her kitchen with a paper bag over her head, leafing through the bound back issues of *The Little Review,* which she edited, thinking, *I did one hell of a job, one hell of a job,* as she feels the evening breeze come through the window beside her, come through the eyeholes in her mask, cool against her moist skin, and she turns and looks out the window as the back yard goes from shadow to dusk to afterglow, and thinks, *He said to take this bag off my head or else he'd take it off for me, I want to see him try . . .*) and waited, as long as he possibly could, pretending he was working, looking through his notes for possible story ideas, tinkering with a few unfinished poems, until it was after nine o'clock and it was dark outside his study windows and there were still no sounds from the kitchen coming up through the register, nothing to indicate that Mary Olive was fixing dinner or that she intended to or that she was even down there at all except that, as the evening grew darker, the light in the kitchen window snapped on and he leaned forward to look out his window at the rectangle of light spilling out on the grass and saw, in the middle of that rectangle of light, her shadow, a tall oblong shadow sitting motionless at the window, a shadow such as would be thrown by a woman sitting on a kitchen stool with a paper bag over her head, then pushed himself away from his desk and got up and went downstairs to find, sure enough, Mary Olive sitting at the counter, reading through the back issues of *The Little Review,* the bag still over her head—she looked up at him as he came into the room, the brown paper face, the black blank eyes, the small ragged "Oh" of a mouth, watching him as he came across the room, but she didn't say anything—ignored her as he went to the cupboard for a couple of packages of granola bars (cinnamon, his favorite; *Thank God*), and, as an afterthought, took the bottle of Jack Daniel's from under the counter, reaching between her legs and the counter to get it but still not saying anything to her, the brown blank face watching him curiously, her body shifting so she could continue to watch him through the eyeholes, and went back up to his study, sitting at his desk to have his makeshift supper; and thought about Don and Sally, the looks between them, the affection between them as Sally lay in bed and Don made sure she had everything she needed before he left—the two of them sharing the words "Just put your lips together and blow" the way that lovers or old friends would—and remembered Sara's phone call that morning, remembered her petulant tone of voice, her ultimatum to him (there was the night, the last time he was in New York to see her, in her apartment on Spring Street, when they were in the bathroom together, getting ready to go out for dinner, while he was shaving as she washed up, both standing in their underwear side by side in the mirror, when he said something, made a crack of some kind, and she poked him in the ribs.

"Don't, Sara," he said.

She looked at him in the mirror, a little girl's smile on her face and mischief in her eyes, and poked him again, harder.

"Don't, I said. I asked you not to."

"You told me not to," she said, and stuck her tongue out at him and goosed him this time.

"Sara!"

She giggled and clapped her hands and began snapping at his buttocks, pinching him, two hands, the tip of her tongue stuck out between her lips like a child intent on winning all the marbles, and he yelled at her, screamed at her, "I said stop it!"

She stopped and looked at him in the mirror, but it wasn't the look of surprise and hurt and disappointment on her face that distressed him: it was the severity he saw on his own face, the set of his jaw, the small mouth, the tone of voice he had used, all of which were identical to Mary Olive the times that he had felt playful and tried to tease her about something, the few times when they were first married when he had tried to play around with her and she had put him down for it, when he was the playful one and she was the disapproving one, and he glimpsed, in that moment, something of what Mary Olive must have felt about him, her annoyance with him, her angers, her disappointments that he wasn't different, that he wasn't better, that he wasn't more of the kind of person she wanted him to be—he understood in that moment something of the deep disappointment one person can have in another, even when, no, especially when, you love that person too); remembered all the trouble he had had in bed with Sara, not just at the beginning but always, all the trouble it took to make her come—twiddling this, rubbing that, the long minutes staring off into space beyond her, studying the posters on the walls or trying to read the book titles across the room as he licked and sucked and fingered away, listening to her slowly, oh-so-slowly mounting whimpers—it was never as good as it could have been or should have been or was supposed to be; remembered holding Sally Pike that afternoon in the back yard, the feel of her plump, full, middle-aged body against his own, the way she draped herself against his stomach and he could feel her, feel her breasts through her peasant blouse, her hips through her buckskin skirt, and thought, *Maybe it's her, maybe it's Sally, maybe she's the one I've been looking for,* thought, *I'm an animal, the woman's sick, you don't know what trouble is,* thought, *It isn't Sally and it isn't Sara and it isn't what's-her-name and it's not even Mary Olive; it isn't that new waitress at The Gables and it wasn't that teaching assistant at Penn State and it wasn't Betty Martinez in the twelfth grade; it isn't any woman who could ever be, it's a yearning that can't be stopped, it's a hunger that can't be filled, it's an emptiness and a lack and a loss that has nothing to do with a majorette's thighs or a movie star's ass or that woman at the checkout counter's tits; when you think of all the women you could have had or might have had and all the women that you won't have, all you're thinking about is your own emptiness and lack and loss of a forever,* and said to himself, Hey, that's pretty good, I wonder if I could make a poem out of it, or a short story; but instead of writing his thoughts down, making a note of them so he wouldn't lose them, he poured himself another glass of Jack Daniel's and munched on another cinnamon granola bar and opened Don's manuscript and started to read.

11
——

MASAU'U

After the Hopi climbed up a hollow reed from the Third World into this, the Fourth World, they traveled over their new home for years, centuries. Some of the stories say they went on their migrations to find the place of the rising sun. Some of the stories say they went in search of the Eastern Star. Some of the stories say they went in search of their true god. Some of the stories say they followed the trail of their white brother, Bahana, because he was known to be clever and intelligent and had told the Hopi he would go ahead and learn as much as possible about this brave new world.

Some of the stories say the Hopi were ordered to go on their migrations by Masau'u himself, that the god of this world told them that they had to travel the length and width of their new land, each clan following a route that looked much like a gammadion or swastika, from the Atlantic to the Pacific, from the tip of South America to the North Pole, leaving their marks and cities and burial mounds wherever they went, learning the boundaries and limits of the Fourth World, before he, the Guardian, would allow them to return to the spiritual heart of the land, the focus of its power, the center of the universe, which was to be their home.

That's what some of the stories say. Or maybe the Hopi, after going to all the trouble to get to their new world, just couldn't settle down again once they arrived. Maybe the Hopi had been without a real home for so long, maybe they had been traveling for so long, that they didn't know when or how to stop. And as so often happens when you start out without knowing where you're going, they found themselves headed back the way they came.

Whatever the reason, here they were again, right back where they started. Not back at the *sipapu,* the opening in the earth they had used to climb up into the present world, because they didn't want to be even that close to the Under World. They were back to the land where Shrike had first met Masau'u—the Skeleton Man: Death—when they received his permission to live up here. It was a land of tabletop mesas rising up from the desert floor, and very little rain. A severe land, a difficult land, a land nobody else would want. They were back to Masau'u's land.

The Chief had seen the footprints since they arrived, enormous footprints in concentric circles on the edge of their camp and beside the springs, as if someone with feet the length of boards was walking around looking for something. Though he assumed they belonged to Masau'u, he had never seen the Guardian. Then one night, when everyone else was asleep, the Chief took a walk out along the edge of the mesa. The mesa rose hundreds of feet above the desert, its bluffs a natural fortification from the outside world. When Shrike first flew up here, to scout this new world for the Hopi, he found a ring of fire surrounding Masau'u's fields of corn and beans and melons, and Masau'u himself sat at a bonfire in the center of the ring, tending the fires, keeping an eye on things. But there was no ring of fire now, no fields; no Masau'u. The Chief tried not to take it personally. He stumbled along the rocks and scrub brush, until he heard footsteps somewhere off in the darkness beside him. And he saw a light.

At first he thought it was the moon rising, a blood-red moon. Then he realized this was no moon. On the edge of the mesa, a little ways ahead of him, was a column of fire the height of a man. The Chief walked toward it, but as he got closer the fire became smaller. When he was three feet away from it, the flames were only a foot tall. When the Chief walked up to it, the fire flickered out. He had started to resume his walk when the flames appeared again, farther along the edge of the mesa. Again he approached them, and again the flames went out as he got closer. The same thing happened a third time as well. The fourth time, however, as he approached the column of fire, he saw a man standing in the middle of the flames carrying his head in his hands.

"Well, I guess I asked for it," thought the Chief.

When the Chief reached the fire, the flames died down but the figure continued to glow. The figure wore an old, shabby woman's dress, the right shoulder exposed instead of the left, and bands of yucca tied around his wrists and ankles. The head was covered with bloody rabbit skins, with large staring eyes and a gaping, horror-struck mouth. It was Masau'u. Besides his head, he carried in his hands a short digging stick. Then the Chief realized it wasn't his head at all, it was a mask. Masau'u put the mask down on the ground and sat on it.

"So, you made it," Masau'u said, motioning for the Chief to sit down across from him.

"Yes, we made it."

Masau'u was a handsome young man with a dark complexion and a strong face. As he talked, the Keeper dug idly in the ground between his enormous feet with the digging stick. "Well, what did you think of it?"

"It's very beautiful. We saw many places where crops would grow, that would be perfect for farming. It must be the most bountiful, beautiful place in the world."

"The purple mountains' majesty above the fruited plain," said Masau'u.

"What?" said the Chief.

"Nothing," said the god, shaking his head.

"I thought I saw you a couple of times," said the Chief. "I saw a torch moving along the hills late at night, but I was never sure."

"That was me. I walk the edge of the world every night,

just to see how things are getting on. It's one of my little duties around here."

"Are you the only god here?"

"No, there's Spider Grandmother and the Little War Twins, and some other ones. But you have to go looking for them. I'm the one who comes looking for you." Masau'u smiled, like a log popping on a hearth.

"Are you the Supreme Being?"

"Who, me? Hardly. Or at least I don't think so. As far as anybody knows, He's up in the sky someplace or other, but nobody seems to know much about Him. At least, everybody hopes He's up there in the sky someplace. If it turns out that I actually am the Supreme Being, or what everybody has always thought to be the Supreme Being, it sort of casts a different light on things, doesn't it?"

The Chief didn't know if Masau'u was trying to be funny or not. Somehow the idea that Death might have a sense of humor unnerved him a bit. The god sat there, his left elbow resting on his knee, his chin cupped in his hand, flicking stones into the night with his digging stick.

"So. You've completed your migrations, you've seen your new world. You've seen what is possible."

"And what's not possible."

"That's cryptic."

"It's a little hard to explain."

"Try me."

The Chief looked off into the darkness. "When we started out on our travels, we were very sure of ourselves. We were sure that we were going to make a better life for ourselves, sure that we were going to become better people. We lived a lot of different places, and we tried to live a lot of different lives. But when it came down to it, we always ended up just repeating ourselves in new surroundings."

"It's interesting to hear that people have the same problems as gods."

"And we found that when changes did come, when we were

actually able to change something about ourselves, it didn't necessarily make us better people. In fact, it tended to make us worse. We might feel good about it for a while, we might find a new tool or a new way to build a house, we might learn something that we'd think would really change the world. But in time we'd realize that we were just fooling ourselves, that any progress was just an illusion, that every gain brought an equal loss, that every plus has its minus."

"It seems to be one of the problems with an unfolding universe that nobody's been able to work out yet," said Masau'u.

"So we want to go back to the way things were. We want to go back to the way of life we had when we started, when we first came to this world. We don't want any more changes."

"You can't unlearn what you already know."

"Maybe not. But we don't want to learn any more."

"Your brother Bahana, the white man, is out there setting up governments, developing art forms, discovering technology."

"Let him. He's good at that kind of thing, he's got the mind for it. We don't. Besides, he told us he'd come back someday and use what he learned to help us."

"Don't hold your breath," said Masau'u.

"We tried to become better people, and so far we've failed. Now we're afraid. We wanted to be better and we don't know how. We wanted to be different and we can't. So now we just want to live with what we know. We want to live here with you."

Masau'u, his chin still cupped in his hand, looked at him. The Chief felt as though Death could see right through him.

"And what makes you think that will be any better?"

"This is our home. This is where we started, and what we started with."

"You can't go home again, to coin a phrase."

"You can't seem to get away from it either. Maybe it's wrong to try. Maybe the only way for us to be better is to admit what we are and live with it. Maybe with a bare-bones existence—"

"Bare-bones?" said Skeleton Man.

"I didn't mean that," said the Chief. "What I meant was, how could we not become better people living in a god-forsaken place like this?"

Masau'u looked at him under his eyebrows.

"I didn't mean 'god-forsaken' either," the Chief said miserably.

Masau'u waved it away. Then he sighed, as if he had known all along it would come to this. "It's up to you. You know how I live. I have my planting stick and my corn and that's about all. If you're willing to live like I do, and follow my instructions, then, yes, you can live here. You can take care of the land for me."

"Will you be our Chief?"

"Not on a bet," said Masau'u. "Besides, that would be an easy way out for you. If you want to be better people, you'll have to do it by yourselves. If you make it, maybe we'll talk about it. But until then, you brought them to the dance, you take them home again."

"But what should we do in the meantime?"

Masau'u stood up and stretched. "Live. Exist. Be. That's about all there is anyway."

"It seems so hard."

"It is," said Masau'u, putting on his mask. A drop of blood fell on the Chief's hand. "But it's better than the alternative."

"How will we get in touch with you?"

"Oh, don't worry about that. I'll be around. You'll see my torch moving around the hills. You'll hear my footsteps."

"I feel so alone."

"You are."

Masau'u was engulfed in flames, a column of fire, a burning bush, and for a moment he danced, a slow, silent, stately dance within the fire, before he flared brightly and went out. The night was darker than before. As the Chief made his way back across the mesa, he was haunted by the image of the god in the hideous mask dancing in the fire. But the more he thought about it, the more he was sure that one of those dead, staring eyes had winked at him.

12

Georg e rumbled down the steps, careening off the banister and landing heavily with his heels on each carpeted tread, to announce his coming, to make sure she heard him, to give her fair warning, and thumped through the downstairs hall into the kitchen. She had moved; she was no longer sitting at the counter, she was sitting at his place at the table, under the circle of light thrown by the wicker-basketlike shade over the table, but she was still looking through the back issues of *The Little Review,* and she still had the bag over her head. As he crossed the room, she looked up at him, the brown blank face, the black staring eyes, the small "Oh" mouth, as if she'd been waiting for him. *Don't stop, just keep moving, you don't need it.* He walked quickly, businesslike, clipped across the room toward the back door, not looking at her, on an important errand and not to be disturbed, his hands extended palms out toward her, his fingers spread, as if pressed against an unseen wall.

"There's somebody up on the hillside," he said, his head lowered, as if bucking against a wind. "I'm going out to see what's going on."

"Maybe it's some more Indians looking for their kachina," came her muffled voice.

"After what you did today, I wouldn't be surprised if it was a war party."

"Maybe I should call the police."

"No!" he shouted, his hand on the doorknob as she started to get up, started to reach for the phone. He spoke calmly, sternly, keeping himself under control; he made sure she could tell that he was keeping himself under control. "I'll take care of it. Whoever's up there has been up there before, I've seen them, I'm sure it has nothing to do with the kachina or any of the rest of this Indian business. And you will absolutely not call the police. Is that understood?"

"Yes, George, it's understood," she said, standing beside the table. The blank brown face stared at him, the room too dark for him to see her eyes inside the mask, though the paper around the small mouth puffed slightly.

I am standing here talking to my wife with a bag over her head. I don't believe this. As if all this was totally natural. Today she beat up some sacred spirits with a broom; she ran two dozen Indian chiefs out of our back yard; she made David Lomanongye cry. Do other people live like this?

He unlocked the door.

"George?"

"What?"

"You said that if I didn't take this bag off my head you were going to take it off for me. And I've still got it on."

"I can see that, Mary Olive."

"So, aren't you going to take it off me?"

"If you want to wear a bag over your head, I guess you'll just have to wear a bag over your head."

"Sounds like you're trying to run away from me."

Why is she doing this? What does she want from me? Does she want trouble that badly? I'm a dangerous man. . . .

"Oh, all right, George, you're no fun at all, I'll just have to take it off myself." She pulled the bag off with a flourish.

"Ech!" said George. She was a bearded lady; a long beard covered the bottom half of her face.

"What kind of thing is 'Ech!' to say to your wife?"

She had undone her hair and pulled it down across her face, tied it over her mouth for a mustache, knitted it under her chin for a beard.

I could kill her.

He pushed out the screen door and headed across the yard, through the glow of the windows, under the branches of the trees, past the lawn furniture still sprinkled with strands of yucca from the whippers during the day.

"It was only a joke, George," she called after him, coming to the screen door after him. "It was only a joke. You used to always tell me you loved me because I was lively and fun. So I was only trying to be lively and fun."

He stopped at the top of the terrace steps, at the edge of the lights coming from the windows; he turned around and looked back at her. She stood in the back door, silhouetted by the lights of the kitchen—it was the first time he had seen her with her hair not in a bun, seen her with her hair long, in years, in maybe twenty years—undoing her hair from around her mouth, clearing it away from her face.

"You know that's not the reason why you do things like that," he said between clenched teeth. "You know that's not it."

"But maybe that's part of it."

He stood gripping and ungripping his fists. He turned and hurried on, down the steps, down across the dark field toward the fence. The Aholi stood up, rose up in the darkness of the wash with a clack of his turtle-shell rattle; his blue head was the color of moonlight, the feathers at the tip of the point glowed like clouds in the night sky. The kachina watched as George bullied his way through the rails of the fence.

Now what?

"And I've had just about enough of you too, goddamn it!" George looked at him. He adjusted his pants around his stomach and walked by the kachina, brushed by him before the kachina could do anything about it, down the edge of the wash and up the other side, climbing up the bank and into the trees.

13

Boulders, a jumble of volcanic, pockmarked boulders the size of Volkswagens, as if thrown there—the result of the peaks erupting? someone had told him once that the mountain was actually a volcano, that there were hot spots on the slopes, that it was just a matter of time before it erupted again, though time in this case was in the millennia—covered the hillside above the wash; the trunk of a fallen tree was silver in the moonlight. He climbed on, zigzagging up among the boulders, up a natural set of steps, puffing, out of breath already, a hundred yards or so; then the hillside evened out, a gentle climb. He slowed down. The trees, the pines, were ancient here, the branches interwoven into a nearly solid canopy high overhead—the night sky, in the few openings of the canopy, a lighter shade of blue, dusted with stars, among the black foliage—the trunks black columns, pillars, each pair a doorway deeper into the woods, farther away from his house; his steps bounced on the forest floor—he had the sensation of walking on a trampoline, the sensation of having to be careful not to bounce too hard—the only sounds were the padding of his own footsteps, the soft crunch of the cushion of pine needles, and of his own breath. He stopped, listened. Something crawled, scurried between the trees, around the trees to his right; then it was gone, it was silent again. He walked on. No, it wasn't silent, his ears were whistling. Was that a shooting star in that patch of sky? A plane? Beyond the scrim of ponderosas, fifty yards to the left, a stand of aspens glowed—*Is there a full moon tonight? Is that why I'm out here giving myself a coronary, puffing around the woods in the middle of the night? Now all I need is a werewolf*—in the bluish light, their white trunks bent, gnarled at the base to keep them upright against the creep of the earth or maybe from the weight of snow in winter, their trunks angled, inclined, gestured in one movement as if frozen in mid-dance or huddled together, whispering among themselves, *Who's that fat guy over there? What's he doing up here?* George walked on.

In half a mile or so he came to a road; it was little more than a path, really, a fire trail barely wide enough for a vehicle, cutting across the slope of the hill. George rested a few moments, leaned against a tree, took out his handkerchief, and wiped off his face—he had thought earlier that it had cooled off some from the heat of the day, but now he wasn't sure, it seemed hotter up here than at the house; his shirt stuck to him, a second, cotton-and-polyester skin—then followed the road south, in the direction in which he had seen the light. This time, when he had seen it tonight, he was sure it was a vehicle, a taillight, he thought (but why only one? a motorcycle?) (and why just a taillight? why no headlights?) (maybe it wasn't a taillight after all—but what else could it be?), and this must have been the road it was on—he hadn't even known this road was here, he had always meant to climb up here, to go for walks around here, explore the area, but he hadn't done it, another thing he hadn't gotten around to, join the list. It was easier going on the fire trail.

Or at least it had been: he came to a fork, a branch heading up, steeply, into the trees: and there were, in the dim light, tire tracks. He looked up the trail; the trail wound up into the trees, into the darkness, toward a rocky area, a small cliff and outcroppings of rock and a red glow, a fire, somebody up there, though there wasn't supposed to be anybody up here, including himself. It occurred to him that maybe he had been a bit hasty when he stopped Mary Olive from calling the police. *You could always go back and call them now. Or just go back. I'll take care of it, oh sure.* "Me and my big mouth," he muttered, then caught himself, listened: if there was somebody up there—what did he mean, if?—whoever was up there (doing what? satanic rites? biker's orgy? hippies?), he didn't want to get involved and, most of all, he didn't want them to know he was around. He stretched his neck, took a deep breath *I'm going to do it, aren't I?* and moved off the fire trail, parallel to the trail, climbed up through the trees and up into the rocks, around the outcroppings. For a moment the glow grew larger, he thought he saw the tips of flames, then it settled down again. He climbed over a rock ledge, peered around the side of a great round boulder: ahead, in a clearing, with only a few old trees nearby, was the fire. *Oh my God what am I doing here?* In front of the fire, sitting hunched over on a rock, was a figure, his back turned toward George, tending the fire, sitting so that, for a moment, from where George was looking, it appeared the figure, a man, was headless. *Is he sitting on his head? Like Masau'u? Maybe he's up here looking for the Aholi, to show him the way back to the Under World. . . .* George's bowels turned to water—*No, not here, it's a long way back to the house with your pants full of shit*—he told himself, I've been reading too many stories. He stood with his cheeks, both top and bottom, clamped tight, rucked fore and aft, until he felt the spasm pass, his stomach, bowels relax. George moved a little closer, hid behind a tree, aware that he stuck out either in front or behind depending on how he leaned, peeked around it. Now the figure moved a little and George could see his head, placed, where it should be, on the man's shoulders, the man sitting on a rock among a clutter of cardboard boxes, some loose papers scattered around, a pile of firewood; at the edge of the clearing was the jeep. In the firelight, against the flames, Don's hair and beard, like a white aura, glistened.

14

Don took the last stack of papers from the bottom of the box nearest to him and began feeding them, in groups of fours and fives, fanning them out like cards in a hand, into the fire, then poked gently at them in the flames with a stick, being careful that none of the burning papers flew away, making sure there were no showers of sparks; when he caught movement out of the corner of his eye and looked around to see George coming toward him across the clearing, into the light of the fire, puffing and out of breath though with a little pleased-with-himself grin on his face— *the last man*—Don wasn't even surprised. *The last man on earth.* George came and stood beside him, looking down at him, tilting his head to try to see Don's face, then moved around the side of the fire a little ways to see him better, away from the direction of the heat. Don didn't look at him for a couple of minutes or so, he kept on feeding papers into the fire; when he did finally look at him, George blinked three, four times, a burlesque of being surprised, mugging between his gasps for breath. *The last man on earth I want to see. He would never understand why I wanted to be alone to do this, why this is sacred to me, why I went to all the trouble to find this spot and lug all this stuff up here so I could be alone to do it; of all the people I know in the world he would understand it least, and of course he's the one who shows up. The world is made so we'll lose, set up so we'll be unhappy, you'd think I'd know that by now, and knowing that why would anyone want to go on with it?* Don motioned, pointed with his stick for George to sit down, then went on tending the fire.

"Phew! That's quite a climb for an old man, ha ha." George

tried to lower himself gently onto a rock but he still landed with an "Oof." He settled himself, stretched out his legs and crossed his ankles, folded his hands across his stomach. "I saw some lights up here and wondered who it was."

"I was afraid somebody might."

"And you were up here the last three nights too."

"I was looking for a safe place to do this," Don rasped, not looking at him, keeping his eyes on the fire. "These rocks were the safest I could find."

"They said on the news you have to be careful this time of year. What is this stuff, anyway?"

"Just some things I wanted to get rid of, old papers."

George nodded. "Phew. I'm still out of breath, ha ha."

Don glanced at him and continued feeding the last of the papers in the box to the fire. *We are lost in a world of phantoms, our minds are Plato's cave, we spend our lives watching Technicolor shadows projected on the insides of our skulls and never know what's really out there, they say that everything you see in a dream is just another part of yourself, we are the building that collapses, we are the driver of the car hitting a telephone pole, we are the pedestrian on the curb watching the broken skull fill up with blood, but the point is, we're the car and the telephone pole and the curb too, and it's the same when you're awake too, it's all just here inside.* He had made a crude fireplace out of some stones, and covered it with a barbecue grill he brought from the house. In the fire, each sheet—he was working his way through the early drafts of *Retold Tales of the Hopi*—caught, flared, curled at the edges, drew into itself like a burning insect, like a charred fist.

"How is Sally?"

"I think she'll be okay. That shot really put her out."

"Doc Harvey said it would."

"Yes."

"He's quite a character, Doc Harvey."

"Yes. A character."

We are lost in a world where we don't speak the same language, where the deadly part is that some of us use the same words so that you think maybe somebody understands, except that we don't use the same meanings, so that just when you think you've finally made contact with somebody you find out you're further apart than ever, an unspeakable gulf, you might say, surrounds us: this man is my friend, he's the closest thing to a friend that I've had since I came to Arizona, since I married Sally and all the people I thought were friends in Albuquerque turned against me, and it doesn't mean a thing, a friendship, a friend, it doesn't make a difference in the face of . . .

George puffed his cheeks, took a deep breath, as if getting a running start at what he wanted to say. "I guess I owe you an apology."

"What for?"

"For criticizing you for trying to keep Sally away from the kachina. I guess you were right. I had no idea it would affect her the way it did."

Of course, George, you owe me an apology; every night for the last four months I've sat in your kitchen keeping your wife company while you were upstairs asleep, I fucked your wife or at least almost while you lay dreaming, of course you owe me an apology.

"What affected Sally had little to do with the kachina. She's been worried about a lot of things lately. What you saw was just the overflow."

"You know she's been worried about you?"

"Yes." Don added more papers; the fire seemed to go out, smoked for a moment, then flared back again. *She's been worried because her husband doesn't want to talk to her any more and moved out of the house, she's been worried because her husband thought more of talking to his best friend's wife in the middle of the night than lying beside her in bed, she's been worried because her husband treated her like dirt.* "She's been worried about my throat."

"She told me about your fight at that party. She asked me to find out what Doc Harvey said the last time you saw him."

"I've already decided I'm going to tell her myself. She has the right to know."

"Yes, I'd think so. She is your wife."

Don looked at him. *My best friend. If I was dying—what do I mean, if—and George came to see me in the hospital, if he stood beside the bed and reached out and held my hand and looked appropriately sad and concerned, what good would it do, what difference would it make, there's nothing anyone can do for anyone else in the face of death, they certainly can't go with you, there's nothing anyone can do to change what's happening to me, there's nothing a friend can do when you're dying because you can't get away from yourself, get outside yourself, you can never become the other, there's nothing in the face of nothing.* George settled himself more comfortably on the rock, reached over, and rubbed his calves; he grinned at the fire.

"This is sort of pleasant, you know? I haven't been out like this, sitting around a fire, since I was a kid. You should have told me what you were doing. I would have come up and kept you company. It's good to get away from things."

Don put the last of the papers in his hand into the fire, watched them without speaking.

George laughed a little, shook his head. "At least Sally's worried about you. Mary Olive would probably be trying to find out what she could do to finish me off, ha ha."

Don looked at him. *He's sitting there like a toad sunning himself on a rock. He thinks he's got the world in control, he thinks what he does matters.* "Mary Olive's a different kind of woman."

"She is that," George said, glassy-eyed for a moment, then blinked. He looked at Don. "I haven't told anybody else about this, but I've been thinking of leaving her."

She set me up, she used me to hurt him, but what difference does it make?

"There's a girl, a young woman, well, I guess she's not so young now either, ha ha; anyway, I've known her for a long time, she's in New York. She's been after me to make a move so we can be together. And I've been thinking more about it."

Don got up and dragged another box of papers closer to him, sat back down, and began feeding more handfuls to the fire. *I did that once, I left a wife for a woman I loved, I know what it is to love a woman that much, or did.*

"But I don't know," George went on. "Mary Olive and I have

been together for a long time. Sometimes it seems like forever, in a good sense, you know? I don't know if I can just walk away from that. If I should."

"We're all just grayling butterflies," Don said hoarsely.

George smiled, nodded, as if he understood.

Don poked at the fire angrily, he wished now he hadn't said anything; sparks flew up and he watched to see where they went, to see that they were out. He was calm again. "The male grayling butterflies are attracted to the females by how dark they are—the darker the female, the more the males are attracted to it. So somebody did an experiment once and made a model of a female grayling, only darker than any female grayling appears in real life. And the males all ignored even the darkest real females and went chasing off after the model."

"Does that mean you think I should stay with Mary Olive?"

"I don't know what it means." Don looked at the papers in his hand, looked at them without seeing them. *It means we're fated to chase after things that we can never have or that wouldn't do us any good if we got them, it means we're condemned by our genes to always look for a dream we can never find.* He tossed the papers in with the others. "But I think you should go after your dream. Without our dreams we're nothing. But what do I know? Here I am, sitting on a mountain in the middle of the night, burning up the best dreams I ever had."

"What do you mean? What is this stuff you're burning?" George reached over and took a few sheets of paper from the box; they were a few pages from *Retold Tales of the Hopi,* some notes for his book on the *Pearl* poet. "This is your work. You mean this is what you're burning?"

"What did you think I was doing, roasting marshmallows?"

"But this isn't all of it, is it? I mean this is just some of your old work sheets and notes, isn't it?"

"It's all of it. I want that copy of *Retold Tales* I gave you back again too. Either that or you can burn it yourself, but I don't trust you to do it. I'm sorry now I ever let you see it."

"But why, Don? Why burn it? It's your work, it's your—"

Life. "Because it doesn't mean anything to me now. Because I just want to get rid of it."

"I can't let you do that. . . ." George reached over and pulled the box of papers toward him. Don pulled it back, glared at him.

"I'm afraid you don't have anything to say about it," Don said, his voice only a sharp hiss. "I'm afraid this is one time your feelings of moral superiority don't make one bit of difference."

"Don, what's gotten into you? You can't talk to me this way. . . ."

"Do you really think these pieces of paper are going to make any difference to anyone a hundred years from now, even ten years from now? Do you think they're going to make any difference to me? Do you really think they're going to make any difference in that last second when you realize there aren't going to be any more seconds, ever?"

"A man's work has value in itself, whatever the work is."

"Oh, come on, George," *you're full of shit* "you don't believe that any more than I do."

"I do believe it."

"When you stop to think that in a hundred and fifty million years there's still going to be a universe going on but everything you and I ever knew is just going to be dust, it seems to me that it doesn't matter what you work at, it all comes down to the same thing, nothing." *He's right, there is value to a man's work, it does make a difference what a person does, and the dumb blind son of a bitch will never know why, he'll never know that's the terror and glory of ever having lived, oh, I did want to be famous.*

"But you've read things that have meant something to you. You've spent years studying the *Pearl;* that has to have meant something to you."

"Okay, George, let's say maybe you're right. Maybe in the world of men some activities are thought to have value. That means that some activities have higher value than others, and that some men have higher value than others too. But then you have to face the fact that you and I are second-rate, third-rate—shit, we're not even on the board. We're undistinguished teachers at an undistinguished school, our pearls of wisdom are thrown before frat kids and police-science majors. And the pitiful little books we've written, or tried to write, aren't worth the paper they're written on."

"I won't accept that."

"Won't or can't?"

"You have no right to insult me this way," George said, standing up. "I've had enough of this."

"I'm not insulting you, George" *you pompous supercilious asshole.* "I just think you're kidding yourself about your own self-importance. And as for your girlfriend in New York, I'd run to her if I were you, because there's not going to be very many opportunities left. I just wish I had the chance to be in love again." *I just wish I could be in love . . .*

"A man has certain moral obligations . . ." George said, stretching his neck, drawing himself up.

. . . with Sally again. "Moral obligations?" Don laughed, a laugh that quickly turned into a cough. "Do you think Mary Olive shares your high moral obligations? Open your eyes, George. Is that what you think she was talking about," *the bitch* "her moral obligations to you, when you found me in your kitchen last night? Is that what you think she's been talking to me about in the middle of the night for the past four months?"

Don stood up and took the grill off the top of the fire, tossing in handfuls of papers, without looking at George. *I shouldn't have said that, I was wrong to say that, I shouldn't have said it that way, to make it sound that way, I'm no better than the people I criticize, I'm worse because I know better.*

"What do you mean?" George said, moving closer to him, around the fire. "What are you talking about?"

"I shouldn't have said that," Don said wearily, feeling the air go out of him. He held the half-empty box of papers at his side as he stared into the smoking fire. "Nothing happened, George, I don't know why I said that, my throat—"

George was beside him. He reached for the box, grabbed it and tried to pull it out of Don's hands, but Don pulled it back again.

"What are you doing?"

"I've had enough."

George grabbed it again, snapped it out of Don's hands this time, away from him, then hit Don with it, against his arm and side, papers flying out of the box like a flock of startled birds and scattering over the clearing, the blow with the cardboard box making more noise than damage. They looked at each other, surprised, almost as if they were about to burst out laughing, Don grinning, shaking his head *How ridiculous, two grown men having a tiff in the middle of the woods, two grown men bopping each other in the middle of the night with a cardboard box, at least we can still laugh at ourselves* then George dropped the box and hit him with his fist, a downward blow in the face with all his weight behind it: Don staggered, grabbed his face, and fell sideways, across the fire, kicking the fireplace, scattering the stones and ashes, a shower of sparks flying up as he tumbled to the ground. He lay on his back next to the fire, squinting from the heat and the pain, his mouth open, blinking, blood running from his mouth and nose; he tried to raise up, to get away from the fire, but he couldn't, he was woozy, he touched his bloodied beard and mustache with his hand and looked at the blood on his fingertips, amazed. George looked around and picked up a stick, a tree branch the length and weight of a baseball bat, and stood over him, his teeth clenched, raised the stick over his head with both hands, ready to smash Don in the head, stood there a moment, frozen, Don staring up into George's hate-wrenched face *He's going to kill me, I'm dead, NO* then George dropped the stick and ran, stumbled blindly away, howling "No no no no no no . . ." away from the fire across the clearing—Don rolled away from the fire and tried to call after him, "George, wait!" but the words came out garbled and painful, his jaw wouldn't work right, maybe it was broken, and his lip, the side of his mouth, was torn, shrieked with pain to move it— howling as if he were the one hit and hurt, to the edge of the rocks, then fell, lost his footing, down the slope.

15

Don saw him fall, disappear from sight—one second he was there, the next second he wasn't—as if he had fallen through a trap door, heard the sound of the rocks and small stones falling, drifting away, then a sickening silence. "George!" he tried to call again, but it was useless. He was weak, trembling; he rolled over on his side, farther away from the fire, and got to his knees, on all fours like an animal, the side of his face throbbing, the strangely metallic taste of his own blood in his mouth; his throat felt seared, there was sweat in his eyes. The fire had scattered and there were small fires starting around the clearing, where the sparks and fragments of burning paper had landed. Don got to his feet, dizzy, and staggered over to the edge of the clearing, peered over the edge of the rocks; he cupped his hand over his eyes as if that would help him in the darkness and tried to see down the slope but he couldn't see George. A couple of the fires around the clearing were getting larger. Don stumbled back to the jeep for the shovel and hurried around the clearing, beat at the flames and shoveled what dirt he could find on them—he decided his jaw wasn't broken, but the skin on his face, around his nose and torn lip, was tightening, as if winched, the pain sharper as the skin got tighter—scattered the stones of the fireplace and buried the coals and ashes until all the fires were out and there was nothing left to smolder. Then he went back to the edge of the clearing and climbed down the rocks to the brush at the bottom and into the trees but though he could see where George had landed, the debris of his little landslide, George was nowhere in sight. Don went on down the slope, through the trees, following George's trail but then he lost it, George seemed to be wandering, not heading back to the trail or toward his house, and Don climbed back up to the clearing and got in his jeep and drove down to the main fire trail. He followed it north for a mile or so—he was sure George couldn't have gone this far—honking his horn, then turned around and headed back, driving slowly, still honking, watching in the darkness up the hillside for some sign of him. Then he turned off the trail and into the woods, down the slope between the pines and across the bottom and out of the trees, out across the field, blue-gray in the moonlight, toward his house. The light in Sally's, their, bedroom was on. He honked his horn—it sounded more like a bleat to him—and from somewhere near the back of the house the dogs came running, their eyes glittering in the light of his high beams, the pack of dogs running across the field toward him, ears pricked, recognizing the horn and the vehicle, tongues hanging out, happy to see him, then skidded to a stop, *en masse,* tumbled over themselves as they realized the jeep wasn't stopping but was coming right at them, and they turned and scattered, again *en masse,* legs flying, tails between their legs, the dogs looking back frantic-eyed over their shoulders as they ran for safety; in front of the cabin, as Don roared by, Cable sat with his mouth open, a smile on his face, the old Labrador glowing in the moonlight, placidly watching the spectacle of the speeding jeep and the other dogs running over themselves to get out of the way. Between the cabin and the house, Sally, in her long nightgown, was already out in the back yard, drifting ghostlike toward the cabin. He pulled up in front of her and got out but fell, his legs collapsed out from under him, weak from pain and shock. She screamed and ran to help him. The dogs came back and gathered around them as Sally knelt beside him, Don sitting up in the damp grass, his legs stretched out in front of him, the dogs sitting in a circle around them like a chorus.

"Don, you're hurt! What happened?"

"There was an accident up in the woods." He could barely whisper, the words garbled from his sore mouth. "George fell down some rocks, I think he's hurt but I couldn't find him."

Sally touched his face with her fingertips, the swelling around his nose and mouth, her eyes full of tears; his nose had stopped bleeding and his lip, where it was cut, torn, was beginning to scab over. "Are you all right? What was going on? I was coming out to the cabin to see you."

"It's a long story, I'll tell you later. I want to get over to George's, I want to make sure he gets back all right. I just wanted to check first to make sure you were okay."

"You did?" She touched his chest, leaned over as she knelt beside him and put her cheek on his chest for a moment. Then she straightened up and studied his face again, the tear on his lip, holding her own lower lip between her teeth as she flicked some of the blood and dirt out of his beard.

"I better call Doc Harvey and have him meet you over there."

"It's the middle of the night."

She put the flat of her hand against his chest; her voice was soft but matter-of-fact. "You know what he'd say if you didn't call him. I'm sure he'd want to look at this, you might need some stitches. And maybe George'll need him too."

"I guess you're right," he whispered. He felt very tired. "Will you come with me?"

"Oh yes," she said, her eyes filling with tears. "Oh yes."

"Go get your clothes on."

She looked at him a second longer, then ran for the house, her nightgown flopping about her, her long braid swinging down her back; the dogs went with her, dancing happily around her, except Cable, who sat where he was, near the cabin, pearl-gray-blue in the moonlight, watching him. Don got to his feet and Cable came over, walking carefully, his legs spread as if walking on rails, and stood beside him, raised his head far enough to fit under Don's hand at his side. Don patted the dog as he thought there was something else he wanted to talk to Doc Harvey about too; Cable burped and licked his lips and followed him, slow and spread-legged, as Don went back to the jeep and eased himself in behind the wheel, to wait.

16

The arm was broken, he was sure of that, but he couldn't tell exactly where, somewhere up near his right shoulder, he thought—could shoulders break? he guessed everything could—maybe the collarbone; his right leg, the knee, hurt too, no longer worked well either. The pain wasn't in one place, it seemed to be all over, throughout his body; he couldn't think straight, couldn't think what he should do.

He thought it was just a matter of going down the hill until he came to the main fire trail again so he kept going down the hill but he didn't come to the trail again and the woods didn't look at all familiar—he must have gotten turned around in the fall—until he found himself at the bottom of the hill in a wash he hadn't seen before that shouldn't have been there in front of another hill he hadn't seen before that shouldn't have been there either and there was nothing to do but climb back up the way he came. He felt faint; he walked hunched over, cradling his right arm with his left, dragging his right leg; he had to keep moving, he was afraid to stop. He tried to find the place where he had fallen, the place where he had landed, but it was gone now, as well as the out-cropping of rocks and boulders where he had seen Don—some-body was hiding things, somebody was playing tricks on him, he'd have to be careful. Around him there was nothing but trees, tall pines. He looked up at a patch of stars; why hadn't he ever learned to read the stars? Why hadn't he been a better Boy Scout? Once he thought he heard honking, Don probably, the jeep, but when he tried to head toward it the honking kept moving away, first in one direction and then the other, until he wasn't sure he had heard it at all. He stopped and listened: there was no honking, there was only the sound of his pulse in his ears, played on a bass drum, accompanied by the throb of his shoulder and leg. More tricks.

Ahead of him, between the black columns of the trees, stood the Aholi, the staff in his right hand and the sacred bundle in his left, looking at him, his head tilted slightly as if studying him, wondering what was wrong, his tall pointed head the color of the moonlit sky. George started toward him and fell, dropped straight down on his knees and howled with pain and toppled on his bad arm and howled again, screamed, unable to get up. The kachina came over to him, the rattle clacking in the darkness, put down the staff and bundle, and helped George sit up, helped brace him against a tree; the kachina touched carefully the shoulder, the leg, looked into George's face, then motioned him to stay where he was. "Where do you think I'm going to go?" George said, but then realized he didn't say it out loud, that the words didn't get beyond his mind, and realized his eyes were closed, and he listened to the clack of the rattle move away through the trees. He didn't know how long he slept, how long he lost consciousness, whether the kachina was gone minutes or hours, or if he had heard the rattle the whole time as he listened to it now coming toward him again. Close up, the kachina smelled the way a large animal might, George thought, a bear perhaps, or a mountain lion. George felt a hand behind the back of his head and opened his eyes to look into the blank eyes, the long black eyes of the mask, the feathers on the peak as wispy as clouds, the tufts of yarn sprouting out of his ears purple in the dim light, as the kachina helped him straighten up and take a drink of water, the freshest, coolest water George had ever tasted, from his jug. "Is that a special formula?" he laughed, but the words didn't get beyond the thinking again because he was crying.

"I could have killed him."

But you didn't.

"I wanted to kill him."

But you didn't.

The kachina looked at him intently, kneeling in front of him, and in the moonlight George tried to see inside the mask, tried to see in the eyeholes at the eyes of whoever it was inside, but the eyeholes were empty, there was no one inside the mask, the mask was empty, the blank empty eyes staring at him, and he tried to scream but he was already gone again, drifting out of consciousness again.

He woke again—after how long? minutes? hours? weren't they the same?—with the kachina helping him to stand, to get to his feet, the kachina taking George's weight, his strong arm braced under George's good arm until George's head cleared and he could move again. Then, his staff and bundle in his left hand, the Aholi helped George down the hill—the opposite direction from the one George had tried earlier—down through the trees to the fire trail. George didn't know how long they walked; he might have passed out again, on his feet, drifted in and out as they walked along; later he only vaguely remembered walking down the road in the moonlight, braced against the kachina, the clack of the turtle-shell rattle as if coming from his own leg, the kachina helping him step by step down the zigzag trail among the boulders to the wash behind his house. When the kachina eased him down on the bank, near the shrine, George fainted again.

The sky, the trees, were gray, becoming grayer when he woke again, woke to the sound of rattles and bells, as he looked up, blinked awake, to see coming toward him, out of the trees, down the other side of the wash, a kachina dressed all in white, with a white bullet-shaped head crested with hawk feathers, two dots for eyes on the mask and one for a mouth, Eototo, carrying his sacred bundle in his left hand; while behind Eototo, standing at the edge of the forest, at the edge of the bank, was the Crow Mother, dressed in a blanket-cape and holding a plaque of bean shoots, the great black wings stretched out from either side of her head. The Aholi and the Eototo embraced and leaned back to look at each other and embraced again and talked excitedly for a moment, softly, their heads inclined toward each other, the Aholi motioning toward the shrine and the house and George. On the bank, the

Crow Mother cried, "*Huu-hu-hu-hu-hu-hu!*"; the morning breeze
stirred her cape and riffled through the black wings. Eototo and
Aholi looked at her and looked at each other and wagged their
heads a little. *Yeh, yeh, we know. Take it easy.* Then the Eototo
reached in his sack of cornmeal and drew a cloud symbol on the
ground in front of the shrine and sprinkled it with water from his
jug; and the Aholi put the butt of his staff on the drawing and
swung the top in a wide arc, singing in a high piercing voice,
"*Ah-hol-li-i-i-i!*" The two kachinas nodded to each other, *Well,
that takes care of that,* and then walked across the wash and climbed
up the bank and followed the Crow Mother back up the hillside,
the Aholi a few steps behind the Eototo, up the jumble of boulders,
into the trees. But as they climbed up the hill, the Aholi, while
the other two weren't looking, looked back and toodled his fingers.
Bye, George.

George lay where he was, watching as the three kachinas disappeared up the hillside, deeper into the woods, then drifted off
again; when he woke again, there was no sign of them, and he got
to his feet and climbed, slowly, up out of the wash, dragging his
bad leg, cradling his sore arm with the other, to the fence, leaning
against the top rail, pillowed on his stomach, as he looked up at
his house. Don's jeep and another car he didn't recognize were
parked beside the trim white frame house—the morning was growing brighter even as he watched, the light stronger as if someone
had lifted a screen, the light on the trees and the hills toward
Flagstaff touched with gold; Don and Sally stood in the back yard,
on the terrace under the twin pine trees, side by side, waving at
him, as Mary Olive, her hair still down from the night before,
hanging loose around her shoulders, came hurrying down the field
toward him. George thought he could probably make it through
the fence without her, but he didn't try.